The Love of
a Cowboy

The Love of a Cowboy

Anna Jeffrey

AN ONYX BOOK

ONYX
Published by New American Library, a division of
Penguin Group (USA) Inc., 375 Hudson Street,
New York, New York 10014, U.S.A.
Penguin Books Ltd, 80 Strand,
London WC2R 0RL, England
Penguin Books Australia Ltd, 250 Camberwell Road,
Camberwell, Victoria 3124, Australia
Penguin Books Canada Ltd, 10 Alcorn Avenue,
Toronto, Ontario, Canada M4V 3B2
Penguin Books (N.Z.) Ltd, Cnr Rosedale and Airborne Roads,
Albany, Auckland 1310, New Zealand

Penguin Books Ltd, Registered Offices:
80 Strand, London WC2R 0RL, England

First published by Onyx, an imprint of New American Library,
a division of Penguin Group (USA) Inc.

ISBN: 0-7394-3539-6

Copyright © Jeffery McClanahan, 2003
All rights reserved

To my husband, George,
who cooked and cleaned and kept the faith

ACKNOWLEDGMENTS

I'm grateful to Robyn Conley, the Book Doctor, who headed up the best critique group imaginable and taught me more than all the classes I took or books I read. Her fingerprints are all over this novel.

I thank the old critique group members who patiently listened and constructively commented—Olyve, Dr. Mike, Diane, Peggye, Ann, Linda, and Jerry.

I appreciate my readers, Ann, Paula, and Heather. They took the time out of busy schedules to read and told me the book was "readable."

And last, I thank my editor Jennifer Jahner and NAL for giving my cowboy manuscript the opportunity to see print. Jennifer's wise direction and shaping turned it into a love story.

Prologue

Dallas, Texas
Monday, December 22, 1997

If Dahlia Montgomery Jarrett ignored the fact that it was her husband she was burying three days before Christmas, it was as good a day as any for a funeral. Sky overcast but no rain, temperature not too hot for her black Ellen Tracy suit. Typical for December in North Texas.

As the obligatory graveside ritual ground to an end, she made a silent prayer of thanks. She had shaken enough hands, said, "Thank you for coming," enough times, been the dutiful spouse. Through it all, she hadn't shed a tear, and was proud of herself. Because she hadn't screamed, either.

The service had been short and uncrowded. Kenneth Jarrett's family was small. He'd had few friends. Some of her friends from work had come, but most only sent flowers. Poinsettias. A touch of the bizarre. Fitting, Dahlia thought.

She moved toward a waiting black limousine, flanked by her father and her lifelong friend, Pegine Murphy. If someone asked her to define her feelings, she could not. How could she find words a mere five days after learning her husband, the man who had vowed to forsake all but her, had died in a violent car collision at four o'clock in the morning with another woman in his car?

Wednesday morning's surreal events had flashed through her mind in snatches a hundred times—the predawn call from the Denton County sheriff's office, weeping and driving against morning traffic to Denton, where she had never been, nearly colliding with a van loaded with Santas who flipped her off in unison when she ran a stop sign.

The morgue scene followed—Kenneth playing on closed-circuit TV like a bad movie. Her knees barely held her through it. Afterward, a young deputy scanning a form on a clipboard asked her if she knew her husband's passenger.

"Passenger?"

"Yes, ma'am. Female, approximately thirty, blond hair, blue eyes, weight one-twenty-seven."

Dahlia shook her head. On Tuesday morning, he had left their North Dallas home for a two-day meeting in Austin. South. No, she didn't know a female rode with him. No, she didn't know why he had been driving a narrow, rural road on the opposite end of Texas from where he should have been.

Female passenger . . . river bottom . . . no ID . . . Would she attempt an identification?

In her mind, Dahlia refused, but her head nodded assent.

Then came the blow that nearly felled her. The woman who had departed life with Kenneth was her coworker Bonnie Gibson. For four years, Dahlia had considered her a friend. They lunched together several times a week, prowled the shopping malls. Three evenings a week, they worked out at a gym, commiserated during breaks at the juice bar about married life and men. And sex. They had shared the most intimate of secrets. She knew the bedroom deficiencies of the deceased woman's husband almost as well as she knew Kenneth's.

Staring at Bonnie's lifeless face, at a visceral level, Dahlia resisted the truth. It slunk in anyway.

Grief, confusion, humiliation, anger—all bunched into a tight knot and lodged behind her breastbone. She hyperventilated, had to be guided to a chair by the deputy. She left the morgue groping for mooring.

She hadn't cried since that day, holding herself together with brittle control.

Thus far, the sheriff's department's investigation had

been typical, she assumed. A 10–50F she heard them say—an accident with fatalities. It appeared Kenneth's Corvette had crashed head-on into a bridge abutment, then plunged into the North Fork of the Trinity River below. Both victims pulled from the murky water were pronounced dead at the scene.

High speed, the cops said. DUI, they suspected. Toxicology results were pending. Dahlia hadn't let herself think of the probable outcome or its consequences.

Since breaking the news to her husband's family the morning of the accident, her only contact with them had been to make funeral arrangements. With her consent, his parents selected the funeral home, the chapel and a grave site in the Jarrett family plot in an old Dallas cemetery.

When the awkward question of her own burial arose, she assured them she didn't expect a spot to be reserved for her beside her husband. His mother's relief came as an audible sigh. No surprise there. Just as Kenneth's WASPy parents hadn't wanted a Catholic, half-Filipino daughter-in-law, they wouldn't want her corpse tainting the family plot some day in the future.

She didn't care, Dahlia told herself. She had her own supporters—her dad and Piggy. They arrived a few hours after being called, having driven from the small West Texas town of Loretta, where she and Piggy grew up.

Now, back at the funeral home, they transferred from the somber black Cadillac to Piggy's fire-engine–red Blazer. Kenneth's friends would be meeting the family at his parents' home for a short reception.

"I dread this," Dahlia said, settling into the Blazer's backseat. "I don't know how I can face them."

Her dad reached back between the bucket seats and squeezed her hand. "Not much longer, sweetheart."

Piggy's fierce gaze reflected in the rearview mirror. Her anger had been snapping and crackling for days. "More to the point, how can *they* face you? Just be glad this little soiree is taking place at *their* house instead of yours. At least we can bail out when you've had enough of the Jarrett charm."

They were silent as Piggy drove. Dahlia stared out, seeing but not registering, stumbling through a labyrinth of memories and warring emotions.

Her husband had been a man of many facets—ambitious, not lazy, sophisticated and suave, handsome enough to have stepped off the pages of *GQ*.

And he had been unfaithful, calculating and mendacious. Countless times she had dismissed how manipulative he was, of others as well as her, or closed her eyes to his selfishness.

Just a few months ago, she had been close to leaving him. He'd had an affair with another woman—not the one who died with him. Even as Dahlia knew a lie rolled off his tongue as readily as the truth, instead of kicking him out or packing her bags, she had let herself believe him when he said it wouldn't happen again.

And why had she done that? Because to her, belonging to some*one* and some*thing* as time-honored as marriage had been more important than a few glitches in probity.

But as diabolical as she knew he could be, nothing had prepared her for both his and a friend's betrayal in one stroke.

They entered the upscale subdivision where Kenneth's parents lived. Large brick homes glided past, their grassy lawns turned to winter's beige and festooned with Christmas decorations. It all looked so normal.

Everyone arrived at the Jarrett home at the same time. As Dahlia entered the two-story foyer, she saw nothing had changed from when Kenneth had brought her here ten nights ago for dinner with his parents and several other guests.

The stairway banister was still draped with thick ropes of green garland and red poinsettias beribboned in gold. A tall, lavishly decorated Christmas tree, unlit, still filled a corner of the living room. Beside this very tree, Kenneth had given her an early gift, a diamond tennis bracelet that brought a gasp from his mother. The presentation, Dahlia saw now, had been nothing more than a performance to make himself appear as a loving husband in the presence of his parents and their friends.

In the formal dining room to the right of the foyer, she could see the Ethan Allen cherrywood table extended to its full length, and food from a caterer laid out. The subdued guests formed a line and filed past.

Piggy went ahead of her, picking up a plate and silverware and surveying the array of fancy cuisine. "Well, this ain't exactly the family dinner in the church basement, is it?" She added some raw vegetables to her plate. "Hmm. I don't see any rice. Did they forget you were coming?"

"Shh. Don't start." Dahlia glanced around to see who had heard. *Rice* was a private joke. It went back five years to the rehearsal dinner before her wedding. Kenneth's mother had asked her if she preferred rice to potatoes, the first of many thinly veiled racial slurs.

I didn't know if you could buy makeup in your color, dear. . . . Did your mother read and write English? . . . If you and Kenneth have children, I suppose they'll be dark. . . .

Dahlia, her father and Piggy ate standing near the fireplace, apart from the group. Piggy assessed the small crowd. "Just goes to show you I'm not the only one who thought he was a jerk. Only a handful of people even care he's gone, and I question their sincerity."

Dahlia's dad spoke up. "Pegine, remember where you are. Show some respect."

"I can't help it, Elton. The whole thing makes me so mad—"

Dahlia stopped her. "Don't, Piggy. I know it wasn't perfect, but I shared my life with him."

"You were too generous, girlfriend. You'd have been better off with a large dog."

"I wanted it to work out. I wanted us to be a family."

Piggy sighed and shook her head. "Let's face it, Dal. You're too nice a person. No match for a scheming sonofabitch."

Another hard truth Dahlia couldn't deny or excuse away.

One by one, Kenneth's friends, for the second and third times, offered their condolences and left.

"Hypocrites," Piggy hissed. "Those bastards knew he screwed around. And you'll never make me believe his hoity-toity mom and dad didn't know it, either. They helped him lie to you, you know."

Piggy ripped into Kenneth and his mother so often, Dahlia frequently tuned her out. Today, of all days, she was too weary to listen. She had been running on adrenaline since Wednesday and as for emotions, she was numb. "I know all that, Piggy. Please don't say any more. It's over."

"If you believe *that*, let me tell you about a bridge in Brooklyn. Personally, I think the fun's just beginning. I'd bet my CPA certificate the IRS was hot on his heels. As underhanded as he was? . . . You may be dead broke and don't even know it."

"I *do* know it. I've been worried about it."

Chapter 1

Two years, four months later

Dahlia Montgomery's patience drew its next-to-last breath on a cold sunlit morning in a godforsaken place named Callister, Idaho, population 635. There, in the reception room of a U.S. Forest Service complex, she and her best friend, Piggy Murphy, waited for their summer employer, Piggy's cousin Jerry. It was the second time in twenty-four hours he had stood them up.

Another snafu. A plague that had become a too-familiar part of Dahlia's once well-planned existence. This latest one, though tiny in comparison to the calamities that had befallen her in the past two and a half years, just might be that infamous straw that collapsed her. Why hadn't she resisted longer and harder when Piggy and Dad nagged her into this harebrained scheme?

Piggy zipped her coat all the way to her chin. "Wonder why they don't turn up the heat."

Dahlia pointed to a sign on the wall. THIS FACILITY IS HEATED BY SOLAR ENERGY, it proclaimed.

"Hunh. Could have fooled me. Feels like they're burning candles."

Yeah, Dahlia thought, and cast a skeptical eye at the golden shafts of sunshine pouring through giant skylights. She pulled her jacket—her *lightweight* jacket—tighter about her and hunched forward. "Jerry should have told us it's still winter up here. We didn't even bring warm coats."

Mumbling a string of swear words, Piggy stuffed her hands into her coat pockets, scooted down and rested her neck on the chairback. Her eyelids fluttered shut.

"It's ten o'clock," Dahlia snapped, tired of hiding her annoyance. They had arrived at eight. She had read two magazines on forestry from front to back and all the brochures on the gray steel side tables circling the room. Two-dozen people uniformed in khaki and green had passed through the front entrance and disappeared up a long hall. A dozen more civilians. No Jerry Murphy. "If the furnace worked we could go back to the house."

"Lean back and take a nap," Piggy mumbled. "He'll show."

"Surveyor helpers. That's a joke. Grunts is more like it. I should have stayed in Loretta and helped Dad."

"Shh."

Dahlia's gaze swept their surroundings. Until now, she hadn't known there were so many shades of gray. Everything—walls, floor, furniture—was tinted to match her mood.

Across the room, in front of a wall of windows, trapezoids of sunlight hopscotched over the salt-and-pepper carpet. She pushed up from her chair and moved to bask in the warmth of one of the sunny patches. Her reflection showed in the window glass. Long curly hair fanned out from her head like a tom turkey's tail in full ruff. She loved her rebellious hairdo, but unshampooed and unmoussed, it looked like the frizz that ate New York. And *that* she didn't love. She turned her jacket pockets inside out, looking for a barrette, a rubber band, something. "I don't suppose you'd have a hair clip," she said to Piggy.

Piggy's eyes opened to half-mast. She pulled a yellow claw clip out of her pocket. "Shazam."

As Dahlia gathered the sides of her black hair into a knot at her crown, she viewed the world outside. Little mounds of thawing snow glistened in brilliant morning sunshine. Water trickled everywhere. Across the street, a brick bank building's digital marquee pegged the temperature at thirty-three degrees.

They had inched into town in a snowstorm yesterday, roads slick, visibility three feet, but today, under clear blue skies, she could see the entire metropolis. The main street was a highway. Boise to the south, who knew what

to the north. Three blocks of buildings, some brick, some
log, huddled on either side of the two-lane road. Though
sunlight glinted off their metal roofs, the structures themselves looked even older and dustier than the ones she
had left behind in Loretta, Texas.

A pair of uncollared dogs trotted past, busy marking
tires. No leash law in this town, she mused. No different
from Loretta.

Something that *was* different was a distant hum of an
engine and the screak and scrape of metal against metal.
Though muted at present by the Forest Service building's
thick windows, the monotonous noise had gone nonstop
all night. And how did she know? Because if she had
closed her eyes in sleep at all, it had been for no more
than a few minutes. "What is that?" she asked the obese
receptionist at a gray desk.

"That sound?" The receptionist—her nameplate said
GRETCHEN and she had on a mammoth ski sweater that
filled Dahlia with envy—plunked a hammy elbow on an
open drawer. "The sawmill. Jobs. Money. They're working three shifts now."

"Sawmill? Is this a mill town?" Another fact Jerry had
neglected to tell them.

"I dunno. The sawmill's the biggest thing we got.
When it ain't running, things get real grim around here.
Most of our folks work over there. Either that or log."

"Log? You mean, as in, cut down trees?" Dahlia knew
little of logging. No sawmills and few trees existed in
West Texas.

Gretchen grunted and slammed the filing cabinet
drawer. "That's generally what happens when they log.
You a tree hugger?"

"Well, no—"

"Good. We got enough of them already." She turned
her back and lumbered up the hallway.

Soon she returned, waddling toward them, carrying a
steaming mug in each hand. On her feet were untied,
all-weather boots the size of shoe boxes. Her steps
scuffed against the tight-napped carpet. She stopped and
shoved a mug at Piggy. "We don't usually serve coffee

around here, but you two look like you could use it. We had some doughnuts earlier, but they're all gone."

Piggy roused and reached for the mug. "Doughnuts?"

With a meek thank-you, Dahlia took the other cup. She supposed she and Piggy did look as if they didn't know where their next meal might come from. They had been wearing the same clothes since yesterday morning when they put them on in a cheap motel outside of Salt Lake City. "I hope you don't mind if we wait here," she said. "We're meeting someone."

Gretchen turned on a Miss America smile. "Hey, you can wait as long as you want to. You're taxpayers, ain't-cha? This building belongs to you."

Considering what had been taken by the IRS after her husband's death, Dahlia felt that could be true. "If you only knew," she mumbled.

One sip of the strong coffee and her stomach rolled and growled. Oh well, she didn't like coffee in the first place, but the mug felt warm against her chilled hands.

A few feet to her right, from behind a closed door, she could hear muffled male voices in discussion. A meeting, she surmised.

Vignettes of her former life flashed in her mind. A surge of longing, unexpected and bittersweet, welled up. A year and a half had crawled by since she had gone home to Dad in Loretta. Simply picked up and walked away from a fast-track job with a top advertising and PR firm in Dallas. She didn't miss Dallas so much, but sometimes she missed the hubbub, the cutting-edge excitement, the exchange of ideas with her former peers, Young Turks with MBAs and BMWs who pursued their goals with the zeal of hungry sharks.

It wasn't too late to go back, and she intended to. Twenty-nine wasn't too old to start over. She had some catching up to do, maybe some classes to take, but just as soon as she got her feet on the ground again . . .

A male voice, suddenly loud, came from behind the closed door. "Now, Luke, the government's policy—"

"No! No way, Ted." It was a louder, angry voice. "I'm not listening to that policy crap. It's one thing to cut

back my allotment, but damned if you're gonna tell me
what to do on my own land. I'm not building no damn
fence between my cows and a drink of water. I'll call
every sonofabitch in Washington if I have to."
    The door burst open. Dahlia jumped sideways a second
too late. A tall, scowling man plowed headlong into her.
She reeled backward, crashing across a table. Her mug flew
from her hand and coffee drenched the image of SMU's
galloping mustang on the front of her T-shirt. Pain ripped
through her hip and elbow as she hit the floor.
    The next thing she knew, she was lying supine and
Piggy, Gretchen and the stranger were hovering over her.
Piggy's voice filtered through. "You okay, Dal?"
    She forced herself up, bracing on the uninjured elbow.
Several other men and women came out of offices, ogling.
    The stranger squatted, slid one arm around her waist
and grasped her upper arm with his opposite hand. His
knuckles nudged into her left breast. "Lord, lady. I'm
sorry."
    As if she were weightless, he lifted her and set her on
her feet. She limped toward a chair and leaned on its
back for support. He brushed at her clothing and petted
her hair. "You all right, ma'am? You hurt anywhere?"
    She could hear the murmurs of onlookers. Embar-
rassment heated her face and she refused to look up.
"I'll be okay in a minute."
    She pushed away the stranger's hands, then slipped
her arm out of her jacket sleeve and examined her
smarting elbow.
    He was there, lifting her arm to look, too, moving long
fingers up and down, palpating her forearm. "Don't feel
any broken bones. Don't see any blood." He turned her
and looked behind her. "How's that hip? Let's—"
    "It's fine." Her palm flew up like a shield. She took a
step back and away from him. Finally, she looked him
full in the face and the connection was as instant as the
skip in her heartbeat.
    He towered above her, an oak tree in a blue-and-white
plaid shirt and a navy quilted vest. His eyes, sober and
intense, were the color of the sky outside, deep set be-

neath a ledge of brow and framed by thick dark lashes. He smelled of masculinity and a hint of woodsy after-shave.

An odd awareness slithered through her, curled itself around her secret places and gave a hard squeeze. She felt weak in the knees, yet she freed her arm from his grasp and skimmed her palm down her shirt front. "Really, I'm okay. Don't worry about it."

His gaze followed her hand and stopped. She looked down. Through the clinging wet T-shirt, she saw distinct impressions of her lacy bra and dark brown nipples. She may as well have been shirtless. Hoisting her chin, she roasted him with a glare and yanked one side of her jacket across her front. *Jerk!*

His gaze moved up to hers, his mouth tipped into a lazy, knowing grin. "I'm usually not so clumsy. I was just so damn mad there for a minute."

He stooped and picked up the pale gray cowboy hat he had lost in the collision and dusted the crown with his fingertips. "Sure you're all right? If you think you oughtta see a doctor . . ."

A cowboy! I might have known. She waggled a dismissive hand and eased down to the chair seat.

"Well, okay then." He turned to the receptionist with a stern look and a pointing finger. "Remind Ted I'm waiting for his call. The minute he finishes that range report. Don't forget."

Gretchen gave him a two-fingered salute. He left in long strides through the front doorway, adjusting his hat as he went.

Piggy stared after him, slack-jawed. "Who the hell is that? He got a posse waiting outside or something?"

Gretchen cackled and went to stand beside Piggy, placing her hands on elephantine hips and dwarfing Piggy's hundred twenty pounds. "He's enough to give a gal a heart attack, ain't he? I usually don't like the looks of a redheaded man, but sometimes it's just all put together real good."

"So who is he? Or who does he *think* he is?"

"Oh, he knows who he is all right and so does everybody else. Luke McRae. Rancher. I ain't seen him so ticked off in months. Him and the range manager must have had a fuss. They do that."

"I think I'm in love," Piggy said, staring at the door.

Not again. Dahlia rolled her eyes and flopped back in her chair.

The phone at the desk warbled. Gretchen shuffled toward it, fanning a plump hand behind her. "It better hadn't be with him. He's left a string of wishing women from Moscow to Winnemucca. I can think of a dozen who thought they could land him."

Piggy frowned. "Mos-co? You don't mean Russia."

A geography moment flitted through Dahlia's mind, making sense of Gretchen's remark. She had to be speaking of Moscow, Idaho, spelled like the Russian capital. Dahlia had seen it on maps, but she couldn't recall ever hearing it pronounced. To most Texas natives, the Idaho city was as distant as the one in Russia.

The receptionist's brows raised in an arch. "Up north, by Lewiston." She yanked up the receiver. "Forest Service. Callister District . . . We ain't got them here. Call Boise." She clacked the receiver back into its cradle. "Pest," she mumbled.

Undeterred by Gretchen's are-you-for-real look, Piggy went to the midriff-high reception desk and found a rest for her forearms. "A dozen, you say?"

"At least. When it comes to women, that man's a heartless hound." Her gaze swerved to Dahlia. "You should go to the doctor. Make him pay for it. He's worth a fortune. McRaes own the Double Deuce ranches. The homeplace takes up a goodly part of this county. No telling what they own down in the Owyhee."

The fortune of a clumsy cowboy was the farthest thing from Dahlia's mind. His perfectly sculpted mouth had made a much more profound impression.

Piggy's brow crinkled into a frown. "You look a little green, Dal. Let's go home. Jerry can find us there."

Chapter 2

"I mean it, Piggy. If an airport existed within a hundred miles of this place, I'd leave today."

Dahlia half limped, half stalked across the wet grass in the front yard of the small house Piggy's cousin had rented for them, their home for the summer. Besides being cold, now she was injured and angry—at Piggy, at clumsy cowboys, and most of all, at her life. The wasteland it had become had brought her to this appalling situation. "This is the last time I let you talk me into doing something this stupid."

Piggy, door key in hand, overtook her, taking two short steps to each of Dahlia's long ones. "You don't mean it, Dal, that you'd just up and go home?"

"In a heartbeat. We haven't been here two days and things are already a disaster. It's the end of April, for chrissake, and it's thirty-three degrees outside. Besides not telling us what we were getting into here, Jerry lied about this house. He told us it was decent."

Piggy unlocked the door and Dahlia breezed past her, headed for the bedroom.

"It is decent. It's clean, got new paint, only two blocks from town. I like it."

"Piggy, when the temperature is freezing, a house with a malfunctioning furnace doesn't qualify as decent. It doesn't have a stick of furniture." She swept an open-handed arc around the ten-by-ten bedroom. Its only furnishings were her army surplus cot and her bags and suitcases. "If we hadn't hauled these cots with us, we'd be sleeping on the floor."

"Jerry told us the house was unfurnished. That's why we brought them. You're not being fair. Maybe he doesn't know the heat's not working. You promised me you'd make the best of this."

"That was before some *cowboy* knocked me down and broke my hip."

Piggy gave her a catlike smile. "Don't forget, girlfriend. I'm not the only one you promised. You also promised your dad."

Ka-pow! Piggy knew right where to place a punch. Dahlia could still hear her dad's arguments: *Chuck's here to help me, Dally. You go and unwind. . . . When you come back from Idaho, Dally, we'll jump into the Christmas season with both feet. . . . Fall is a better time to look into that mail-order idea you've been talking about. . . .*

Dad. Her fortress. Her Anglo connection to the human race. Since before she was born, he had owned and operated the only grocery store in Loretta, Texas. The Handy Pantry, in all its outdated, small-town glory. What would she have done if he and the rundown little store hadn't been there for her after the catastrophe her husband's life and death left in her lap?

Tears filled her throat. She swallowed hard, recognizing she was skirting the edge of self-pity. *If you waste all your tears on nothing, you won't have them when you need them.* It was a voice from long ago, spoken in the soft, rhythmic accent of her Filipino mother. Get a grip, she told herself.

She sank to her knees, opened her big suitcase and dug for dry clothing. Even the front of her jeans was wet, and she smelled like coffee. "Okay, forget it. I'm not going home. But you have to admit this is ridiculous. We don't even have a place to *sit,* for crying out loud."

Another rush of tears filled her eyes. She ducked her head to hide them as she hooked the front clasp of a pink lace bra. A turtleneck sweater was the warmest thing she had brought. She wiped her nose with the heel of her hand and pulled the burgundy garment on, catching her mane of curls in its neck. She freed them on a sniff, then pushed to her feet and peeled off her wet jeans and panties. "My hip's killing me." She turned her back to Piggy. "Do you see a bruise?"

"Oooh, that's gonna be a good one. You must have hit that table on its corner."

Dahlia stepped into pink lace panties to match the bra she had just put on. "Dumb, unconscious cowboys. Is there anyplace in the universe they're not worthless? I'm surprised I didn't break something. Then what would we have done?"

She zipped herself into clean, dry jeans and slipped back into her jacket. "Listen to me." She began counting off on her fingers. "Number one, you may think this is fun, but I nearly froze last night. And I want to take a bath. If we're going to stay here, this house has to have heat."

"Hey, didn't I help you fool with that stinky oil thing for an hour last night? We'll find somebody to fix it. Chill out." Piggy broke into a laugh. "Chill out. Get it?"

Dahlia threw an exasperated look at the ceiling and ticked off a second finger. "Number two, I'm not staying in this place if we don't get some kind of window coverings. I don't intend to provide this town with four months of daily strip shows.

"And number three, I'm hungry. All we've swallowed for a week is gas-station pizza and Pepsicola. If it takes my last penny, we're going to buy some groceries. I presume the stove and refrigerator work. We sure don't need to spend money eating out. I've got less than twenty dollars to last 'til we get a paycheck."

"Relax. I've still got a fifty tucked away. And we can always fall back on plastic."

"Plastic? Are you kidding?" Dahlia strode to the bathroom, ripped off a strip of toilet paper and blew her nose. "You seem to forget my plastic is long gone." Yet another fact that was enough to make her weep. Once she'd had more credit cards than her purse would hold. Bankruptcy had left her with none.

Piggy moved from propping up the bedroom doorjamb to the same posture in the bathroom doorway. "Look on the bright side. We're better off than the Russians. We've got toilet paper. So why're you so weepy?"

"I'm not weepy. It's just tension."

"And is that not why we're here? A little tension relief? A change of scenery? You've sat around in Loretta for over a year and done nothing but work twelve-hour days and feel sorry for yourself. That's long enough."

"Bite me, Piggy. I don't feel sorry for myself. Work never hurt anybody. And this is definitely a change of scenery." Dahlia squeezed past her. "C'mon. If I don't eat, I'm going to faint."

As she trekked toward the kitchen, guilt nipped at her for being churlish toward the one person who had been her unwavering friend since kindergarten. In the entire world, only Dad and this zany redhead cared about her. The truth of that, as piercing as a needle, brought a swell of comradeship and she stopped and looked back. Piggy, right on her heels, ran into her. They laughed—through thick and thin they had always been able to laugh—and Dahlia wiped her eyes with her sleeve. "I suppose spending a summer in the wilderness isn't so bad. Looks like it'll be cool."

"Atta girl. You can't say that about West Texas. The way I look at it, this is a chance to expand our horizons."

"I can just imagine."

In the kitchen, Dahlia rummaged through the cabinets, looking for peanut butter. "I still say we're too old for this nonsense. It was one thing to go off and do something crazy for the summer when we were kids, but that was a long time ago. I know absolutely nothing about surveying and neither do you. What if we screw up? Jerry will hate us."

Piggy popped the tops on two cans of Pepsi. "Jeez, we're college graduates. How hard can it be? This may be our last chance for a goofy adventure together. Like you say, before long, we'll be old and too decrepit. We'll have to get serious and get real jobs or something."

Dahlia found the giant jar of peanut butter and a box of saltines, her first food since yesterday afternoon. Her mouth watered. She fished a plastic spoon from a sack on the counter. "I remind you, Piggy, you could have already had a real job. Why you didn't take it, I still don't know. I gave mine up for a good reason."

"Oh, gimme a break. You're not gonna lay that martyr-helping-my-dad trip on me again, are you?"

The sarcasm hurt. Dahlia's spine stiffened. She was glad, no, eager, to help her aging father, but there was no fooling a friend of twenty-five years. Helping Dad was only part of the reason she had moved home. In truth, the manner of her husband's death and all that followed had whipped her. Admitting it was as painful as a leg cramp.

"I *was* helping him. Until I let you drag me off on this wild-goose chase." She resumed heaping peanut butter onto a cracker. "You're not kidding anybody either, you know. Staying in Loretta? Keeping books at the cotton co-op? That couldn't exactly be classified a career move." She thrust a cracker toward Piggy. "Here. Have some lunch."

Piggy took the cracker and licked off the peanut butter. "You're the career girl. I went to college to kill time. I'll be mad forever 'cause I didn't join the Navy and see the world. Threw away all those years learning number crunching when I could have been sailing all over with a boatload of horny guys."

"A boatload of horny guys. Every woman's dream."

Piggy reached for a second cracker. "Couldn't have been any worse than marrying Kenneth Jarrett. Crook. Self-centered asshole extraordinaire. As far as I'm concerned, that Corvette and the North Fork of the Trinity River bridge did you a big favor."

"Stop saying that, Piggy. Lightning's going to strike you. And I might be standing beside you when it happens."

"It already did, remember?"

Dahlia did remember. Piggy's senior year at UT. Her fiancé of two years left her at the altar and Piggy's attitude about men had made a hundred-eighty-degree turn.

"Anyway," Piggy went on, "we're not gonna discuss the asshole of assholes this whole summer, right? We're

gonna resolve one more time, here and now, that what
he did wasn't your fault. His estate's settled, the lawsuit's
settled, the IRS is off your back. You couldn't be more
cleansed if you ate a whole package of laxative. It's time
to stop beating up on yourself. Elton thinks so, too.
That's why he pushed you to come with me on this trip."

"I'm more than cleansed. I feel like I've been skinned."

"So? Now you grow new skin. Make a fresh start."

As she always did with Piggy, Dahlia felt herself re-
lenting. She sighed as some of the deep anger that had
become so much a part of her sneaked back into its dark
hole. "Well, at least I've got something of a reprieve.
For four months, you won't be trying to push me into
bed with Mick Ivey."

Piggy giggled. "I'll find somebody else. . . . Maybe
you don't know what you missed with ol' Mick. Dorinda
Parsons says he's a regular Roto-Rooter."

Dahlia felt herself blush, but she couldn't keep from
laughing, too. "For chrissake, Piggy, that's disgusting. I
don't believe she said that."

"Would I lie? He's not a bad guy, you know. I remember how moon-eyed he was over you in high school. He
still has a crush on you. You think he comes into the
Handy Pantry all the time because he's shopping?"

"He comes in to buy beer, and lots of it. He can forget
it. If there's anything I don't need, it's a cowboy Casa-
nova who's a drunk to boot. . . . Besides, I'm not like
you. I couldn't handle recreational sex."

"Pity. It doesn't hurt nearly as bad as the other kind."

"We're a pair, aren't we? The princesses of love gone
wrong. We should be in a soap opera."

Piggy's mouth twisted into a bitter smile, and she
shrugged. "You know what I always say about the battle
of the sexes. Take no prisoners. Then you don't have to
worry about their feed and care." She dipped a plastic
spoon into the peanut butter and scooped out a spoonful.
"Speaking of men, did you get a look at that long, tall
sucker who ran you down? The once-over he gave you
would fry a burger."

Did she get a look at him? Like a brand, the blue fire

of his eyes had seared his image on her brain. She still felt the heat. His gaze had done more than peel off her shirt. It had touched her at a deep level she hadn't known was there. An uneasiness still drifted around inside her. Life with Kenneth had left her tough and resistant to men, she had told herself. But then, she hadn't met one who so unapologetically sized her up, made her feel so, so . . . *female*. Being that exposed was a new and frightening experience.

She didn't dare tell Piggy, or anyone.

"Don't forget, Piggy, we didn't come here to chase men."

"Well, no, but that doesn't mean . . ."

"These is real good tires, Luke. Might outlast your truck."

"Think so?" Sipping coffee, Luke leaned on an elbow on a worktable and watched Holt Johnson's teenage employee mount the last of a set of new tires on his aging 4x4. He had known Holt his entire life, had played on the high-school basketball team with the Exxon station owner's youngest brother.

Holt stuffed a dirty rag into the rear pocket of his blue coveralls. "You seen the new Fords?"

"Nope. Not looking." It would take the sale of forty fat steers to pay for a new rig. Luke didn't make a purchase that costly without careful thought.

Holt poured himself a cup of coffee from a filthy urn. Luke grimaced and told himself it had to be cleaner on the inside. The station owner rambled on about how many miles the last set of tires had lasted on Luke's battered Ford and jawed about cattle prices, which he couldn't possibly know a damn thing about. In twenty years, he had scarcely left the service station as far as anybody knew.

Though Luke participated in the conversation, his mind stayed on the woman he had knocked flat earlier in the Forest Service offices. Another newcomer. Outsider. The Forest Service kept bringing them in, as if enough weren't coming on their own.

Like swarms of grasshoppers, migration from south to north had moved across Oregon and Washington for years. City people—retirees, movie stars, Silicon Valley new rich. He had eyed the encroachment from across the state line, thinking, *Better thee than me,* but his security had had a short life. Soon *they* discovered Montana, then Idaho. Now they came in a stream, as if a gate had been left open. Now he understood the bumper stickers he saw every time he went to Oregon: DON'T CALIFORNICATE OREGON. Somebody oughtta make one for Idaho.

No doubt the woman was one of them. He wondered if she was the kind who would try to sue him. You never knew these days, especially with folks from California. Filing a lawsuit seemed to be their solution to life's problems. Last fall, a Los Angeles woman had crashed into a small bunch of Double Deuce cows trailing home from summer grazing. With no clue what "open range" meant and no interest in learning, she had sued and he'd had to pay a lawyer to defend the ranch.

The black-haired woman didn't look to be hurt, but he had offered to take her to a doctor all the same. He guessed that was all he could do. Issue closed.

But it wasn't closed, not in a distant part of his mind. Her being an outsider or filing a lawsuit wasn't what nagged him. What kept coming back was the memory of round breasts, nipples peaked and unusually dark behind a lacy bra under that wet T-shirt. He did love the sight of a shapely female form strategically covered by skimpy lace. An edgy feeling crept through him. The crotch of his jeans grew tighter.

Christ, he had gone without too long. Otherwise, his cock wouldn't be twitching in his britches in the Exxon station's garage over some woman he'd seen for no more than a minute. Being aroused by women he didn't know was a luxury he could neither afford nor allow. He had learned the hard way the pitfalls of giving in to his more primitive urges without thought. A painful, expensive lesson that hadn't ended yet.

"Looks like you're all fixed up. Too bad about the Circle K, eh, Luke?"

"Hunh? . . . Oh, yeah. Dang sure was." Luke set his empty mug on the worktable as the rack holding his truck lowered.

Holt scrubbed a forearm across his brow, leaving a black streak. "What if the buyer does like they did over in Montana?"

"How's that?"

"A fella in here the other day told me some stockbroker from back East bought a ranch over there. Brought in a bunch of sick buffalo. Spread a disease all over the place."

Tales of that nature had floated around the Northwest ranching community for several years. Sometimes the curse was TB, sometimes it was brucellosis or one of a dozen other plagues that chilled a rancher's blood. As the owner of a substantial herd of carefully bred and nurtured beef cattle, Luke never stopped studying or vaccinating— or following up rumors of a new outbreak. "That's just a story, Holt, but with these dudes and flatlanders coming in here, it could happen."

Holt ordered the teenager to back the Ford out of the shop and led Luke inside to the cash register. "I heard it was a computer nerd from Seattle that bought old Tuffy out. They say the guy's never seen a cow up close."

"Yep, that's what they say," Luke answered absently while writing a check, his thoughts dominated by the black-haired woman. She was foreign looking. A hybrid mix of some kind, but he couldn't put his finger on it. Oriental? Too tall. Indian or Mexican, maybe. Her light-colored eyes were deceiving, green being a recessive gene. Well, whatever her breeding, she couldn't be bringing anything worthwhile to Idaho.

"Why didn't you buy it, Luke?"

"Lord, Holt, I've already got more to do than I can say grace over. Not that I wouldn't have been interested. But it happened so fast, I didn't know about it 'til it was over. Guess Tuffy was more desperate to sell than I thought."

The red-faced station owner shook his head wearily and tucked the Double Deuce check into a greasy cash drawer. " 'Preciate your business, buddy. Things is changing, ain't they? Not like they was when we was in school. I ain't so sure I like all these new folks."

Luke looked into Holt Johnson's face and saw the fear common in the eyes of many of the old-timers around the county. He suspected it showed in his own eyes if anybody looked close. "We can't kill 'em, Holt, much as we might like to. Guess a man's got to learn to roll with it, else get mowed down."

Leaving the service station, Luke turned south toward Boise and a two o'clock meeting. The sale of Tuffy Keeler's ranch pressed on him heavily. Like the Double Deuce, the Circle K had been a family operation for a over a hundred years. Good friends, good neighbors, the Keelers. What did a computer nerd need with a cattle ranch?

He had intended to look into buying it when he first learned Tuffy had decided to sell out, though it would have meant a staggering debt. But with a cold, wet February and March, calving had been harder than usual. His free time and mental energy had been used up the last few months with trips to Oregon, taking his seven-year-old son to a Portland specialist and arguing with his ex-wife. The new doc had recommended his son be put into a special school for mentally and physically challenged children, the idea had gone down like sour milk until he found such a place in Boise.

To make matters worse, his ex-wife wanted their two daughters to spend the summer with her in Boise, which was bound to be trouble with a capital T.

He shifted in his seat, combating the discomfort brought on by thinking about the woman at the Forest Service, puzzled by the charge of lust she had set off in him. He hadn't seen his lady lawyer friend in weeks. That had to be his problem. While he was in Boise today, maybe he would have time to pay her a visit.

In the idleness of the two-hour drive, he pictured Belinda Hughes. Tall and thin, long yellow hair pinned up in a roll on the back of her head, she looked cool and untouchable in a mannish suit. But stripped bare, hair loose and draped over her shoulders, she was hot as a woodstove in January and more than a little kinky.

The contrasting images excited him. He enjoyed bringing the deputy attorney general down off her pedestal. He could call her today and she would "clear her calendar" and meet him at her house in the foothills outside Boise. He liked that. It was more convenient than making dates and maneuvering to keep them.

Belinda took him into her bed for nothing more than fun and blistering sex; he went for the same two reasons. Neither of them had ever been disappointed. They refrained from boring each other with sentimental platitudes, phony expressions of affection or personal problems.

If they discussed anything at all, it was politics. She droned on about women's lib, double standards and equality of the sexes. Sometimes he listened, other times he tuned her out. He didn't like her much and didn't tell her he did. They weren't even friends in the way he defined friendship. None of that was important. He was glad she didn't let emotions get in the way of what satisfied them both. Their two-year-old affair was a perfect arrangement for a divorced, confirmed bachelor.

Despite Belinda's political views on the exploitation of women, she wasn't above using feminine favors to advance her career, so he knew others preceded and followed him when it suited her agenda. He didn't care and it felt good not to.

Deceit and hypocrisy. Typical of his experience with women. He had fought it for the nearly nine years he had been married to Janet. He saw it in the women closest to him—his mother and how she had taken decision making at the ranch from his dad, and his two sisters, the way they manipulated their husbands into living somewhere the men didn't want to, doing jobs neither of them liked or knew how to do.

Steeped in negative thoughts about the opposite sex, he decided not to call Belinda Hughes after all, for their affair did have a flaw. As physically satisfying as he found sport with her to be, invariably, he left her bed feeling like a key without a lock, the part of him above the waist longing for something more.

He usually tossed off the emotion as a temporary weakness and pushed it out of his mind until he needed her again. He was in no mood for that empty feeling today. In two hours he would face a counselor about his son's future, a hard enough truth. He didn't need to be reminded that thoughtless sex and human weakness were responsible for the little guy entering the world with a damaged brain.

Chapter 3

"Should we?"

"Supper club? That's a redneck bar if I ever saw one." Dahlia stood beside Piggy in front of Carlton's Lounge & Supper Club, each hanging on to two plastic grocery sacks bulked with necessities.

Dark had descended. Except for foot traffic in and out of the town's two bars, the main street was deserted. From a high, narrow window beside Carlton's front door, inviting golden light spilled out onto the sidewalk. As revelers came and went, loud country music blurted through the doorway.

"The perfect place to find Jerry."

"I wonder if the food's fit to eat."

"It's too cold to go back to that house."

"Only one drink, Piggy. I don't want to make a night of it. If we're going to stay in that quaint little cottage, we have to do something about the furnace. And we *have* to find your cousin. We can't just hang out."

Piggy shrugged. "Whatever."

They stowed their groceries in the Blazer and headed for the supper club. As they opened the door, a blast from the jukebox hit them full force and Dahlia jumped.

They stood for a moment, letting their eyes adjust to the gloom. A layer of cigarette smoke floated above them. Evidently, the smokeless environment movement had yet to arrive at Carlton's. Even stronger than the smoke, the tang of masculine sweat pervaded the air.

An antique bar ran the length of one side of the corridorlike room. Tall stools lined up along the front of it, all of which were occupied by cowboys and suspendered

stout men Dahlia thought might be loggers. Most of them
looked as if they had rolled in the mud outside. Wearing
clean jeans, a sweater, and Nikes, she felt overdressed.

A TV sat on top of an avocado-green refrigerator in
the far corner behind the bar. Baseball players darted
and leaped across the screen in silence, the broadcaster's
voice no match for the jukebox. A dozen pairs of eyes
turned toward them. In the middle of pouring whiskey,
the bartender, the lone female, flicked a glance their way.
Dahlia made a silent groan. As much as she hungered
for a real meal, she wished she had balked at the choice
of places to have it.

Though the bar stools were filled, the tables were
empty. Piggy took the lead and they threaded their way
to one against the wall opposite the bar. The two-foot
Formica square sat spotlighted beneath a Coors sign
hanging on the paneled wall.

"We may as well be on stage," Dahlia grumbled. "All
we need is a drum roll."

As they sat down, the men whistled and hooted.

"Close enough," Piggy said.

A monumental urge to bolt darted through Dahlia.
She leaned forward and yelled to be heard over Garth
Brooks. "This is *worse* than a redneck bar. Let's leave."

"Wait a minute. The testosterone's knee-deep. This
could get interesting."

Dahlia was too hungry to be intrigued by wading in
male hormones. Through an amber-lit doorway at the
rear of the room, she could see a few customers dining
at tables covered with red-and-white checked cloths. The
aroma of searing meat wafted past, mingling with the
barroom's earthy smells. An acute pang clutched her
stomach.

The bartender brought a plastic bowl of unshelled peanuts. "Whatcha drinkin'?"

"Margarita," Piggy said.

Dahlia ordered white wine and dug into the peanuts.

Soon, two more drinks appeared, sent by one of the
men at the bar. The bartender pointed him out. He gave
them a toothy grin and tipped a greasy gimme cap.

A short while later, several margaritas and glasses of white wine were lined up in front of them, all bought by different bar patrons, and Piggy was doing her best to keep up with them. Dahlia concluded the men weren't being so friendly, sending them free drinks. She and Piggy were being slugged with alcohol and her fun-loving pal didn't care.

She asked for a Coke, shelled peanuts at a fast pace, and watched with trepidation as Piggy downed another margarita. Two had evaporated before Dahlia persuaded her to transfer into the restaurant to eat.

They had just been handed menus when a tall silhouette with a cowboy hat appeared in the doorway. Dahlia's stomach thumped. Her every female instinct went on alert. She didn't want to look at him, but if doing it should strike her blind, she couldn't keep from staring at the cowboy who had mowed her down.

The restaurant's young hostess met him with a molar-showing smile. He draped an arm around her shoulder, removed his hat, and held it to his midriff by the crown. His head bent and he nodded as the hostess whispered to him. He chuckled wickedly. His girlfriend, Dahlia thought, and felt a letdown.

Anyone born and raised in West Texas recognized Wranglers as the uniform of cowboys, but at the time of her fall, Dahlia hadn't noticed how well his fit him. Faded and soft, they molded around muscled thighs, cupped the subtle masculine bulge below his trophy belt buckle. *Trophy belt buckle? Not a rodeo-er!*

The hostess rose on tiptoes and whispered to him, then giggled, bumped his long thigh with her hip and led him toward a table in the far corner. To Dahlia's bewilderment, she resented the hostess.

As his boot heels thudded across the wood floor, Piggy's gaze followed him, too.

"You look like an owl," Dahlia whispered. "Will you stop?"

Piggy leaned on one elbow studying him, tapping her bottom lip with her forefinger. "I'm picturing him naked, stretched out on a king-sized bed in a Marriott some-where. Champagne. Black satin sheets. I bet he looks like . . . Who was that statue we saw that summer in Rome? The naked one with—"

"Shh. It was David. And it was Florence."

"He's the real deal, you know? Cowboy through and through."

"Humph. That means he's broke or in debt up to his ears."

"Gretchen said he's rich."

"Then he's probably a drunk with two or three illegiti-mate kids somewhere."

"What the hell? I don't want to keep him. I just want to—"

"Piggy. Stop it."

He cast them a glance. Piggy waved. A few minutes later, the hostess, long faced and sullen, came to them and pointed back toward him. "Mr. McRae over at that table wants to know if you want to eat supper with him."

"Certainly," Piggy said, rising and picking up her drink.

Dahlia sprang from her chair to protest. *Thunk.* Her knee struck the table leg. A full water glass tipped over, the condiments in the middle of the table clattered, and she felt her face flame. Under the glowers of the two other dining couples, she scooted jars and silverware to the corner of the table. The waitress hurried over with a towel and began to sop up water.

"I am so sorry," Dahlia gushed, dabbing with her nap-kin. "My knee bumped and . . . I'm just so sorry."

Shooting her a malicious glare, the waitress gathered the four corners of the wet tablecloth, making a bundle of the condiment jars and silverware, then stamped away in a huff, dripping a trail of water.

Dahlia smiled at the two staring couples and lifted her shoulders in an apologetic shrug. For lack of an alterna-tive, she followed in Piggy's footsteps. Her tipsy pal was already seated and Luke was standing when Dahlia reached his table.

"Luke McRae." He offered his hand, his glacier blue eyes freezing her in place. "That's not the first time something got spilled in this joint."

Words failed her. Nodding, she shook hands woodenly, her slim hand lost in his large one. She barely mumbled her name.

"It was real rude of me not to introduce myself this morning. Sometimes talks with the Forest Service make me forget my manners."

He spoke in a deep, soft drawl with an unfamiliar cadence. Neither Texan nor Southern—just slow and easy. And seductive. She hadn't noticed his voice in the Forest Service reception room. "Oh, that's okay."

She hooked a clump of flyaway, crinkled hair behind her ear. Her mind stumbled for a clever remark, but all save idiot conversation eluded her. "You don't like the Forest Service?"

"They've got their rules. Sometimes they get a little heavy-handed is all." He grinned. "Say, it's good to see you moving around. I've been worried about running you down ever since it happened. Least I can do is buy you supper."

For some reason, Dahlia believed he had, in fact, worried about her. Looking up at his wide shoulders, for an instant she felt so safe. If a fire-breathing dragon leaped from the kitchen, she was positive Luke McRae would slay it. "Oh, that isn't necessary. Really."

He pulled out a chair. "Yes, it is. Here, sit down." He spoke with such authority, she sat without further contention.

The hostess brought menus again, a blessed diversion, though after Dahlia read it, she didn't know why one was needed. The fare was steak. Period. French-fried or baked potatoes. Lettuce and tomato salad with French or ranch dressing.

While they waited for their meal, Luke ordered another margarita for Piggy, and a double shot of Jack Daniel's, neat, for himself. Dahlia asked for a Coke and found herself wondering how much he had already drunk.

The conversation revolved around Texas, for which Dahlia was glad. With a nerve jumping in her stomach and having to keep an eye on a friend who must be on her fifth margarita, Dahlia was too distracted to concentrate on anything that required much thought.

When their food arrived, as if she hadn't been tormented by hunger for two days, she picked at it. Her appetite had fled.

Luke gave her a questioning look, his knife and fork poised above his plate. "You don't like steak?"

"Yes, uh, yes, I do." The meat could have been cardboard for all she knew. Her attention was devoted to his hair—slightly wavy, but cut to control it, mussed in front. Not quite red, not brown either, but somewhere in between. Cinnamon, she decided. Even in the dimly lit room, she could see a tan line across his forehead where his hat fit.

"My friend Dahlia loves steak. She's a meat expert." Piggy's voice had become a slur. "She's a butcher. She can turn a cow into hamburger in three minutes." Piggy held up two fingers.

Dahlia cringed.

"Yeah? A real butcher?"

She opened her mouth to talk, but Piggy spoke first. "As we say in Texas, there ain't no such thing as a pretend butcher. It's like a calling. Something you either is or you ain't."

"Hunh. You look so—well, so ladylike."

Before Dahlia could reply, Piggy reared back, her glass balanced between thumb and forefinger. "What, you think ladies can't be butchers? It's not a gender-restrictive occupation, you know." Butchers and restrictive came out mushy. Dahlia planted her elbow on the table edge and covered her mouth with her palm. Any minute now, she would strangle the person who had led her into this humiliation.

"Well, there you go." Luke sliced off another bite of well-done steak. "Looks like we're all sort of in the beef business. Where'd a pretty gal like you learn butchering?"

Oh, dear God. Could he get any cornier? "Well, I—"

"She learned it at her daddy's knee. They're a family of butchers." Piggy broke into a booming laugh.

I'll kill you, Piggy. I'll just kill you.

With the end of dinner came another round of drinks. It appeared Luke fulfilled at least one of Dahlia's expectations of cowboys. Piggy began to tell bawdy jokes and throw out suggestive remarks. Uninhibited sober, drunk she was downright raucous. And tonight, not amusing. Dahlia wanted to slide under the table.

Luke chewed on his toothpick, sipped at his whiskey and made a few naughty comments of his own. Dahlia began to fidget. What had they gotten into?

With his attention turned on Piggy, Dahlia felt out of place. She could see him and her friend winding up in bed somewhere. She'd be lying if she said she wasn't disappointed, but then, men often overlooked her. She had always suspected she didn't give off the right vibes.

She couldn't debate it now. Now, she had to save Piggy from Piggy. She mentioned they had groceries in the Blazer, suggested they drink up and go home. Neither Piggy nor Luke heard her.

A lighted Budweiser clock hung on the wall across the room. Its hour hand crept past ten. They were the only customers left in the restaurant.

At eleven, Piggy launched Lucille Ball's Vitameatavegamin routine. She had spent years cultivating an impressive repertoire of Lucille Ball antics. It came from when they were younger, when Dahlia followed her into so many ill-fated adventures, Piggy's mom dubbed them "Lucy and Ethel." Piggy had taken the nickname to heart, even to the point of lightening her auburn hair to a carrot color. The cook came out of the kitchen to watch and listen and he and Luke roared with laughter.

Thirty more minutes. Luke ordered another double shot and another margarita. Piggy looked as if she would tip off her chair any minute. She let the margarita sit and took up ice water, a sure signal to someone who knew her as well as Dahlia did that she'd had way too much to drink.

Dahlia had drunk so much Coke, she felt she sloshed

when she walked, despite making three trips to the ladies' room. She'd had enough of this fun-filled evening.
The rented cottage, their frosty home away from home,
took on appeal. She rose, lifted her jacket from her chairback and pulled it on.

Luke looked up. "Where you going?"

"Home. She's had more than enough to drink. Thank
you for dinner." Dahlia moved to her friend's side and
put an arm around her waist. "Come on, Lucy. You've
been on stage long enough." Dahlia struggled to stuff
her into her coat. Her body was as rubbery as cooked
spaghetti.

Luke stood, too, dragging his vest off his chairback.
"Lucy? I thought her name was Peggy."

"Her name is Piggy. With an I. It's short for Pegine.
It's Irish." Dahlia had made that explanation so often, it
flowed from her mouth automatically.

Luke dug a money clip from his pocket, peeled off
some bills and dropped them beside his plate. "She looks
pretty limber. You need some help?"

"No, thanks. I can manage if I can just get her to
the car."

"I can handle that." He picked up his hat from the
neighboring table and put it on, then came around and
scooped Piggy off her chair. Dahlia stared up at him,
dumbfounded.

The hostess zoomed to where they were, her eyes large
with question. Luke gave her a wink and a devilish grin.
"Guess this little gal's had one too many." He headed
toward the door. Dahlia grabbed up their purses and
followed.

Luke carried Piggy through the front room, ignoring
the chorus of wolf whistles and rank suggestions from
the crowd seated at the bar. Dahlia, needing to feel use-
ful, edged ahead of him and held the front door open.
Piggy's head lolled backward as she sang with the jukebox all the way outside.

"Where you parked?" Carlton's door swung shut behind them.

The temperature had dropped. Dahlia zipped up her

jacket and pointed at the Blazer parallel parked across the street from Fielder's. Until they arrived at the passenger door, she didn't remember the keys were in Piggy's purse. Luke stood by shivering with Piggy in his arms while Dahlia dug into an unfamiliar handbag. She gave him a thin smile. "Sorry. Poor planning."

Door open at last, Luke positioned the life of the party on the Blazer's passenger seat. Piggy mumbled something about being cold and sleepy.

He resettled his hat and looked at Piggy. "I wouldn't want her head tomorrow. Where'd you say you're staying? Tom Baker's old house?"

No. No way. "Well, yes, I think that's it, but you don't need to—"

"If you couldn't get her into the car, how will you get her out? I'll just follow you."

Absolutely not. No drunk cowboy is coming to our house. "No, really. You don't have—"

But he was already crossing the street, striding toward a lone white pickup.

Chapter 4

Dahlia parked the Blazer in the carport attached to the cottage. Luke's pickup pulled in behind it. The little white rental, its windows unlit, loomed ghostlike in the chilled black night. Their headlights and the relentless screech from the sawmill not far away were the only signs of life.

Piggy was out. With the temperature so cold, leaving her to sleep in the Blazer wasn't an option. Dahlia had never felt more isolated, acutely aware she didn't know another conscious human being within two thousand miles. The man she had thought to be a dragon slayer before he consumed so much Jack Daniel's now seemed more like the dragon himself. She had to keep him outside.

She killed the engine and went back to intercept him. "Really, you don't have to—"

"You already said that." He slid out, gripped her shoulders and set her aside, out of his way. "Your front door locked?"

"Well, yes, but—"

"We can't get in if you don't unlock it." He opened the Blazer's passenger door, lifted Piggy out and started toward the front stoop.

By the time she grabbed their two purses and the four plastic sacks and reached the stoop, he was waiting, a scowl on his face. She stepped past him and shifted the bags to dig into Piggy's purse for the key.

The porch was roughly four feet square, barely large enough for the three of them. The air seemed charged by his nearness. He was just too damn close.

"Sugar," he said from behind her, "this little gal didn't weigh much when we started out, but she's getting heavier by the minute. And it's awful cold."

Uneasiness blossomed into annoyance. She hated men talking down to her, but even more, she hated having one who was a stranger call her phony epithets.

She fumbled with the old lock in the dark, her fingers cold and stiff. Finally opening the door, she reached inside and flipped every switch on the wall. Light flooded the porch and living room. Thank God the lights worked better than the furnace. "Thanks again for your help. If you'll just put her down, I can get her inside."

As if he hadn't heard, he carried his load through the doorway, shooting a derisive look from the corner of his eye. "Don't worry, sugar. I haven't hurt any pretty girls in a week."

Okay, so he knew she didn't trust him. What was wrong with that? "I usually don't let strange men into my house in the middle of the night," she said to his back.

"Most folks don't think I'm strange. Where's her bed?" She could hear a shiver in his voice. The temperature inside the house felt even colder than outside and she could see their breath when they talked.

Luke was about as cold as he had ever been and this woman was testing his patience. He followed her down a short hall leading from the living room to a bedroom. She switched on the light and fussed with arranging a sleeping bag on an army cot.

"This is her bed?" He surveyed the small bedroom. Besides the cot, all he saw was a cardboard box and a couple of suitcases. He laid his burden on the sleeping bag and straightened. "Why're you keeping it so cold in here?"

The black-haired woman looked up and he nearly drowned in the green depths of her eyes. The thing that had been twisting inside him all evening gave a hard yank.

"Our heater doesn't work," she said.

Uh-oh. He sure didn't need to get roped into a furnace repair job at midnight. Thumbing his hat back, he planted his hands on his hips. "You mean you're staying here with no heat?"

She shrugged and played with her coat zipper. "Well, it's temporary. We haven't gotten around to it yet."

"You just camping out, or what?"

She blinked at him. "I suppose you could say that. Sort of."

Lord, these two women were kooks. He looked at the floor and shook his head. "In cold country, sugar, one thing you don't want to be without is heat. It's freezing out there now and it'll be *real* cold before morning."

His tone must have sounded harsh because those soft-looking lips that had been teasing him for hours clamped into a pout. She lifted her straight little nose and sniffed at him. "It really isn't your concern, is it?"

He guessed he had pissed her off. Women. They were always ungrateful, and nothing you did was ever good enough. "Nope. Just neighborly advice. Your friend there"—he tilted his head toward the drunk one, wishing he had just left them at Carlton's and gone home—"you oughtta throw another blanket on her. Hypothermia can come on quick when somebody's dead drunk."

She frowned and looked down at her friend. Hell, he was wasting his breath. These two probably didn't know sic 'em about hypothermia. He wondered how long they had been staying here without heat.

"What's wrong with your furnace?" He could kick himself for asking. He didn't have time to concern himself with it. The meeting in Boise had gone on longer than expected and he had stayed in Carlton's too late. If he hit the road right now, it would be nearly two o'clock before he got home.

"Well, I don't know much about it, but I think it takes oil and the tank may be empty."

She was shaking a little. He couldn't tell if she was nervous or cold. Those berry-colored lips turned down at the corners and dark crescents showed under her eyes. She looked tired and lost, but her elevated chin told him she was too proud to ask for help.

He felt that yank in his chest again and blew out a

long breath. *Shit.* She might look like she had just lost her last friend, but he guessed she had found herself a furnace repairman. "The tank out back?"

She made a little sigh and nodded, grateful after all. He saw that in her eyes, too.

Passing through the living room, he noticed the fireplace and stopped. "Guess you don't have any firewood, huh?"

"Firewood?"

"It'd be a little warmer if you'd build a fire."

Her eyes widened as if a lightbulb had clicked on. "Oh. Well, actually . . ." She lifted her arms and let them fall. "No, we don't have any wood."

He strode to the back door, gritted his teeth and charged into the freezing dark. Christ, he'd be lucky if he didn't have pneumonia by the time he got away from here.

The porch light came on, lighting a path to a rusty storage tank. Glad she had enough thought to turn on a light, he hoisted himself up on a ladder rung on one side of the stand and knocked on the tank's steel wall with his knuckles. A hollow sound pinged. "Yep. It's empty," he called back to her.

Under a window, he saw ricked firewood covered by a black plastic sheet. He yanked back one corner. "Here's a cord of wood, all split. Didn't you know this was here?"

"N-n-no," she said from the porch in a shivery voice. "We d-d-didn't lift up the plastic."

"Looks like you got some kindling, too." He picked several logs from the top of the pile, cradling them in the crook of his elbow, then bent over for some kindling sticks. He passed by her, his eyes watering from the cold, carrying the firewood back through the doorway. "Cover that wood up. You don't want it exposed to the weather."

He was shivering worse than a cold dog. Sinking to one knee in front of the fireplace, he checked the damper and laid a fire. She wasn't behind him, so he hoped she was outside re-covering the woodpile like he told her.

Hearing her footsteps, he turned and looked up at her. "You got a newspaper?"

She left the room and came back with a paperback book.

He ripped out the pages and stuffed them under the kindling. "You got matches?"

She shook her head. Nope, no matches. Having a match to light a fire when the temperature's freezing would be too simple. He sighed and stalked outside to his pickup. He kept a work coat stashed behind the seat. He put it on, then found a book of matches in the jockey box.

Back inside, he lit the paperback pages. Fire flared and crackled and he placed a split log on top. Just the smell of burning wood made the room seem warmer. He looked up at her and she wiped one eye with her fingertips. Lord, was she crying?

"That'll get going in a minute." He stood, pulled his handkerchief from his back pocket and wiped his hands. He felt mean and was glad of it. As sweet as her body looked in that wine-colored sweater, mean might be the safest way to feel. He still had a wet-T-shirt memory floating around in his head. "Being from Texas and all, guess you girls don't know much about getting along in cold weather. Didn't anybody tell you it won't get warm around here 'til July?"

"July?" Her eyes rounded. Her black lashes looked like little brushes.

"I'm surprised Tom rented you this place with an empty oil tank. You should've made him fill it up. I know him. I'll call him tomorrow."

"You don't have to. I mean, we can buy our—"

"Nope. I'll call him. It's not right he rented you a place with no heat. Stove oil has to come from down the road a ways. Unless it's an emergency, you'll be lucky to get a delivery tomorrow.

"You could go up to the ski lodge and spend the night, but it's thirty-eight miles and it's a little late. I expect there's black ice on the road. Besides, your friend in there"—he tipped his head toward the drunk one's bedroom—"doesn't exactly look like she's game for the trip."

She crossed her arms and lifted her chin. "We survived last night, Mr. McRae. Despite how it looks, we aren't helpless and we aren't stupid."

The sassy comeback amused him. "Then I guess you'll make it 'til the oil truck shows up."

Her lips pursed. He felt like an ass. "Look, I didn't mean to make you mad, but I need to get home. I could use a cup of coffee if you've got some. I've had a little too much to drink myself and I've got a far piece to drive."

Dahlia was too happy he was leaving to be mad. Besides being drunk and high-handed, he was so rude he wouldn't even let her finish a sentence. If coffee would put him on his way, she would make him a gallon. "As a matter of fact, we do."

Before she could move, he strode toward their kitchen, the pounding of his boot heels echoing in the house's emptiness. She had no choice but to follow.

The kitchen light seemed uncommonly bright in the white room. Walls, ceilings, cabinets—all were painted sterile white. Even the kitchen floor was covered with a white-on-white patterned vinyl. The entire house smelled of fresh paint.

Luke looked around. "Tom must have found a sale on white paint."

"At least it's clean," Dahlia said, parroting Piggy's earlier comment. "Sorry I can't ask you to sit down, but as you can see, we have no chairs."

He stood in the kitchen doorway, his gaze roving the empty living room. "You don't have any window curtains, either."

"We intended to buy shades in town today, but there weren't any. We have to go shopping somewhere."

He came back and stood over her while she spooned out coffee, his hands splayed on his hips. A wave of tremors rippled along her nerves. She had never experienced anything so crazy as this unnerving physical attraction and she didn't like it.

"You'll have to go down south, to Boise, to buy house goods. They've got some of those big stores down there." He headed back to the living room. "Let's don't waste that fire."

Dahlia followed. He squatted and leaned forward on the balls of his feet, added another log to the fire. His coat and vest slid up, showing a plain leather belt. Wranglers stretched taut across his narrow butt and muscled thighs.

He looked up and caught her staring. His lips curved into a slow grin that was almost a smirk. "Like what you see, sugar?"

Moscow to Winnemucca. Annoyance pecked at her. "Don't flatter yourself. And stop calling me sugar."

He stood and warmed his palms in front of the fire, an amused expression playing across his face. "What should I call you? What's your name again? Della?"

Della? Peggy? Was he teasing? Did he really not remember their names? "Dahlia," she said sharply. "Like the flower."

Pop! The overhead light went out. She jumped and glared up at the dark light fixture mounted on the ceiling. In an instant, the ambience had changed. The fire glowed orange, and a long yellow bar of light spilled from the kitchen doorway. The living room became as intimate as a cocoon, almost cozy. It even felt a few degrees warmer.

He stared at the ceiling fixture, too. "Guess an extra lightbulb would be too much to hope for."

She bit down on her lower lip as their gazes connected.

"Flower, huh?" He offered her his open palm. "Well, pretty flower, I won't bite. Come on over here and warm up."

Though her fingers and toes had gone numb, she hesitated. Finally, she sidled up beside him, holding her palms out to the precious warmth. It seeped into her and her tensed muscles began to relax. "I don't think I've ever been so cold."

Their arms were almost touching. She sensed he was waiting for her to look up and she did.

"There's better ways than this to get warm," he said softly.

Her heart went off on another wild tangent as a too-vivid image of twisted bedsheets and bare muscular arms and legs darted through her mind. For the first time since she and Piggy had arrived in this place, she was glad her bed was a cot. "And I suppose you know all of them."

"Not all. But a few you might like."

With a silly titter, she returned her gaze to the fire, hoping a display of amused indifference didn't appear to be as bogus it was. "Really, I don't know what you must think, Mr. McRae, but I'm honestly not interested."

He straightened and adjusted his vest, like his pride might be hurt, then turned his back to the fire and crossed his wrists behind himself. She turned, too, duplicating his stance. His vest front slid back, exposing his belt buckle. She couldn't read what it said, but could make out a bucking horse.

"Fire feels good," he said.

She recognized the call for a truce and smiled without looking at him. "Yeah." Then she had to ask, "Do you rodeo?"

"Me?" He barked a laugh. "No ma'am. Fact is, I don't much like rodeos."

"Oh. I just thought . . ." Her gaze traveled to his fly. It seemed to be bulging. Her heart thumped. *Did he . . . ? No, of course not . . .* "I—I mean, you have a buckle."

He grasped the ornate silver oval with one hand, tipped it up slightly and studied it. "It's old."

She sneaked another glance at his fly. It *was* bulging. She inched away from him. "You, uh, used to rodeo, then?"

"No, ma'am. It's from high school. Saddle bronc. You know what that is?"

"I'm from Texas," she said dryly. "You must have been good at it, one time anyway."

"It was a dare." He flashed a cocky, one-sided grin. "You see, in a way, I hustled it."

She waited for more, but he didn't follow up. "You can't tell just part of a story. How did you hustle it?"

His shoulders shrugged in a self-deprecating way. "When we were kids, my brother and I used to make a little spending money catching mustangs down in the Owyhee and training 'em for ranch horses. After a few summers of that, riding a rodeo horse is easy. A saddle bronc's not a wild animal. It's just a poor tortured athlete."

He paused, stared out the living room window at the darkness and added an afterthought. 'Course, when you're a kid, everything's easy."

His concern for rodeo animals surprised her. That wasn't the attitude of most cowboys she had known. She wondered what the Owyhee was. This was the second time she had heard someone speak of it. Yet coupled with the distant expression in his eyes, it was his last remark that intrigued her most. "You said that as if you're ancient."

His gaze came back to hers. "Thirty-three. Thirty-four in a couple of weeks. In case you get to where you *are* interested."

His pupils were dilated in the low light and outlined in pale blue, his lips were parted and looked . . . well, kissable. All at once, he cleared his throat and reached for her jacket. "It'd be warmer if you'd take your coat off and let the heat touch your skin."

She lifted one shoulder away from his grasp and pulled the jacket tighter about her. "I'm warm enough."

He grinned and dropped his hands. "Smells like that coffee's about ready."

In the kitchen, she took two heavy mugs from the cupboard and set them on the counter. "We may not have chairs or shades, but we do have cups."

He picked up a mug and looked at it. "This true?"

"What?" She glanced at the empty cup in his hand. It was Piggy's favorite, white with a cartoon line drawing of a naked couple engaged in vigorous sex. The skinny, knobby-kneed male wore a cowboy hat and boots. Scrawled underneath, in red cartoon lettering, was COW-BOYS DO IT BETTER.

Dahlia felt her whole body flush. She wasn't a prude. No one could have a lifetime friendship with Piggy and her wild brothers and be so much as narrow-minded, much less prudish. But after defusing the conversation in front of the fire, this was more than she wanted to hear. "I wouldn't know. It's a joke."

"I've never thought sex was a joke." He looked pointedly into her eyes. "Pleasing a woman in bed's serious business. I *never* do it wearing my hat and boots."

Damn him. He knew he was making her nervous, maybe doing it on purpose. He probably came on to all women this way. No doubt he had already classified her as being no different from his other groupies. The thought upset her, and not knowing why upset her even more. She jerked the mug from his hand and clunked it on the countertop. "You're pushing your luck, Mr. McRae."

He picked up the mug and read it again. His thick, red-brown brows drew into a V. He poured the mug full of steaming coffee and handed it to her. "Good art," he said.

"It's a crude cartoon, and I think you've gotten the maximum mileage from it."

He picked up the second cup and poured coffee for himself. He blew on the hot liquid, then sipped, squinting across the cup rim. "A butcher, huh? Guess they grow butchers different in Texas."

"My dad owns a small grocery store. He taught me to cut meat when I was a teenager. I'm very good at it, but of course, I do other things, too." For some reason, she wanted him to know something about her, but she stopped short of telling him her more prodigious accomplishments. In light of what her life had become, they seemed trivial.

"Nothing wrong with that. A good butcher's practically a dinosaur." He gave her another cocky grin. "I'll bet that's not all you're good at, is it darlin'?"

"Cute. Is that come-on usually effective?"

"Come-on? If you want to know the truth, I don't like talking a thing to death. I'd rather get right to the point. How about you?"

She couldn't keep from frowning. The Mrs. Baird's

Bakery truck driver was the only man in Loretta who flirted with her, and she didn't flirt back. Trading innuendo with this handsome fool was almost fun—but dangerous. "I prefer talking it to death."

"Ain't that just like a woman? Make a complicated thing out of what Nature made simple."

"Mr. McRae—"

"Call me Luke, darlin'. He nodded toward her cup. "That coffee's getting cold."

She pulled the mug toward her. "Don't call me darling." She took a jar of hazelnut Coffeemate from the cupboard and dumped three heaping teaspoons into her coffee.

His mug stopped in midair and he gave her a puzzled look.

"I'm not a serious coffee drinker," she said.

"I can see that." He drained his mug and reached for the carafe. "Mind if I have one more cup? Cold and wet as it is, the road home might be tricky. I don't want to fall asleep while I'm driving."

"Do you live in another town?"

"Nope."

"You said you had a long drive."

"Not another town. About forty miles north of here. In the high country. Takes nearly two hours to get up there. Slow road." He took another sip, his eyes showing as blue slits.

"Oh. I thought we *were* in high country. . . . Well, you might as well take the rest of this coffee with you. I'll just have to pour it out. We have some Styrofoam cups."

"Okay. If you're sure you won't drink it. That'd be real good."

She pulled a tall cup out of the cupboard. As she began to fill it, he leaned his elbows on the counter, watching, and his upper arm brushed hers. A warmth rolled up her arm. Her mind flew back to the restaurant, when she had mentally stripped off his shirt and would have let her musing go farther if seeing his belt buckle hadn't stopped her. She missed the cup rim and poured hot coffee on his hand and coat sleeve.

He swore and jerked back, coffee dripping from his fingertips. A steaming puddle spread on the counter.

"Oh! Ohmygosh!" She grabbed a sheet of paper towel, wiped his hand and scrubbed at the wet stain on his coat sleeve. "I'm so sorry. Are you hurt? I don't know why I'm—"

He stilled her hand with his. "It's okay. I'm not hurt."

"But it's coffee. It'll stain."

"It's all right." He reached for more paper towels and mopped up the puddle. "Looks like your saddle's slipping a little, darlin'. You tired or something?"

"I'm fine."

He scooted the soaked towels into a wad. "Where's your trash?"

She dumped oranges from one of the plastic grocery sacks and thrust it toward him.

"You didn't say. What are you girls doing in Callister?"

"We're working on a surveying job for the Forest Service."

His eyes narrowed. He tossed the last of the soaked paper towels into the grocery bag. "You work for the Forest Service?"

"Well, no. Not *for* them. It's a subcontract. We're working for Piggy's cousin. He's a surveyor."

His fists jammed against his hips. "What's the government surveying around here?"

She had no idea where they would be working, but the folksy, drunken cowboy had vanished. In his place was a hard-jawed, scowling man who was definitely less friendly. She gave him a blank stare. "Is—is it important?"

"Being an outsider, you wouldn't understand. Here, we're surrounded on three sides by the government. Congress is filled up with featherheaded fools who think the West ought to be preserved for spotted owls and timber wolves. Yes, ma'am. Nowadays, everything the Forest Service does is important."

"Oh . . . Well, I—I've never been around the Forest

Service. What I mean is, I think they may be down at
Big Bend. Or they may be over in East Texas, because
there's trees over there. But I live in West Texas, which
is a long way away from East Texas and Big Bend both
and . . ." She stopped herself. She was babbling like
a loon.

And he was staring at her with a pained expression.
He shook his head as if to clear it. "I got to git," he
said, "or I won't be home before daylight."

The abrupt change in him threw her even more off-
kilter. He moved toward the front door and she followed,
though she felt as if she had been following him all evening. "Listen, thanks again for dinner and for helping
me. And Piggy. She's—I suppose I should say . . . well,
you caught us at a bad moment. We aren't really like
this."

He stopped. His laser gaze bored into her eyes and
held her. "*You* are."

Her stomach rose and fell. "You forgot your coffee."

She left him waiting on the stoop and quickstepped
back to the kitchen. When she handed him the Styrofoam cup, his fingers touched hers.

"I left enough wood on the hearth to hold you 'til that
oil truck gets here. Be sure to add a log after a bit. That
fireplace won't heat the whole house, but it'll keep you
from freezing."

She watched steam curl past his nose as he sipped and
she knew. Knew without a shred of doubt, no matter
how much Jack Daniel's he had drunk or if ten feet of
snow fell or a mountain had to be moved, tomorrow they
would have a full oil tank. "I will. Listen, thanks again
for helping us."

His mouth curved into a slow grin. "You bet. I always
try to help out damsels in distress."

*Damsels? I'll just bet you do, all the way from Moscow
to Winnemucca.* She smiled.

"There you go, darlin'. I knew you could smile. . . .
Well, guess I'll be seein' you." With a tug at the front
of his hat brim, he stepped off the porch, then looked

back at her. His voice lowered to a deep purr. "If I were you, sugar, I'd be careful about which cowboys I served coffee to in that mug."

"It's a joke, for crying out loud."

But he couldn't have heard her. His long legs had already taken him across the yard to his pickup. He didn't break stride until he stopped to open the door.

She exhaled a long breath, its trail limned in the feeble porch light. "Good grief," she whispered.

She went back inside and to her room, pulled the extra blanket off her sleeping bag and draped it over Piggy's still body. Piggy snored away, unconscious to being on the brink of hypothermia.

As shadowy quiet stole through the empty house, she thought of how Luke McRae seemed to fill the small space.

And she had looked and sounded like a dumb klutz.

If she had a reputation for anything, it was for her cool head. When all around her screeched in hysterics, hers was the rational voice. Emotional ups and downs didn't paralyze her productivity. Hormonal ebbs and flows didn't drive her to do irrational things. Ever. What had happened to all of that? This tall stranger had wiped out her unflappability as if it had never existed, and her hormones must be rioting.

She went back to her room, rolled up her sleeping bag, took it to the living room and spread it on the floor in front of the fire. Then she turned off the lights, added another layer of clothing and sweats and burrowed into the sleeping bag.

Though she was worn out, sleep didn't come. Luke McRae and his sexual remarks kept sneaking into her thoughts. Was he teasing her or was he serious? She was sure he had been aroused there in front of the fireplace. Did he really think she would just up and . . .

Piggy would. Piggy would already be in bed with him, and tomorrow would be joking about mindless sex. Dahlia had never had mindless sex in her life. Her physical relationship with Kenneth had been on a more elevated plane, or so he said.

Piggy's drunken snore resonated from the bedroom. *Oh God. Four months.* She must have been insane to let Piggy and Dad talk her into coming here. If only she were home, warm and safe in her own bed, around people she had known all her life, where failings of the male species were common lore and she didn't have to guess at the motives.

Yet even as she wished for home, she found herself wondering if and when she would see Luke McRae again and at the same time, fearing she might.

Piloting his old Ford north, Luke let the hot coffee slide down his throat and warm him from the inside out. Weariness settled on him. He had been up since four-thirty this morning and he was unaccustomed to drinking so much.

The green-eyed woman wouldn't leave his thoughts. It was too strange running into her twice in one day.

What was even stranger was getting a hard-on in front of her fireplace. She didn't look anything like the Nordic types who usually turned him on. And she was nervous— just about the most nervous person he had ever met. And serious. She had hardly smiled all evening. He wondered what she would call fun.

He sighed. It didn't matter. Unless she froze to death in that house, it was doubtful he would ever hear of her or see her again, which was just as well. His associations with women were better left out of town.

In Callister, folks pried into their friends' and neighbors' lives for entertainment. His hell-raising marriage and ball-busting divorce had put his whole family on the receiving end of gossip in a way few McRaes had ever been. The opinions of the bigmouths in town meant no more to him personally than a bunch of magpies squawking, but he would be forever making up for the hurt and embarrassment he and his ex-wife had brought down on his innocent family members.

Janet had been away from the Double Deuce, if not out of his hair, for five years now and the busybodies had moved on to juicier victims. Her exit had restored harmony to life at the ranch, and he would fight a pack of wolves before he would let it get screwed up again.

He finished off the coffee and thought about the green-eyed woman's fingers touching his when she handed him the cup. And the way he had lingered a few extra minutes at her front door, hoping for . . . what? An invitation to stay over? He chuckled. Hell, she didn't even have a bed.

Then he wondered if, back in Texas, she might have a husband she had forgotten to bring up. When it came to lying, he wouldn't put anything past a good-looking woman.

You said that as if you're ancient. Her words in that soft Texas drawl hung in his memory.

Ancient. That's how he felt, all right. Older than dirt, older than his years. When was the last time he had felt young? Or been allowed to be young? A father at nineteen, a ranch manager at twenty-four, it seemed he had been an adult forever. His one brief excursion into the frivolity of youth had been when he played basketball for a year at college.

Well, so much for that. A man could waste all night thinking useless thoughts. He would be home soon. A couple hours' sleep, breakfast with his kids and his mom and dad, then a decision on what to do about his son, Jimmy. The seven-year-old's needs were as relentless as winter in the mountains. Putting him in a boarding school 170 miles from home was a resolution of long-range consequence, and Luke would make the decision only after he had slept on the question.

He clicked on the radio to see if he could pick up a station. Static hissed as low, green light illuminated the cab. Most of the time, besides being dark, the long night ride from town to the Double Deuce was silent and lonesome. Radio waves, like a lot of things, didn't penetrate the mountains. Once, he had paid the trip no mind, had used the time to think and plan, but nowadays, it seemed like getting home took longer.

Turning down the volume to quiet the noise, he left the radio on. The light and the monotonous hum of the old Ford's engine were company.

Chapter 5

Dahlia had to run, if for no other reason, to clear the cobwebs of sleep.

After stoking up the fire, she tugged her ski jacket over the three layers of clothing in which she had slept and tiptoed out the front door. At home, she ran at least three days a week, a mile in the summer when the eighty-degree mornings steamed the Texas landscape, two miles or more in the cooler winter months. It did more than keep her trim and fit; the runner's high kept her spirits from plummeting further into a black hole.

Achy and stiff from sleeping on the floor, she jogged toward the end of the block. A long block later, slapped awake by the chilled daylight air, her blood was singing through her veins. She shifted into an easy lope, sucking in the cold, fresh air, exhaling visible plumes.

Luke McRae. Cowboy. Jerk. He had baited, teased and maybe insulted her—she still wasn't sure. One thing she was sure of: He had turned her into a bumbling fool and she wouldn't let that happen again.

The shrill scraping noise from the sawmill cut through the still morning. Except for a few barking dogs and the crunch of her footfalls on the unpaved road, it was the only sound.

Men. For two years she had kept them at a distance. Too busy at the grocery store to cater to a fragile male ego—that was the excuse. The truth was, the years as Kenneth Jarrett's wife had left her untrusting and afraid. Common sense told her every man out there wasn't as deceptive as he had been, but she considered herself too naïve to know the difference. So she worked hard at helping Dad and clung to the ideal of someday meeting someone as trustworthy and giving as her father.

If she continued to meet men like Luke McRae or Mick Ivey, she would probably give up altogether. Grow old alone, dress funny and raise cats.

She made a right turn and pushed herself two more blocks, pumping her arms. Her eyes watered, nose ran, lungs burned. She felt better already. Another right turn and she was on her way back to the cottage with one goal—a bath and a shampoo, regardless of the temperature in that house.

When she tiptoed back inside, Piggy hadn't surfaced. The fire had warmed the living room to bearable. She gathered her robe and toiletries, set her jaw and went to the frigid bathroom.

A showerhead hung over the undersized fiberglass tub, but the bathroom was so compact, without a plastic curtain, taking a shower would have doused the entire room. She filled the tub with hot water and poured in bubble bath. Lavender-scented steam rose and mingled with the strong smell of fresh paint.

Sinking into the bubbles, she drew her knees up to her chest and washed fast, passed up shaving her legs.

Shampooing her hair presented a shivery challenge, but she would endure great inconvenience for the sake of her curly hairdo. It represented freedom and defiance. Kenneth had insisted she wear a smooth bob, no longer than just below her ears. Looked more professional, not quite so earthy, he always said. Every day, she regretted she hadn't restyled it while he was alive. It still grated thinking how she had allowed him to dictate her very appearance. Letting a dead man have that much influence in her life was sick, Piggy said, but Dahlia had argued that her hair obsession was about survival, no different from Piggy's promiscuity.

Her teeth were chattering and her skin had taken on a purple hue by the time she finished rinsing away the shampoo, but the triumph pleased her. She took her mousse, her hair pick and portable mirror to the warmth of the living room and set about the detangling.

Piggy shuffled into the living room and wilted cross-legged on the floor in front of the fireplace. "Where did we get fire?"

Dahlia grinned. *Lucy* looked like hell this morning. "A gremlin brought it."

Piggy squinted at Dahlia's hair. "Hey, you're wet."

"You should try the tub. It's not too bad if you're quick."

Piggy nodded and rubbed her eyes with her fingertips. "Since I'm numb, I won't notice anyway."

"I'm fixin' to make tea. Do you want coffee?"

Piggy lay back, spread eagle on the hardwood floor. "I think I'd throw up. No kidding, where'd the wood come from? You chop up your cot?"

"There's a pile in the backyard. It was hidden by a big sheet of black plastic. Hot chocolate, then?"

Piggy grunted. "Don't feed me. Just shoot me. Put me out of my misery."

"It's tempting." Dahlia went to the kitchen. She returned with tea, hot chocolate and a package of bran muffins and sank to the floor.

Piggy groaned and reached for a muffin. "So many men, so many margaritas."

"And you drank all of them."

"At least I didn't—"

"Only because you didn't get the chance."

"You know I didn't mean to be an ass, Dal. Am I wrong, or were we the only women in that bar last night?"

"Except for the employees. And the couples in the dining room."

"Wow. I think I'm gonna like it here."

Dahlia studied her for a moment, recalling a day from childhood, playing in the big oak tree still growing near the patio in Dad's backyard. Piggy had wanted to grow up and be a pirate. Dahlia wanted to marry someone just like Dad and have six babies. So much for childhood fantasies. Dahlia's life hadn't come close to how she had expected or wanted it to be. Never had she planned to become Dahlia Do-nothing.

Before they finished breakfast, an Amoco stove-oil delivery truck came and filled their oil tank. When they tried to pay the driver, he waved away their money and told them it was all taken care of. They didn't know who had paid for it, the landlord or Luke McRae. The truck driver gave them instructions for igniting the furnace and soon divine heat filled the cottage's five rooms.

An hour later, like a specter emerging from the mists, a Suburban appeared in the driveway. Hail Jerry Murphy.

"Where the hell have you been, Jerry?" Piggy slugged his shoulder as he came into the house. "We waited two hours at the Exxon station on Sunday, then again yesterday at the Forest Service. If I hadn't had the key and the address of this house, we would be sleeping in the Blazer."

"Yeah," Dahlia added, "thanks a lot. We were ready to pack up and go home."

Jerry laughed. "Would you believe, stuck in traffic? . . . Dal, baby! It's been a few." He swept Dahlia into a dance position and waltzed her around the living room. "Love the hair, babe. You look like Cher. Hell, you look better than Cher."

After a couple of turns, Dahlia wrenched from his clutches with a laugh. She slugged him, too. "You haven't changed a bit, Jerry. You're still full of bull."

They loaded into his Suburban. He drove them thirty miles uphill through wet snow and thawing mud to just below the snow line. "Wolf Mountain," he announced. "We'll start here."

"Get real," Piggy said through chattering teeth. "It's so steep, you can't stand up straight."

Jerry's voice took on a warning tone. "Dammit, Piggy, don't do this to me. I've got a deadline and heavy penalties if I don't meet it." He jabbed a forefinger against her collarbone. "*You* wanted this job, cousin. I told you from the first, this is physical, outdoor work. If you're gonna flake out on me, do it before we start so I can hire somebody else."

Dahlia sighed, zipped up her jacket and stepped out of the backseat—into mud past her ankles.

"This is the end of the world," Piggy groused. "Who's gonna come up here to know if it's surveyed or not?"

"Some logger type wants to trade this whole mountainside with the Forest Service for access to his trees. It's been surveyed before, back in the forties. C'mon, I'll show you how to find the old section corners." Jerry lit out toward a gigantic evergreen tree.

Piggy tramped after him, mumbling. Dahlia followed in grim silence as the reality of what was expected of them sank in. It looked like a long, hard summer ahead. And cold, too.

It was late afternoon when Jerry dropped them off back at the cottage. He asked if they had good gloves, sturdy boots and long underwear. Also cell phones. When they said they didn't, he groaned and told them to take tomorrow, get their stuff together and meet him at the Forest Service offices at daylight Friday, ready to start. As an afterthought, he mentioned they would have to go shopping down in Boise, 130 miles away.

For the first time since they left Texas, Dahlia and Piggy perfumed and got made-up, readying for a shopping trip to Boise on Piggy's credit cards.

Piggy put on jeans and boots, but not Dahlia. She donned a tan broomstick skirt and fussed over a top to match it. Wearing skirts made her feel feminine. She wore jeans only when she did something where a skirt would be inconvenient.

Piggy leaned a shoulder against the doorframe as Dahlia tried on her third top. "Wear that green shirt, the one with the fancy embroidery around the neck."

"It's too low-necked—"

"Wear it. It shows off your boobs. If we meet any new men, you'll be irresistible."

"I don't want to show off my boobs. I'm not trying to be irresistible."

"If I was a thirty-six-C, I'd wear the green one."

The bickering between them could go back and forth all day. Dahlia gave up and pulled on the long-sleeved deep green velour shirt. It was slightly darker than her eyes. Its V neck almost but didn't quite show cleavage and it did flatter her full bosom.

"Bright lights, big city," Piggy sang as they left Callister in chilly, brilliant sunshine. Besides necessities for work, their shopping list included items that, in Dahlia's mind, were necessities of life—window shades, a shower curtain and some odds and ends for the kitchen. No matter what Piggy said, Dahlia planned to cook. Eating out was extravagant.

Twenty-two miles out of town, the Blazer came to a choking, leaping halt. Piggy nursed it off the highway onto the shoulder. They opened the hood and stared into the engine well, brains anesthetized by the confusion of hoses and wires.

As they contemplated their options, a white pickup slowed and pulled off the highway, crunching to a halt on the gravel behind the Blazer. Dahlia recognized the driver in silhouette even before the vehicle stopped—the square set of wide shoulders, the shape of a head and hat. Her heart made a leap and she bit down on her lower lip.

Luke slid down from the driver's side and sauntered toward them like the temperature was eighty instead of forty. His denim jacket hung open, showing a tan button-down shirt. His long legs filled a pair of clean Wranglers. Dahlia found herself wondering who, if he wasn't married, put the sharp crease in them.

He stopped at the Blazer's left-front fender, planted his fists at his waist and looked down at the engine. A toothpick dangled from the corner of his mouth. "You girls have a breakdown?"

Piggy arched her eyebrows. "We like to look at engines so much, sometimes we just have to stop wherever we are and do it."

Dahlia willed her pulse to settle down. "Maybe you'd let us use your phone."

He gave her a tolerant look. "My phone's a long way

from here." He bent forward, jiggled and adjusted a few wires and hoses. "Start it up," he told Piggy.

Dahlia stuffed her hands in her pockets and waited as Piggy followed his directions with no results. Finally he said, "You're not going anywhere in this rig right now. Looks to me like a bad fuel pump. Holt Johnson at the Exxon's got a tow truck. I'll take you back to town."

Dahlia found her tongue and stepped forward. "But that's a lot of trouble. You're going in the opposite direction. If you could just send somebody—"

"Two women sitting on the side of the highway all by themselves is a dumb idea." He hitched a thumb toward his pickup. "Get in the truck."

Without further argument, shoulder to shoulder, Dahlia and Piggy marched toward the passenger door of the 4x4.

"Who made him king?" Piggy grumbled. "Ordering people around like—"

"Shut up. He's right. I don't want to sit on the side of the highway."

Dahlia yanked open the passenger door, lifted her foot to step up and stopped still. A small boy huddled by the steering wheel stared at her, clutching a toy horse in a choke hold.

He was perhaps five or six. Pale and freckled, red haired. Thick, wire-rimmed glasses magnified small sky-blue eyes set into the flattened face of mental retardation. Dahlia stood in the doorway and tried not to stare. For once in her life, Piggy made no smart-aleck remark.

Luke slid behind the wheel. "Scoot over here close to me, son. We're gonna take these ladies back to town."

Son. A warmth encircled Dahlia's heart as her petty, self-indulgent problems shriveled.

The child scrambled close to Luke's side. Luke put an arm around his narrow shoulders, whispered something to him, then peered across the cab at her, already shifting gears. "Get in. We're wasting time."

Dahlia climbed into the sanctum that smelled of hay and leather, an uncommon aroma in her life, but not unpleasant. Piggy followed. The struggle to avoid crushing Luke's son while straddling the floor-mounted gear-shift in her long skirt presented problems. She tugged one way and squirmed another, feeling awkward and clumsy. She could see Luke was watching.

When she settled at last, he angled a look down at her. "Lord, I thought I was gonna have to help you."

She felt her cheeks glow. Even the sound of his voice sent unfamiliar sensations snaking through her.

The boy, squeezed against his father's side, began to cry. Luke stopped, slid out and lifted and carried him to the front of the pickup. Thin legs curved around Luke's waist as the frail-looking child sobbed against a wide shoulder. Dahlia couldn't hear them above the diesel engine's clatter, but she could see Luke talking and rubbing his son's small back with his fingers. He dug a handkerchief out of his rear pocket and wiped the boy's teary eyes, then cleaned the tiny glasses.

"What do you think is wrong with him?" Piggy chewed on her thumbnail and watched.

Dahlia couldn't tear her gaze away from the tender scene before them. "Some kind of birth defect. Down's syndrome, maybe."

"He doesn't look the same as Hamlin's little boy."

Dahlia nodded, recalling an acquaintance in Loretta whose child was a victim of Down's. "No. He doesn't."

Luke carried his son, perched in the crook of his arm, back to the pickup and opened the door. "This is my boy, Jimmy. He doesn't see many strangers, so he gets excited." To Jimmy, he said, "These ladies are nice, like Aunt Kathleen and Aunt Brenna. We're gonna give them a ride. That okay with you, pardner?"

Jimmy nodded, his lower lip pushed out, then buried his wet, red face against Luke's neck.

"I know we're crowding him," Dahlia said. "He—he could sit on my lap."

"How about that, son? Wouldn't you like that? She smells awful good, just like Aunt Kathleen."

Dahlia felt her heartbeat kick up again. Dear God, couldn't she be around this man without a physical reaction? And she made a mental note of the perfume she was wearing.

Jimmy hesitated, then cautiously eased down from Luke's arms and crawled onto Dahlia's lap. A keen trembling vibrated through her. She had seldom held a child. As a teenager, when many of her friends baby-sat to earn extra money, she had worked in Dad's store.

She had wanted a child when she and Kenneth first married, but he said the patter of little feet wouldn't mesh with their busy lifestyle. Too distracting, too confining. In time, she had replaced her desire for motherhood with a career.

She had to fight the urge to wrap her arms around this stranger's little boy. As her brain struggled for logic, Jimmy looked up and offered her his horse.

At the Exxon, they all went inside, where Piggy made arrangements for the Blazer to be towed. While no one watched him, Jimmy had gone to the snack machine. Now, he pounded its front viciously with both hands. Luke strode to him, squatted beside him and grasped his hands. Jimmy let out a scream so shrill, Dahlia jumped. Luke spoke to him in a low voice. When Jimmy calmed down, Luke dug coins from his pocket and showed him how to get a candy bar from the machine. Dahlia took it all in, fascinated by Luke's gentle patience.

As Holt Johnson pulled away in the tow truck, Piggy came out of the ladies' room drying her hands on a paper towel. "We're screwed for going to Boise if it really is the fuel pump. They don't have one here. Can't get it 'til late tomorrow."

Jimmy had sidled up to Dahlia and clutched a wad of her skirt in a chocolate-stained hand. Luke saw and pried him away. An egg-sized brown spot was left on her skirt.

"Damn, I'm sorry," Luke said. "I'll buy you a new one."

Dahlia laughed. "It's washable. Let's just call it even."

Luke gave her a conspiratorial grin. "But my coat was old and dirty."

"Did I miss something?" Piggy's glance shifted between them.

"Not a thing," Luke said. "Lemme use that towel, Red."

"Sure thing, Slim." Piggy handed over her damp paper towel.

Luke squatted to wipe his son's face and hands. "You say you girls were on your way to Boise?"

"Yes." Dahlia and Piggy answered in duet.

"If you want to, you can ride with me and Jimmy. We're headed to the feed store and to an appointment, but if you don't take too long, I've got time to haul you where you need to go."

"We were going shopping," Dahlia said. "We don't want to be any trouble. I mean, it sounds like you have things to do."

"Suit yourself. Wouldn't offer if I thought it'd be trouble."

They stood in strained silence while Dahlia's heart pounded against her breastbone. Then she remembered the oil delivery. "Oh," she said, "oil came yesterday. I think we owe you money—"

"Nope. It's Tom Baker's responsibility. He agreed he should have filled up the tank when he rented you the place."

Dahlia couldn't think of anything else to say. She still didn't know who had paid for the oil.

Piggy piped up. "Me, I'm up for bumming a ride to Boise. It's Wednesday already. My cousin will skin us alive if we aren't ready to work Friday morning."

Above Dahlia's protests, they set out again as Luke's passengers. Jimmy rode on Dahlia's lap. Not far into the trip, he dropped off to sleep against her breast, wee glasses askew. She removed them and stroked wayward curls off his face.

Luke said little. Sneaking sidewise glances at the Tom Selleck profile and stern jaw on her left, Dahlia could see that the solemn man to whom those features belonged wasn't nearly as laid-back as the gregarious cowboy in his cups on Monday night.

While Piggy filled in the silence with blather, Dahlia's mind was busy, considering the irony of a physical specimen as perfect as Luke being the father of an imperfect child.

Chapter 6

Luke had closed his ears to the freckle-faced bigmouth about five miles out of Callister, but he couldn't ignore the sweet-smelling brunette whose left shoulder and hip pushed against his right arm and thigh. All dressed up, she looked like one of those TV models for women's stuff. Her skin was golden and didn't have a mark of any kind. He could see the slope of ample breasts subtly rising and falling with each breath, the lace edge of her bra showing where Jimmy's head twisted her shirt. The sight of his son's cheek resting there shook him clear to his boots.

He couldn't find a place to put his right hand, so he hooked his wrist over the steering wheel and stared straight ahead, his arm a barrier between himself and this mysterious lure. Jimmy had taken to her, too, which was puzzling. Lord, Lee Ann Flagg had been hanging around the Double Deuce for years, like family, and Jimmy would hardly talk to her.

Most of the women he spent time with would have been put off by his son, wouldn't have held him on their laps and finger combed his hair as if he were normal. The little guy's own mother wouldn't even do it.

"Jeez, my tongue's tired," the redhead said. "If nobody's gonna talk to me, I'm going to sleep." She scooted down in the seat and closed her eyes, and Luke thanked the Lord for small favors.

Dahlia found the silence oppressive. "How old is Jimmy?"

"Seven." Luke's gaze stayed glued to the highway.

"Seven? Oh . . . I thought he was younger."

"Most folks do."

"He seems small for his age."

"Yes, ma'am, he is."

"Does he, uh, go to school?"

"My mom and I teach him. . . . Least we did."

His reply sounded defensive, but he spoke with such stone-faced emotion, she couldn't be sure. Except for Dad, she wasn't accustomed to men who had so little to say when given the opportunity to vent. In the sophisticated world in which she had functioned in Dallas, most of the men she knew were self-absorbed egomaniacs enamored with the sounds of their own voices. She had been married to one of them. "He lives with you, then?"

They had reached the outskirts of Boise and a crossroads with a stop sign. As Luke braked, he turned his head to face her. The muscle in his jaw twitched. "Yes, he lives with me." His tone said "How dare you intrude?" A few beats passed and he added, "I make it policy not to talk about my kids with people who don't know 'em."

A parade of emotions showed in his eyes, not the least of which was pain, and she saw she had stumbled onto something complex, something that ran as deep as her own weaknesses.

But "weakness" wasn't the right word, not for *this* man whose upper arm touched and warmed hers. "Vulnerability" was more accurate. The difference between the two words hadn't been defined and separated in her mind before, but looking into Luke McRae's troubled eyes, it was. Her curiosity became as rampant as her pulse rate. "Do you see Piggy and me as some kind of threat?"

She felt the movement in his thigh as his foot shifted from the brake to the accelerator. As the pickup moved forward, a corner of his mouth curved into something that lay somewhere between a grin and a smirk. "You always this nosy?"

Anger sparked. "It's called conversation. In the civilized world, we do it all the time."

He didn't reply, just glanced at his sleeping son. "He's

probably getting heavy. We'll be at the feed store in a minute."

"No problem." *Jerk.* Dahlia drew herself up and stanched the emotion threatening to spill everywhere. Shifting away from touching him, she jostled Jimmy, who murmured in his sleep.

In reality, the "feed store" was a farm supply offering a large variety of products, some of which she and Piggy needed. Jimmy appeared to be in familiar surroundings. He made a beeline for the back of the store. Luke followed. Soon they heard another of the little boy's shrill screams.

When Luke brought him back, the seven-year-old was eating a candy bar. He ran to Dahlia's side, hugged her legs with soiled hands and buried his chocolate-smeared face against the front of her skirt. Luke's brow drew into a frown, but his eyes begged for understanding.

She forced a smile. "It already needed to be washed."

While Luke had a conversation with the clerk about supplements, Jimmy was picking up boxes of products that might be toxic, scattering a display of folded T-shirts. Luke saw, but did nothing about his son's behavior.

In the Handy Pantry, Dahlia had been on the opposite end of this scenario. Empathizing with the merchant, she squatted to Jimmy's level and caught his frenetic hands as she had seen Luke do at the Exxon station. "Look, Jimmy, let's put all these shirts back the way we found them." She folded one as he watched. "These don't belong to us. It isn't nice to make such a big mess. I know you're a nice boy, so help me, now."

One by one, he handed over the shirts he had piled together. When they finished, she put her arm around his shoulder and gave him a hug. "That man talking to your dad is going to be so glad we did this for him. Doesn't that make you feel good?"

A glance from the clerk said thanks.

Luke's business took a short time. When he finished, he guided them to a display of thermal underwear and all-weather boots. After making recommendations, he busied himself with placating Jimmy while she and Piggy made purchases. After they left the feed store, he dropped them off at Kmart and told them he would pick them up in two hours.

They completed their shopping well before he returned and waited on a bench on the sidewalk outside the store. The day had turned warm, so they shed their coats and lazed in the sunshine.

"That kid's something else," Piggy said of Jimmy's behavior. "Do you think he's spoiled, or does he act so bad because of . . . you know, the way he is?"

"I don't know. Maybe both."

"He sure likes you, girlfriend." Piggy glanced at Dahlia's skirt. "And you're covered with chocolate to prove it."

"Puppies like me, too," Dahlia said with a laugh. She had laughed more today than she had in a long time, felt a lot of emotions she had feared might be dead.

They saw Luke's pickup and reached for their bags. He took them to McDonald's for lunch and guided them to a booth inside. After what she had seen of his son so far, Dahlia was glad. She couldn't imagine trying to manage the undisciplined child in a more traditional restaurant.

As he ate, Jimmy rocked from one knee to the other on the seat. Near the end of lunch, he said, "Zoo, Daddy," and made a loud growling noise.

Luke looked at them across the table, his eyes pleading again. "I take him to the zoo when we're in Boise."

Sensing a wisecrack ready to burst from Piggy, Dahlia gouged her with her elbow. "Zoo's good. That'll be fine."

Before they left McDonald's, Luke bought Jimmy an ice-cream cone. A premonition sent Dahlia to the ladies' room where she dampened some paper towels and stuffed them into her purse.

The Boise zoo was plain compared to the exotic, well-funded Fort Worth and Dallas zoos, but they did see Northwest forest denizens she and Piggy hadn't seen in real life. Jimmy was beside himself with excitement, racing between exhibits. He sought her hand often as they strolled through the manicured pathways, and a few times, while she hung on to one of Jimmy's hands, Luke hung on to the other. *Just like a family . . . Don't be insane, Dahlia.*

While Luke had revealed few facts about himself, Dahlia saw he was far more interested in the zoo animals than she and Piggy were, and what's more, he knew obscure facts about them. He even became talkative. At the elk pen, he said, "Elk have ivory eyeteeth. The Indians used them for jewelry. They're range animals. I hate seeing 'em penned up like this."

"You don't say." Piggy bobbed her cocked head.

Dahlia seared her with a glare and whispered, "Stop being so rude." To Luke, she said, "That's very interesting. We didn't know that."

They looked down on two black bears eating something unidentifiable. "Bears are like hogs. They eat just about anything."

"Imagine that," Piggy said.

Before Dahlia could glare at her again, Luke removed his toothpick and fixed her with a hard look. "I'll tell you one thing, Red. If you meet one on that surveying job, I hope you stay downwind. They're almost blind and they can't hear too good, but they can smell to beat hell. And they clock at thirty miles an hour."

Piggy scowled and clamped her mouth shut. Dahlia hid a grin. Few people halted Piggy's tongue.

At the snack bar, Luke steered them to a table and he and Jimmy went to the counter to order drinks. He returned from the pickup window with a Styrofoam cup of hot coffee and two of hot water with tea bags. Dahlia didn't have the heart to tell him that when they asked for tea, they expected *iced* tea.

Jimmy had a cup of hot chocolate and a chocolate bar. He danced on one foot, then the other. Luke peeled the candy, Jimmy grabbed it and ran to the far side of the room to watch tropical fish in a wall-sized aquarium.

"He might not be so hyper if you didn't feed him so much sugar and chocolate," Dahlia said.

Luke stared at her as if she had accused him of child abuse. "You got any kids?"

Dahlia squared her shoulders and stared back. "Well, no, but I haven't been living under a rock. Everyone knows that children's sugar intake should be controlled, some more than others'."

The staring became a contest.

"I just mean," she said, breaking away and dunking her tea bag, "if he already suffers from a handicap, you shouldn't do things that don't inure to his optimum benefit."

A reddish eyebrow shot halfway up Luke's forehead. "Inure to his optimum benefit?"

Piggy frowned at her. "What the hell does *that* mean?"

Dahlia touched her temple with her fingertips and shook her head. "Forget it. I apologize. I shouldn't have said anything. It's none of my business."

"You're right about the last part." Luke shoved his toothpick back into the corner of his mouth.

The trip home began in heavy silence. Jimmy sat on Dahlia's lap. Luke was pensive and seemed preoccupied. Dahlia stewed, wondering if her remarks had angered him.

After a while, Piggy said, "Hey, Jimbo, look here. You and I've got matching hair." She lifted a strand of her own hair and held it next to Jimmy's. "Whaddaya think?"

He laughed and touched her hair with both hands.

"Can you sing? You know any songs?"

Jimmy nodded with such enthusiasm his bangs flapped.

Piggy sang a Barney song that Dahlia supposed she had heard from one of her many nieces or nephews. Jimmy followed along, then Dahlia began to sing, too. Luke stared straight ahead.

At the end of the song, Dahlia said, "All right, Jimmy!" and taught him to high five. They spent the rest of the trip singing children's songs and high-fiving. Luke didn't comment or join in.

When they reached the cottage, he dutifully helped them gather their packages from the back of the pickup. A part of Dahlia wanted to understand why he seemed so disturbed, but a more rational part asked her why she cared.

As she reached for the last bag, she looked up at him. "We appreciate your help. I hope you don't think I was judging you with what I said about your son. I can see how much you love him."

Luke's jaw twitched. "You see, he doesn't have much to look forward to. I don't spend as much time with him as I ought to, and sometimes I lose patience with him, so I have a hard time telling him no. That's not an excuse. It's just a fact."

"It doesn't help him when you overindulge him." *Good grief, Dahlia. Is your tongue disconnected from your brain? What do you know about raising children?*

"You a psychologist of some kind?"

She puffed a laugh. "Well, I passed Psych One and Two."

Luke pushed back his hat and glared at her as if he wondered why she would dare have an opinion.

Jimmy leaned on the pickup's windowsill. " 'Bye Dal-la."

In a tiny voice, he had said her name slowly, in separated syllables, and her heart overflowed.

" 'Bye, Jimmy. We had fun today, didn't we?" She sought Luke's eyes, but he was staring at something across the street.

He reset his hat and opened the door. "Scoot over, son. Let Daddy get in." He started the pickup. "We need to get on. It's getting close to suppertime."

Dahlia stood in the driveway embracing a giant Kmart sack and watched him back out and drive away.

Piggy's voice came from behind her. "Strange dude is all I can say."

Later, sipping hot chocolate and lounging in the new webbed aluminum lawn chairs they had bought, Piggy stretched her legs and held her socked feet in front of the fire. "Today has to go down as one of the more bizarre days of my life."

"Me, too," Dahlia said.

"I'll say one thing for Luke. He's got the patience of a saint. Gives *macho* a whole new image."

"It's odd that Jimmy lives with his dad, isn't it? Where do you suppose his mother is?"

Piggy shrugged. "Divorced, probably. Who isn't?"

"Something bad has happened there. It shows in Luke's eyes."

Piggy studied the contents of her cup. "Speaking of eyes, he's got that gleam in his when he looks at you. You know that, don't you?"

"Who, Jimmy?"

"Don't be dense. The Marlboro Man."

"What gleam?"

"Like some kid let loose in Baskin-Robbins with a fifty-dollar bill."

Dahlia's heart leaped. She left her chair and went to pick up a Kmart sack resting in the corner of the room. "I'm tired. I'm going to bed."

"Trust me. He likes his women soft and sweet. Like you."

Dahlia did trust her. Piggy was an expert. Practically everything Dahlia knew about men and sex she had learned from Piggy. "You're the one who's interested in him. In the restaurant, you—"

Piggy waved away her comment. "You know me. I like all men. How long's it been for you? I'll bet you don't even know."

"How long what?" Dahlia set her jaw and yanked a new blanket from the sack.

"Since you got laid, goofball."

Dahlia felt her cheeks burn. She tore the plastic package from around the blanket. "I keep records of a lot of things, but not that."

"I can figure it out, you know. You haven't even gone on a date since you moved back to Loretta." Piggy hunkered forward, set her mug on the floor and began to count on her fingers. "This is May. That makes it two years and five months since Kenneth nose-dived into the river. You've already told me he wasn't a stallion in the bedroom, so I've always doubted he was capable of boinking you at the same time he was boinking Bonnie."

Dahlia rolled her eyes. Why had she ever discussed her sex life with Piggy? She unfurled the blanket and gave it a vigorous shake. "Just drop it."

"I'm right, aren't I?"

Dahlia wadded the blanket into her arms. "My relationship with Kenneth was more—more intellectual."

"Sure it was."

"The whole world doesn't revolve around sex, you know."

"But it does, girlfriend. In all cultures and at all levels." Piggy sat back in her chair. "Luke will be back, you know, with rubbers in his pocket. He's got your scent. The question is, what're you gonna do with him?"

A tremor shimmered through Dahlia. "Piggy, for God's sake. This is dumb. He's a *cowboy*."

Piggy opened her palms. "Simple question." Her brown eyes sparked with mischief. "I'd bet my CPA certificate you'd never forget a lusty dance on a mattress with that long-legged sucker."

"Yeah? Well, your credentials are safe. There's no danger I'm going to become one of the Moscow-to-Winnemucca crowd." Dahlia raised her chin and strode toward her bedroom. "You know something, Piggy? You really should stop betting your CPA certificate. Someday somebody's going to take it away from you."

Dahlia. Why would somebody name their kid after flowers?

Irritation grated inside Luke. One nosy woman's presence had made a hard day harder. First she had distracted him with lips that looked like ripe berries; then she had laughed and talked to Jimmy in a soft, deep-throated voice that made him think of sexy words whispered from bed pillows.

Inure to his optimum benefit? Who the hell talked like that? Not some bimbo in town on a summer job.

Well, he didn't have to worry about it. Running into

her and her friend today was a fluke. He didn't go into Callister that often, so it wasn't likely to happen again.

Belted into the passenger seat, Jimmy sang and pounded his plastic horse on the windowsill. Luke watched him, remembering how Dahlia had hugged him and laughed with him like she really meant it when the little guy got the hang of a high five. Luke's heart swelled a little as it always did when the kid learned anything new, even something small.

And he was jealous. It was childish, but he resented the hell out of her, a stranger, being able to teach his son to do a simple thing, a task others, including himself, accomplished only with a lot of effort. That very reason was why he had taken Jimmy to Boise today, to be looked over and poked at by a damn committee for enrollment in a school for the mentally challenged.

Dahlia's picking at his failure to discipline his son had been as hard to swallow as a toothpick. He hated for an outsider to be right. Luke knew he spoiled Jimmy. Everybody at the Double Deuce spoiled him. Nobody ever said no to him. That was part of the problem. Lack of discipline was why he didn't learn.

Luke's eyes and nose stung. His throat felt thick, like a fist had knotted in it. He must have one of those allergies people were always complaining about. Damn spring weather anyway. He shifted, pulled his handkerchief out of his back pocket and wiped his nose and eyes. Then he stuffed it back, reached over and ruffled the thick hair that curled around Jimmy's undersized head. "You're gonna hurt that horse, son. Let him rest and teach me your new songs."

Jimmy scooted close and started over. Luke sang with him, correcting him when he missed the words. As much as he wanted to encourage Jimmy, he wanted to distract himself from thoughts of the raven-haired outsider.

Chapter 7

"Listen. There's a diesel in our driveway." Dahlia cocked her ear toward the front door.

Dressed in sweats and thick socks, she and Piggy had taken their tea and coffee to the new aluminum chairs in front of the TV and settled down to watch cartoons. If Piggy was anywhere near a TV on Saturday mornings, watching *Sylvester and Tweety* was a must. Thursday, in an episode that would have made *I Love Lucy*'s producers envious, they had managed to make the TV work by replacing a frayed cable running from an antenna on the roof.

Friday, dressed in their new cold-weather gear, they had accompanied Jerry to Wolf Mountain. After spending a day in instruction on the use of surveying instruments, Dahlia felt more confidence in her ability to do the job to which she and Piggy had committed themselves. There even seemed to be much to like about the work.

"Ohmygosh, that must be Jerry. I don't want him to see me without a bra." Dahlia dashed to the bedroom to change her clothes—out of Callister's view. Besides repairing the TV cable yesterday, they had installed new pulldown shades on their bedroom windows.

Dahlia stepped out onto the front stoop into a penetrating chill. The sun had yet to climb high enough to chase away the morning fog or the front yard's shadow. To her surprise, she saw Piggy helping Luke McRae unload furniture from the back of his pickup. Already sitting on the grass were two reclining chairs, and Luke was lifting a folded card table over the tailgate's edge.

"Mornin'." His face broke into a wide grin. "You just get outta bed?"

"Wha—what are you doing?"

Piggy's forearms rested on the back of an ugly brown recliner. Stuffing poked out from a slice in the vinyl upholstery on one arm. "Stop acting like you just got here from Neptune. It's furniture."

Dahlia blinked in confusion. Luke strode toward her, carrying the card table under one arm and two metal folding chairs under the other. He wore a tan suede blazer over an open-collared dress shirt and Wranglers, dark blue in their newness. "Thought you girls could use this."

"Where did it come from?" Dahlia held open the front door and flattened her back against it to stay out of his way. The faintest whiff of his aftershave floated by her as he passed.

"Bunkhouse. It's pretty well used, but it'll work."

"Come over here and pick up the other end," Piggy called out, stooping to lift the front of the recliner.

Dahlia stamped to where the chair sat in the middle of the yard. "Piggy, no. I'm sure he bought the stove oil. I don't want to be obligated to him any more than we already are."

"Pick it up. We need something to sit on that feels better than lawn chairs."

Dahlia let out a loud sigh and lifted the thick back of the brown chair. In tandem, they carried it into the living room. Luke came with the second one. On his last trip, he brought a lamp, its primitive base made of horseshoes welded on edge. Spying an empty cardboard box they had saved in a dining room corner, he brought it into the living room and turned it upside down between the chairs. He set the lamp on top, then dusted his palms. "There you go. How's that?"

Dahlia laughed. "Martha Stewart would be impressed."

"Who's that?" Luke dug a toothpick from his shirt pocket.

"Never mind." Dahlia glanced down and saw his boots,

brown ostrich quill that still had a shine of new on them. He was dressed up. Why? And for whom? A niggling annoyance plucked at her.

Piggy offered him a cup of coffee, but already on his way to the front door, he said he'd had enough.

Piggy made no effort to see him out, so Dahlia followed him. The least they owed him was courtesy. "This is really nice of you—"

His palm came up and stopped her. "No big deal. You were real good to Jimmy. I figure I can do you a favor."

"I know you don't know us. I promise we'll take good care of your things."

"Sugar, that stuff's old and beat all to hell. Unless you burn it to heat this house, you couldn't hurt it."

With no warning, he grabbed her arm, drew her outside, onto the shaded stoop and pulled the door shut behind her. Her gaze shot to his face. "Is—is something wrong? What is it?"

A fierceness glinted in his eyes. "They want him put in a school. That's why I took him down to Boise the other day. So they could look at him."

The truth slammed into Dahlia. His coming here this morning had nothing to do with the loan of a few pieces of battered furniture. What she saw in his eyes was frustration. And pain. Emotions to which, she suspected, he would never give voice.

Though she and Piggy had been with him most of Wednesday, when he left them at Kmart, he didn't say where he went. "They" had to be counselors or teachers or doctors or who knew who else. She thought of the gentleness he showed with his son and how difficult taking care of him day after day must be. Having someone think he wasn't meeting the boy's needs would be more than a proud man could stand.

But what did he want from her? Approval? Her blessing? He was looking at her as if he expected some kernel of wisdom to fly from her mouth. She searched so hard for one that a nerve began to quirk in her left eye. "That—that should be a good thing. They'll be more objective than you are. I'm—I'm sure they'll help him."

He released her arm. Turning away, he stuffed his hands into his back pockets and stared across the street. "It's a boarding school. He's never stayed away from home."

She wanted to reach out, touch him, ease the worry she could plainly see. Instead, she wrapped one chilled arm around the porch post. "If it's a boarding school, I'm sure they have people who have dealt with that before."

He lifted the flap of his shirt pocket and tucked away his toothpick. His eyes swept the street in both directions. "I haven't been down this street since I was a kid." He tipped his head toward the vacant house. "I used to know the people who lived over there. They left. Couldn't make it."

The moment of weakness was gone so quickly Dahlia wondered if it had really happened.

"It's a struggle for folks to get along here," he said. "Being an outsider from a rich place like Texas, I expect you don't know much about that."

Dahlia thought of her dad's tumbled-down house and the long hours he worked in the grocery store because he couldn't afford to hire as much help as he needed. "Texas hasn't been rich for a long time. For most people, it never was. This place doesn't have an exclusive on hard times. I haven't found life to be easy anywhere."

He turned back to her, his size and nearness invading her space. His eyes probed hers. "Who are you? Really?"

The confidence to answer that question had been missing for a long time. She gripped the porch post tighter, felt its sharp edge cut into her breast. "N-nobody you need to worry about."

His hand clamped tightly around her arm. He drew her so close his clothing brushed hers. Minty breath touched her mouth and she found herself staring at his perfect lips. Giddiness danced through her.

"Don't tell me lies." He gave her a little shake. "You're not a grunt who dogs a surveyor through the brush for minimum wage. You're not a butcher, either."

She glowered up at him, indignation spiking. "I don't

have to lie about anything. Take your hands off me. Who
do you think? . . ."

The rebuff died in her throat. He was leaning toward
her, so slowly she had time to see the shine of his freshly
shaved face. She caught a breath. His hand moved to
bracket her jaw and his mouth settled on hers.

She stood frozen, letting him taste her, paralyzed by a
rush of emotions—fear, desire, a jolt of excitement.

Then she shocked herself by sliding her own tongue
against his. A low groan left his throat. She made a half-
hearted effort to pull away, but his arm banded her waist.
His hand left her jaw, crawled beneath her sweatshirt
and cupped her breast. His thumb brushed her nipple,
which had grown embarrassingly taut. A primal message
rose from a place low in her stomach.

Stop this, Dahlia. You don't even know this guy.

Sanity fought its way to the surface. She pushed
against his wall of a chest with both hands. Balling a fist,
she struck his shoulder. "Are you crazy?"

If her feeble blow affected him, he didn't show it. He
neither moved nor let her go. His mouth hovered above
hers. He took her hand down and pressed it against his
fly. He was hard! The heat of him radiated through his
jeans.

"Feel this," he said huskily. "This is what happens
every time I see you."

The words swam at her through a hazy pool. Her
heart galloped.

"Go with me to Boise. We'll go to a floocy restaurant,
get a fancy room at—"

"No." She pushed against his shoulder and jerked back
her hand.

His eyes narrowed. "No? You kissed me back, lady.
And it was more than just a peck."

Guilty, guilty, guilty. "I didn't mean to. But even if I
did, that doesn't mean I'm going off to . . ." Suspicion
struck her. She stepped around him, off the porch, onto
the grass. "Is that why you did favors for us? Brought
furniture? You thought that would get me into bed with

you?" She huffed a sarcastic laugh. "Did you honestly think I was so cheap?"

"No. I just now thought of it. The way you kissed me."

She tore her eyes from his face, stared at the dew-laden grass and shook her head. "Look, you've got the wrong person. I'm—I'm, uh . . . My life's sort of a mess right now. I'm not ready for something like this. There are plenty of women—"

"What'll it take for you to get ready?"

She sucked in a breath and kneaded her fingers where he had held them in his viselike grip. "Nothing. Don't take it personally. You're an attractive man. It's—it's me."

A long, tense silence followed, giving her heartbeat a chance to slow. She looked back up at him. He was a good six inches taller than she was, and standing above her on the stoop, he was a giant. "Where, uh, is Jimmy? You don't have him with you today."

He stepped down to her level. "He's in Boise. I took him yesterday. He got so hysterical when I left him, I worried over it all night. I'm headed down there. Since you got along with him like you did, I thought you might go with me. You could sing a song with him or something. It might make him feel better."

Oh. Her lips formed the word, but no sound came. An arrow of tenderness stung her, and she swallowed to keep tears from springing, dead certain the man scowling down at her wouldn't appreciate tears. The urge to give him a hug was powerful, but she didn't dare. "I—I know that was hard. I know it took courage."

"Yeah, right." He stalked toward his pickup.

In less than a minute, he was out of sight. She stood there in the yard, staring up the road, noticing for the first time in a while that she was cold.

Good grief. She braced a hand against the porch post and took some deep, cold breaths. She had to calm herself before she went back inside to face Piggy.

"I think we should have flaked out," Piggy said.

They sat in the Blazer in the Forest Service parking

lot, shivering. It was Friday. All week they had braved
snow, freezing temperatures and more ice-cold mud than
either of them ever imagined existed in the world. They
knew the definition of bearing trees, brass caps, blaze
lines. New phrases were becoming commonplace in their
vocabularies: metes and bounds, range and township.

They also knew how to retrace an old survey over
ridges and canyons and what they had to do if brush and
trees obstructed their paths. Piggy's question, "What are
we gonna do with these machetes and chain saws?" had
been answered.

Every muscle and sinew in their twenty-nine-year-old
bodies ached. Dahlia had played tennis in college,
worked out in a gym in Dallas. More recently, she
jogged, put in long hours in the grocery store hefting
beef and pork carcasses, boxes of produce and cases of
canned goods, but she had never done so much relentless, strenuous physical labor. Neither had Piggy. Jerry
laughed and called them cream puffs, told them to take
the weekend off and recover.

For Dahlia, accompanying the week of physical challenge had been the memory of Luke's kiss and her hand
pressed against his manhood. And the glimpse into the
all-too-human man he had shown her when he let his
guard down on her front porch. As much as her work-
weary body looked forward to crawling into her sleeping
bag every night, she couldn't find rest until she had re-
played the scene on the stoop and contemplated the
next one.

And she thought of Jimmy McRae. A dull-witted little
boy alone in big new world of strangers, rules and education, without the protection of his very capable father.

On Wednesday evening Luke had called and invited
her to dinner for Saturday night. She supposed he got
the phone number from Information. She had declined.

On Saturday, they hauled their filthy clothing to the
only coin-op laundry in town. "R and R is what we
need," Piggy said as they watched the dryers spin. "Entertainment. We deserve it after the week we've put in.

There's a band at the Eights & Aces Saloon tonight and
I haven't been dancing since the last time I went to Billy
Bob's with Bill Porter."

With reluctance, Dahlia agreed to the outing.

As she usually did for a boot-scootin' Saturday night,
Piggy duded up. Blue satin Western shirt with black
fringe, skin-tight jeans belted by silver *conchos* and
stuffed inside a tall pair of high-heeled boots. And half
a pound of sterling silver hanging from her ears.

Dahlia put on a long-sleeved white silk shirt and sedate
black slacks. She sat down on one of Luke's recliners to
strap on her black patent leather, high-heeled Ferragamo
sandals. They had cost a week's pay. She had sacrificed
many things since leaving her well-paying job in Dallas,
but some luxuries, like Italian shoes, couldn't be given
up.

"Far out. Fuck-me shoes. You're finally coming out of
it," Piggy said.

"Shut up, Piggy. These are all I brought." Dahlia went
to the bathroom and gussied up her wild hair, pinning
the sides back with green crystal hairpins.

At nearly nine, they arrived at the Eights & Aces. As
soon as they entered, Dahlia recognized it for what it
was—a honky-tonk, just like in Texas. And the place
was packed.

A wooden dance floor the size of a tennis court dominated the room. A four-sided bar squared off one end
against a low stage on the other. A long banner stretched
between two wooden posts, and tuning up under it was
a six-piece band, Rocky Mountain Electric. A jukebox
on one corner of the stage struggled to be heard above
the buzz of the crowd.

Dahlia and Piggy pushed their way through the crush
and lucked into an empty booth at the edge of the dance
floor. A layer of low-hanging smoke blurred her vision,
but Dahlia could see they were surrounded by cowboy
hats and bill caps. No question. The Eights & Aces Saloon was a working-class gathering place. They tagged a
waitress and ordered Coors Lights.

The band exploded to life with a thundering drum and

a growling bass guitar, in a raucous rendition of "Truck Drivin' Man." A collective cheer and whistle surged from the crowd and dancers began to scoot and spin around the floor.

Soon, a bearded, stubby-legged cowboy they had seen at the Forest Service offices ambled over and asked Piggy to dance. Dahlia sipped her beer and watched, feeling out of place as usual. Hoedowns in honky-tonks hadn't been part of her social life since college. *What social life?* Though she had grown up with country-western music, Kenneth had refused to listen to it. Music illiterates, he had said.

At the end of a clattering version of "Boot Scootin' Boogie," the band took a break. Piggy, breathless and perspiring, led her partner back to the table and they flopped onto the seat. She introduced him as Pete Hand, range inspector, fence rider and Forest Service horse wrangler. Also part-time steelhead fishing guide. Only Piggy could learn that much about somebody in a milieu where conversation couldn't be heard.

The party in the booth behind them left, to be replaced by a tall, attractive couple. The woman's carrot-colored hair hung to her waist and she wore jeans, a plate-sized belt buckle and a silver-studded Western jacket that screamed Santa Fe style.

She rounded the end of Dahlia and Piggy's booth and slid into the empty seat beside Dahlia. "Mind if I sit down?" She nodded toward Pete. "I want to ask my cousin Grizzly a question."

"Not at all," Dahlia said.

The newcomer stuck out her right hand. "Name's Kathleen Adams. What's yours?"

Dahlia said her own name, then Piggy's. The lanky redhead threw Piggy a curious look. "What's that again?"

"P-I-G-G-Y. This little piggy went to market, this little piggy—"

Kathleen tilted her head back and shrieked with laughter. "That's different. Where you from?"

"Texas."

She turned back to Dahlia. "Texas. You too? You look Chinese."

The comment, put so bluntly by a stranger, caught Dahlia off guard. *They all look alike.* Instant dislike erupted in Dahlia's mind. "Uh, actually, my mom was Filipino."

Kathleen turned her attention to Piggy's new friend. "Say, Grizzly, you been out to look at our fences yet?"

"Too cold. Figured you still had snow."

"Mud, mostly. You'd be doing us peons a favor if you'd get out there pretty soon. The whole north line between us and the government has to be rebuilt. My brother's been in such a snit for the last three weeks, nobody can stand him."

Kathleen's companion, blond and tanned, striking in a white polo shirt and pleated jeans, dragged a chair from a nearby table. Straddling it, he rested his forearms on the back, a Coors longneck dangling from his left hand. An impressive diamond wedding band circled his ring finger. "And my friend," he said, placing a hand on Pete's shoulder, "it's pure hell riding for the Double Deuce when John Wayne's pissed off."

Dahlia's ears perked up. She felt Piggy's toe dig into her shin under the table.

Pete laughed. "Serves you right, tenderfoot. Ol' Luke's a tough 'un, all right. Him and Ted went at it again last week over the new grazing rules. I thought somebody was gonna have to touch off a couple of rounds to settle 'em down."

"Wouldn't have done any good. Luke McRae catches bullets with his teeth."

Dahlia felt Piggy's kick.

The blond man stood and leaned over the table. "Where'd a hairy-faced old fart like you find these lovely ladies, Pete?" He thrust his hand toward Dahlia and drawled in an exaggerated imitation of a cowboy, "Dave Adams is my handle, ma'am, and I'm just passing through, lookin' for my wagon train."

Everyone laughed. Dahlia, then Piggy, shook his hand and said their names again.

Kathleen gave him a frozen stare and clacked her empty beer can on the table. "I've told you not to make fun of my brother. He's had a bad week. You're mad 'cause you're six years younger and can't keep up with him."

Dave arched his eyebrows at Pete. "See how they stick together?" The band resumed with a rafter-rattling number. Dave raised his voice to a yell. "A poor outsider like me doesn't stand a chance. The only place I come out on top is in bed."

Kathleen sprang to her feet and dragged him off his chair. "Let's dance. You're embarrassing me."

Watching as they melded into the dancing crowd, Pete chuckled. "Now, there's a pair to draw to." He turned to Dahlia. "Don't pay no attention to what she said. She's got hoof-in-mouth disease, but she's good people."

"Exactly who are they?" Piggy asked.

"Part of the McRae clan. Kind of like royalty in these parts. Kathleen's one of the princesses. The pretty blond is her husband. At the Forest Service, we call him Cinderella."

"We know about them," Piggy said. "They're ranchers."

"They're more than that. Around here, they're a legend."

"That Dave sure doesn't look like a cowboy."

"He ain't. He was a tennis player somewhere over in Washington. Kathleen drug him home to work on the ranch. Luke McRae's got his hands full making cowboys out of his two sisters' husbands. I think old Dave must be coming along though. I heard it's been months since he's had to walk back to the barn."

Dahlia tucked all that information away.

Dave and Kathleen returned, and as Dave latched on to the passing waitress, his attention went to the front entrance. "Well, I'll be dipped. Speaking of John Wayne . . ."

Dahlia looked up. Just inside the door, dimly visible through the smoky haze, stood Luke. He appeared to be surveying the crowd. Panic was her first reaction, and to prove it, she tipped over her beer can with a clatter. Fortunately, it was empty.

One of his hands rested on the shoulder of a woman standing in front of him. She was too far away for Dahlia to make out her features, but she was dressed in jeans and a short fringed jacket. *Rodeo queen.* The memory of the kiss on the stoop flew into Dahlia's mind. Again. A green imp hissed in her ear. She craned her neck to see if this blond threat also wore a trophy belt buckle.

"He must be lost," Dave said to his wife. "I didn't think he knew this joint was here."

"Maybe Lee Ann talked him into coming to hear the band," Kathleen mumbled.

"I thought she'd hooked up with some dude from Oregon. I wonder what she's doing with Luke."

Dahlia wanted to know, too. If Luke's sister and brother-in-law knew this Lee Ann, she must hold a position a notch above the groupies.

"I don't know, but it'll make Mom happy," Kathleen said.

Another cryptic remark Dahlia couldn't fathom.

Kathleen stood on her knees on the booth seat, stuck her fingers into her mouth and released an earsplitting whistle. She waved her long arms over her head like a signalman directing a jumbo jet. "Luke," she yelled. "Over here."

Luke spotted her, hitched his chin and he and the woman moved toward them.

Damn. When Dahlia turned down his dinner invitation she had told him she would be too exhausted by Saturday for a night on the town. She didn't like being caught in a fib, even an unintentional one. Hemmed in by Luke's sister, she couldn't escape the booth and flee to the ladies' room. And while she was considering what to do, Piggy's toe under the table gouged so hard it felt as if it had broken skin.

Luke approached the table glaring at her, calling her a liar with his eyes. Dahlia refused to be intimidated by a man who had propositioned her as if he had no girlfriend. She raised her chin and glared back.

His girlfriend wasn't unattractive—square faced with

prominent cheekbones and thin lips. Long, bleached-blond hair, parted in the middle and hanging straight did nothing to make her look more feminine, Dahlia thought with satisfaction. The interloper's close proximity revealed she did indeed wear a silver belt buckle, a figure of a bronze calf roper etched in its center. *Calf roper?*

The woman greeted Kathleen and Dave like they were old friends and struck up a gossipy conversation. Yes, she was more than a groupie, Dahlia concluded.

Standing behind Dave, Luke gripped his brother-in-law's shoulders with both hands and dug in his fingers. The dominant male gesture wasn't lost on Dahlia, particularly since Luke sent her a heated glance while he did it. "Don't forget, hoss," he said to Dave. "We're sorting cattle in the morning."

"Ow, ow." Dave scrunched up his shoulders. "Tomorrow's Sunday, boss man. A day of rest."

"Those cows don't know that," Luke said. "Don't you forget either, Sister." He pointed a finger at Kathleen. "I want to see your butt in the saddle at daylight."

Someone called to him and he moved away, guiding his short companion with a hand on her back. He touched his hat to Dahlia and Piggy, but didn't show so much as a flicker of acquaintance.

"That was my brother," Kathleen said. "Sorry I didn't introduce you, but you never know what kind of mood he's in."

A black cloud formed within Dahlia. Left alone while her group danced, she barely endured the next few songs. She turned down three invitations to dance, hunkered in the corner of the booth and peered at the dance floor, intending to torment herself by watching Luke dance with his blond date. She didn't see him.

When Piggy and Pete landed again, she told them she had a headache and wanted to go home. Pete volunteered to give Piggy a ride, so Dahlia left in the Blazer.

Back in the cottage, she changed into sweats, stoked up the fire and settled in front of the TV with a blanket. The irony of having Luke's sister sit down beside her loomed in her mind.

You look Chinese.
Well, so what?

Channel-surfing took her to an old Western. *High Noon.* She had seen it before. She had seen *most* old movies before, a disgusting commentary on her social activities.

She couldn't stick with it. In Gary Cooper, she saw Luke McRae, but watching Grace Kelly, she didn't see herself. The blond actress didn't "look Chinese."

Having somebody question her ancestry was anything but new. Besides Chinese, she had been labeled Indian, Mexican, Middle Eastern, even Hawaiian. But she hadn't heard direct comment about it since Kenneth. He used to add a footnote about her appearance when he introduced her to new people, as if he thought he needed to apologize for her not being one-hundred-percent Anglo. His infidelities had been with blondes. Once, Dahlia had even considered bleaching her hair.

Silly, fawning Dahlia. Always trying to please.

She had gone out of her way to try to make his family and friends see her Anglo side over the Filipino. Why had she done that? Kenneth's mother had been in touch with her only once since his death. Dahlia wished now she had flaunted her own mother's ethnic customs and language at Kenneth's WASPish parents.

Oh, Dahlia, get over yourself. . . .

She awoke to Piggy shaking her shoulder. "Hey, girlfriend."

Dahlia came out of a deep sleep, her hip aching from her leg being twisted in the chair. "What time is it?"

"Late. Or early, depending on how you look at it. You should have stayed for the fight."

"Who had a fight?"

"A couple of tree fallers."

"Tree fallers?" Dahlia creaked to her feet. One foot tingled.

"Yeah. You know. Big guys who cut down trees." Piggy raised her arms and flexed her muscles. "Tough bastards. Something about a girl and a pool table. Luke's sister's a hoot, isn't she?"

"Yeah, a real hoot."

"I didn't see him anymore. He must have left."

"I didn't ask." Half asleep, Dahlia padded toward the bedroom, dragging her blanket behind her.

"Then I won't tell you the girl he was with is his neighbor and his old high-school girlfriend," Piggy called after her.

"Okay, don't tell me." Stiff everywhere, Dahlia eased down to sit on the edge of her cot, then swung her legs into her sleeping bag.

Piggy clicked on the overhead light, flapped out a white T-shirt and held it up. "Pete bought me this."

Dahlia raised her head and squinted to read it. An ugly vulture covered the front. I SURVIVED BREAKFAST AT BETTY'S ROADKILL CAFÉ was its message.

"Pete and I went to breakfast with Kathleen and Dave. I found out what's wrong with Luke's kid. They call it FAS. Fetal alcohol syndrome. Luke's ex-wife—her name's Janet—is a drunk."

Dahlia's eyelids clicked wide.

"She was drunk the whole nine months she was pregnant with Jimmy. Kathleen told me."

Dahlia lifted her head, wide-awake now. Could this guy get any more complicated? "That's insane. No woman in her right mind would do that."

"Kathleen told me something else, too. Jimmy may not even be Luke's kid, but they don't know. When Luke found out his wife was pregnant, his mom wanted him to do that paternity test thing, but he wouldn't."

"His sister told you all that? We just met her."

"It's no big secret. Everybody in town knows it." Piggy laughed. "Hell, when it comes to gossip, this place is no different from Loretta."

Dahlia flopped her head back to her pillow and stared at the ceiling. Definitely too complicated.

"Well, I'm hitting the sack. My feet think I've gone crazy." Piggy flipped off the light. "If I'm asleep when you get up, don't let the day start without me. I'm going fishing with Pete.

"By the way," Piggy called from her bedroom, "Luke's

got two more kids besides Jimmy. Two daughters who live with him. They're thirteen and fourteen. He must have gotten married when he was an infant. He can't be much over thirty."

Thirty-three, thirty-four in a couple of weeks.

Dahlia felt her eyebrows knit together. Definitely too complicated.

Chapter 8

"If you keep turning him down, he'll quit calling."

In the backseat of Jerry's Suburban, while Piggy nagged, Dahlia pawed through her lunch cooler. Luke had called last night with another dinner invitation, but she had declined before he could say where.

A cold deluge held them captive on an isolated, rugged road, halfway to the top of Wolf Mountain. Deafening, giant raindrops slapped the Suburban like angry hands, and rivulets washing down the windows blurred the landscape. Wind gusts rocked them.

"Shit." Jerry hit the steering wheel with the heel of his hand. "We're gonna have to quit."

"He's got a girlfriend, for crying out loud," Dahlia said. "From the gossip you hear, more than one. Besides, food isn't what's on his mind."

"Who y'all talking about?" Jerry asked.

"Nobody you'd know." Piggy cocked her head at Dahlia. "Did he make a move on you or something? And where was I?"

Dahlia concentrated on the layers of her ham-and-cheese sandwich. She hadn't told Piggy about the incident on the front stoop. "Arranging furniture."

Piggy's eyes narrowed. "You mean when he brought the furniture? In broad daylight and you didn't tell me?"

"Oh, stop it, Piggy. He just kissed me."

Jerry made a high-pitched *heh heh heh.*

Piggy reached across the back of the front seat and slapped his shoulder. "Butt out. This is girl talk."

Wind howled. Rain pounded harder. "That's it." Jerry cranked the engine. "Y'all got all your gear?"

That question got Piggy's attention. "We're leaving?"
"Can't work if we can't see, babe. Besides, I don't want you two cream puffs to drown."
"Awesome. Just let me put my machete in my purse."
Dahlia gave her a wry look and gathered up their lunch trash. "Do that, Lucy. You never know when you'll need a manicure."
Piggy sighed. "I wonder if it's gonna be like this tomorrow. Pete was gonna take me for a boat ride up the Snake River."
"*That'll* put a pucker in a new place." Jerry pushed a cassette into the tape player.
"Who says?"
"The Snake River ain't the Brazos, Cousin. Last I knew, you couldn't even swim."
"I'm not planning to swim."
Piggy and her cousin sniped at each other all the way back to town. Dahlia closed her eyes and did her best to hear Ricky Van Shelton in the background.
In Callister, the weather was no kinder. Clouds hugged the ground. Through a cold, gray drizzle, the town looked gloomy and static, buttoned up against the elements. Jerry dropped them off at the red Blazer in the Forest Service parking lot.
As soon as they arrived at the cottage, Dahlia built a fire. Piggy prattled on as if their conversation on the mountainside hadn't been interrupted. "Even if you kissed him back, it doesn't mean you have to sleep with him. But you do have to eat."
"There was more to it than that. He wanted me to go to Boise, to a hotel."
Piggy stared at her a few beats, then tilted her head back and laughed.
Dahlia turned up her palms. "What's funny about that?"
"That's why you've been in a blue funk for two weeks. And I thought you were homesick. I told you he'd be back."
"I don't know what to do."

"You are so anal, Dahlia. If you like the guy, why can't you just go with the flow and have a good time?"

"It's not that simple. I can't just . . . do that. I have to think about it before I make a decision."

"So much for spontaneity. . . . Okay, let's analyze this. On the A side, you're healthy, unmarried and horny, though you won't admit it. On the B side, he's unmarried, looks like Adonis and is probably hung like one of his bulls. One side offsets the other. I fail to see the problem."

Dahlia gasped. "For crying out loud, Piggy, I knew better than to mention this to you. If I wanted to become a notch on some guy's bedpost, I could do it back home in Texas. Like with Mick Ivey. Just forget it. Are we going to rent movies or not?"

Saturday dawned in struggling sunshine. The world outdoors dripped, but a promise of improvement peeked through breaking clouds. Boat in tow, Pete came to pick up Piggy.

In one way, Dahlia was glad. She loved Piggy like a sister, but after weeks of her in-your-face personality, Dahlia looked forward to some time to herself. Despite the everlasting battle she fought against loneliness, she often enjoyed being alone.

The beautiful day and the physical exertion of the job they had taken on had her spirits soaring higher than they had been in months. An evening confined to reading or watching TV in their bare house held no appeal. Nor did dining out at Carlton's or Betty's Roadkill. She wanted a good meal in a nice place, and for a moment she wished she had accepted Luke's invitation to dinner. Oh, well. The Blazer sat idle in the driveway and Piggy expected her to drive it. Who needed an escort?

She showered leisurely, put on matching blue lace panties and bra, then slipped into one of the two "going out" dresses she had brought—embroidered rayon gauze, also blue, with cap sleeves, a sweetheart neckline and tiny pearl buttons down the front. Its gored skirt fell

from princess styling and struck her above the knee—
the ultimate floaty, feminine dress, designed for a hot
Texas summer. She didn't care if she froze wearing it.
She felt good, like the old Dahlia who enjoyed dressing
up and going out, even alone.

Primping finished, she strapped on the sexy Ferragamo
sandals and hooked a pair of huge silver earrings in her
ears. Last, she splashed on True Love, a fragrance that
reminded her of her dad's flower gardens. Though she
had given up the spendy Estée Lauder cosmetics for a
brand Dad stocked in the grocery store, good perfume,
like Italian shoes, couldn't be substituted.

Studying the map the Forest Service had supplied, she
found Indian Mountain Resort, called the "ski lodge" by
the locals. The thirty-eight-mile road to it was marked
as a scenic drive.

As she shrugged into the stadium coat she had bought
off the markdown rack at Kmart—besides the jacket she
came with, it was her only coat—she thought of how she
had changed. Once, she would have stayed home before
going out wearing a coat that didn't complement her
dress. The thought brought a smile. In Dallas, fashion
savvy had been so important she would drive to the mall
or risk a trip to some drugstore in a bad part of town
late at night to buy the right color stockings to wear the
next day.

She drove slowly, enjoying the scenery along the steep,
winding ascent to Indian Mountain. The roadway was
clear of snow, but on either side, dirty patches thawed
beneath towering evergreens. Water ran in every ditch
and crevice, and she regretted wearing her best shoes.

The pinks and blues of sunset colored the sky by the
time she found the ski lodge. Her expectation had been
of something primitive. A log and gray stone hotel
flaunting a rough-hewn elegance was a pleasant surprise.
Sprawled at the foot of several long ski runs, the massive,
trilevel structure made the resorts where she had skied
in New Mexico look pitiable.

She parked the Blazer nose in against the long front
deck. The parking lot was wet from water trickling from

high snowbanks surrounding it. As she picked her way on the rickety high heels to the deck steps, the cold bit into her feet and legs—thin stockings weren't much protection—and it occurred to her the temperature would drop after sunset and the roads might be hazardous going home.

Oh, well. This is a hotel. If the roads are dangerous, I'll rent a room.

Independence. Decisiveness. *Yes!* The old Dahlia was back.

The hotel's interior looked like a ski lodge should, she thought—rustic, homey décor with walls of varnished stacked logs aged to a golden hue. In the sunken dining area, chunks of wood burned in a mammoth gray stone fireplace. Open-beamed ceilings soared above the huge room, but low light and dark furnishings exuded an air of intimacy. Dahlia could imagine red-cheeked, sweater-clad skiers sipping hot drinks and enjoying the ambience. She counted a couple dozen tables, but only three were occupied.

A cute and flirty young waiter seated her at a table for four and she asked him where the customers were to fill this large dining room.

"It's off season," he told her. "In the winter, we're full of skiers. In the summer, we get tourists, but May's the pits." He informed her the special for the evening was fresh grilled trout just brought in this morning from a nearby fish farm.

Breakfast had been tea with milk, lunch, a hunk of sharp cheese. She was famished, and smells from the kitchen had set her mouth watering the moment she entered. She ordered the trout and a bottle of champagne.

By the time her meal was served, the other two customers had departed, leaving her sitting alone among empty tables and chairs. The waiter bustled as if he were rushed to serve twenty diners. The pink trout steak was the size of her hand, an inch thick and slathered in butter and garlic sauce. She took her time and savored each bite. Growing up around the grocery business, then living with Kenneth, she had become something of a gourmet.

Along the back of the dining room, a wall of windows allowed the scenic outdoors into the room. Dusk had dimmed the light to mauve. In the middle of the window wall, a wide bypassing door opened onto a wooden deck. After she had eaten enough, she put on her coat and went outside.

The deck extended the length of the long building. In warmer weather, it would be filled with tables for dining, she surmised, but this evening, its vacancy exaggerated its expanse. Ignoring the cold chilling her knees and feet, she strolled toward the rail, her high heels making a hollow *clonk*.

Like an airfoil, the structure thrust into space, far over the brink of a steep cliff. She leaned on the waist-high wood railing, pushing her face into the waning light. The thin, cold air stung her cheeks and brought tears to her eyes.

A vast, frozen lake filled the foreground of the stunning view. Lights, tiny as stars, winked from homes on the lake's far end. Beyond, layer after layer of snow-covered ridges lay like giant plump pillows between stands of frosted dark green trees. A string of jagged peaks stood against the horizon and clutched at the sky with mammoth fingers. Never had she felt so small or heard such silence. She could be the only person alive.

A whispering breeze rose from below and echoed across the grand vista. It came to her as if she were its destination, and as delicate as a fairy wing, it touched her face. An eerie sense of place, of belonging, stole through her, hummed at her center in perfect harmony with her soul. She breathed in the chilled air and held it inside her lungs as if by so doing she could grab on to the moment and store it within herself.

The rare feeling flicked away as quickly as it came, and she realized her hands were cold. As she tucked them into her armpits, her ring mounting caught on a thread from her coat. She pulled back her hand, snapped the stray thread loose, then held out her hand to study the artistic arrangement of diamonds and sapphires. It had been her wedding set, but she'd had it redesigned.

She didn't allow herself to think of her marriage much anymore, but in quiet moments, her mind tricked her. Now, as her gaze froze on the ring, her memory spun backward to the events that had left an indelible bruise on her soul.

It was the week of Christmas again, two and a half years ago. Monday, ten days before the holiday. She and Kenneth had quarreled when he refused to postpone his trip to Austin. He accused her of nagging and stormed out of the house.

That evening, he made an uncharacteristic effort to make up with her, and they made love for the first time in over a year. She had never told anyone, not even Piggy. He had been tender and attentive, like when they were first married, hadn't worried about birth control as he usually did, even told her he thought she would be beautiful pregnant. The next morning in the bathroom, while dressing for the day, they kissed and held each other like lovers and she told him she hoped she *was* pregnant. She wished him a good trip and told him to hurry home. They would have the best Christmas yet.

Less than twenty-four hours later, the call came from the Denton County sheriff's office. Like a death spiral, her life plunged into one long nightmare. Of Kenneth's company records, what the SEC didn't seize, the IRS did. Every day brought a new and shocking revelation of duplicity. The toxicology report revealed drugs as well as alcohol. Their auto-insurance company rejected the claim for Kenneth's totaled sixty-thousand-dollar Corvette. The bank holding the large note sued. Bonnie Gibson's husband filed a wrongful death suit on behalf of their three small children.

Dahlia had had no choice but to defend Kenneth. Her own survival depended on it. She dealt with all of it in the manner of the professional she had been back then, keeping most of the gory details a secret from her dad. The culminating moment came when the IRS claimed her home and all that was in it. Bankrupt, she stoically walked out, handed over the keys to a government agent and left town.

Things were better now. Calmer. She no longer felt she might snap at any minute. Loretta was quiet. No one expected anything heroic from her. She worked hard in Dad's store, lived in Dad's old house that didn't even have a dishwasher and took life one day at a time. She had even grown accustomed to the inconvenience of having no credit. Only Piggy knew all that had happened in Dallas.

Now, she took a deep breath and thought of the ring. It and her car—a jazzy BMW Z3—were the most valuable material possessions she owned. A Dallas lawyer had salvaged the car from her bankruptcy and she had kept the ring hidden through her trials with the IRS. The ring held no sentimental value. The four-carat center diamond had been more a statement of her husband's success than a gift of love and affection. She didn't wear it often, and lately, she had considered selling it to repay her dad.

She suspected her dad had dipped into his retirement funds to pay for her education, had done so again when she chose to have an expensive wedding. She worked and helped, of course, but he had borne the majority of the expense. Money wasted. The education was going as unused as her wedding dress, which was stored in a box in his attic, and the marriage had been . . . well, there were no words to describe what her marriage to Kenneth Jarrett had been.

Guilt tweaked her. With the salary she had earned in Dallas, she could have already paid Dad back. But obsessed with trying to please a man who didn't love her and his family who didn't respect her, her own caring, undemanding father had been pushed to the back burner. Yes, when she returned to Texas, she *would* pursue selling the ring.

Luke sat on a stool in the Hearth Room, a small dark bar between the Indian Mountain Hotel lobby and the restaurant. He sipped at a double shot of Jack Daniel's and watched some politicians yammer at low volume on

the TV. The whiskey had begun to seep into his blood-
stream along with a lazy lonesomeness. His kids had gone
to Boise to visit their mother, his folks and his grandmother
had gone to Twin Falls to visit relatives. His sisters and
their husbands, as they often did, had disappeared 'til
Sunday night.

He gave the housekeeper the weekend off. No sense
making her hang around to cook for just him. After a
long day working with his colts, he had cleaned up, come
here and devoured a good steak dinner.

He didn't like throwing away an evening in a bar, but
that ranch house had seemed awful empty. He wished
he had gone to Boise. Down there, he could have called
Belinda Hughes or any of several other numbers and
found more than company for supper.

"Hit you again, Luke?" The bartender, married to a
cousin on Luke's mother's side, approached with a bottle
of Jack Daniel's.

"No thanks, Cal. I'm gonna go when I finish this one."
Luke looked around. No one else had entered the bar
since he dropped in. "You could close this joint up. Sharon'd probably be glad to see you come home early."

"I'm gonna be busy here a while. Got a convention
coming in on Monday. Some club studying Sioux history.
They've got a little party planned." He slid the Jack Daniel's bottle back into its slot and began to wipe down the
counter. "Heard you took Jimmy down below to some
school."

"Yep, I did."

"Bet that upset Aunt Claire."

Luke's mother's good-bye to Jimmy on the front deck
had been emotional and teary. "She's getting over it. It's
the best thing. We miss him, though."

"What's Janet up to these days?"

Luke swallowed a sip of whiskey, waiting for its bite
to smooth out the kink in his gut that always followed
the mention of his ex-wife's name. History—he and Cal
shared some. The Hearth Room had been Janet's favorite haunt. Countless times, Cal had called the Double

Deuce at odd hours asking for somebody, anybody, to come and get her—*too drunk to drive down the mountain . . . drunk and on the peck.*

Janet met men friends in the Hearth Room, but Luke didn't ask about them, and Cal, being a gentleman, had never volunteered information. "The kids tell me she's answering the phone in some beauty shop."

"Guess she spent enough time in 'em to know how," Cal said.

Luke felt himself grimace. In the nine years Janet had been his wife, she had poured more money into her appearance and wardrobe than most of Callister's citizens made. His mother told friends she didn't know how one woman could spend so much money on herself and still look like she belonged at Mustang Ranch instead of the Double Deuce.

Suddenly, Luke had enough of the Hearth Room, and kicking back in his recliner in his cabin with Louis L'Amour seemed like a good thing. He quaffed the last of his drink and set the heavy glass on the black bar top with a *thunk*. "I'm gonna go." He dug out his money clip and paid, then shrugged into his coat. "You tell Sharon hello for me. Aunt Josie, too,"

He left the bar by the dining room doorway, strolling to catch a parting glimpse of the view he loved through the windows on the far end. The sun's last rays reflected off a new storm moving in from behind Little Horse Ridge. Wide swaths of purple and dark blue slashed across the sky.

Unlike the restaurants in Boise, he felt comfortable here. The ski lodge resembled the hundred-year-old house he called home. Sterling Mountain, barely visible in the distance, backed up to the Double Deuce. The majesty of its high, jagged peaks never failed to inspire him. The mountains were a part of him as much as he was a part of them.

At the dining room's exit, the waiter, Fred Smith's boy, David, and the cook, Roger Gilbert's fat little wife, Nan, were sitting in a booth, playing cards.

"You two poison all the customers?" Luke asked.

Nan crossed her arms over a round, apron-covered belly and laughed. "We can't go home 'til we get rid of our mystery lady."

"Mystery lady?"

"She's real glamorous looking. We think she's a tourist, up from California. Maybe a movie star, but we can't place her."

Luke looked around. He saw only a glass and a champagne bottle on one of the white-clothed tables near the fireplace. "Where'd she go?"

David nodded toward the double glass doors in the window wall. "Out." He snickered. "Communing with nature."

Luke glanced outside, saw the backs of a pair of shapely legs. His gaze traveled up to a skirt extending only a few inches below the bottom of a thick coat. Lord, she had to be cold. A cascade of black ringlets hung down her back. He almost swallowed his toothpick. He would recognize that hair for the rest of his life. *Jesus.*

What the hell was she doing here? Her refusing his invitation to supper smacked him square in the ego. Women liked him. Most didn't tell him lies to get out of spending an evening with him.

Settling his hat on, he told the waiter and the cook he'd be back in a minute. He dropped his toothpick into an ashtray and headed for the glass doors.

Chapter 9

"If you came to go skiing, you're late. The season's over."

The bottom dropped out of Dahlia's stomach. She spun around, toward the unmistakable sardonic drawl. Luke McRae's shoulder leaned against the doorjamb, his coat pushed back, his fingers stuffed into jeans pockets. *Damn.*

"Just my luck," she said. "A day late and a dollar short, as they say."

With lionlike grace, he pushed off from the door facing and sauntered toward her. A loose off-white coat with a Hudson Bay stripe hung past his hips. His gray hat brim hid his eyes and emphasized his lean cheeks. A warm rush slithered through her.

He stopped in front of her and stared down, eyes hooded, his face all sharp planes and shadows in the low light. Her memory leaped to the kiss on the front porch and her heartbeat stepped up. The only time she had seen him since that morning had been at the Eights & Aces Saloon the night he had the blond calf roper hanging on his arm. Regrouping took a second. "What are you doing here?"

"I'd say this is more my territory than yours." His gaze made a lazy hundred-eighty-degree sweep of the deck. "Where's your third arm? Saturday night? I'd expect a couple of party girls to be whooping it up at the Eights & Aces."

"We aren't party girls. Piggy went out. With someone we met at the Forest Service. Pete Hand. Maybe you know him."

"I do. Good man."

"She needs that. She's known her share who aren't."

His stare penetrated all the way to her spine. "And how about you? What do *you* need?"

She had opened the door for that one. "Nothing."

"You're lying to me, darlin'. For about the third or fourth time."

His voice had gone soft and low, a mixture of accusation and seduction. *Damn him.* She jerked back toward the lake view. "It's odd how you keep popping up."

He leaned forward, too, bracing his forearms beside hers on the rail. He had a pocketknife and a wooden match stem in his hands. "I didn't pop up. I'm guessing I got here first." His long fingers worked at whittling a sharp point on the match stem. He gave her a sidelong glance, his dark auburn eyebrows arched. "Lost my toothpick," he said, as if she had asked.

"Don't you have a date waiting? Or something?"

He smiled his smirky smile. "If I did, would you care?"

Care. She had done her best not to after seeing him with his girlfriend. She made a little gasp, speechless again.

"Truth is, I tried to get a date with a pretty brunette. Wanted to bring her up here for supper and show her what a good place this is, but she turned me down. Told me a lie, to boot. Told me she wasn't usually hungry at night." He turned his head and faced her. "You must've got hungry after all."

Did he expect an explanation? Why did every conversation with him feel like a contest? A smart-ass retort refused to gel, so she settled for something trite. "It's a woman's privilege to change her mind."

"Yep. Guess it is." He closed his knife, straightened and slid it into his left pocket. "You ski?"

What did *that* have to do with anything? She tore her gaze away from his pocket—and his fly—and looked out over the landscape. "There isn't much skiing in Texas. I did it a few times when I was in college. Ruidoso, and Aspen once. You must have skied all your life."

He leaned on the deck rail beside her again, his arm

touching hers, the whittled match stem lodged in the corner of his mouth. "Nope. Never had the time. All I come up here for is to eat. College, huh? SMU?"

"How'd you know that?"

"I read it on your shirt, that day at the Forest Service. What's it stand for?"

Dummy. How could anybody not know what SMU stood for? But then again, how could an ignorant cowboy who had probably never been out of the Frozen North know anything about a prestigious Texas college? "Southern Methodist University. Class of ninety-three."

"Ahh. A graduate. Lemme guess. Art. School teaching, maybe."

Her ego smarted. "Business. I'm an MBA."

"Ahhh, an *advanced* graduate. I knew you weren't a butcher in Podunk, Texas."

Jerk! She wanted to yank that match stem from his mouth and stab him with it. "I'll have you know, Loretta is a bigger town than Callister. And I used to live in Dallas."

"Bigger butcher shop, huh?"

"I didn't work in a butcher shop. I'm a . . ." She stopped; she was no longer anything. "I *was* a marketing specialist. In advertising."

He tucked back his chin. "Were you, now? That sounds like a hefty paycheck. Gave that up to work on a survey crew, huh? What happened? A shark bite you?"

"*What* are you talking about?"

"Isn't that what they call it—swimming with the sharks? Guess one of 'em spooked you. So you cut and ran to the beach." He undulated a hand through the air in a swimming motion. "Or in this case, the high country."

The truth of that statement cut deep. Except for Piggy, who didn't count, no one ever chided her this way. Emotion knotted in her throat. She pulled her cloak of pride tighter and lifted her nose. "For your information—"

Uh-oh. Luke straightened, shoring up for the tongue-lashing that was bound to come. Before she could launch it, snow began to float down.

"Ohmygosh! It's snowing. I didn't know it was going to snow. I won't be able to get home. I wouldn't have come up here if—" A snowflake landed on the tip of her nose. Her fingertips flew to touch it. "Oh!" Her eyes rounded, then she laughed. "I don't remember the last time I saw it snow. But it shouldn't be doing this in May."

She was a confusing woman. He had poked at her on purpose, venting his anger. Ten seconds earlier she had been ready to give him a cussin', now here she was laughing like a kid over a few snowflakes. Why the hell he found that intriguing he didn't know, but there it was. "Well, darlin', when you're halfway to the North Pole at seven thousand feet, it snows in May."

She held her palms open to catch the large flakes. Her eyes sparkled. God Almighty, she was a pretty thing. He had thought so that day she and her mouthy friend went to Boise with him, but tonight, standing here with white snowflakes on her shiny black hair, her full lips wet and red, the taste of them lingering in his memory, she took his breath. All he could think about was kissing her again. Well, truth be told, he was thinking about more than that.

"Are we really halfway to the North Pole?"

"Forty-fifth parallel. The marker's up the road a piece." A few black corkscrew curls feathered against her cheek. He reached out and pushed them back, then touched her earlobe and earring. She didn't jerk her head back or bat his hand away, so he changed his tone to serious. "Why wouldn't you come eat with me tonight?"

"You know why."

Yep, he did. Releasing a long sigh, he dropped his hands. He wasn't sorry he had kissed her on the porch that day, but he wished he could take back the crude invitation. "What, you thought I'd jump you? Like on the front porch?"

"Not necessarily."

"Scared you'd jump me?"

She rolled her eyes and turned back to the lake view. "Women jumping. I've heard that happens to you often."

"When it comes to McRaes, you could hear anything in Callister, most of it not true."

"Whatever. I assure you I have never *jumped* a man in my entire life."

"Maybe not, but you did kiss me back pretty good that day."

"I shouldn't have done that."

He couldn't see clearly in the fading light, but he was sure she was blushing. He chuckled silently. "Nothing wrong with it. I've been thinking about it ever since."

"If you had told me at the beginning you were on your way to see your son, I would have known you were stressed out and—"

"Stressed out?" Not a phrase he used or associated with himself.

"Upset, then."

He removed his match stem. "You would have gone that day, hotel and all, if you'd known I was a little bothered about my boy?" He flicked the match stem into space, then crossed his arms and braced his butt against the deck rail so he could see her face. Damned if he was gonna talk to her side view. "I should've been smarter. Should've mentioned him first."

She didn't look up. "That's not what I meant and you know it. I'm just saying, I might have been more sensitive if I'd known you were . . . a little bothered."

"Sensitive. Now, there's a college word."

She did look up then, firing him a look that would fell a buffalo. "Do you have something against people who go to college? What I was trying to tell you is I'm sympathetic, as I imagine most people are."

You bet. He had more sympathy than he knew what to do with. Everybody felt sorry on the surface. Pity from *her* cut deeper than a skinning knife. "I don't need or want anybody's sympathy. I got past crying in my beer a long time ago."

"There's no reason to be such a stoic, you know. It's normal for someone to feel for a father of a challenged child."

Challenged child. Dumb-ass term. He could feel his

lips sneaking into a smirk. "That's another one of those *college* words. Some of that politically correct crap. Doesn't help Jimmy much, but I guess it makes the do-gooders feel easier. You don't have to dance around words with me. I can handle plain talk."

"I don't dance around. But even if I do, it's because you say obnoxious things that make me lose my train of thought. I think you do that to hide your feelings. I think you can't handle plain talk at all."

Damn her for that smart mouth. And damn himself for not being able to leave her alone. How had she wormed under his skin? Agitation that had simmered for two weeks boiled over. He straightened and jammed his fists against his waist. "How's this for plain? A few years ago, they called him mentally retarded. That was a bitter pill, but I swallowed it because that's what he is and that's as clear as you can say it." He huffed a laugh. "Challenged. That's a goddamn cruelty joke. It doesn't come close to the way it is."

Her eyes went wide. She didn't move. He had shocked her. Good. He intended to. Then he realized he was looming over her. He took a step back and stuffed his hands into his coat pockets. Christ, what was it about her that got his back up? He never got aggressive or shot off his mouth to a woman, especially one he wanted to bed.

Though Dahlia was stunned by his words, the almost imperceptible sag of his wide shoulders didn't escape her. "That's cynical. I know political correctness has a phony ring, but it's just words."

His lips twisted into a sneer. "No. It's more than that. It's propaganda. And those school people are experts at it, trying to cloud people's thinking so they can't see or don't have to deal with the truth of things. Giving people false hopes."

He turned and stared off toward the mountains, but she had the feeling he wasn't seeing them. "Well, here's the truth about my son. No matter what *they* call it, no matter how big a check I write 'em, it won't make any difference."

A pair of gloves came out of his pocket. He used them to scrape off snow that had accumulated on the deck rail. She gave them an envious glance. Her fingers felt like Popsicles.

"The day won't come when he takes the reins at the Double Deuce like McRae men have always done. He doesn't know he has a heritage that's over a hundred years old. Can't dress himself, can't comb his hair unless somebody shows him how every time. Can't eat a meal or even . . ." He paused and stared at her, his eyes a bleeding wound. "He can't even take a piss without help."

As straight as a javelin, his pain went to her core. She had suspected his cantankerous streak shielded a tender heart, but she didn't dream it was also a broken one.

He stuffed his gloves back into his pocket. "He'll never live on his own. Never have a woman. And if he tries, those politically correct assholes, they'll call him perverted. . . . Hell, he may not even get to be twenty years old."

"R-really? What's wrong with him?"

"Heart. Takes a long paragraph to explain it. And you know what I've thought about every day of my life since he was born? . . . It was preventable. If I could have just . . ." His jaw hardened. He clenched a fist and shook it.

Just what? She had seen women hysterical over any and everything, but she had never been close to so much raw emotion in a man. Kenneth hadn't even been capable of such depth of feeling.

The gossip she had heard about Janet McRae's drinking hurtled into her thoughts. Like a gust of chilling wind, understanding swept through her and she saw his torment: the proud father at the birth of a son and heir, the devastating discovery his offspring had been born less than whole, the despair at learning why. Without a doubt, this was a side of him rarely revealed. Had she somehow unleashed this festered rage? Or was it simply long overdue?

"Just what?" She had to know what he thought he

could have done that would have prevented his son's tragedy.

"Jimmy's mama didn't want any more kids." He braced his hands on the deck rail and spoke to the empty space in front of them. "Hell, she didn't want the two we already had. But she was a regular fertility goddess. Just look at her and she'd get pregnant. That third time, she went clear off the deep end. Wanted to have an abortion. Looking back, maybe it'd have been just as well if I hadn't stopped her."

Compared to this moment, Dahlia's interaction with all other people, even with her husband, seemed superficial. Mentally, she reached out to touch his forearm. "If—if abortion was what she wanted, how did you keep her from it?"

"Money. An MBA oughtta know money's the number-one motivator in all the world. In school, they teach you all that shit about fear and hunger and so forth, but it's really money. I bought her off. Me and my dad. Mom wonders to this day how we came out of the fall sale that year with no cash. Janet agreed to give birth as long as she didn't have to take care of another kid. Then she went on a world-class shopping trip. I made a deal with a devil, but I figured it out too late."

Dahlia could hear her own breathing. Her thoughts crashed into each other. *Jimmy may not even be Luke's kid.* "I don't understand. If things were that bad between you, how—how did she get pregnant?"

A bitter smile quirked one side of his mouth. "The usual way. I'm not without sin in this." He heaved a sigh. "What the hell. It was a long time ago. It's not your problem, darlin'."

She was darlin' again. A door had slammed shut.

She drew a calming breath, unable to leave it alone. "I know about Jimmy. Your sister told Piggy."

He turned toward her slowly, his eyes narrowed. "What is it you think you know?"

"That—that he doesn't have Down's. That it's fetal alcohol syndrome because his mother . . . drank."

The muscles in both his jaws twitched. "That little sister of mine—I'm gonna put a half hitch in her tongue yet."

"She wasn't being malicious. I'm sure Piggy asked her questions. If you want to talk about it, I don't mind listening. And I don't spread tales. Everyone needs to unburden sometimes."

"Laying blame on somebody else's doorstep, you mean." He shook his head. "I said more than I intended. Bad thing, letting Jack Daniel's do my talking. Jimmy's not something for you to worry your pretty head about. And neither is my ex-wife."

The snow had changed from a few gentle flakes to a swirl about them, and her feet felt like stumps, but she couldn't bring herself to disrupt the first time he had said anything significant about his life. "You obviously have strong feelings about putting Jimmy into school away from home. It would be hard for any father to do, but the important thing is improving the quality of his life, isn't it?"

"It is. Where that boy's concerned, you won't hear me argue against something that helps him. We've covered it. That's the end of it."

He was impossible. She gasped and started to wheel away.

Unexpectedly, he caught her coat collar and drew it together under her chin, tipping up her face with his thumbs. "Don't do that. I don't like it when you to turn your back on me."

His hands, warm and more gentle than his firm voice, framed her face, his mouth close. "Kiss me," he murmured. "You know damn well you want to."

No. Yes. I don't know. Before she could swallow the flutter in her throat, his head bent and his mouth covered hers. She grasped both his wrists to pull away his hands, but just like that morning on the stoop, she couldn't make herself stop him.

He sucked at her lips, drew her tongue into his whiskey-sweet mouth. Taking her arms around his neck, he pulled her closer. Unable to think of anything but the pleasure swimming around in her body, she locked her hands behind his neck and kissed him back.

His hand moved down to the small of her back, pressed her against the solid evidence of his desire, but she made no attempt to push away. They kissed for a long time.

"Dahlia," he murmured, raising his lips from hers. "As pretty as the flower. I looked up a picture."

Her name, spoken in his husky baritone, rolled off his tongue like a song rehearsed a thousand times. It was the first time she had heard him say it. She drew a shaky breath, forcing her own voice. "We shouldn't be doing this."

"Why not? You like it. So do I." He slid his arms beneath her coat, his palms holding the sides of her breasts. "You know what I want. This place is as good as any."

His thumbs brushed her nipples. The flutter in her throat plunged lower, considerably lower. "You don't know anything about me. I don't know anything about you."

"I'm easy to know. A simple man. I play straight-up, all cards showing."

He was anything but simple, and she suspected he wasn't anywhere near showing all his cards. But standing here in the warm circle of his arms, her feet freezing, her secret places blazing, she was dangerously ready to believe anything he said. She looked into his eyes. "I'm lousy at card playing."

"It comes natural between a man and a woman, darlin'. One of those things that's meant to be."

A vision of their naked bodies plastered together under warm bedcovers skipped through her head. Piggy's forecast came back to her and she wondered if he did have condoms in his pocket.

Of course he does. All men have condoms in their pockets, especially if they're cowboys. "I should go home before the roads get slick."

He smoothed his hands up and down, his thumbs pressuring the sides of her breasts. His lips, too sculptured to be on such a masculine man, tipped into a smile, lazy and slow. "You're too late, darlin'. It starts freezing again the minute the sun dips."

She chewed on half her lower lip. "This is crazy. You can't . . . Just because you want to doesn't mean you . . ."

The swirling snow had become a veil between them. He glanced up and around. "Let's go inside before we get buried. We can dance while you think it over."

Think it over! She didn't dare. *There's nothing as seductive as having a sexy guy look you in the eye and tell you he wants to screw you.* Piggy's words, frighteningly true. "Dance? Where?"

He tipped his head toward the door. "There's a dance floor in the bar."

She nodded, gave a thin smile. "Oh. Well, maybe dancing would warm up my feet. They're frozen."

He offered his arm. Tucking her hand into the crook of his elbow seemed the logical thing to do. His hand covering hers, his gaze traveled down to her sandals. "I'll just bet they are. We'll sit down and I'll rub 'em."

She angled a dubious look up at him.

He winked.

Damn him. Here she was again, letting herself be led in a direction she hadn't planned to go. Or had she?

Chapter 10

Luke had cooled down to a simmer. His jeans felt a little less binding. He was pretty sure she was thinking about what he had said, but he had already figured out she wasn't one to take decision making lightly.

He had told the waiter to bring her check, her bottle of champagne and some toothpicks into the Hearth Room. She attempted to outgrab him for the check, saying she would pay for her own dinner. Brushing her hand aside, he gave David a fifty.

As he helped her out of her coat, he let his gaze slide from her hair to her ankles. Her dress was thin-looking and showed her shape. The neck wasn't especially low, but he could see the swell of golden, supple flesh that moved when she breathed and cleavage that made his tongue itch. Lord, she was all woman, soft as a kitten and sleek as a high-blooded filly. He swallowed and told her she was wearing an awful pretty dress.

She said, "Thanks," and rubbed a palm up and down one arm, an action that pushed a breast up and into a soft mound above the neckline of her dress. "It's really not right for this climate, but . . ." She looked up then. The corners of her mouth twitched in a smile, like she wasn't used to hearing compliments, which was hard to believe.

"After being grungy all week, I felt like wearing something pretty. I didn't bring many clothes, so . . ." She shrugged.

He turned to Cal and asked him if he would be bothered by some music. The bartender turned down the TV, saying he had too much to do to be watching TV anyway.

Luke placed his hand at the small of her back and guided her to the jukebox, pulled her against his hip as they studied the titles, and she didn't resist.

It felt comfortable having her close beside him. He still sensed unhappiness in her, as he had that first night he met her, and he found himself wanting to put a smile on her face. He poked some quarters into the coin slot and told her to pick what she liked. She shook her head, so he did the choosing. When Willie Nelson broke into "My Heroes Have Always Been Cowboys," he curved his arm around her waist and eased her away from the jukebox's neon glow. He asked her if she liked the song.

She smiled. "It would be traitorous for a Texan not to like Willie."

"That wasn't a yes or no, was it? Something tells me your heroes aren't cowboys."

"Well . . . Actually, no. They aren't."

He told her he was afraid of that and asked if there was anything a lonesome cowboy could do to change her mind. She laughed and said if he helped her get off this mountain without wrecking her friend's Blazer, she would rethink her opinion. Rethink. Another expression he didn't often hear. He liked the way she talked.

He shuffled her in a circle around the dance floor, being careful not to step on her exposed toes. She followed the steps, but she was stiff as a plank and told him she hardly ever danced anymore because back home there wasn't a place to do it.

He thought he might be able to tease her out of being so uptight, so he leaned back to where he could see her face. "That town that's bigger than Callister? No place to go dancing?"

She frowned and gave his shoulder a little punch. "Loretta's full of Southern Baptists. They don't dance."

"Sounds like you're not one of 'em."

"I grew up Catholic. Like my mother. She was Filipino." Her eyes narrowed. "Don't tell me you didn't wonder about that."

He grinned. One of his questions answered. "Nope. I

won't tell you I didn't wonder, but what I thought was, whatever the cross, it turned out just fine."

Pulling her closer, he placed his chin against her temple. In her high heels, she fit the length of his body. Her soft curls tickled his nose as he breathed in her scent, the same perfume she had worn that day they went to Boise. Bringing her hand between them, he pressed her palm against his chest, covered her hand with his and told her she smelled real nice, like the flowers in his sister's greenhouse.

"Thanks," she said. "I guess."

The soft thrum of bass seemed to fill the room as he moved her around the dance floor. Their thighs touched and he willed himself to control the lust that surged. He thought of the night he met her, when she had told him she was named after a flower, so he told her he liked her name and thought it suited her.

"Thanks, again."

"Filipino, huh? You born in this country?"

She pushed away from him. That straight little nose shot up in the air. "You think I sneaked in?"

"Hold on. All I asked is where you were born. No need to be so touchy."

"Loretta, Texas. And I'm not touchy. To my downfall most of the time, I'm disgustingly agreeable."

"I hadn't noticed that."

"What you *noticed* is I'm only half white."

He could see fire in her eyes and he scrambled to explain himself. "You're wrong. You're making the question out to be something it wasn't."

"Oh, really? And how am I making it out?"

"Like me wanting to know is one of those racial things. So I'm guessing you see being a mixed breed as some kind of flaw."

"Mixed breed?" She pushed against his chest, but he tightened his arm around her waist and didn't let her escape.

"Let me go. I knew you'd be a bigoted sonofa—"

He laid his finger on her lips. "Nobody calls me that,

darlin'. You don't know any such thing. You're all excited for no reason." He slipped back into the music's rhythm, rubbing his right hand up and down, smoothing out the kinks in her spine. She moved with him, but he could feel her reluctance. "Crossbreeding makes a good animal. Most of the time, you get—"

"You're incredible. And insulting. If it weren't for the—"

"Shh. You're not listening. Producing high-quality animals is what I know about. It's what I do. Fact is, people aren't much different. You're an example of an exotic mix that turned out good." He smoothed his hand down her arm. "Real pretty, soft skin. Golden coloring. Small boned, but not the least bit fragile. Your body looks and feels strong."

He picked some curls off her shoulder and rubbed them between his thumb and fingers. They felt like silk. "Thick, healthy-looking hair. I'd say, on the whole, you'd be a superior brood animal. If you were a mare, I'd put my best stud on you."

Before he could stop her, she wheeled out of his arms and marched toward their coats, her high heels clicking like castanets across the wooden dance floor.

He strode behind, grabbed her arm and pulled her to a halt.

She jerked free and glared up at him, eyes clear and stark. "What is it? You've already made your desires plain. You want to check my teeth before you hobble and mount me?"

"What's wrong with you? I paid you a compliment."

She glanced away and let out a heavy breath. "I've never thought of being biracial in quite—in the way you described."

"Well, there you go. A different way to look at it."

The music ended. He was out of quarters and he figured they were finished dancing anyway, so he reached for her hand. She balked and glanced toward the doorway, a wary look in her eye. "C'mon," he said, tugging on her hand. "Let's sit down. For the time being, you got no place else to go."

She let him lead her toward the small round table

where his hat and their coats lay. "I just told you what I see. No hidden meanings, no insults." He squeezed her hand. "But if you don't believe me, while we're finishing off this champagne, I'll let you call me all the dirty names you know."

"I didn't mean to say that. I don't usually call people names." She sank into the chair he had pulled out for her. "I know I don't look like everyone else. You can't help but notice."

"You know what? Cows and horses come in all kinds and colors, but they're all still cows and horses." Watching her smooth her dress and flip her hair back, he filled their glasses. "I don't like that word, biracial. It's a politician's word. Doesn't mean a damn thing when it comes to making it from one sunup to another."

She angled an almost-civil look at him. "What is this, Luke McRae's homespun philosophy?"

He grinned. She wasn't such a bad sport after all. "And I don't need to check your teeth. I'd bet they're just fine."

She huffed a laugh and shook her head. "Anyway, it isn't important. Everything's been upside down for so long, I don't know who I really am myself. Someday, when I make that discovery, I'll be fun."

"You're fun now, darlin'. And I'm guessing you know exactly who you are, but you got your spurs tangled up for some reason."

"My spurs are not tangled."

"Looks like it to me. Fact is, it sticks out like a bear-clawed stump." He lifted the champagne bottle into the light from the jukebox and checked its contents. "Tell me something. You having a private party or drowning a demon?"

"Maybe I'm not doing either. Maybe I like champagne."

"Let's talk about that. Champagne's a social drink. You might see a dressed-up lady keeping company with a bottle of beer or even a shot of whiskey, but it's real unusual seeing one all alone with a whole bottle of champagne."

"It's nothing as melodramatic as you seem to think. I don't drink much, but I've been in a good mood all day. I felt like celebrating. Champagne makes me feel special."

"Now, that's a crying shame it takes a bottle of liquor to make a woman feel special. She oughtta have some fella doing all he can to make her think she's a queen."

She smiled, ran her hand underneath her hair, shook it back, then asked him if he was applying for that position. As he gazed into her jewel-like eyes, he feared he *could* be. Before he stepped into that trap, the weight of his past experience pressed down on his shoulders and he shoved the picture of himself as any woman's bootlick out of his mind. Been there, done that. Spent a fortune, bought nothing. No woman would ever put a ring in his nose again.

He cussed himself for spouting things he didn't usually say, for sounding like some moonstruck kid. "I'm just telling the way things oughtta be, not the way they are. I've heard every excuse there is for drinking. I've never known hooch to make anything better, but I've sure seen it make things worse. And I didn't learn that in college."

"You went to college?"

He filled the two glasses the waiter had left. "You think I'm too dumb?"

"Of course not. It's just that . . . well, I guess I'm surprised. I don't know why I should be, really. Loretta's a farming and ranching town. A lot of people I went to high school with went on to Ag School—"

"I didn't go to Ag School." He took a sip of champagne, watching her face over the rim of the glass. A discussion of his college days would have to include his ex-wife, a road better left untraveled. So he grinned, set down his glass and unwrapped a toothpick. "I gave up chewing snoose for toothpicks. I like these minty ones. They taste good with champagne."

She leaned back and propped her elbow on her hand, her glass poised in air, putting distance between them. "You changed *that* subject in a hurry. And you had to be angry before you talked about your son. Why is that?"

"I'm not mad at anybody. I just don't want to relive

old history. Most of the time it's not worth the breath it'd take to tell." He winked again, reached under the table and picked up her foot.

Dahlia tried to jerk it back, but he held a firm grip and started unbuckling her ankle strap. Her shoe hit the floor with a thump and her foot was swallowed in the warmth between his thighs. It felt wonderful.

"Lord, this foot feels like a chunk of ice." He rubbed it back and forth between his palms.

She closed her eyes as warmth crept back. "You can't do this. This is a—"

"Real nice feet," he said. "I like 'em."

She took a deep breath as her whole body began to relax. "They're size tens. Not especially dainty."

"My granny would say you've got a good understanding. And her old sayings are always right." He began to knead the sole with his thumbs. "So while I'm warming up these size tens, why don't you tell me what you've run off from. Old boyfriend, maybe?"

"I get it. I tell you my secrets, but you keep me guessing about yours. This probably isn't the clever thing to say, but I don't have any old boyfriends."

Now he was rubbing her toes, and feeling was seeping back in stinging prickles. She closed her eyes and flexed her ankle from pure delight. He reached under the table, grasped her calf and lifted her other foot to his lap. She almost slid out of her chair. "This is outrageous. You shouldn't be doing this."

"Old husband, then. These days, everybody's got a used spouse laying around."

She jerked her foot again and glanced away. "You know, I really don't discuss my life with new acquaintances."

"Humph. Must have guessed right about the husband."

"If you must know, my husband's—" Dahlia stopped. Only two people had ever heard her discuss Kenneth: Piggy and, ironically, the woman who died with him in the car crash.

Luke's hands halted and he glared at her. Both her feet hit the floor. "You're married?"

"Deceased," she blurted, adjusting herself in her chair and setting her glass back on the table. "My husband's deceased."

"You mean dead."

She gave him a level look. "That's what deceased meant the last time I checked. He died in a car accident. Two and a half years ago."

His toothpick rolled from one corner of his mouth to the other, his gaze locked on her face. She couldn't tell what he was thinking, but she waited for the oh-you-poor-dear expression and the gush of sympathy she had come to expect and hate when people heard she was a widow. Or from him, if not that, a tacky remark.

"That's too bad" was all he said. He picked up her left hand and studied her ring. The candlelight sparked in the large center stone. "Wedding ring, huh?" His gaze settled on her eyes. "Nice trophy."

Not liking what his expression and the remark implied, she took back her hand, slid it out of sight under the table. "I wouldn't call it a trophy. Consolation prize is more like it."

"What's that mean? He screw around?"

She felt a tic in the corner of her mouth. It was one thing to say her marriage had been on the rocks, but quite another to say her husband had preferred sex with women other than herself. "Look, I'm not into reliving old history, either. Besides, it isn't fair to delve into my life when yours is off-limits."

"I'll tell you this much. I didn't cheat. Not once. I've never wanted but one woman in my bed."

Everything inside her stilled. The statement conflicted with the gossip she had heard. "I've been in this town only a few weeks and I've heard a half-dozen stories about your girlfriends."

"Uh-huh. And that's what they are, too—stories. Tell you what. I'd rather talk about the future. Figure out what happens after this is empty." He picked up the champagne bottle and set it back down.

"That's easy. The snow will stop and you'll help me get home, like you said."

"A nighttime trip on a snow-covered mountain road could be real trying for a gal from Texas, even with four-wheel drive. I didn't see snow tires on that Blazer. This little squall will be over by morning. By then they'll have the roads—"

"Stop right there." She raised her palm like a traffic cop. She didn't have nearly enough experience to be playing these boy-girl games. "Maybe I should make things clear. Just because—"

"What happened out on that deck's already made things clear. Seems to me the when and where's been decided, too."

Damn him! She shouldn't have let him kiss her. Shouldn't have kissed him back. Shouldn't have allowed the intimacy of his hands on her feet and legs. He was just another cowboy. And a devil on top of that. And how could she have been so dumb as to come to a ski lodge in the Frozen North without thinking about the weather? She fixed him with narrowed eyelids. "You promised you'd help me get home."

"Yes, ma'am, I did. And I'm not backing up on that." He removed his toothpick and gave her a slow grin. "But look around. Hotel in the mountains practically all to ourselves. Snowy night. Flatlanders from down below pay big bucks for this atmosphere."

"Well, not me. I'm not swept off my feet by atmosphere."

"You sure?"

"Piggy will worry if she comes back and I'm not home."

"All that willpower. You're a tough lady, darlin'. But that kiss out on the deck told me you want it. I'm sure of that much."

Inside she flinched. "I'm not tough. I told you, I'm not looking for a relationship."

"Neither am I, sugar. Neither am I."

"Then what are we talking about?"

She waited for his answer, but he only sighed and re-filled their glasses. "I haven't paid close attention to the weather report today, but winter's last gasp in the high country could be a thirty-minute fuss or an all-night hell-raising. Guess all we can do is play it by ear."

His tone had gone from soft and seductive to matter-of-fact. Was he giving up? And why did she feel disappointed? "Fine." She took such a large gulp of champagne, it bubbled into her nose. "We'll just . . . what you said, play it by ear."

They discussed the differences between ranching in Texas and Idaho, a safe, sterile topic. He told her he enjoyed a visit with a woman who understood the business end of ranching. He was a gentleman, charming, showing no trace of the bitterness that had erupted earlier when he spoke of his son. She told him her plans to start a mail-order business in gourmet foods, omitted saying her own ambivalent attitude crippled her progress.

Tension drummed between them. *That kiss out on the deck told me you want it. I'm sure of that much.* What was wrong with wanting *it*? Wasn't a normal twenty-nine-year-old woman who hadn't felt a lover's arms in years entitled?

Then the bottle and their glasses were empty and Cal wanted to know if they were about ready to go. She felt warm and fuzzy, and yeah, a little drunk. Her traitorous mind kept wandering to the rooms upstairs.

The late news came on TV and Cal turned up the volume. The weather report forecasted another twelve hours of storms. Time stopped. She was in a forties movie, a lone adventuress stranded by the elements in a place she might never be again. "This does seem like a nice hotel. I suppose you, uh, stay here often."

"Nope. Never have. No reason to."

"I suppose, if, uh, it's still snowing, the wisest thing to do would be, uh . . . to, well, to wait until morning." *Dear God.* An alien had taken hold of her tongue.

Luke nearly swallowed his toothpick. It was the damnedest thing, how things sometimes happened when you least expected. Hell, all he had come here for tonight was supper.

He'd had half a hard-on ever since the kiss out on the deck, but hearing she was a widow and had had an unhappy marriage set him back a pace. God knew he could relate to a bad marriage. He couldn't keep from wondering what had gone wrong with hers. He thought of how he seemed to want to tell her things he normally didn't discuss. He thought of how gentle she had been with his son, caring even, how Jimmy had taken to her at once. And he thought of her fierce pride when she told him her mother was Filipino.

In a flash of intuition, he saw that with her sex might not come for free like it did with most of the women he knew. She had aroused in him some weird urge to protect her, which he didn't need. He had enough to protect already. Besides that, fooling around with a woman so close to home could only lead to trouble. So why didn't he do the sensible thing—put on his coat and see that she got home? This snowstorm didn't amount to diddly, and letting her think it did suddenly seemed like a chickenshit thing to do.

He challenged her with a steady look, giving her a chance to renege, in a way, hoping she would. At the same time, he thought about the softness of her lips and the silken heat of her mouth.

Aw, hell. Why keep arguing with himself? Two weeks ago on her front porch or two hours ago out on the deck, he'd had no second thoughts. Against his better judgment, violating his own rules, he had pursued her. He knew what he wanted, and it looked like she wanted the same thing. It was nothing more than sex, and learning she had been married put the situation in a new light. "We could do that. If that's what you want."

She nodded, reached down for her shoes and stood up.

No need for more conversation. He rose, picked up his hat and scooped their coats off the chair. Then he clutched her elbow and guided her from the restaurant.

Chapter 11

Hugging her purse, Dahlia lingered barefooted in front of the lobby's bulletin board where Luke had parked her. Her expensive but useless shoes hung from her fingers by their heel straps. She watched as he paid cash for a room. No credit cards for Luke McRae. A pouch of gold dust seemed more fitting.

He pocketed his money clip and came toward her, a key card in his hand. His gaze drilled into her. "You take birth control?"

Unh. There *was* that aspect of sex, wasn't there? She ducked her chin and shook her head.

"Wait here." He strode toward the men's room down the hall.

She made a mental sigh. What had she expected, roses and chocolates? He had made it clear romance wasn't part of this equation. Good grief, he had compared her to a brood animal.

And still she was drawn to him.

She stared unseeing at the notes and posters pinned to the bulletin board. Her pulse pounded in her ears. Never had Goody-Two-Shoes Dahlia done something this brazen, and if she had to explain it now, she couldn't.

He returned and without so much as a glance, grasped her arm and ushered her toward the elevators. Inside the car, he reached for her hand and interlocked his fingers with hers. They lurched upward on a soft whir. She held a white-knuckled grip on her shoes and purse.

"You should have worn some better shoes," he said.

"Uh, yeah." What else could she say? He was right.

The ping signaling their arrival at the second floor

sounded like a cathedral bell. A start darted through her. He must have sensed it because he gave her hand a squeeze.

As they stepped into the amber-lit corridor, his hand slid underneath her hair and settled at the base of her neck. A possessive gesture—Psychology 101. She gripped her shoes and purse tighter, put one foot in front of the other and let him herd her to the end of the silent hallway. As he plugged the card into the lock, she dared a glance at him. He was tight-lipped and firm-jawed. She pictured the two of them, poised for a bungee jump off a high bridge.

Don't be dumb. It's just sex.

He went in ahead of her, laid their coats and his hat on the dresser and switched on the lamp. A king-sized bed, its width emphasized by a spread of dark blue and green stripes, took up most of the room. She stood in the hallway, immobilized by the sight of it.

He straightened. "You gonna come in?"

With a gulp, she entered the chilly, floral-scented room.

A heating unit hung on the wall under the wide window. He went to it, squatted and fooled with the controls. She heard a click and a rustle, felt warm air. He stood and opened the draperies and she could see a blurry view of the frozen lake.

He turned, his hand held out to her. She crossed the room in a robotic daze and stood beside him, still clinging to the coats and her purse and shoes as if they were lifelines that could save her from this insanity. He took them and laid them on a table that was squeezed between the bed and the window. "These must be getting heavy," he said.

Tears pooled in her throat. *Oh, please don't let me cry.* She swallowed and glued her eyes to the almost indistinguishable lake view. "I've never seen it snow like this. It's beautiful."

"But not as much as you."

"You don't have to flatter me. I—I don't expect it. I mean, I've already agreed to—"

He lifted her chin with his knuckle. "If I didn't think it, I wouldn't say it."

Instinctively, she knew that was true.

His lips brushed her eyes, her cheek and settled on her mouth. His hands came up and cradled her face as his tongue slid into her mouth in a lush, deep kiss. Sensation flooded her, so warm and sweet she would have recognized it if she had felt it before. She couldn't keep from arching her back and leaning in to him. And when she did, his hands slid down, his arms went around her and he pressed her against his body. He felt so solid and strong, so male, and she couldn't keep from comparing him to Kenneth, who'd had fewer muscles than she did.

He ended the kiss on a ragged breath, his mouth an inch from hers. "Dahlia," he whispered, "I've wanted to fuck you since the first day I saw you."

Shock bolted through her. And excitement. No man had ever said such a thing to her. "R-really?"

His mouth took hers again in a kiss so hungry it sent a shiver up her spine. His hand glided down her front, wedged between her legs, and as if it had a mind of its own, her pelvis lifted to it. A deep hum left his throat, and he rubbed her in slow circles through her dress. "This is all I've thought about for weeks. Hot and tight around my cock."

She froze, colliding head-on with reality. This wasn't Kenneth who had watched TV during lovemaking, if one could call it that. The man whose hands were now stroking her most intimate place was a virile animal to whom sex was a blood sport. Making love with him would be nothing like what she had known. Kenneth had had boundaries. This earthy cowboy would have none.

His fingers moved up to the tiny pearl buttons that arched over her breasts. "These work?"

Her hands flew to undo them. She wouldn't put it past him to yank them open. "Let—let me."

He stepped back, his gaze dipping to her fumbling fingers. When she finished, he reached for the front of her dress and eased it open. Her breath faltered as his knuckles skimmed her skin. "Beautiful," he murmured, staring at her breasts.

Her nipples felt tight, and she glanced down. They were protruding in dark peaks through her blue bra's thin fabric, and for an insane moment she wished they were the rose color of a hundred-percent Anglo woman's. She fought to keep from crossing herself with her arms.

He slid her dress off her shoulders and goose bumps popped out on her exposed flesh. "You're perfect," he said. He cupped one breast with a large hand, bent down and kissed the swell of flesh above the lacy edge of her bra.

The obvious gap between his experience and her own finally tore its way to the surface and sent her mind reeling. Gretchen's remarks about his women came roaring up. He had done this hundreds of times. Thousands. He *knew* how attractive he was. He *would* have a herd of women. Hundreds. Thousands. Tens of thousands. Anger flashed, at him and at herself. *I've never wanted but one woman in my bed.* How had she let herself accept such a lie?

Drawing back, he frowned. "You're shaking."

Shaking! Her stomach was churning so fast, she thought she might be sick. Pushing away from him, she jerked her dress back upon her shoulders. "I—I can't do this. Downstairs, I thought I could, but . . ."

Luke stared at her in disbelief, his groin throbbing. She looked up at him, eyes wet, her lips swollen from his kisses. She was gripping the front of her dress in a fist. Had he scared her? Women were never afraid of him.

"This has no meaning. We're not"—her shoulders lifted on a deep breath—"not in love."

Shit! He should have listened to the little voice that warned him she was as unpredictable as the weather. She was about to bolt. While his horse sense said good riddance, a more basic part of him wanted pretty damn bad for her to stay.

He hitched a hip onto the tabletop beside him, the pounding need ebbing a bit. "Love. That's a mighty tall horse to climb on, sugar." He reached for her hand. "You don't think a man and woman can enjoy each other just because they want to? Without so many strings?"

She shook her head. "I know people do. But I—I'm not one of them. Actually, I'm pretty dull. Now that I think of it, I don't know why you'd want to sleep with me. I'm not very experienced. What I mean is, I don't know a lot of ways to . . . My husband and I didn't . . . Piggy says I'm sexually repressed."

Sexually repressed. More college words. She'd done it again—gone off jabbering, like that night she poured hot coffee on him. Her being so nervous threw him a curve. In his experience with good-looking women, most weren't nervous when they had some poor devil hot to trot. Most took full advantage of all that power. He mustered a smile, trying not to make things worse. "That was a lot of words just to say you want to back out."

"This is a really nice room. I know it's expensive and you've already paid for it and . . . I know I agreed to stay over, but . . . I'll reimburse—"

He sliced the air with his hand, stopping her. "Forget it. I won't croak over the cost of a hotel room."

This had gone downhill faster than a hog on skates. A mistake from the git-go. Being fully dressed and hard as blue steel with a sexy woman who had rejected him didn't leave him much dignity, but if any man knew how to deal with life's disappointments, he did. Grabbing on to his pride, he pushed off the tabletop and went to the dresser where he had laid the room key, his hat and their coats. "I'll see that you get home. This storm's not so bad. We'll forget this part of the evening."

Her chin dropped to her chest. Her shaking fingers worked at buttoning her dress. He felt a little shaky himself.

"This couldn't go anywhere, you know. I'm going to be here only until the end of August. I'm really sorry. I don't blame you if you think bad things—"

"You're a lady who changed her mind. That's all I'm

gonna think." He settled his hat on his head, his composure coming back. Damned if he wanted to dissect the situation. Or hear an apology.

She reached for her purse and held it tight against her chest. Her shoes still lay on the table. Did she plan to leave without 'em?

"This is terrible."

He heard a catch in her voice. She was gonna cry for sure. *Shit.* He had lived his whole life in a houseful of women, but he still didn't know what to do if one broke down and bawled.

He laid the coats and key on the dresser and went back to her. A clump of shiny, ebony hair curled at her collarbone. He wanted to bury his hand in it. Instead, he reached out and tucked it behind her ear, letting his hand linger on her neck. "Being scared cuts both ways, you know."

She sniffed and shrugged off his hand, her purse still bonded to her chest by crossed arms. "I wouldn't think you'd be afraid of anything. Especially with . . . with women."

"What, you think I just hop in and out of the sack without considering what I'm doing?"

She looked up at him, her head tilted. Her eyes told him that was exactly what she thought. No telling what she had heard. Tall tales about him and women went around Callister as regular as clock hands. She had been in town long enough to hear ten or twenty.

She looked so soft and smooth, he wanted to touch her, so he ran his fingers up and down her arm, ignoring the little quick intake of her breath. "Acting on instinct's such a simple thing in animals, but people make it complicated. When you said you wanted to come up here, I thought you felt the same pull I do, but if that's not true—"

"No. I—I do feel something." Her eyebrows drew into a tent. She reminded him of a wild creature, cornered and defensive. "But I'd rather us be friends. I'm not sure we could be if . . . if we did this."

"Sugar, if two people can't please each other in bed

and be friends, who can?" Silly question. He had yet to meet a woman who would allow sex and friendship to go together, so he added, "But you seem upset about it. We can discuss it some other time."

She stood there without moving, hugging that damn purse, those clear, green eyes as luminous as jewels. Did she really want to stay?

He lifted her chin with his fingertips. "Dahlia, I wouldn't try to tell you this is more than it is. If you want to go, we'll go. Fact is, it's probably a good idea. But it's your call."

Her lips trembled. Lord, she had the most kissable mouth. The taste of her lingered like heat from a smoldering fire, and he couldn't shake the want. As tender as he knew how, he placed a kiss at the corner of her mouth. "I've never expected a woman to do something she didn't want to. I'm not good at throwing around flowery words, but I'll make you one promise. If you stay, you won't be sorry."

The spark Dahlia had felt from the first flared. It *was* her call. Despite her conscious mind, an arcane thing inside her had chosen him above all others. It was as simple as he said. Instinct. Sex. Natural, normal parts of life. Nothing to go witless over. She drew in a deep breath. "Okay," she said, her voice a squeak.

A smile softened the grim set of his mouth, but his eyes were solemn. He took off his hat and reached for her purse. He laid them on the table and she went into his arms.

His embrace swallowed her. His mouth angled across hers and his tongue plundered. She felt light-headed, intoxicated by the heady mix of Polo and being desired by a such a masculine man. His erection pushed against her stomach, his hands gripping her buttocks and moving her back and forth against it. Heat filled the empty places she had denied were there, and this time, she didn't fight it. She slid her arms around his ribs and hung on, finding an anchor in the strength of his well-honed muscles.

He walked her backward until her calves bumped the edge of the gymnasium-sized bed. His thumbs slipped under the neck of her dress and bra strap. "Do something about this. I don't want to bust these fancy buttons." She frantically undid them for the second time.

Then, in a tangle of hands, arms and mouths, the top of her dress was shoved down around her waist and her bra, his shirt and T-shirt were flung across the back of a chair and he was caressing her breasts and teasing her nipples with his tongue and something was tugging at her down low and she didn't think she could ever get enough of all of it.

They sank to their knees on the mattress. He bent her backward across his arm, latched his mouth on to one nipple. Heat sizzled through her, throbbed between her legs. She clasped his head to her breast, astonished at the primal greed driving her.

Together they fell back. His hands moved everywhere, touching, stroking, rucking up her skirt. "Sweet Jesus," he muttered, "stockings."

The tabs that held them popped free. His hand slid her lace bikini panties to her ankles and off, but when the same hand smoothed up the inside of her thigh, panic shot through her. She grabbed his wrist, squeezing her eyes shut and wondering again, as much as she had thought she wanted this, if she could go through with it. "Wait," she said.

He pulled back and looked down at her. His eyes glittered, pupils dark as sapphires surrounded by a blue halo. "Don't tell me you're gonna stop me."

Her breath came fast and shallow. "It's just that it's— it's been a . . . real long time."

His mouth took hers in a painfully tender kiss. At the end of it, he whispered, "It'll be okay. I'll take care of you."

She believed him. Dear God, she believed him. With a whimper, she loosened her grip, and he twisted his wrist free.

His palm covered her mound and pressed and made a slow circle. "Let me play with you . . . make you hot."

She whimpered again. If she grew any hotter she might ignite.

His fingers worked gently into her pubic hair, parted her and eased between her layers.

"Oh—"

"Feel good?"

"I think so." The weak remnants of denial melted in the pleasure of his languid strokes.

"You're wet—"

"I know. I'm sorry—" The room began to spin; she was coming apart.

He laughed softly and gently bit her neck. "Don't be sorry."

Abruptly, the magic ceased and she gasped. He rolled to his back and struggled to push down his jeans and shorts. She rose to her elbow and helped him shove them past his narrow hips. His erection sprang free, huge and alive. With no hesitation, she curved her fingers around the pulsing thickness.

"It's all yours," he choked out, "but don't pump."

She didn't, but she let her thumb graze the slit on the damp tip of him.

"*Shit.*"

In an instant, she was on her back and he was crouched over her, bumping her thighs apart with his knees and kissing her like he could eat her alive, the broad, hot head of his penis pushing into her.

Pain! Deep and sharp and unexpected. She stiffened and grunted to keep from letting out a yelp.

"Oh, Jesus." He braced himself on his elbows and held himself still, his body taut and trembling. "You're tense, sweetheart." His voice sounded as tight as her body felt. "Relax a little. Let me get it in."

She *wanted* him to "get it in," but her body apparently had other ideas. She had never imagined "it" might not work. Anxious and upset, she squirmed and pushed herself against him. "Just do it. Just do it."

"Shh . . . shh. Not so fast. I don't want to hurt you."

His hand skimmed over her hip. He reached between them and she felt his fingers parting her, exploring. Intense sensation whooshed through her. Her muscles contracted, and with a helpless sob, she arched to him. His penis pushed into her, and mindless, shattering tremors crashed through her.

Then she was floating, the world coming back in bits and pieces and she was stretched and filled from side to side, top to bottom with Luke McRae, and she was certain he must be all the way inside her womb. The pressure was incredible and wonderful and she couldn't remember why she had denied herself this.

"I damn near didn't make it through that," he said, his voice husky in her ear.

She was beyond answering, beyond thinking of anything but him. She couldn't hold him close enough, couldn't take him deep enough. She ran her hands down the valley of his spine, dug her fingers into his taut buttocks.

His lips brushed her eyelids, the corner of her mouth. "Sweet," he murmured. "So good."

He reared above her and began to rock. Her mind emptied, and as if she had known it forever, she found his quick, steady rhythm. His thrusts reached up high inside her, touching a place her husband had never found. She could feel it starting again—the deep throb, the voluptuous desperation, like she had melted and become a part of him and he a part of her.

His arm slid under her hips and molded her to him. "Put your legs around me, Dahlia."

She obeyed. He slid deeper, moved faster. She kept up, panting and racing to a repeat of the intense sensation that before tonight she had only imagined.

Her second orgasm was even more explosive than the first. It crashed through her in waves. Her deep muscles clutched at his hot flesh in a frenzy of contractions. Her neck arched and her mouth jerked open in a silent scream.

His powerful arms crushed her to him. With a groan, he plunged and shuddered and the scalding spurt of him flooded her.

Then it was over. Awareness returned in gauzy layers. They were wet and slick and still joined, and she could feel his breath against her neck. Slowly her muscles relaxed, and he shrank from inside her with imagined suction. She felt the lift of his body from hers. Her eyelids weighed a hundred pounds, but she forced them to open and saw him looking down at her.

"You okay?"

She nodded once, her mouth dry and unwilling to form words. He rolled away and sat on the edge of the bed, leaving her raw and sore and sticky. And exposed. She sat up behind him, tugging her crinkled dress to cover her nakedness.

"That was a little rougher than I meant it to be." He cocked a foot across his knee and pried off a boot. The muscles in his wide back rippled with the movement of his arms.

The cartoon on Piggy's mug and his smart-aleck remark that first night he came to her house popped into her mind. Well . . . at least he wasn't wearing his hat. Every part of her grew cold as the realization that she had become one of his groupies trickled in.

Swearing, he tossed his boot backhanded past the foot of the bed, then hunched forward and rested his elbows on his thighs. "You don't have to worry. I don't have any diseases."

Diseases. That rational concern hadn't entered her mind. "I didn't think you did," she said to his back. "I—I don't, either."

"I can't remember the last time I didn't use a rubber. What about you?"

"Me? I don't have sex. I mean, I didn't . . . I—I haven't been with anyone since my husband."

He looked at her across his shoulder, his eyes as cold as their arctic color. "You said he's been gone two and a half years. You telling me you haven't fu—uh, you haven't done it in two and a half years?"

The question reminded her what a desert her relationships with men had been, including the man she had married. She pressed her fingers against her lips, holding back a sob.

He turned away, cocked his other boot over the opposite knee and pried it off. "Jesus Christ," he mumbled again. "When was your last period?"

Her face burned with embarrassment. "I'm sure it's too late in the month for me to get pregnant. I—I'm practically religious about keeping up with my . . . cycle."

His head jerked back to face her. She couldn't label what she saw in his eyes. "Why? You just said you don't screw around."

She had never felt so dumb. "Kenneth was so adamant about not wanting kids. I, uh, had a reaction to birth-control pills. I . . . We used the rhythm method. I've just never stopped keeping up with my . . . schedule."

His expression was flat, as if he had never heard of the rhythm method of birth control. A few seconds passed. "You got off a couple of times, didn't you?"

Got off? Pain washed through her, as biting as alcohol poured on a wound. She wanted to mean something to the only man who had taken her to a place she had never been. But it would be foolish to let herself believe she was anything more than another conquest. They had little in common, and he had shared nothing but his body. She bit back tears. She couldn't let him see her cry. It was just sex, wasn't it? "Uh, yeah . . . a couple."

He stood, yanked up his boxers and jeans, tucking himself away. He dragged his shirt off the chairback and held it out to her. "You, uh, need the bathroom?"

She nodded and curled to the edge of the bed, wincing at the deep ache between her legs. The musky scent of sex surrounded her. She felt cheap and disappointed, stunned and exhilarated. And puzzled—she was sure he had gone into the men's room downstairs to buy condoms.

Her stockings were bunched around her ankles. Holding her dress against her breasts with one arm, she peeled them off, then reached for his shirt. No more than this meant to him, she couldn't bear having him see her nakedness. As she rose to her feet, blessedly, her crushed skirt slid to cover her hips and her skewed garter belt. He stood there watching her, his fly yawning, his hands on his hips.

Unable to organize thought and speech, she padded to the bathroom.

Luke stared after her. As soon as she disappeared behind the bathroom door, he sagged to the edge of the bed. Christ, what had he done? He had ravaged her, oblivious to caution and *pre*caution. He longed for the empty feeling that usually followed fun and games in a king-sized bed. He *wanted* to feel his normal MO—that urge to get dressed and get the hell out.

He wanted that because what gnawed at him now was worse, something he couldn't name, and that made it plumb scary.

Unbidden, a string of women paraded through his mind. They all had two things in common: They knew the ropes, and no matter what happened in their beds— and it had always been *their* beds, never *his*—they kept one eye glued to the assets of the Double Deuce. He had never kidded himself that any one of them cared more about him than about his checkbook.

The woman in the bathroom didn't fall into either of those slots. He might not be the first man to have her, but he would bet the ranch he was the second. Hell, she probably had been a virgin when she got married. The onus of that realization fell on his shoulders like an anvil, as disturbing as it was satisfying. "Jesus Christ," he muttered. He yanked off his socks and stuffed them into his boot top, rubbed his forehead with thumb and fingers.

Possessiveness surged, like it had out on the deck and in the bar. It felt strange and downright uncomfortable. For a crazy millisecond, he wondered if his daughters would like her or if she would like them.

He squelched that thought. If he ever brought a woman into the lives of those girls, his ex-wife's explosion would make Mount Saint Helens look like a firecracker. Nothing would set Janet off faster than for her to think he was attempting to replace her as a mother. Never mind that Tabasco, his favorite bull, had better parenting instincts than she did. It was wearying to think of the trade-offs he made to prevent her uprooting their daughters' lives and trying to move them back to Boise. He had walked on eggshells for five long years.

Dahlia. Delicate like her name. And vulnerable. What could he say to her? He stared at the closed bathroom door, heard the water stop running, didn't know what to expect when she came out. If she belted him, it would serve him right.

The door opened slowly, and she paused in the doorway, her slender body silhouetted in the bright bathroom light. Her hair was all messy and sexy. His shirt hung off her narrow shoulders, past her cute little bottom, the cuffs hiding her hands. He liked seeing her in it.

The pretty blue dress was draped over her arm. Without looking at him, she took it to the clothes rack and hung it on a wire hanger. Tenderness ached inside him. As much as he wanted to ignore it, he couldn't. He went to her, framed her face between his palms and kissed her. "I'll buy you a new one."

To his surprise, she laughed. "That's the second time you've offered to buy me clothes. It's just wrinkled. I'll send it to the cleaners and it'll be good as new. I should have taken it off, but I didn't have time."

Damn, she was likeable. He laughed, too. "I guess I was pretty hot. I was primed ever since out on the deck. When you touched me, I lost it."

She rose on tiptoe and placed a kiss beneath his jaw.

His heart squeezed. He felt himself stir again, but it was too soon—she needed some time. Shit, who was he kidding? He was the one who needed it. "You're a special woman, Dahlia. You've got a sweetness about you. You make a man glad he's a man."

Swollen lips smiled up at him. He could see where his whiskers had reddened the skin around her mouth. He wished he hadn't been so hard on her.

"Really? What a nice thing to say. I think I could say the same about you."

"I'm sweet?"

"In a rough sort of way. I think you don't want anybody to know the gentle, nice person who hides behind so much cynicism."

"I don't know how you could think I'm nice after the way I . . . after the way this happened."

"You didn't twist my arm. We both came up here for the wrong reasons."

He stared at her for a long time, a new set of emotions churning inside him. He wanted her again all right, but in a different way. "Maybe not," he said softly.

He placed his hand on her neck and brushed his thumb over her smooth cheek. "It can be, *should* be, better than it was, Dahlia. . . . Not that it wasn't good, but it can be . . . not so, I don't know, rushed, I guess."

She shrugged, sort of resignedlike, and he wondered if it had ever been good for her. "You could show me," she said, "if you want to."

"Lord. Right now, there's nothing I want more." He kissed her then, gently filling her mouth with his tongue, and just as gently, her tongue played with his. When they parted, he moved his hands to the shirtfront. "Can I see you?"

She looked down and nodded.

He eased the shirt off her shoulders. It drifted to the floor. She stood there and let him look at her. Her body was long and slim, like his. He could see why they fit together so well. The amber lamplight played over larger-than-average breasts, round and plump with nipples high and pronounced and dark as chocolate. He could feel his throat thickening again. "You're so beautiful. I know I've already said it, but . . ."

At a loss for more words and fearing what she might see in his eyes, he pulled her against him and tucked her head against his shoulder, felt her tremble against him. She wrapped her arms around his middle and they held each other, her breasts burning against his middle. It had been a long time since a woman had simply held him.

He kissed her deeply, sinking to a place in his mind he usually didn't visit during sex. She kissed him back in kind, and he opened himself to let softness seep from her into him. When they had to stop for breath, he led her to the bed and pulled back the covers. She scooted in and sat there, her arms wrapped around her knees, watching as he dug in his jeans pockets for the two rubbers he had bought downstairs. He tossed them on the table by the bed. She glanced at them, then back up at him, and he knew her thoughts.

"I like my kids, sweetheart, but I don't want any more."

She picked up one of the foil packets and read it. "Your granny would say this is shutting the barn door after the horses are gone."

He had to laugh. She didn't seem concerned about the risk they had taken. With any other woman he knew, he might suspect a trap, but instinctively he knew she was too honest. So if she wasn't worried, he wouldn't worry, either. He shucked his jeans and shorts and slid into the bed. "She might, at that."

As he pulled the covers over them, she snugged her body to his as if she belonged there. He reached up and clicked off the light. Usually, he liked the light, but for some reason, tonight he wanted the darkness. Maybe he wanted to make it easier on her.

"I lied when I said I couldn't remember the last time I didn't use a rubber," he said. Then he added something he probably couldn't have said in the light, something he hadn't told another living person. "It was the night we made Jimmy. It was my fault. I knew she wasn't on birth control. I was mad and horny and didn't care. Of the mistakes I've made, that was one of the biggest."

She snuggled closer and held him tighter, as if she understood the weight of the hair shirt he had worn for seven years. "How long were you married?"

"Not quite nine years. . . . You?"

"Not quite five."

"Your husband's name was Kenneth? Why didn't he want kids? Mine are just about the best thing that ever happened to me."

"He was career oriented. He thought they'd be in the way." She paused, and he waited, toying with the silky curls that tickled his nose. "I wanted a houseful," she said softly. "But he sort of had a thing in his mind about the . . . We never discussed it, but I believe he didn't want his children to be mixed race."

Her voice held a note of sadness, and for some damn fool reason, he wanted to wipe it away. Caution, practicality and fantasy warred in his head as he searched for a reply. "If it was years ago and I was starting over, I'd be proud for you to be the mother of my kids."

"Thanks," she said, "but you don't have to say anything. I'm past it now, though I used to spend hours wondering why Kenneth felt that way. To this day, I don't know why he married me. As time passes I'm finding it harder to know why I married him."

"In my case, that's one question I know the answer to."

"Was your wife pregnant?"

"What do *you* think?"

"Didn't you love her?"

"I was a kid. And a dumb one at that."

"Sometimes it's hard to swallow what life gives you. But you learn to. The luck of the draw, I think they say in poker."

He thought again about her sensitivity to being half white, how much the man in whom she had put her faith must have hurt her, and he vowed to tread softly. "Know what? Right now, I'm feeling pretty damn lucky drawing this hand. I told you downstairs how I felt about race. And I meant it when I said you're all I've thought about since the first day I saw you."

She rose on one elbow. In the snowlight, he could make out the outlines of her high cheekbones, the fullness of her lips. "What you actually said was slightly more graphic." She smiled and kissed him. "But yeah, me, too."

His heart made a little bump. She trusted him in a way no one had in a while, if ever; he knew it.

He began to touch her sensitive places again, reveling in her soft sighs and throaty moans. When she seemed embarrassed, he held her and told her it was okay to enjoy.

She wanted to explore his body. He wasn't used to giving up the lead in bed, but trust seemed to be contagious, and he lay back and let her gentle, questing hands learn his intimate parts. When he could endure no more, he stopped her and buried his face in her rain-smelling hair, shaking with new and unfamiliar needs.

"I want to tell you something," she said. "I couldn't tell you at first, but now I can. I've never . . . It's not that I didn't know how it felt, but never with . . . Kenneth didn't—"

"Shhh. I know. That man was a damn fool." He found her mouth with his and their lips clung in heart-hurting tenderness.

He prepared her with his fingers again, making her whimper and tremble until she teetered on the edge of orgasm. He crawled between her open thighs, his naked cock stretched and eager. She took him easily this time. Her hot, tight sheath gripped him in climax the moment the head of his penis pushed into her. He squeezed his eyes shut and held his breath. As soon as she finished, he moved up high on her body and they rocked together in a silky rhythm. She lifted her knees, and he penetrated to her deepest place. A frantic little noise burst from her throat and she came again, her deep muscles convulsing around him. He lost control. Release thundered through him, blinded him and took his breath and nothing had ever felt so right.

Chapter 12

Dahlia awoke in the circle of Luke's arms, their legs tangled, his hand loosely cupping her breast. She could hear his deep, regular breathing near her ear, feel his even heartbeat against her back.

Brilliant sunlight filled the room. Last night, they hadn't closed the draperies on the wall of windows. She could see a snow-covered landscape against a cloudless electric-blue sky and in the distance, snow-covered mountains.

She would kill for a toothbrush.

A few feet away, her blue bra hung by one strap from the back of a chair and Luke's tan shirt lay across the seat. Her stockings were strewn six feet apart in grayish wads on the teal-blue carpet. She couldn't spot her panties, didn't know where they had gone after Luke swept them away.

She had a driving urge to shower. She hadn't washed before going to sleep. Her cheeks warmed at the memory of how they had both drifted off with him inside her.

What to do next was the question. Of all the bedroom adventures she had heard from Piggy as well as some of her other sexually active friends, morning-after etiquette with a stranger was a detail they hadn't covered.

One thing was without doubt—she had to go home. Though she suspected Piggy had spent the night with Pete, if she returned to the cottage and found Dahlia and the Blazer missing, she might assume the worst and be frantic. Dahlia carefully moved body parts—his and hers—and eased out of bed. He didn't stir.

Covered with his shirt, she went to her dress hanging

in the corner of the room, finding her panties on the way. She gathered them, the wrinkled blue dress, her purse, her stockings and garter belt and tiptoed to the bathroom.

Her hair looked like she'd been out in a windstorm. The sight of it in the vanity mirror made her glad Luke had been asleep when she left the bed. On a tray on the counter, small bottles of courtesy shampoo and conditioner sat alongside a bar of soap. She sniffed their fragrances, and finding the pear scent pleasant, dripped several tiny drops of shampoo in her hand, added water and scrubbed at her teeth with her finger. Then she swished the perfumy mix in her mouth and rinsed. Her mouth felt better, but it wasn't a teeth-cleaning method she would recommend.

Showering and washing her hair, she wondered what Luke would think when he awoke. What would last night mean to him? A one-night stand? Did she want it to be more? She didn't know. She stayed in the shower until she ran out of unanswerable questions to ponder and tender places to wash.

With no cosmetics except lipstick, she traced a light coat of the burgundy shade onto her lips. Then she dug a ball-point pen from her purse, picked tangles from her wet hair and dried it standing under the overhead heater. When she had made herself as presentable as possible, she eased the door open.

Luke was awake, lying on his back, his hands locked behind his neck, his biceps bunched, round and hard as baseballs. Dark, reddish brown hair lined his armpits and covered his muscular chest like a pelt. It whorled down and disappeared under the sheet and blanket caught at his waist. His nipples showed as tan buttons, and she remembered how at one point in the night she had wantonly licked them and he had groaned and shuddered.

"You've got your clothes on," he said. "What's wrong?"

He looked sexy and dangerous with his hair mussed and whisker stubble framing his lips. She loved his lips even more now that she knew their taste, knew the pleasure they could deliver. Suppressing the erotic memory fogging clear thought, she shrugged. "Nothing. I have to go home. You were sleeping—"

Before she could finish, he threw off the covers and stood, unconcerned for his nakedness. She swallowed a gulp and made no attempt to stop her greedy eyes. She hadn't really looked at all of him at one time last night, but in the bright sunlight, she thought him magnificent—stomach taut and flat, waist narrow, hips even more so, the thickly muscled legs of a man who had spent his life on horseback.

And he was aroused. She didn't see how he could be after last night, but his erection protruded from a thatch of dark brown curls.

He had to know she was staring, but he stood there letting her look. As intimate memories raced through her mind, a quickening low in her belly startled her and she glanced away. She had already been reckless enough. Now, going home was what she had to think about. "I— I left soap and shampoo on the side of the tub."

He came to her and pulled her close. His skin felt warm and soft, his lips brushed hers with the sweetest of kisses. "What is it? . . . Sorry?"

This morning she had a new attitude about sex and men. Of the myriad emotions she felt, sorry wasn't one of them. "No."

"Then what?" His eyes probed hers.

She shook her head. "Nothing. Really. I'm not sorry, no. It was—*you*—were wonderful."

A twinkle softened his gaze. "You were pretty damn good yourself." His head tilted toward the bed. "I guess, since you're all prettied up, you wouldn't be interested in crawling back into that bed and letting me kiss all the places I missed last night." She could feel his hardness against her stomach and a newfound shamelessness thought of doing just that. She resisted the lustful urges and curled her hand around his neck, drew his face down to her and kissed him again. "Piggy doesn't know I went out. She'll be worried."

He angled his head toward the phone. "Call her." His

palms framed her face. He kissed her cheekbone, her nose, her eyelids. "Let's don't go yet. Take a shower with me."

"I already—" She stopped and smiled into his eyes. "You're a terrible influence."

"We don't have to check out of here 'til noon."

She sighed. "Well . . . okay."

A few minutes before noon, they left the room, his wrinkled shirt and her wrinkled dress covered by their coats, and headed for breakfast. They and one other couple shared the hotel dining room. A waitress came with a coffee carafe, but before she could fill Dahlia's cup, Luke covered the rim with his hand.

"I know you don't like coffee. What would you rather have?"

"Uh, tea," Dahlia answered, surprised he remembered she wasn't a coffee drinker.

He ordered eggs, sausage and biscuits with gravy and she let him tease her into having the same. A heavy breakfast was a novelty. She usually had a cup of tea and a snack. They sipped while they waited for their food.

"Your friend at home?"

"She didn't answer."

"She with Pete?"

One thing Dahlia didn't do was discuss Piggy's affairs and liaisons. "I don't know. Maybe. What do you do on Sundays?"

"Um, kind of a slow day. If Mom's around to roust them out of bed, the family goes to church. I use the time to go through the mail, pay some bills, grab a little privacy in my cabin."

"You don't go to church with them?"

"Darlin', I'm in church with every sunrise and sunset, every time a calf or colt comes into the world, every time the seasons change."

She smiled. "That's poetic. You keep showing me sides of you no one would guess were there. Or is that another of your granny's old sayings?"

"Granny McRae wouldn't be poetic. What she would

say is, 'I don't need a damn shiny-faced flatlander to tell me there's a Higher Power.' "

Dahlia laughed, wondering how it would be to have a feisty grandmother.

"How about you? You a churchgoer?"

"Not so much anymore. When I was a little girl and my mother was alive, she took me to the Mexican church. It's the only Catholic church in Loretta. But after she passed on—well, the grocery store's open on Sundays, so—"

"You lost your mother when you were little?"

"When I was twelve."

Luke's eyes took on an odd expression of earnestness. "What happened to her?"

"Pneumonia. It started with the flu. She believed in tribal remedies, so she didn't trust doctors. By the time she went to see one, it was too late. Actually, I don't know if it was the pneumonia or a reaction to the antibiotics that took her life. I've never discussed it with my dad. It's too painful for him."

"That's tough, a young girl growing up without a mother. Who raised you?"

"My dad. He's the only family I have. My mom's relatives were all killed in the Philippines during World War II. My parents were older, so my dad's parents, except for his mom, were all gone by the time I was old enough to know them. Like me, he was an only child, so . . ."

Dahlia shrugged the serious discussion away. Growing up, she had envied her friends who had mothers and families, even envied their sibling rivalries. Now, except for how it affected her dad, she no longer had strong emotions about her mother's absence from her life, and she had substituted Piggy's large family for her own. "Flatlander. That's a word I hadn't heard until I came here. That must be what I am."

He chuckled. "Sweetheart, you're worse than a flatlander. You're a foreigner. Where is Texas anyway?"

She laughed, enjoying his teasing. "You have a log cabin?"

"Yep. Me and Davy Crockett."

She laughed again. "I've never been in a log cabin. Tell me about it." She sat back for the waitress to serve their food.

She watched his long, efficient fingers as he busied himself buttering a biscuit. She liked his hands. It was obvious they were working hands, but they had a masculine grace about them and he knew all sorts of erotic things to do with them. "Nothing much to tell. It used to be one of the bunkhouses. When I quit school and moved back home, I turned it into a house for me and my family."

"So you did go to college. Why didn't you want to tell me?"

"Does it matter?"

"No, but it isn't unreasonable that I would want to know."

"University of Idaho, up in Moscow."

"And something tells me you weren't an Ag major."

"Nope. Biology."

"Biology. Really?" Now some of the remarks he had made became clearer.

"Genetic research in large animals is where I was headed."

"But you'd need a master's or a PhD."

"Sometimes things don't work out. But when one thing doesn't, something else usually does. In a way, ranching's the same thing."

As she sliced a bite off a piece of sausage, Dahlia tried to apply that philosophy to her own life, but couldn't make it match, had lost track of how long it had been since something had "worked out" for her. They ate in silence until she became aware he was watching her and looked up. He had stopped eating, as if he was waiting for her attention.

"I'm not going around with anybody," he said.

The statement and the urgency she thought she saw in him surprised her. They held each other's stare for several seconds while the meaning of what he had just told her sank in. She didn't know where he was leading her, but sheer joy danced all over her insides. She nodded. "Okay. Good. I mean, I'm glad."

They finished breakfast and left the hotel. He helped her into her coat and remarked how cold her feet were going to be. Outside, he asked her for her keys, told her to stay on the deck and left her. He returned in Piggy's Blazer, parked it near the steps and brought her a pair of battered rubber boots. "Put these on," he said, standing on the snow-covered ground below the deck. He began to unbuckle her strappy high heels.

She hung on to the deck rail and let him change her pretty, expensive shoes for ugly, practical boots that swallowed her narrow feet and she laughed. "These are yours? Where did they come from?"

He tilted his head to the right, taking her sight to his white 4x4 parked only a few vehicles up from where she had left the Blazer. She wondered if it had been there yesterday afternoon when she arrived,

"In the high country," he said, "you never know when you'll need more clothes. I keep extra boots and a coat in my truck."

"I can see the wisdom in that." She laughed again. Her heart softened. He was hard and blunt to the point of being crude. And gentle and honest and responsible. If she had ever met a man who could be counted on in a pinch, she suspected this man was he. Luke McRae, cowboy. A man who lived the Code of the West.

She shook those dangerous thoughts away. Last night had been just sex and she had best not forget it. She looked out at the white landscape. "Will we have any trouble getting home?"

"Nah. Sun's out. Roads are plowed and sanded. A few miles down the mountain it'll be slush." He escorted her to the driver's seat of the Blazer, her steps crunching in the frozen snow. When she was seated and belted in, he leaned into the window, cupped her jaw in his palm and kissed her. "No need to hurry. Just take your time. Don't stomp on the brake. If you slide, steer into it. Don't worry. I'll be right behind you. I'll look out for you."

A downhill, ice-covered road should have terrified her, but his telling her he would take care of her was all the assurance she needed. "Okay."

The drive down the mountain was tense and slow, but uneventful. She even had a chance to admire the scenery as the snow became more sparse with each descending mile.

When they reached the cottage, Piggy hadn't returned. Luke walked her into the house and checked the thermostat. "Looks like your furnace is working now. Want me to build you a fire?"

"No need. I know how." She handed him his boots.

He pulled her into his arms "Good. I don't want you to freeze 'cause I'm gonna be back." He kissed her long and deeply, then rested his forehead against hers. "Damn. Wish I could take you home with me."

Damn. To her dismay, she wished it, too.

Chapter 13

"I have to have a dress." Dahlia hung up the phone, excitement bubbling over. It was Thursday and almost two weeks since she and Luke had spent the night at the ski lodge.

"Where's he taking you?"

"Something political. A dinner and dancing. It's black-tie."

"Oh, wow," Piggy said. "We'll take off work tomorrow. Go shopping in Boise. Jerry thinks it's gonna rain anyway."

Their boss's forecast proved to be accurate. The following morning broke with leaden skies and pouring water. Jerry canceled work until Monday.

They left Callister early and found the Towne Square Mall in Boise. Scouring the racks in the Bon Marché, they saw nothing that caught Dahlia's eye, so they moved out of the department store into the mall.

Piggy was the one who first spotted the world's most perfect dress in a boutique's window—a red silk sheath, elegant in its simplicity. When Dahlia tried it on, it smoothed down her body to her knees, touching in just the right places. The color enhanced her skin and eyes. A strap of silk circled her neck and held the front in place while the open back showed her skin to the waist. The salesclerk gushed oohs and aahs and Piggy wisecracked it could do double-duty as a nightgown.

An obscene price tag hung on the wisp of fabric, but Dahlia paid it. Then they dashed back to the Bon Marché for red shoes and, of course, red lace underwear.

The chariot in which Luke came for her was a white

Explorer with a logo on the side—a Black Angus cow's head inside a wreath of green letters spelling out DAM RANCHES, INC. As soon as they were seated inside it, he leaned across the console and kissed her, smiled, then kissed her again and told her she looked pretty and he couldn't wait to get his hands on her. She couldn't wait, either, and tried to recall a time she had been happier.

He had rented a room at the Evergreen Inn in Boise, where the dinner was being held. If the elegant hotel wasn't Boise's poshest, it looked like it should be. He left her alone to bathe and dress while he handled some kind of business. After a self-indulgent soak in an over-sized marble tub, she put on makeup, pinned her hair into a chignon, then donned the red dress. For jewelry, she added only gold hoops to her ears. Anything more would have been too much.

Waiting for Luke's return, she opened the draperies and looked over the small city of Boise. When she heard the click of the door's lock she turned toward it, and from all the way across the room, she saw his quick intake of breath. His stare pierced her to the bone, and at that moment, the dress, the shoes, the lingerie—the whole package became worth every penny it had cost.

Downstairs, in one of the banquet rooms, they took seats at a table with another of Luke's siblings, Brenna, and her husband, Morgan. Brenna was congenial, but soft-spoken, the opposite of the younger sister Dahlia had met at the Eights & Aces. Brenna remarked that Luke rarely attended these functions, but when he did, he usually came alone and left as soon as he wrote the check he felt was the reason for his being invited.

Typical enough to be trite, the banquet consisted of a meal of chicken and peas, unfunny jokes and boring speeches, but it didn't matter. Her attention was on her tall, taciturn escort.

The party's roster was impressive. Idaho's two senators were present, along with lesser politicians and representatives from most of the state's business communities. They mutually brownnosed and glad-handed, but not Luke. Instead, the politicians sought him out, asking for his opinions and, just as Luke's sister had said, for donations.

Luke didn't hesitate to state his mind or tell them what he expected for his money. She admired his frankness and how, if his words were negative or critical, he softened their bite with a self-deprecating grin and a slap on the shoulder. There appeared to be no issue important to Idaho's agricultural industries on which he wasn't current and well versed. She didn't have to observe him long to conclude that the foolish cowboy she had first thought him to be didn't exist.

As soon as the meal and the speeches ended, they moved into the ballroom. An older man whisked her away to dance. He was replaced by a younger man when the song ended, and so it went for the evening. Dahlia had the heady sense people were watching her, was certain she saw them discussing her.

Luke stood back and said nothing, but every time she glanced in his direction, his gaze was glued to her. She had a hard time keeping her eyes off him, too. He looked so handsome, broad shouldered and trim in a black jacket and a white banded-collar shirt. And Wranglers.

The party waned and the band announced the last number. When they began "Lady in Red," she felt someone grasp her waist, and she turned. Luke. He moved her to a quiet corner of the dance floor.

"I was starting to wonder if I was gonna get to dance with the belle of the ball."

She'd had several glasses of champagne and the abundance of male attention had her ego soaring. From somewhere, a bad-girl chuckle left her throat, and as sassy as Scarlett, she teased him in an exaggerated Texas drawl, asking if he was jealous.

"Damn right. I don't take to sharing my woman."

His woman. The very thought took her breath.

Back in their room, they had no sooner closed the door before he was kissing her like there was no tomorrow. She kissed him back with the same heated desire, and they furiously undressed each other and fell onto the bed. They slept little, dozing or talking between sessions of searing lovemaking. Each time, she thought she had been drained of desire, of emotion, but when he began murmuring to her, touching her, kissing her . . .

Summer came and progressed. With Luke's daughters spending the summer in Boise with their mother during the week, he made trips to town to see Dahlia. Having no privacy in the cottage and no bed except the cot, his visits often ended in the carport with steamy sex in his pickup's front seat and his oath to buy her a real bed.

On weekends they fished in high-mountain streams or from Luke's boat on beautiful lakes. They dined in good restaurants, traveled to the San Juans to watch whales and to the Oregon coast to fish for salmon.

And they made love with a passion she had only read about—in the boat tied up on a deserted beach, in the Jacuzzi tub in a luxury condo in Sun Valley, on a sleeping bag in the sunshine beside a trickling stream, an experience from which Dahlia came away feeling wicked and earthy.

Luke kept her separated from his life at the ranch. She had accompanied him on a few visits to see Jimmy at the boarding school in Boise, but otherwise, he made no attempt to include her in a relationship with his family, a fact that sorely troubled her.

By August, the survey work was nearing completion. She attempted to discuss with him that she would be leaving Callister soon, but he put off conversation about her departure. Their lovemaking took on a desperate quality, as if every time would be the last. When he told her he wanted to show her the Double Deuce before she went home to Texas, she could scarcely contain the thrill.

He came early, with Jimmy, on Saturday morning to pick her up. She had dressed in jeans, a polo shirt and the cowboy boots Luke had bought her. He had said they would take his son horseback riding because it was one of the few things the boy did well. Now that he spent so much time at the school in Boise, when he came home to visit, Luke made it a point to take him riding.

The day was sunny and warm, but as they climbed out

of Callister Valley, the temperature cooled and the scent of pine filled the air. Jimmy sat close to her and jabbered about his horse. Soon he dozed off against her side and Luke explained that the little guy slept a lot because of his heart ailment.

To say the trip was scenic was a gross understatement. In some places the ever-climbing gravel road had been sliced out of a steep hillside, leaving sheer rock walls soaring on one side and fathomless forest descending on the other. At times, dark green evergreens with trunks three feet wide lined the roadside.

When they had traveled for what seemed like forever, the forest thinned, revealing an expanse of sunbaked hills and brush-filled ravines rolling down from a faraway backdrop of saw-toothed mountains. Slender-trunked evergreens, tall and straight as sentries, guarded the foot of the mountains and she knew by now the trees were called lodgepole pines.

Luke slowed at a steel cattle guard across the road and pointed out a fence corner anchored by piles of large rocks and reinforced by barbed wire. "That's our southwest corner," he said. A while later, he stopped atop a crest in the road. "This is it. Sterling Valley."

His low tone reflected reverence and adulation, and she knew in her heart the exquisite landscape that lay before her was a far more captivating contender for his affection than a mistress or any mere human being could ever be.

"My grandfather from five generations back named it," he added. "Proved up on it in 1840, before Idaho was a state."

She gazed out over the vast valley of grass baked to tan by summer sun and rainless skies. On the far side, it gave way first to scattered boulders, then to long fingers of jutting granite and limestone. And finally, all of it converged to a distant dark blue peak topped by white, looming brilliant against the electric-blue sky. "Your family owns all of it?"

"Everything you can see. That's Sterling Mountain way over there. The snow on top never melts entirely."

She felt drawn to the place herself and rolled down her window for a clearer view and a breath of the clean, silent air. "I don't know what to say. It looks like a calendar picture."

Looking down, she saw corrals and barns, a row of buildings made of logs, their metal roofs glinting like mirrors in the sun. Luke's pointing finger directed her gaze uphill and off to the right of the barns, to a rambling house of logs and stone. "There's the ranch house."

"Why, it looks like the ski lodge," she murmured.

He chuckled. "A lot of people say that. It's way older than the ski lodge. The second generation grandson, James, built it."

"Jimmy's namesake?" she asked, and Luke nodded. "Wow," she said, overwhelmed. The power and strength of generations in one spot with a common goal pressed on her, and she wished she could imagine how it felt to have so much family and know its history.

"We'll stay in my cabin." He showed her a steep-roofed log structure nestled in a pine grove nearer to the barns than to the ranch house. "I don't live in it anymore, but it's still my favorite place. Now, my kids and I stay in the Big House with Mom and Dad. Things are easier that way."

"Big House?"

"The ranch house. We started calling it the Big House when my girls were little. They changed homes so often, they got confused, started calling the ranch house the Big House and the cabin the Little House. Big House just kind of stuck."

Dahlia didn't miss the unwitting reference to his unhappy marriage. She knew from gossip his children had known their share of emotional trials.

He distracted her from her thoughts by pointing across the valley to two more houses barely discernible on a distant ridge. "There's where my two sisters live. When they got married and brought their husbands here, the ranch built houses for them."

At the bottom of the hill, they rumbled across a cattle guard, through a stone and log gate and parked at a corral where a ranch hand had horses saddled and waiting. Jimmy had awakened and he began to bounce on the seat when he saw the saddled mounts. Luke had to calm him down before they entered the corral.

The horseback ride turned out to be shorter than anticipated. They hadn't reached the other side of the valley before Jimmy's energy began to fade. He cried to go home, so they turned back. At the corral, the child was so worn out, Luke had to almost drag him off the saddle, and Dahlia thought again about the patience and gentleness with which Luke treated his brain-injured child. Some fathers would lock Jimmy away, but Luke nurtured his son with a loving fierceness that touched something at the very base of Dahlia's soul.

At the Big House, she followed as Luke carried Jimmy through a wide front door. The entry was huge and dim, with varnished log walls and creaking oak floors and a heavy staircase of peeled poles. And it smelled of lemon oil. Natural light spilled from a wide door opening to a great room. She sneaked a sidewise glance and saw a massive stone fireplace and chimney taking up one wall and thought again of the ski lodge.

She felt as if she had entered a time capsule. Old photographs and paintings in ornate frames lined the entry walls. Directly in front of her, as if he were standing post, hung a life-sized oil painting of a white-haired man clad in a plaid kilt. Looking into his face was like looking into Luke's.

A middle-aged woman wearing an apron and a jolly smile met them. "Jimmy's plumb tuckered out," Luke told her, then performed introductions. "Ethel runs things around here, keeps us organized. You two get acquainted while I put this boy to bed."

As Luke carried his son upstairs, Ethel put out her right hand and Dahlia shook it. The woman kept smiling and looking like she expected comment, so Dahlia swept her hand passed the photographs and paintings. "Who are all these people?"

"McRaes," Ethel answered as if glad to be asked. "All of them. The big one is the ranch's founder. He was from Scotland."

Obviously, Dahlia thought, but she didn't say it.

Ethel strolled along the row and told Dahlia the name of each frame's occupant. She stopped and pointed to a grainy black-and-white photo of a man with mutton chops, a solemn face and a stiff collar. "This is who built this house," she said. "We still use some of the furniture he had shipped from Europe. It came around the Horn."

JAMES A. MCRAE, Dahlia read on a brass plate attached to the bottom of the frame and wondered if the letter A stood for Alan, which she knew was Luke's middle name. At the end of the row they came to a framed photograph—an enlarged snapshot, Dahlia could tell—of Luke and an older woman on horseback. Luke's mother. Like a heavy cape, a sense of foreboding crept over Dahlia. Claire McRae's temperament and her battles with Luke's ex-wife were common lore. "Oh, here's Luke. Is this his mom with him?"

The one-who-ran-things stepped back, her arms crossed over her apron. "Yes, ma'am. She's *really* the one who runs things around here. I just follow orders."

Dahlia couldn't tell if the housekeeper spoke out of awe or dislike, but the picture of the arresting, straight-spined woman astride a huge horse left no doubt Ethel's statement was fact.

Luke returned and ushered the two of them into a restaurant-sized kitchen where he began dragging food from an oversized double-door refrigerator. "You hungry?" he asked, and Dahlia shrugged and said, "Sure."

"I'll make us a lunch. We'll do some exploring in the Jeep. Have a picnic." He turned to Ethel. "Jimmy went to sleep. He be okay with you for a few hours?"

"You know he will," the housekeeper said, still smiling.

With Ethel's help, Luke made cold roast-beef sandwiches, then grabbed two apples from a basket in the center of a round oak table in one corner of the kitchen and took a hunk of cheese and some Cokes from the refrigerator. He and Ethel packed all of it into a brown grocery sack. Swinging by a closet in the dining room, he plucked a bottle of wine off the shelf and some Styrofoam cups and stuffed them into the sack.

They loaded the lunch and a bundle that looked like a sleeping bag into the back of the Jeep and set out, winding uphill toward the imposing Sterling Mountain.

"Your parents aren't home?"

"They went to Salt Lake, for Mom to see a doctor. Won't be back 'til the middle of the week."

"Oh," Dahlia said, puzzled. Would Luke have invited her here if his parents were home? She doubted it, and a glum feeling settled on her. To undermine her enjoyment further, thoughts of returning to Texas and leaving him battered her.

Before she could fall into despair, they came to a huge granite outcropping and Luke told her that from here she could see the whole valley all the way to the Snake River and this was a good place to stop and eat lunch. She could and it was.

It was also a good place for lying back and lazing in the sun, and after they had eaten the sandwiches and drank most of the wine, they did that. With Luke cushioning her neck with his arm, they were soon kissing, tongues dueling, hands caressing each other's intimate parts and building heat.

"It's been too damn long," he whispered, his eyes dark and stormy.

She loved seeing passion in his eyes and knowing she had put it there. They hadn't made love for more than two weeks. The last time she had seen him, she had been having her period. "I know."

"There's a better place." Lithe as a cat, he rolled off the boulder to his feet, then turned and lifted her down. They loaded back into the Jeep and proceeded uphill. Tension, thick and hot, drummed between them. They didn't talk, but when he wasn't shifting gears, he clutched the inside of her left thigh and she hung on to his hand.

A two-track trail off the main road soon appeared, and Luke made a sharp turn onto it. Dahlia began to hear the distant roar of rushing water. He parked, slid out and went to the back of the Jeep. She followed. He pulled the bundled sleeping bag out of the cargo hold and told her to grab the lunch.

There were still apples and cheese in the sack, and Cokes and some of the wine. She gripped the sack and trailed behind him as his long legs ate up the rough terrain. They rounded a cluster of boulders, and right in front of her, water bubbled out of the hillside and tumbled downhill. In its unhindered trip, it had washed clean and eroded to a smooth surface tiers of flat, tan rock that stairstepped down the mountainside. Vapor rose above it and Dahlia could feel heat and dampness.

"Steam," Luke said, "from the hot spring. There's a dozen of them around here."

Her gaze traced the water's steep downward path to a pool at the foot of the hill. Evidently man-made, it was a rock-dammed portion of a stream. A swirling cloud of mist hovered at its surface. Luke reached for her hand and led her down. Her heart was pounding when they reached the bottom, whether from the hike or anticipation of things to come, she didn't know.

They stood in a shroud of warm mist. She saw through it that they were in a green bowl of ferns and plants secluded by hillside and giant dark green trees. Slivers of sunlight checkered through the tall evergreen canopy on one side. The water's roar drowned out sound. The smell of fertile earth, so rich she could taste it, filled her nostrils. An eerie feeling came over her. She had never been in a place that stimulated every sense at one time.

Without a word, Luke began unsnapping his shirt buttons. A flash of pure, dark lust spiked inside her. Her gaze locked with his and she pulled her own shirt over her head and off. In a minute they were naked as nymphs.

Her nipples tightened as the warm, humid air whispered over parts of her body outdoor air didn't usually touch. She closed her eyes and basked in the spine-tingling sense of freedom coursing through her. From the center of her being to the tip of every hair, she felt alive, charged with desire.

"Look," Luke said huskily, and she opened her eyes. He was standing a few feet away—all long bone and thick muscle and *that* part was long and thick, too, thrusting like a column from his groin and visibly throbbing.

He reached down and took himself in hand. "See how much I want you?"

She felt herself flex deep and low. Her mouth went dry and she drew in a long, slow breath, unable to take her eyes off his engorged penis.

Then he was there, his arms wrapping around her like a straitjacket and his mouth slamming down on hers. It was a violent kiss, out of control. Her head spun, enveloped as she was in a cloud of passion and pink Chablis. His hand burrowed into her hair and held her head. His tongue thrust deep, and she sucked it like candy. Her nipples ached for his hands, his mouth, and she rubbed the rigid little points against his hair-roughened chest, reveling when he groaned.

She smoothed her hands down his sculpted body, over his narrow buttocks, around to his erection. While his tongue plumbed her mouth, she brushed the velvety shaft with her fingertips, stroked the smooth, bulbous head, cupped his hairy scrotum in her palms. He tore his mouth from hers and swore on a ragged breath.

She could think of nothing but pleasing him. She trailed her mouth down to the base of his throat, licked the quick pulse beating there, bent her head and found his nipples with her tongue and licked and nipped. He shuddered.

Spurred on, she sank slowly to her knees, licked her way over his solid abdomen, past his navel and down. His breath sharpened. "Aw, God, Dal . . ."

She moved on, caressing his buttocks, pressing her face against his groin and breathing in his musky scent. His penis jutted beside her cheek, a pearl of moisture glistening on its tip. She had to kiss the swollen thing. She closed her hand around it, licked away the salty drop and molded her lips over the plump head, ran her tongue around the rim.

He hissed through clenched teeth; his fingers dug into

her shoulders and he moved himself away. "I'll come," he said and brought her to her feet. He gripped the backs of her thighs and lifted her. Instinctively, her legs locked around his waist and she clung to him.

He carried her to a water-washed bench of flat rock and tipped her back onto the hard surface. Water, nearly hot, sluiced underneath and around her, wetting her body, soaking her hair, filling her ears with sound, but the steamy temperature didn't compare to the sizzle in her blood.

"You make me crazy," he growled. "Fucking you is all I think about, day and night."

It wasn't poetry, but it was Luke. Whatever. It was all she thought about, too. She planted her heels on the edge of the rock, opening herself to receive him. "Put it in."

"Not yet." He leaned over her and pinned her wrists beside her head. Warm water trickled over her arms and hands, her feet, and down there, it pummeled her gently, teased her intimate parts with its ebb and flow. Her mind moved to another plane, fixed on the sensations between her legs.

"I can't get enough of you," he whispered. He nuzzled the hollow of her arm and inhaled deeply. "I want to breathe you in, swallow you up, save you inside me."

She wanted no less, and as his mouth moved to her breasts, she arched her back, offering them to him. He took her nipples one by one and sucked her hard, pressing each rigid crest against the roof of his mouth, sending spikes of lightning dancing straight to where the warm water tormented her.

He moved down, his hot mouth trailing over her body's swells and hollows. The stubble of his afternoon beard scraped her stomach. He placed his palms on her inner thighs, spread them wide and stared down at her. "Beautiful," he murmured.

She made no attempt to cover herself, wanting his eyes to worship her. She came up on her elbows, hair and body soaked and dripping, and shamelessly watched as his fingers stroked her feminine layers. The dual sensations catapulted her to depths of lust she had never known. "Luke, now . . ."

"Not yet . . . Not 'til I kiss you everywhere . . . make you come twenty times." His head bent down and his tongue trailed the edge of her pubic hair. "So sweet," he whispered, and two fingers slid into her.

Her breath caught.

"Relax . . . Just enjoy." His fingers worked upward, stretching and touching something so good it had to be forbidden. Her anxious muscles clutched at his fingers as they pushed deeper. His mouth moved along her inner thigh murmuring sexy words she could only partially hear over the sound of the rushing water. ". . . eat you 'til you scream my name . . . hear you beg . . ."

Then his mouth was there, between her thighs and she watched as his tongue traced her cleft. Her pulse drummed in the top of her sex. She could feel that odd tension, the delicious pressure, her deep muscles clenching inside, and she whimpered.

His fingers withdrew, and he placed a hand on her breast, gently pushing her back. "Lie back." His hands slid under her buttocks and he lifted her to his mouth.

He kissed her with gentle suction and probing tongue. She wallowed in an erotic haze of wine and ecstasy and warm, trickling water, letting him do anything and everything. His tongue thrust deeper, rougher, pushed her higher. Her head thrashed from side to side and she did cry his name and beg. Then, as soft as warm silk, he drew the tiny, ripened core of her sex into his mouth and a world of sparkles exploded behind her eyes. She sobbed and gripped his wet hair in her fists, panting and gasping as orgasm after orgasm crashed through her.

It wasn't enough. Emptiness clawed at her. Her woman's sheath wept for his hot flesh; her womb ached to be washed by his semen. "Inside me . . . Hurry. I need you inside me." She panted the words, yanking him up by his hair and opening herself to receive him.

He didn't fail her. With a savage curse, he drove into her. She came again, her breath hitching, her deep muscles milking him with quick, strong contractions. He

pumped once, twice, swearing and straining. She felt the
spurt of him, heard his savage outcry as he plunged over.
At the end of it, he collapsed on top of her, shaking
and gasping.

She, too, was shaking. She had never known emotion
so deep, passion so hot, sex so raw. Tears gathered in
the corners of her eyes, trailed down her temples, washed
into the clear pool below, and she sobbed, torn asunder.
She loved him. She had tried to deny it for weeks, but
she loved him to the depth and breadth her soul could
reach, like in the poem. "Oh, Luke—"

He gathered her close to his chest. "Did I hurt you?"

"No, but—" Unable to put her feelings into words,
she kissed him fiercely and he kissed her back.

"Aw, God, sweetheart . . . That nearly killed me. . . ."

"We're all wet," she said on a sniffle.

"Shh, shh. We're okay. Don't cry now." He scooped
her into his arms and carried her to the warm pool.

Chapter 14

"You guys went to the hot springs?" Luke's sister Brenna slanted Dahlia a wise grin. The slender strawberry blonde dumped salad from a plastic container into a wooden salad bowl in the kitchen of Luke's cabin. She and Morgan had brought Jimmy and a large basket containing four T-bones and all the fixings for supper and invited themselves to stay. Luke said they were being nosy, but Dahlia didn't mind. She had liked Brenna from when they first met at the political fund-raiser in Boise back in May.

Learning a member of Luke's family suspected what she and Luke had been doing at the hot springs, Dahlia felt herself blush. "Uh, I'll do the garlic toast."

"Hey, don't be embarrassed. Morgan and I've enjoyed the hot springs ourselves." Brenna talked as she unloaded the basket of food. She produced a canning jar filled with what Dahlia assumed was salad dressing and rummaged in the cupboard as if she knew how to find what she was seeking. "When you're up there, it's like you're Adam and Eve and you're the only people in the whole world." Brenna pulled a small carafe from the cupboard and set it on the counter with a clunk. "Every time we go, I think I'll get pregnant. The atmosphere just seems right for it."

That remark brought a quickening of Dahlia's pulse as she thought of her and Luke having had sex twice without condoms. She watched as Brenna poured salad dressing from the canning jar into the carafe. "Is that home-made?"

"Hope you don't mind. I'm sort of into cooking."

"Not at all," Dahlia said. "I'm sort of into cooking, too, or at least I used to be." She turned away and slid the bread into the oven. "Is that what you want, to get pregnant?"

"Morgan and I've been married six years. It's time we had kids if we're ever going to. We've had all the tests. No reason why I shouldn't conceive, they say, but it never happens."

Dahlia glanced outside through the window in the back door at the McRae sibling who obviously had no problems conceiving. He was showing Jimmy how to tie his sneaker.

Brenna looked out, too. "The teaching never stops. It's so tragic. My brother's a wonderful father. Jimmy devastated him. Devastated the whole family, really. Somebody should strangle that child's mother."

"Luke hasn't told me much about his ex-wife."

Brenna laughed. "He wouldn't. He never discusses his feelings about anything, but I know he's got 'em." Brenna put the finishing touches on setting the round oak table at the end of the kitchen, then gave Dahlia a pointed look. "Take you, for example. He hasn't said a word about you to any of us, but he's brought you here. That's never happened before."

That tidbit from Luke's sister made Dahlia giddy, and she let go of a self-conscious giggle. "He's such an attractive man and this is such a wonderful place. It's hard to believe he's never brought home a female friend."

"Girlfriend, you mean? He doesn't have girlfriends. At least not the call-up-and-ask-for-a-date type. He's always kept his women stashed in Boise. Or somewhere. I've never met a one of them except when he used to go around with our neighbor. She didn't really count though. He mostly went out with her for Mom."

"I see," Dahlia said, caution restraining comment.

"You've probably heard about his ex-wife and our mom."

"A little." Dahlia was growing uncomfortable, but she couldn't control her curiosity.

"I was still in high school when Luke and Janet got

married. I'll never forget the hurricane that went through this family. He was such a kid. Mom saw through her from the first."

"Saw through her?"

"Janet thought by marrying my brother she had captured a seat on a gravy train. What she didn't know when she trapped him was that life at the Double Deuce is more hard work and survival than wealth and glamour. Every day of the time she lived here, she resented that."

"Why did she stay so long? And why did she have kids?"

"The kids were accidents, all three of them. She begrudged them, too. As for staying, she had nowhere else to go. She'd probably still be here if Luke hadn't caught her in a motel room in Boise with a logger. Who she later married for about a year."

Brenna looked out the door again and sighed. "Look at that." Jimmy was sitting on Luke's lap, his head on his father's broad shoulder. "Jimmy adores his dad, bless his heart. Morgan and I'll take him home with us soon as we eat"—she wiggled her brows up and down—"so you and Luke will have some privacy."

The men brought in the steaks, and while Luke took Jimmy to the bathroom, Brenna opened the bottle of wine she had brought. Luke and Jimmy returned and all of them sat down to eat.

While they visited over the meal, Luke cut off bites of his own steak, putting them on his son's plate and cajoling him to eat them. Brenna buttered his potato, broke a slice of toast into pieces and arranged it beside Jimmy's meat. The three of them, Luke, Brenna and Morgan, carried on conversation as if their constantly directing Luke's son was not a distraction.

Dahlia began to understand how much time and persistent attention taking care of Jimmy required and the fact that it had been Luke who had cared for him since the day of his birth. Her respect and admiration for the man doubled again.

Soon Jimmy said he was sleepy, and Luke laid him on

the sofa with a pillow, an afghan and a stuffed horse. He was asleep in no time.

Brenna opened a second bottle of wine, and with no embarrassment, regaled them with a graphic recount of her and Morgan's latest visit to the gynecologist. Dahlia was ill at ease at first with such a frank conversation about an intimate subject with people she hardly knew, but at the same time the openness made her feel accepted. Like family.

Then Brenna remarked that since Luke seemed to be the only McRae who was fertile, he had better get married again and have more kids if the old-fashioned custom of having a McRae son inherit the ranch were to prevail.

Luke cut her short. "That's not funny. Three kids is enough for anybody."

"But you're only thirty-four years old," his sister argued. "You've got plenty of time to have more kids. God knows, you wouldn't have any trouble finding a wife."

"Cut it out," Luke said. "No more kids."

Dahlia winced at his sharpness, and the feeling of belonging disappeared.

When supper ended, Brenna and Morgan left, taking Jimmy with them and leaving Dahlia and Luke standing at the cabin's front door. "It seems that everybody looks after Jimmy," she said.

"They do. And I appreciate it. He can't take care of himself and I can't be here every minute."

He went to the kitchen, returned with what was left of the dinner wine and set the bottle on the glass-topped coffee table. A CD player and speakers were tucked into one of the bookcases. He turned it on and inserted a CD.

To Dahlia's surprise—she expected to hear something country—the haunting strains of Enya filled the room. "This is Brenna's music," he said, as if he didn't want to admit he might like it, too. He drew her into a dance position.

"It's great. I love it," she told him, and melted into his arms.

They moved to the music, swaying in place. His thighs rubbed against hers, the heat of him radiated into her body. She thought of how alone they were, the primitiveness of their lovemaking earlier in the afternoon and the need began to build again.

"Let's go to bed," he whispered against her ear.

Dahlia sank into a soft pillow and brushed Luke's bristly cheek with hers. Her heartbeat gradually slowed. She was drained of energy, but she was where she wanted to be forever, safe and whole, sharing Luke McRae's bed, miles from the rest of the world. Time could stop.

A symphony of crickets thrummed through the open windows, punctuated by the *hu-hoo* of a nearby owl and the wail of a distant coyote. The night was as soft as the music, and black, the moon and stars hidden by clouds that hinted of rain. The cabin's metal roof popped like an exploding firecracker and she jumped.

"Shhh. It's just cooling off. When the sun goes, so does the heat."

"Not like Texas." She strummed his ribs with her fingertips. His skin was smooth and moist. He smelled of clean sweat, *his* smell. "That was incredible. Was I loud?"

He braced himself on one elbow and pushed strands of hair off her face. One corner of his mouth eased into the lopsided grin that had become so endearing. "Woke up the dogs. Didn't you hear them barking?"

"No, I didn't." She smiled into the eyes that just moments ago had been dark and turbulent with passion. Now they were turquoise and calm, a tropical lagoon after a storm. She touched his lower lip with her forefinger. "You bring out my basest instincts, Luke McRae."

He bit down gently on her fingertip. "You're the damnedest woman, Dahlia. All a man could ever want."

His body shifted. She tightened her hands on his ribs. "No, don't. Don't move yet. Stay inside me."

"I couldn't move if I wanted to." He settled and placed his warm lips near her ear.

She wanted to tell him she loved him, but she didn't dare say it first. She believed he loved her, too, so why wouldn't he tell her, especially at a moment like this? "Today was wonderful," she whispered.

"Hmm," he said.

A long creak of the front door hinge rent the ambience. Her pulse quickened. "Luke? Was that—"

"Luke?" It was a coarse female voice.

His head jerked up. The front door closed with a *thud!* A butterfly swarm took flight in Dahlia's stomach. "Who—who is it?"

"Where are you, Son?"

Footsteps scuffed up the hall on the thick carpet. Luke twisted to look behind himself. Dahlia looked past his shoulder. A tall female shape filled the open doorway, silhouetted in the hall light. *OhdearGod.* Dahlia's heart stuttered.

Click. Blinding overhead light flooded the room, obliterating all vestiges of the loving moments that had just occurred. A gray-haired woman stared from the doorway. "Wha—what's going on here?"

Dahlia buried her face against Luke's thick biceps. He didn't move. "Go back to the living room, Mom."

The silhouette turned abruptly and left the doorway, muttering obscenities.

Luke sprang to his feet, shut the bedroom door and rounded the end of the king-sized bed.

Dahlia groped for the bedsheet and clutched it against her chest. "God, Luke. What should I do?"

"Nothing. I'll take care of it."

His jeans lay in a pile on the floor. He grabbed them and jerked them on, his belt buckle and pocket change clinking and jangling. He disappeared into the hall and pulled the door closed behind him.

"Who's with you?" His mother's voice crackled with indignation.

"Where's Dad?" The front door hinge creaked again. "Dad, you got back early."

Oh, no!

"Not *too* damned early, from the looks of things," the mother spat. "Where's Jimmy? Is he here? I hope you haven't left him alone in the Big House."

Dahlia waited for Luke to tell them his sister was looking after his seven-year-old son, but the next voice was the dad's. "Claire, you *know* what those doctors said about getting upset. What's going on here, Son?"

Dahlia scanned the bedroom. Her jeans lay crumpled on Luke's chair a half-dozen steps away. No shirt, no bra. Where *were* they?

Oh no! They were on the sofa in the living room where Luke had started undressing her. A manic urge to wrap up in the bedsheet and streak from the cabin careened through her head.

"Who *is* that girl?"

"Cool it, Mom."

"What's going on, Son?" Luke's dad repeated.

"Nothing. Just keep Mom in here, will you?"

Dahlia scrambled from the bed, headed for her small duffel bag on the floor near the bathroom doorway. Luke's warm essence trailed down the inside of her thigh, but she didn't take the time to stanch it. Before she could dig out a change of clothing, the bedroom door opened. Luke was back, holding her bra and shirt in one large hand. She winced, picturing him gathering up her underwear while his parents watched.

He shut the door with a clap and locked it. "Put your clothes on. I'll take you back to town."

She dropped the duffel, grabbed the bra and polo shirt and lunged across the room to her jeans. She was shaking so badly, her foot missed her pants leg. Luke came to her side and held her steady while she skinned the jeans over her bottom, sans underwear. She crammed the bra into the jeans pocket and yanked her shirt over her head. "My boots, Luke. They're in the living room. And my purse."

"I'll get 'em," he said, stuffing in his shirttail. He slipped through the bedroom door opening again.

"That's the girl from the Forest Service, isn't it? The one you've been taking to the ski lodge."

Oh God, no. How did his mother know that?
"I hear about the two of you every time I go to town.
You take that slut—"
"That's enough!" Luke's voice, a bark. Dahlia had
never heard him speak so harshly. "She's no slut. I don't
want to hear any more of this. I'm not a kid. This is
where I live. What I do here's my business."
"Claire," Luke's dad said, "the doctors *told* you not
to get upset—"
"I hope the Flaggs don't find out about this. This will
break Lee Ann's heart." The mother's coarse voice lowered to a stage whisper. "Good Lord, Son. Have you no
shame? It hasn't been a week since you brought her here
for a respectable dinner with your family."
What? Dahlia felt her eyes bug.
"Cut it out, Mom. I mean it." Luke returned to the
bedroom, carrying the boots and purse and wearing a
dour expression. "You okay?"
No, she wasn't okay. No part of this was okay. Especially not after hearing he had brought his old girlfriend
to dinner with his parents just last week. Still, Dahlia
bobbed her head, dropped to the edge of the bed and
pulled on her boots. "Get me out of here. Before your
mother has a stroke."
He caught her hand. "Come on. Looks like you're
about to meet my folks."
"*No!* Luke!" She dug her heels into the carpeting. "I
can't meet them like this."
"Then what do you want to do, sneak out the window?" His arctic stare brooked no argument. Her fingers
ached in his tight grip. Her mind raced, headed nowhere.
"Why can't we just, just . . . well, just walk past them?"
He hesitated a few seconds, as if he might be considering that as an option. Then, he said, "No. We can't do
that." He tugged her down the hall and stopped just
inside the living room. "Mom, Dad, this is my friend
Dahlia. Dahlia Montgomery."
From her seat on the sofa, a sixtyish woman with wiry,
iron-gray hair glared. A tall, white-haired man with star-
tling blue eyes—the eyes from the portrait in the Big

House entry—stood in the middle of the living room, his brow furrowed in puzzlement.

Dahlia cringed, clutching the lifeline Luke's hand had become. "Uh, uh . . . how do you do?"

With obvious effort, the matriarch pushed herself up from the sofa and stood, her fists knotted at her hips, the malice in her eyes as piercing as a honed icicle. She came closer, within inches, and glared up at Luke. Tall as she was, she was a good six or seven inches shorter than her son. "You didn't answer me, Son. *Is* this the girl from the Forest Service?"

Dahlia had been in Callister long enough to know that to the local ranchers and loggers, being associated with the Forest Service or any branch of the federal government was akin to sitting at Satan's knee.

Luke's grip tightened on her hand. She shot a look up at his profile. His jaw muscle wasn't just twitching—it was jumping. "Yes," he snapped. "She is."

His mother must have seen his anger, but she was undeterred. "Your ex-wife should have taught you about getting involved with outsiders. And your daughters? Have you thought about the stories they hear about their father shacked up in the hotel where they go skiing?" Her head jerked toward Dahlia. "You, young woman, might feel more at home some place that rents by the hour."

Dahlia quailed, stunned by the venomous hostility.

"I said cut it out, Mom."

Luke's dad came to his wife's side and placed his hand on her elbow. "Claire," he said quietly, "let's go up to the house." He looked at Luke. "Where's Jimmy, Son?"

"Jimmy's fine. He's with Brenna and Morgan."

Claire jerked away from her husband's touch, her lips pressed into a flat line. She moved toward the front door, and Luke's dad followed, carrying his hat and guiding his wife through the doorway. "We'll see you in the morning, Son."

The front door's closing brought silence—except for Enya's seductive voice crooning from the CD player. Dahlia drew a breath for what seemed like the first time.

Her purse slid off her shoulder and hit the floor with a *plop*. She wilted onto a chair near the door and clasped her heated cheeks with her palms. "Oh my God. I can't believe this happened."

Luke knelt in front of her. "It's not the end of the world. It'll be okay."

Her nose stung, but she forced herself not to cry. "How can it be okay? They think I'm a—"

"I'll set it straight tomorrow, after Mom settles down."

"Take me home," she said in a voice that came out tiny. "Please. Just take me home."

"C'mon," he said, picking up her purse and handing it to her. "It really will be okay."

She didn't know how her weak smile looked, but she knew how it felt—pitiful and helpless.

Dahlia wedged herself into the corner of the passenger side as Luke's pickup bounced down the Double Deuce's long driveway and remembered for the first time, in her frantic hurry to get dressed, she had left her panties on the floor in Luke's bedroom. Only a dire threat could make her return to retrieve them.

Like a horror mask, Claire McRae's angry visage loomed in the night's blackness. She wished she could teleport, zip to the cottage in town without having to think or endure a two-hour ride over the rough road ahead. Every nerve had balled into a knot at the base of her neck. Her heart and dignity ached from a dozen lacerations. It was a toss-up which had her more upset— being thought a slut by the mother of the man she loved or learning he still saw an old girlfriend.

The pickup slowed, eased across the cattle guard that spanned the ranch's stone gateway. They turned left toward town. She glued her sight to the dual fans splayed over the narrow road by the headlights. Only after they had traveled several miles did her neck and shoulders begin to relax.

Luke spoke first, his voice sounding tight and artificial. "Boy. Blacker than the inside of a cow tonight."

"Why didn't you stand up for us, Luke?"

He looked at her across his shoulder. *"Us?"*

His answer confirmed what she had feared for weeks. To him, there was no "us." Her throat felt like she had swallowed a tennis ball, but she pushed on, a glutton for punishment. *"Us.* As in you and me. Why didn't you stand up for us as a couple?"

His eyes swerved back to the road, his lips moving in a swear word. "I don't know, Dahlia."

Waiting tears spilled over her eyelids. Trying to stop them brought a hiccuping sob.

The pickup jolted to a halt. He shifted out of gear, pulled her across the seat and wrapped both arms around her, cradling her head against his shoulder. "Don't do this, Dal. C'mon . . ." His fingers slid beneath her hair. "Hush, now."

He soothed and petted her until her sobs turned to sniffles. Then he hooked a knuckle under her chin and dabbed at her wet face with an ironed handkerchief that smelled of fabric softener. "Don't cry, now. I guess we can't blame Mom for flying off the handle. I know how *I'd* feel if I found one of my girls . . . well, like she found us."

Dahlia pushed away. "That's ridiculous. It's not the same thing." She yanked her purse to her lap and dug out a Kleenex, mopped her cheeks and blew her nose. "We're adults and we were in a private place. She ripped into us like a chain saw. How can you ignore that?"

He thumbed his hat back and rested his elbow on the steering wheel. "Mom acts on reasons she thinks are good ones, Dahlia."

"Really? And what good reason does she have for insulting me? What's worse, you didn't defend me."

"I told her you weren't a slut. Seems to me that's defending."

Good grief! Can he really be so obtuse?

"I know what Mom did wasn't right, Dal. She'll calm down. It just takes a little time."

"And *then* what?"

A quick anger flared in his eyes. "Nine people count

on me keeping things running smooth and I go out of
my way to do it. I'm not gonna go into a long-winded
explanation, but I depend on my mom a lot. She can
make my life hell, but in the ways that are important,
she makes it easier. There's *some things* I'm not gonna
screw up, for you or anybody else. I never said I would."

His words cut like whiplashes. He had never spoken
to her in anger. She fought back another gush of tears.
"No, I guess you haven't." She stuffed the ragged Kleenex into her purse. "Let's go on. It'll be daylight before
you get back home. No doubt she's watching the clock.
If you're late, she might paddle you."

His gaze held hers in a long, seething look, but gave
no hint what he was really thinking. They were at some
kind of crossroads. She waited for him to tell her a direction to go, but he only sighed and shifted into gear. They
inched forward.

Silence. A few more miles, giving her time to consider
how little she really knew of Luke and the way he lived.
He seldom discussed what went on in his daily life, didn't
talk much about his kids. She knew every curve and
plane of his muscular body, yet he had always maintained
a peculiar distance. From the beginning, he had been a
rugged mountain, wider and higher than she could reach
across or see over.

In for a penny, in for a pound. She cleared her throat.
"What did your mother mean by 'I hope the Flaggs don't
find out about this?' "

"Mom's blowing smoke. Flaggs are neighbors. They
join up with us on the east. They've been in Sterling
Valley almost as long as we have."

The evasive answer set off a hiss of jealousy, not just
of the blond calf roper hanging on his arm at the
Eights & Aces Saloon months ago, but of all Luke and
the neighboring rancher's daughter had in common. "Do
you still date Lee Ann Flagg?"

"Date? You're the first woman I've taken out in
years."

"But you took *her* home to dinner last week."

His head jerked toward her, his eyes glowering. "I drove down to get the mail and she came by, on her way home from town."

"Well, that's convenient." Dahlia winced again, wondering where this strange bitch inside her had come from.

"Up here, we can't afford not to take neighboring serious, Dahlia. It was suppertime, so I asked her to eat. She's a good friend. There'll never be a time she's not welcome at our table."

Or in your bed? "Your mother must think you're more than good friends."

"That's just Mom. I don't like talking about this, Dahlia, but since I figure you've already heard it from that bunch of know-it-alls at the Forest Service, I'll tell you. Lee Ann and I had something going on a long time ago. It didn't mean as much to either one of us as it did to our families. Mom's wanted me to marry her since we were kids, but I guess I'm not cut out for marriage. I figure Janet and I drug that institution through enough dirt to last a lifetime."

He reached across the bench seat and gripped her arm. "We don't need to be arguing about Lee Ann or anything else, Dahlia. We've always got along. C'mon now. Don't be ornery. Come sit close to me."

No. He had mopped the floor with her feelings. She freed her arm. "I'm okay."

Clear thinking crept in without mercy, bringing a vivid depiction of how life at the Double Deuce must have been for Janet McRae. No doubt Luke's mother had kept the peerless Lee Ann Flagg around in spirit if not in body. In those days, did Luke stand up to his mother on his wife's behalf? Or did he leave her twisting in the wind while the Wicked Witch of the Double Deuce Ranch picked at her bones?

The question left Dahlia grim and overwhelmed as yet another truth sank in. She should have listened when she heard words like "old-fashioned" and "tradition." And *clan.* McRaes were a clan in the old-world sense. A half Filipino from Texas breaching such chauvinism was no more possible than scaling the stone walls of an ancient

Gaelic castle barefoot. His marrying Lee Ann Flagg would be a tribal union, and after the face-to-face meeting with Luke's willful mother, Dahlia didn't doubt for a minute it could still happen.

She had been so blind. And stupid. All summer, she had let his activities be her clock and calendar, counting the hours between his visits. Her heart raced at his touch. The sight of his narrow hips and muscular thighs in his tight jeans filled her head with erotic imaginings. Happiness would be to spend the rest of her life at his side, in his bed. Having his babies.

Reality squeezed her heart one more time. She was too late. He already had babies with someone else. They were almost grown and he didn't want any more. He had a life apart from her of which he hadn't so much as hinted she would ever be a part. While she would recover from the embarrassment of being surprised in his bed by his parents, she might never recover from letting herself fall head over heels in love with yet another man who didn't return her affection.

And if tonight's incident did nothing else, it made another fact as clear as the hot-springs pool. Even if tomorrow he said the three words she longed to hear, so long as his mother presided over the Double Deuce ranch, a future together for Dahlia Montgomery and Luke McRae was no more likely than a blizzard in Houston.

At midnight, Luke parked in the cottage's driveway, slid out and headed around the front of the pickup, but Dahlia didn't wait. She stepped down from the passenger seat, slammed the door and stalked across the skimpy lawn toward the front stoop.

"Dahlia, hold up—"

She stopped and faced him. Another time, she might have been inhibited by her tear-swollen eyes and the streaks of black mascara that must be trailing down her cheeks, but tonight, vanity seemed a shallow indulgence. "Hold up for what?"

His straw Resistol came off and he held it in front of him, working the brim. "I know it doesn't look like it, but they don't tell me what to do or who to see."

"I agree. It doesn't look like it." She groped for the doorknob. If she didn't get away from him, another fit of tears would destroy her.

"I know it's hard for an outsider—"

"Don't call me that." She could scream. She and Piggy had been called outsiders a hundred times since arriving in this backwoods burg. Anybody whose great-great-grandpa hadn't come here on a wagon train was labeled "outsider."

He raised his head. "I wanted you to see the ranch, Dal. It didn't turn out like I planned, but I'm not sorry you came. I hope you're not either."

"Your ranch is beautiful," she said softly.

"I'll call you tomorrow, okay? You'll feel better after you get some sleep."

He stood there, hat in his hand, looking more helpless than she had ever seen him. In his eyes, she saw a plea, like that day in the service station when Jimmy had smeared chocolate on her skirt. Could he be in as much pain as she was?

She sniffed and shrugged. "You've got the number."

"Right. I'll call."

She nodded, a deep ache in her throat. Turning into the doorway, she left him standing in the yard.

As Luke's old Ford crawled up the main street, except for the lights and noise from the two bars, town was deserted. The saloons tempted him not the slightest. Though he felt lower than a snake's belly, he had never been one to throw liquor on his sorrows, not even when troubles had him buried so deep he couldn't see out.

Dahlia. Her name and her tears were a whirlpool in his thoughts. He guessed he should have done something different back in the cabin, but what? Anything he might have said would have made a bad situation worse. When his mother was pissed off, arguing with her was like squaring off with a grizzly. He had seen slithery bankers and hard-bitten cowboys buckle in the path of her gray glare and caustic tongue.

Leaving the lights of town behind him, he headed north. His truck had made the trip from town so many times, it performed by rote and that gave his mind freedom.

His life was too damn complicated for an outsider like Dahlia to understand. His mother, a smart woman who knew the cow and horse business inside and out, had been the hub of the Double Deuce since the day his father gave up that role. To Luke personally, she was more. She had been both gentle teacher and surrogate mother to Jimmy since infancy.

He had weathered many of Mom's storms, so one more wasn't what filled his thoughts. What caused a knot in his chest was this whole thing with Dahlia. From the first, like a sorceress, she had drawn him, and as if he were powerless, he had let her. The minute he left her he started plotting the next time he could get to town to see her. Hell, his gasoline bill had doubled.

And hadn't taking her to the ranch for a weekend proved he was under a spell? He never, *ever* took women to the ranch.

Then he had compounded the error, taking advantage of his employee Ethel by asking her to watch Jimmy so he and Dahlia could spend time alone. He never, *ever* involved the ranch's employees in his personal life.

By anybody's definition, Dahlia was a distraction. And *that* he didn't need—never, ever. He had no room for "relationships," a dumb word anyway.

He drove through the Double Deuce's gateway at two a.m. Luck was with him—the Big House was dark. He headed for the cabin. His blue-eyed heeler, Frosty, and his border collie, Bingo, began to bark from the front deck before he arrived. So much for not waking the household.

As he entered the bedroom, he saw Dahlia's pink panties on the floor beside the bed. He picked them up and rubbed the silky fabric between his thumb and finger. Muttering swear words, he stuffed them into his jeans pocket.

As he slid into bed, Dahlia's scent surrounded him, bringing back a memory of her body molded to his, and he missed her.

Another worry cropped up. She had told him sex without a rubber was okay, but he wondered. Her monthly schedule had become almost as familiar to him as it was to her, for he enjoyed making love without . . .

Whoa! At what point had screwing become making love?

Shit. He should have stayed away from her.

Chapter 15

Birds. A million of the shrieking little fiends lived in the trees surrounding the cottage. Once Dahlia's ears tuned in to their chittering, even if she wanted to, she couldn't go back to sleep. *Dumb birds.* She groaned, burrowed deeper into her sleeping bag and covered her head with her pillow.

With wakefulness came thought. Yesterday, she had expected to wake up today in Luke's arms and they would spend a quiet morning making love in the pastoral setting of Sterling Valley. A far cry from waking alone on a cot in a bare bedroom of a tiny old house. What a difference a day, an hour, a minute, even a split-second, could make in a life. Who knew it better than she? Irony was her old friend.

A memory from long ago eased into her thoughts— Filipino superstitions. As a child, if she went to bed unhappy, in a musical mix of languages, her mother told her to hurry to sleep because magic happened in the night. In the morning, the thing making her sad would be gone.

Magic hadn't occurred while she slept. Last night's scene in Luke's bedroom had not been a bad dream. Opening her eyes wouldn't cancel out the tall silhouette standing in the bedroom doorway or the angry shrew waiting in the living room.

Dahlia pulled her sleeping bag tight around her, guessing the temperature to be in the forties. She loved these bracing mountain mornings and slept with her window wide open. The clean, dry air was addicting. August in

Callister was nothing like August in Loretta, where the temperature and humidity often equaled each other. *Texas. And home.* She would be returning in two or three weeks. Would she long to come back here? Would she come back to visit Luke? After last night, would he want her to?

Pots and pans banged from the kitchen, clashing with a George Strait ballad in the background. Piggy cooking breakfast. Or lunch. Or who knew what?

Growing more awake, Dahlia remembered she was naked from the waist down. After she and Piggy had talked into the wee hours, exhausted, she had shed only her jeans and crawled into her sleeping bag. The skin of her inner thighs stung from having been chafed for hours by the damp seam of her jeans and she smelled like stale sex. The flimsy fiberglass tub and shower in the tiny bathroom beckoned like a luxurious spa.

Throwing open the sleeping bag, she willed her feet to the hardwood floor and stripped off her shirt. She was sore all over. Besides not having been horseback riding in years, sex at the hot springs had been a workout— delicious, but a physical stretch all the same. And it had happened without birth control at a marginal time of the month.

Dumb, dumb, dumb.

Oh, she was sure he'd had condoms—he always did. But ever since that first time at the ski lodge, he had relied on her to tell him when their use was necessary. Yesterday, they had both been so hot, he didn't even ask her if it was safe and she hadn't cared if it wasn't.

Dumb, dumb, dumb.

She groaned her way to her feet, then padded naked to the closet for her robe. Kneeling beside the suitcase where she stored her underwear, she rooted beneath the clothing for the calendar on which she kept a record of her menstrual cycle.

During her marriage, keeping the calendar had been more than birth control. It had been a record of the days she might be fertile, her own secret plan for an accident. She had been so lonely. Even when her husband wasn't absent in body, his mind had been off in some computer nirvana. She had thought a child would fill an empty corner in her heart. The planned accident never happened—she had always chickened out.

This morning, the calendar confirmed what she suspected, and she felt a stab of panic and guilt. Her hand went to her stomach and she sat back on her heels remembering yesterday afternoon. Aroused beyond reason, she had wanted Luke's seed released into her body, with no barrier, latex or otherwise.

It had been a driving desire, not the same as when she had wanted a baby with Kenneth. Then, it had been a goal rather than a passion, like going to a store to buy a coveted doll. With Luke yesterday, it had been the most powerful craving she had ever felt, something emanating from the very core of her self, something she might never feel again.

It wasn't the first time they had pushed the envelope. All summer, the days her period was due had been nail-biting times. Besides losing all her inhibitions when it came to making love with him, she lost her good sense, too.

Fear surged. Was life growing inside her at this very moment? Luke wouldn't be happy. He might not even be supportive. She drew her hands down her face, closed her eyes and said a silent prayer, promising to be forever chaste if she were allowed to squeak by this one time. Then she rehid the calendar in the bottom of her suitcase.

The alarm clock on the floor by her cot showed ten. *Ten.* And the phone hadn't rung.

She pushed herself to her feet and plodded with head-jarring footsteps to the bathroom. Dropping her robe in front of the mirror on the medicine cabinet door, she saw her breasts rosy with abrasions. Whisker burns!

She touched a hickey low on her stomach and recalled the exact moment Luke had put it there. They had both been so carried away. She fought back tears. "God, Luke . . ."

Don't think, the swollen face in the mirror told her. *Run. Far and fast. Until you drop.*

Instead of showering, she went back to the bedroom. Pulled on her sweats and tied on her Nikes.

As Luke closed the cabin's front door, the hinge creaked and he considered dead bolting the door. When Janet lived here, the doors had always been locked against his family members.

He had just come from breakfast at the Big House, which turned out to be less silent and awkward than he had expected. His grandmother had been present, which postponed the inevitable. Then, after the meal, the sweet little old lady, God bless her, lingered to visit, so he had been able to make his escape.

On second thought, he rejected locking the front door and went on into his office, which was really the converted front bedroom. The Big House had a real office but it was his parents' domain. He guessed it would be his someday, but he didn't like its antique fussiness.

He preferred the simplicity of his own space he had put together himself after Janet left. Comfortable cowhide furniture fit the look of the cabin's yellowed-with-age pine plank floor. On his walls hung photographs of some of his prize bulls and horses along with some original Western paintings—investment art. On his bookshelves, alongside his eclectic collection of reading material sat pictures of his daughters.

Here and there were Indian artifacts he had collected from all over the Double Deuce. They kept him humble, not letting him forget that McRaes were newcomers. His distant grandfather may have staked his claim over a hundred fifty years ago, but the Sioux had preceded him by many generations.

Dahlia's line buzzed busy, so he tackled the week's worth of mail he had let accumulate on the corner of his desk, slicing through envelopes with a vengeance.

Making an easy escape from the breakfast table didn't mean he had dodged questioning from his family. Sure enough, he hadn't finished opening the mail before he heard a tap on the front door, followed by footsteps in the living room.

"Son?"

"In here, Dad."

His white-haired father strolled into the office and eased down into the easy chair opposite the desk. "Shorty tells me you got more hay while your mom and I were gone."

Luke folded his arms on the desk, digging in for the first barrage. "I bought extra. In case we see a late spring."

Nodding, his dad took his pipe from his shirt pocket and began to pack it, a process Luke knew would take a minute or so. He went back to slicing open envelopes with his pocketknife.

Pipe lit, his dad spoke. "You and your lady friend caused a hell of a stir up at the house."

"No reason for it. I don't claim to be a monk."

"I think what upset your mother is you brought her here. And frankly, I'm a little surprised at that myself. You haven't brought a girl here since you were a boy."

"Is the Double Deuce off-limits to my friends?" Though Luke knew his easygoing father didn't mean to pick a fight, he couldn't keep his tone from being combative.

"You know better than that. Lord, even if we do have all these shareholders, for the most part, this ranch is yours now. I'm just reminding you the long shadow you stand in."

"That painting on the wall stares me in the face every day." Even if he wanted to, Luke couldn't forget. The Scot immigrant's visage was embedded as deeply as his genes in the McRae psyche.

His dad chuckled and dug into his jeans pocket for his lighter. "I expect he would be proud of you. What you've accomplished here is not to be sneezed at. You've put the ranch on firmer ground for those who'll follow you."

Dad always preceded criticism with a compliment. He referred to the decisive action Luke had taken a few years back that freed the ranch from the grip of salivating bankers.

Parasitic moth larvae had been discovered by the Forest Service on Sterling Mountain, including the part that belonged to DAM Ranches. Racing time, Luke hired a logger to clear the affected area and burn the diseased slash. He used the logging proceeds to pay off the ranch's notes and to purchase the winter pastures McRaes had leased for years in the more temperate southern part of the state. Now, DAM Ranches, Inc., the Double Deuce's parent company, ran virtually debt free, one of the few family-owned cattle operations left that could make the claim.

"It was no big deal. Mostly timing and luck."

"I don't think so. You had to make a hard decision I wouldn't have made. If it had been left to me, the bugs would've got the whole mountain. But I fear you've stepped in your own trap, Son. While you've made the ranch more secure than it's ever been, you've also made it more demanding. Buying more land, adding stock. Selling bulls, selling horses."

"We're living in complicated times." Luke absently scanned a stockman's association newsletter. "Half the country wants to regulate us out of business. We can't afford to be standing still."

His dad sighed. "Don't know what they think they'll eat if they succeed. Guess it's not good enough nowadays for a rancher to be just a good cattleman." He pointed his pipe stem at the computer setup on the table behind the desk chair. "Who would've thought you'd be using that thing to run a ranch?"

Luke glanced at the multicolored Microsoft flag undulating across the black monitor screen. He had always been quick to use any tool that improved the bottom line. The computer had become invaluable, all the way from following market trends to keeping records of breeding history and tracking his steers' weight gain to keep abreast of disease and state-of-the-art treatments. At times, he even participated in on-line bull auctions. "Gotta keep up. That's what happened to the Circle K. Tuffy kept doing things the same old way."

"I hear the new owner's bitching about the deer eating his rosebushes."

"No doubt." *Investor.* Of all the interlopers pushing into Idaho, investors were the worst. They paid inflated prices for the land to dodge taxes and pump up their financial statements and give themselves bragging rights at some country club a thousand miles away. They had the money to buy politicians who legislated sweeping changes. Every property-owning citizen of Callister County had become the unwitting victim of out-of-state investors who didn't care a whit about the people who depended on the land for livelihood. Then, to add insult to injury, they brought in stupid animals like llamas or emus.

"You can rest easy, Dad. I don't intend to be forced to sell the Double Deuce. Or to turn it into a subdivision."

Luke couldn't resist that little jab at his parents. Ten years ago, they had come close to putting the ranch on the market. He had given up a master's in biology to prevent it. Now his focus was on the ranch's business, his kids and his family. Anything that diverted his mental energy was unacceptable. And that made a resolution of what was going on with Dahlia more pressing. An association that went beyond occasional fun *had* to be a doomed one.

"All I'm saying is when you choose your friends, I hope you use the same sound judgment you use with everything else."

"Okay, Dad. We're finally to it. I know this is really about Dahlia and the Forest Service."

Bushy white brows pinched together. "You know as well as I do, since that 'Wilderness' legislation, the Forest Service hasn't been our friend—"

"Dahlia's not a Forest Service spy." Luke leaned forward for emphasis. "She's from Texas. She couldn't care less about government grazing."

The older man harrumphed and drew on his pipe.

"She's not political. All she's doing is helping a surveyor for the summer. She's going back to Texas in a few weeks."

"That'll make your mother feel better."

The purpose of his parents' trip to Salt Lake leaped

into Luke's mind. "How *is* Mom? What did the doctors say?"

"Not much."

"Did she tell them about the stumbling, the falling?" His dad leaned on one chair arm, dug his knife from his pocket and worked on his fingernails. "They told her to use a cane. I doubt she will. She still thinks she's gonna ride again. We're going back down there in a month."

Luke wondered what he wasn't being told. He knew his mother had quit riding horseback, but he didn't know why. He couldn't imagine her being unable to sit a horse. She was lean, looked to be a good physical specimen. If it weren't for her gray hair, most folks wouldn't guess she would be sixty in November.

His dad sighed and rose to go. Luke followed him to the front door. "She's waiting for you," the patriarch said. "You might as well go on up there."

After his dad drove away, Luke gave himself a few minutes to think. Lord, how he dreaded the coming argument with his mother. He wished he could call back his youth, when she had laughed and told jokes and life for both of them had seemed like more than hard work.

In his childhood, a special bond had existed between them, rooted in their common love of animals. In those days, Mom trained horses. People brought their colts from miles away for the Claire McRae handle. His dad would tease her and call her horses-in-training luxury animals that ate up, tromped down or shit on everything in sight. She would argue that horses had souls, were better than people and without them, man might still be living in caves.

Then, the second summer after his marriage to Janet, fate played its hand. He and Matt, his brother three years older, came home from the Owyhee, bringing a mustang stallion—a superbly muscled bay, faster than the wind. At supper they bragged he could outrun any fancy-blooded horse their mother trained or owned.

The next morning at the barn, Mom, ever a competitor, led out her powerful palomino gelding and challenged their stallion to a race across the pasture behind the corrals.

Sensing a threat, the stallion snorted and pranced and threw his head. Mom's gelding squealed and fishtailed when she saddled him. Dad watched from the fence, said they were headed for a horse wreck.

Matt tried to back out, but Luke, no stranger to a dare, went to the tack room, hauled out his own saddle and made clucking noises at his brother. That was all it took to kindle Matt's courage. He pushed Luke aside and swung his saddle onto the stallion. Helping his brother cinch up, Luke glimpsed a strange light in his eyes and recognized it as fear.

Seconds into the race, the nameless stallion blew up and flipped Matt over its head. Three days later, death took the twenty-four-year-old anointed heir and nothing and nobody had ever been the same.

Dad shot the stallion and put the palomino up for sale. Mom turned hard. Soon, Dad lost interest in the ranch. Like an avalanche, management fell on Mom's shoulders, then ultimately, on Luke's. His notion of becoming a scientist got lost in grief and necessity.

Ambling to the far edge of the deck, he reached up to hang on to an overhead beam and watched the landscape change colors as the climbing sun burned away the haze. From here, he could look down and see the corral and the fenced twenty-acre scene of the accident. No day went by that he didn't remember it at least once. He and his mother had never discussed it, but how they had goaded Matt into the fatal ride, innocent though it had been, both linked them and stood between them.

Luke drew in a deep breath, letting the cool, crisp air clear his head. *Mom.* She had the strength of a titan. Without a word of complaint, she took care of Jimmy. She was always there for his daughters. A meal was ready when the time came, his clothes were washed and mended, he slept in a clean bed every night. He owed it to her to listen to what she had to say. He guessed he may as well go on up and get it over with.

He reached inside the cabin door and plucked his cap

from its wooden peg, then set out on foot. As he trudged up the hill to the Big House, he asked his herd dogs, Frosty and Bingo, if a man ever got too old for an ass-chewing from his mother.

Chapter 16

Returning from a full-stride, three-mile run, Dahlia staggered through the front doorway, heaving for breath.

Piggy glanced up from the Boise newspaper to which they had subscribed for the summer. Piggy had to have cartoons. "Hey, girlfriend. How many miles?"

Lacking breath to answer, Dahlia held up three fingers as she passed through the living room. She stripped, turned on the shower as hot as was bearable and let the prickly spray wash off the scent of Luke McRae.

After showering, she took a pick to her wet tangles. Her hair was no longer a flurry of black ringlets from scalp to tip. Her perm had relaxed and grown out. Luke loved her hair, had begged—no, ordered—her not to cut it, so she hadn't so much as trimmed it all summer.

Piggy came over and leaned on the bathroom door facing. "You need a trim and a new perm. Looks like a two-hundred-dollar job doesn't last any longer than one for fifty."

Dahlia glanced at her friend. Since yesterday morning, Piggy's coppery hair had been cut and frizzed into a cap of tight curls. Dahlia had seen it last night, but she hadn't been up to asking questions. "Okay, I give up. What happened to your hair?"

Piggy tugged at a springy tuft. "I didn't think you were gonna notice. This is the fifty-dollar job. I thought I'd save a buck or two. Two and a half hours at Dr. Frankenstein's yesterday, better known as Tami's Hair & Nails. Should have known not to get a haircut and perm in a place like Callister."

"Yep. Should have known . . . Did I miss a call from Luke?"

"I had the phone off the hook 'til a while ago. Since we were up all night, I didn't want it to wake us. I saved you some breakfast."

Dahlia didn't want food, but she followed Piggy to the kitchen and poured herself a cup of coffee. She tamped down her annoyance at the phone being left off the hook with heaping teaspoons of French vanilla Coffeemate. Wilting onto a chair at the card table, she propped her chin on her palms and watched a spider scurry across the windowsill and disappear into a crevice. She wished she could follow it.

A paper plate scooted between her elbows. Centered on it was an orange clump embellished with something red and something green. "Eat," Piggy said, and handed her a plastic fork.

Dahlia took a bite, then almost spit it out. "What *is* this?"

"Salsa and eggs. Mostly salsa. And spices, tons of spices. It's all we had in the larder. We haven't bought much at the grocery store lately."

"I guess it's just as well. I guess we'd just have to throw it away when we leave."

"Jeez, you've been around him so much you're starting to talk like him. Luke does that, says 'I guess' before everything."

"I guess he does."

They looked at each other, Piggy's freckled nose wrinkled, and they broke out laughing. A welcome release of tension. How drab her life would be if she didn't know Piggy, Dahlia thought. "You look like Orphan Annie," she said.

"Thank God you haven't lost your sense of humor. Last night, I wasn't sure you'd ever laugh again."

"This is an act. I should get an award."

"I've got something to tell you, but you're so upset, I hate adding fuel to the fire."

"Tell me anyway."

"After Tami finished screwing up my hair, we went to

the Eights & Aces. Kathleen and Dave were there, bombed and loose-tongued as usual. Did you know Beauty-Shop Tami and Tennis-Bum Dave are cousins? And Tami and Luke's ex-wife are buds."

Dahlia's head began to pound. "What?"

"Why are you so big-eyed? Who's kin to who around here is like a maze. It's a lot worse than Loretta."

"What if Dave tells Tami what happened at the ranch?"

"How would he know? And if he did, why would he tell?"

"Piggy, you don't understand. The McRaes all live close together. They see each other all the time. There's no way Luke's whole family isn't going to know. Luke says Dave gossips worse than an old maid."

Piggy pulled one side of her lower lip through her teeth. "Oh, crap. I see what you mean."

"I shouldn't have gone to that ranch." Dahlia massaged her aching eyes with her fingertips.

"So he tells. What difference can it make? Luke hasn't been married for what—five years? Nothing will come of it."

"It's his kids, Piggy. Luke and his ex-wife still have some kind of fight going on over custody of his kids."

Silence fell between them. If anybody knew of dramas involving broken marriages and child-custody battles, Piggy did. Her oldest brother had been in the middle of one for years.

After a few minutes, Piggy sighed and stood. "Well, you can't put the genie back in the bottle. And why should you want to? I don't see what's wrong with sex between two grown single people who love each other."

"Yeah. Why isn't it that simple?" Dahlia felt her throat filling again. "Damn. Let's drop it, okay?"

"Sure. Let's do something to get our minds off the Marlboro Man. Let's go do laundry. The only clean shirt I've got is this one." She pulled at the seams of an oversized T-shirt hanging to midthigh. TEXAS DIRT SHIRT was printed across the front.

Dahlia wiped away a tear and took her plate to the trash.

"There's nothing on the boob tube tonight," Piggy said, "so we should stop by the service station and rent a couple of movies when we finish. . . ."

Luke had missed Dahlia. Her line had been busy the half-dozen times he had called her, and now she didn't answer.

He strolled out to the deck. The noon sun didn't have its usual warmth. A cold front banked in the western sky. The calendar showed August, but the air felt of fall. He made a mental note to hire a high schooler to split and stack firewood.

A glance toward the barn reminded him that all summer he had put off chores that needed doing. The barn had to be stained before cold weather set in, but he had spent so much time with Dahlia, he hadn't put out a request for bids.

He dropped lazily to sit on the edge of the deck, dug out his pocketknife and picked up a stick to whittle. Frosty came and lay against his thigh. Luke scruffed his hair. "Snow's just around the corner, Frost."

Frosty whined and hid his eyes with his paw. Luke wished he could whine, too, but who would listen? He had to make it a clean break with Dahlia, let her get on back to Texas. If she were out of his sight and out of his reach, he could *put* her out of his mind. Yep, he should do that all right.

Road noise sounded from the distance and he looked up. A late-model Cadillac slowed and turned between the stacked rock stanchions at the county road. Janet, bringing Mary Claire and Annabeth home. School would be starting in another week.

Her maroon El Dorado stopped in the gravel turn-around in front of the Big House. A stranger sat behind the wheel. Janet was the only McRae who had ever owned a Cadillac. Luke drove up from the cabin in his old Ford truck, arriving in time to help Mary Claire and Annabeth clamber out of the Caddy's backseat.

Dad emerged with a big grin from behind the house.

Mom and Ethel led Granny McRae and Jimmy out onto the deck. Everyone was glad to see the girls come home. Both his daughters hugged him, but Annabeth clung a few extra seconds. "I missed you, Daddy. I'm glad to be home."

On coltish legs, she bounded up the six deck steps, knelt in front of Jimmy and opened a plastic sack. "Look, Jimmy. I brought you some animals."

Mary Claire, on the other hand, ignored Jimmy and said a few terse hellos. Then she wrapped her arms around numerous department-store bags and sacks and strode into the house.

Annabeth jumped to her feet and slid a long, bony arm around her grandfather's waist. "Did you give Chico oats while I was gone, Grandpa?"

"Now and then, sweetheart. He still has a lot of grass. We don't want him to get too fat. What he needs most is somebody to ride him. Your dad and Shorty haven't had time."

Janet had emerged from the car on the passenger side, leaving her companion behind. Luke stood by his truck and watched as she picked her way in fancy high-heeled shoes across the gravel driveway.

"Hi, Luke," she said, angling a look up at him. Her blue eyes seemed faded, like old jeans.

"Janet." He touched his cap bill with his finger.

"I must say, you're aging well." She gave his stomach a couple of proprietary pats and let her hand linger.

Luke stepped back as if a scorpion had landed on him. Their last encounter had been a year ago in a judge's office in Boise, settling the third blowup over custody of the girls. It had cost him several thousand dollars. He hadn't had carnal thoughts about her for years. When he saw her nowadays, all that went through his head were dollar signs with wings.

At forty-one, she appeared a little weathered, but God and any number of highfalutin cosmetic companies had favored her—she still looked like a fancy doll. She should. When she had been his wife, with his mom often reminding her she was eight years older than he, slapping on grease from a drawerful of jars and bottles had been a continuous ritual. She spent hours on her long bleached hair—he couldn't remember if he had ever known its *real* color—while tasks she should have been doing were being handled by his mother or Ethel. He guessed she would always be a good-looking woman, but she had never held up her end of any bargain she ever made—including marriage and motherhood.

She hoisted her chin. "The girls hated coming back to this god-awful place. They wanted to start school in Boise."

"Uh-huh. I'll bet."

"Well, they *did*! I promised them we'd discuss it."

"You can consider *that* discussion closed."

Janet's companion climbed out of the Caddy and came over and her act changed. "This is Tony," she said, lowering her voice and giving him a sly smile. "Tony Scarpello. He just moved up from San Francisco. His family's in wine."

Uh-huh, and wine's in him, Luke thought, detecting a yeasty odor. A thousand dollars said she had picked him up in a bar. Janet reeked of Listerine, a poor disguise that she, too, had been imbibing. Not even her strong perfume hid it.

The familiar mix of smells hit Luke like a glove across the cheek. A red heat crawled up his spine.

The boyfriend stuck out his hand. If he knew no love was lost between Janet and her former family, he didn't show it. Luke shook hands, eyeing him with narrow-lidded skepticism.

The guy looked ten years younger than Janet. A frizzy black ponytail was banded at his neck. He wore loose-fitting slacks and soft shoes and had on what Luke figured they called a designer shirt—somebody's name was plastered over the front. Luke didn't hesitate to admit his curiosity about his ex-wife's boyfriends. Sooner or later her flings affected their daughters in some way.

Janet's voice burst into his assessment. "I bought the girls school clothes. I charged them to *you*."

"Nothing new about that." Luke put a lid on his anger and leaned against the fender, studying his ex-wife's attire—a storm of loud colors, a lot of straps on her shoes and a lot of bracelets clicking on both arms. That was how Janet had always dressed—with a lot of everything. Needless to say, in the nine years they were married, she had been inside the barn less than a dozen times.

"They were wearing absolute *rags*. They need nice clothes, even in a place as backward as Callister."

She scowled and waited, poised to pounce. When he refused to take the bait, she turned her attention to her boyfriend. "Come on, Tony. I'll introduce you to my son. And my daughters' grandparents, such as they are."

She led Ponytail up to the deck like he was a pet horse and made the introductions, gushing with phony affection over Jimmy.

Luke turned away. He couldn't stand seeing her pretend to care about their son when he knew it to be a lie. Mom and Ethel showered Jimmy with attention, but the little guy had enough smarts to know neither of them was his mother.

Janet pointedly ignored Ethel. That rankled, too. Janet, who had come out of a sewer herself, had always practiced her own caste system.

He couldn't hear what passed between his parents and Janet, but he didn't need to. He could imagine what his mother would say to her. Soon, obviously pissed off, Janet clonked back down the steps, nearly losing her balance, but Ponytail caught her.

The boyfriend went back to the El Dorado's trunk where he began to dig out some more sacks and shoe boxes. Janet stalked to where Luke stood and jammed her fists against her waist. "I see everything's the same as it always was. Your mother's still a mean bitch. I don't know how poor Mary and Annabeth stand it."

She wheeled around, stamped to her car and reached for the door latch.

Enough was enough. In one giant step, Luke leaned on the El Dorado's door with the heel of his palm, making it impossible for her to open it. "Janet," he said, keeping his voice too low for the family to hear, "if I ever again see those girls in the car with you or anybody else who's drunk, they'll never spend another day with you. And there's not a judge in Idaho that'll make a difference. Got that?"

He shot a glare at her companion.

Ponytail piped up, "Now, wait just a minute—"

Luke pointed a rigid finger at his nose. "Drop it, mister. You're poking in something you don't know anything about. And don't you ever forget, those are my kids you're hauling around. If a hair on their heads gets out of place while they're in your company, you'll have me to answer to and you won't like it."

Janet gasped and sprang up in his face, blowing Listerine and gin. "You don't tell me what to do anymore, Luke McRae!" She pointed a crimson-tipped finger up at his mother. "And neither does that hateful old bag! I hope she falls off her goddamn high horse and breaks a leg."

She flipped her loose blond curls. "You self-righteous asshole. Someday I'll get something on you. And when I do, I'll get my kids again. And you'll wish you'd never met me."

I already do, Janet, I already do. He lifted his hand from the car door. "Janet, you have a nice trip back to Boise. . . . And one more thing. If we ever do this kid exchange again, it'll be on your turf. I don't want you coming here anymore."

"Fuck you!" She jerked open the car door and plopped into the passenger seat. "Get in, Tony," she commanded.

Ponytail moved around to the driver's side, slid in without comment and cranked the engine. As they pulled away, Janet stuck her upper body out the window, smiling and waving both arms. " 'Bye, kids. Be good girls now. I'll see you Thanksgiving."

Luke looked around. Who was she trying to impress? Mary Claire already had taken her loot into the house and Jimmy was wrapped up in his newly acquired plastic animals.

" 'Bye, Mom." Annabeth lifted a limp hand in a half wave.

Only when the Cadillac passed through the front gate did Luke feel his blood pressure lower a few notches. He gathered the shopping plunder and took it up onto the deck.

Chapter 17

"I don't understand why he hasn't called." Dahlia was disgusted with herself the minute the words left her mouth.

She and Piggy were resting under a canopy of amber-leafed oaks on a mountainside where they had stopped to eat lunch.

"Maybe his mother killed him." Piggy gathered their lunch trash and stuffed it into her backpack.

"Don't say that. You know I hate jokes about death."

"Sorry, Dal. It slipped."

"The stuff we've heard about his out-of-town girl-friends—do you think he's been seeing somebody else while we—"

"Get real. I know he's a stud, but holy cow."

"I can't believe he hasn't been able to find five minutes to call me." She picked up a dried twig and snapped it in half. "God, I don't know how I got into this."

"Chemistry? Or maybe you were just plain horny."

Dahlia slowly shook her head. "At first I thought his having so much family was neat. His loyalty to them and that ranch seemed so noble. Now, here I am again, pushed behind everything else in someone's life. Just like with Kenneth."

"Phooey. There's no comparison between Luke and Kenneth. And you can't say Luke's doing that. You've been with him every weekend. He's come to town during the week to see you. That couldn't have been easy. The trip alone is a killer."

"You want to know what's wrong with the whole thing, Piggy? It's not his mother—who would hate anybody except Lee Ann Flagg—or the ranch or his kids. He doesn't *need* me. That's what's wrong with it. It's like, if I'm there, fine, and if I'm not, that's okay, too."

"Luke reminds me of my oldest brother," Piggy said. "He's a warrior and a survivor. His perspective is different. You won't see him diving off a cliff for the sake of a woman."

"Humph. And I guess you won't see him making a commitment to somebody in town for the summer." Dahlia felt tears welling in her throat, swallowed to gain control. "Men like him take what they want and go on to the next hot body, don't they?"

"There's more to Luke than that."

"You've always been on his side. You're the one who should have been sleeping with him. You would have been able to do it and forget it."

Piggy sat up, spread her hands and laughed. "Hey, you know I would have. But *you,* girlfriend, were the one he wanted."

Dahlia huffed, remembering how he had pursued her. And seduced her. "Yeah, right."

"Here's a riddle. If he showed up today and said, 'Dahlia, marry me and live with me forever at my ranch at the edge of nowhere,' would you?"

Dahlia stared at the ground between her feet. What *would* she do? The possibility seemed so far-fetched she hadn't let her thoughts venture into that territory. "I don't think I'm going to have to answer that."

"He's got love in his eyes when he looks at you, Dal."

"Well, it's not on his tongue. He's never said it. In fact, lately, he makes me feel like spoiled fish."

"As always, you're beating yourself up for no reason."

"Even if he did ask me, and even if I weren't so damn mad at him, I don't see how it could work out. Dad will be seventy-eight this year. He's grown to depend on me in the grocery store, you know."

"So you're saying it's okay for *you* to have family loyalty, but not Luke?"

Dahlia gave her a narrow-lidded look. "Okay, smart-aleck—"

"He-e-e-y!" Jerry's yell from up the hill ended their discussion. He made a windmill arc with his arm, motioning for them to follow him.

"Jeez," Piggy grumbled, forcing herself to her feet. "We've still got to hike all the way back down to the Suburban after we climb to the top of that hill."

They returned to the Forest Service offices late in the afternoon, collapsed into the steel armchairs in the employee break room and joined in the end-of-the-day camaraderie. "This is the hardest work I've ever done in my life," Piggy whined, bringing laughs and jokes about the shortcomings of Texans.

"Hey!" Gretchen shouted from the reception desk. "Dahlia Montgomery! Phone!"

Luke. Dahlia's weariness fled. Her feet scarcely touched the floor on her way to the lobby.

"It's long distance," Gretchen said, handing over the receiver. "They said it's important."

"Oh?" Dahlia hesitated, stopped by a sudden shot of anxiety. "Dahlia speaking," she said in a tight voice.

"This is Chuck Moore, Dahlia. You've got to come home. It's your dad. He's . . . well, I don't know any other way to say it, hon. He had a stroke."

A few seconds passed before her brain gears engaged. "Is—is he okay?"

"He's in the hospital. You can come home, can't you? I can look after the store, but I can't sign checks. Payday's Friday and vendors are waiting—"

"I just have to get a flight," she broke in, her mind scrambling. Her father's absence from the Handy Pantry was an urgent situation. Most of the employees lived from payday to payday and the wholesalers required either check on delivery of goods or payment within ten days. "He can't sign checks?"

"No, hon. He can't."

The words dropped like stones in her stomach. Chuck told her a few more bits of information: can't talk, can't move his right side, don't know what's going to happen. She repeated she was on her way home and hung up.

On rubbery knees, she returned to the break room where all held questioning looks. She motioned Piggy outside, leaving them to wonder. "Dad had a stroke."

"Oh, no. He's not—it wasn't a *bad* one, was it?"

"I don't know. It sounds bad. I have to go home." Her words came out in spurts, keeping time with her thudding heartbeat.

"Shit-house mouse," Piggy muttered, her eyes turning shiny. "I'll go, too."

"You can't. You have to help Jerry finish up and you've got the Blazer. You'll have to get our things back to Loretta." In her mind, Dahlia was already organizing. For all her floundering over mundane problems, her cool head prevailed in a crisis.

Piggy frowned and sniffed away what had almost been a tear. Though her wisecracking pal tried to appear jaded and tough, Dahlia knew her heart was a cotton ball, especially where Dad was concerned. He had always treated her like a second daughter.

"He'll be okay," Piggy said. "I know he will. Look at the shape Old Man Clark was in. They gave him physical therapy and now he's out square dancing."

Just then, Pete Hand swung out the door behind them and hooked an arm around Piggy's neck. "Sweet lips. Let's go."

"I can't," she said. "Dahlia's dad—"

"You go on," Dahlia told her, knowing Piggy wanted to spend the free time she had left in Callister with Pete. The two of them probably had planned to join the Forest Service crowd at Carlton's for happy hour. Beyond that, the last thing Dahlia needed while packing and recapturing her wits was Piggy hovering and gushing false confidence. "There's nothing you can do. Just leave the Blazer with me. I'll have to wash some clothes."

"What's going on?" Pete asked.

Before either of them could explain, the beep of a horn drew their attention. They looked across the two-aisled parking lot and saw Luke's white pickup near the back corner, almost hidden by employee and government vehicles.

"Well, whaddaya know," Piggy said, casting a sly glance in the Ford's direction. She dug the Blazer's keys out of her jeans pocket and handed them to Dahlia.

Relief swept over Dahlia. Luke would put his thick, strong arms around her and tell her in his deep, soft voice everything would be all right. God, how she needed that. The anger she had felt at him since Saturday night vanished.

Yet as joyful as she felt, she didn't know what to expect. He had never appeared like this at the end of her workday.

Piggy gave her a see-how-smart-I-am look. "You stewed three days for nothing. I told you he'd get his head straight."

With a quavery laugh, Dahlia glanced down at herself. A day of chasing a surveyor up and down mountainsides always left her filthy and disheveled. She hadn't let Luke see her in that state. "I look awful."

"You look great. Go get 'im." Pete tugged at Piggy's hand.

"Listen, Piggy, when I get back to the cottage, I'll try to book a flight for early tomorrow. You can take me to the airport, can't you?"

"No problem," Piggy said. "I'll run Jerry down, tell him we can't work. But when tall, freckle-faced and handsome over there finds out you have to leave, I'll bet *he'll* want to take you."

Dahlia stared across the parking lot at Luke. She had never asked him to do anything for her. Taking a calming breath and stuffing the car keys into her pocket, she hurried to meet him.

By the time she reached his pickup, Luke was outside, holding the passenger door open. He, too, had on work clothes—a blue snap-button chambray shirt, his wavy, cinnamon hair turning up at the collar, and faded Wranglers that fit him like paint. The awareness that always turned her into a fumbling fool when she saw him slithered through her. If it weren't for the circumstances, she might strip off her clothes, crawl into his pickup bed and wait for him.

"Looking for me, stranger?" She hoped she sounded upbeat.

"Hi," he said. No kiss, no enthusiasm. He usually chuckled when she made goofy remarks and he always kissed her hello.

Questioning with a glance, she planted her foot on the pickup's floorboard. He put his hand under her elbow, boosted her up into the cab and closed her in with the smells everpresent around him—hay, leather and Polo.

She watched his grim face as he rounded the front of the vehicle. Her mind raced. She knew his kids had returned over the weekend. Had something happened to one of them? Or to some other family member? The notion that he would be a comforting element for *her* began to dissipate.

He scooted into the driver's seat and twisted to face her, laying one arm across the back of the bench seat and resting the other elbow on the steering wheel. His straw hat lay between them, a barrier to her moving closer.

She managed to paste on a smile. "What's up?"

"I, uh, wanted to talk to you, Dahlia."

His tone was low, his eyes solemn and unfathomable. In a flicker of paranoia, she wondered if he had purposely placed his hat between them. She scrunched up her shoulders. "I like talk. Let's talk."

"I've been thinking about what's going on between us, Dal."

The happiness from a few minutes earlier resurged. No wonder he was so serious. He wanted to discuss their relationship. "Oh, Luke, I've thought about it, too, and—"

"Aw, hell, Dahlia . . ." He turned to face the windshield, hunched his shoulders and tucked his hands between his knees. "I've got some problems, sugar."

Premonition flew into her mind. *I don't want to hear this.* Her heart began a rapid rhythm. She, too, jerked her head to stare at the windshield.

"Janet found out about the cabin."

"And that's a problem?"

"It's the girls. They live with me, but Janet's the one with legal custody. She sicced her lawyer on me. Wants 'em brought back to her house. I gotta take 'em to Boise tomorrow."

Dahlia winced inside, hating the idea of causing trouble for his children. And at the same time, she quelled the urge to scream curses on empty-headed Dave Adams and malicious Beauty Shop Tami. "I see."

"It's a damn mess. Not something I can't get handled in time, but knowing my ex-wife like I do, if I don't put the kibosh on it right now, it could turn into a regular rodeo."

"Exactly what are you, uh, putting the kibosh on?"

"Well . . . they're saying I'm immoral and some other stuff. . . ."

They? Other stuff? The odd catch in his voice caused her to glance back at him. For an absurd instant, she was distracted from the catastrophe evolving in her own life by worrying what could be upsetting him so much.

". . . school starts next week," he was saying. "If the girls enroll down in Boise, it'll be just that much harder later to get 'em back up here. Those kids have been through a lot. Been shuffled back and forth between houses. Seen stuff kids don't need to see. They're my flesh and blood, Dahlia. My responsibility. I can't let *anything* compete for my attention to 'em. They need me too much."

And I don't? My only living relative is lying in a hospital. Dahlia wanted badly to say it, but she couldn't risk his pity. "N-no, I suppose you can't."

"But it's more than that. I've got a lot to do right now. Morgan got a job in Boise. Him and Brenna are leaving the ranch, moving Labor Day weekend. Winter's coming on. It takes all of us to get ready and I've been wasting so much time, I haven't been holding up my end. All of a sudden, my back's against the wall and we're gonna be going into cold weather shorthanded."

Dahlia knew Luke's brother-in-law was a lawyer who had political aspirations and she knew Luke's sisters

helped with the ranch work. "Morgan got a job? Practicing law?"

Luke went on as if he hadn't heard her question, spilling more words than she had ever heard from him at
one time. "Coming from Texas and all, I know you don't
understand it, but up here, if a cowman gets caught by
the weather, he could lose everything. Mother Nature
doesn't give two hoots about my silly social life."

Silly social life? Wasting time? Dahlia felt as if he had
punched her with his fist. Bitterness boiled up. "Could
we get to the point, Luke? You aren't the only person
in the world with problems."

Her truculent words hit home. Hurt clouded his eyes.
"Well, yeah. I just think we oughtta, well . . . take a look
at what we're doing. This got a little hotter than I ever
expected it to. The way things are in Callister, if we keep
this up, it'll wind up hurting my kids and my family. And
I have to ask myself if having a good time's worth it. I
mean, that's about all either one of us was after, wasn't
it? We both knew you were in town just for the summer, right?"

"Well, I . . ." She couldn't finish. Her throat had
closed. What was left to be said anyway? How could
what she meant to him be any plainer? She had been
naïve, convincing herself he loved her. In truth, she was
but one more in a long line of women he took and dis-
carded to suit his fancy, just another Moscow-to-
Winnemucca groupie after all. She felt the snap in her
chest as her heart broke.

Her survival instinct, that salving discipline life had
forced her to hone, switched on. She began to pretend
she was an observer in this drama rather than a partici-
pant. "Actually, it's just as well. It's time I got back to
Texas anyway." She was proud of her self-control and
cool delivery when her every body part wanted to shrivel.

"And I think that's what you *should* do. Maybe let
things cool down, clear our heads a little."

She heard relief in his matter-of-fact reply, and why
not? She was giving him a free ride—making a conve-

nient, peaceful exit. No big scene, no demands, no shootout in the street.

"But we can stay in touch," he added hastily. "You'll be here a little while longer. I thought we'd—"

Thought we'd what? Meet in some alley and knock off a quickie? "I, uh, I don't know if I'll have time. I may go back sooner, Luke. The surveying is practically finished. There's, uh, really no reason for Piggy and me to hang around after the work's done." She took a fortifying breath. "Like you said, we've had a good time. And you're right, winter is coming and silly me—I left my ski clothes in Texas."

"Speaking of skiing, if I can get things calmed down with Janet and get these lawyers off my ass, maybe we can get together up at the ski lodge before you go."

So it wouldn't be in an alley; it would be in an expensive room in a nice hotel.

"Sure." She swallowed the mushy bubble growing in her throat. "Just call when you can work it into your schedule."

Luke winced at the icy retort. She was mad. And hurt. Or both. He didn't want *that* any more than he wanted to hurt his family. But he was in no position to make her any promises, had been careful not to. None had been expected from her, either. So why did he feel this sensation like panic?

He wished he could call back the past few minutes and start over. Practicing this speech all the way into town hadn't kept him from bungling it. He had whined like an orphaned calf, sounded like a pompous asshole.

His gaze traveled over her. Even with dirty jeans, a torn T-shirt and no makeup, she looked pretty. He liked her hair pulled back and braided.

He could see the rise and fall of the delectable, full bosom he had kissed all over just Saturday. The hot-springs pool sprang into his memory—their hands gliding over each others' bodies, his tongue catching water droplets off the dark tips of her breasts. . . . He felt a twitch in his shorts. He wanted to take her in his arms and . . .

Jesus. He shoved those thoughts from his mind. This was no time—

"Look, Luke. I'm in sort of a hurry. I need to get home. I've got . . . laundry to do."

"Dahlia, I—"

Her raised palm stopped him. An ache in his chest displaced the one in his groin. Her head shook sharply one time. "Let's don't do this," she said. "You've been very clear."

She pulled on the door latch and slid one leg outside, turning back to face him. Her eyes glistened. *Tears. Jesus.* He cussed himself again.

"Why do I feel like I'll never see you again?" she said softly.

His mouth went dry as a gravel road in August. "One of these days, I'll get it all straightened out, Dal."

"Are you asking me to wait?"

Yes. No. Jesus. He snapped his gaze back to the windshield. "No. I guess I don't have the right to ask you anything."

She nodded and slid the rest of the way out. The door closed with a soft click. He watched her cross in front of his truck, her chin level. She went to Piggy Murphy's rig, dug into her pocket, pulled out keys. Blood swished inside his ears.

Stop her, you dumb bastard.

But he *had* to let her go. Allowing a woman to become a disruption to life at the Double Deuce was lunacy. What he felt was lust, juvenile obsession, nothing more. In time, it would wear itself out.

The Blazer backed out and moved down the street. Not once did its driver look back. "Goddammit," he muttered, watching it disappear, kneading his lower lip between his fingers and thumb.

Women. A diabolical joke Nature had played on men. He wished he could live without them, without that Lorelei between their legs. But he was weak and it was sweet, as hard to resist as a bear trap baited with honey. And just as treacherous. Once a man gave in and chased it, anything could happen. Wasn't that what had gotten him into nine years of pure hell in the first place?

And hadn't what happened this morning underlined that point?

After he had spent all day yesterday on horseback, Mom had cornered him in the barn the minute he returned. Hadn't even waited 'til he unsaddled Roanie before she landed on him. Apparently, Annabeth had told her what went on all summer at Janet's house and set Mom off again. Then there had been an ominous message from Brad, the family lawyer, telling him Janet wanted their daughters returned to her immediately.

Puzzled as much as angry, Luke had called Brad back at once and learned the rest of the story. Somebody told Janet he had been found in bed in the cabin with a Chinese prostitute. The lawyer couldn't guess the origin of such an outrageous tale, but Luke knew the pattern. The gossip had passed from his own sister to her husband, then to the beauty shop where it had been altered and embellished and handed over to Janet.

Mom's rant couldn't have motivated him to end things with Dahlia, but Janet's threat to prevent their daughters starting school in Callister was a horse of a different color. It seemed that saying good-bye to a fling going nowhere anyway wasn't just the easiest thing, it was only thing. But this afternoon, he wasn't as certain as he had been this morning. A flap with Janet wouldn't last forever. A few dollars and she would probably crawl back into a Boise bar. Maybe he should follow Dahlia home. . . .

A bang jerked his mind back. The range manager's assistant had slapped the Ford's front fender as he passed. "Hey, Luke. How's it going?"

"Good, Carl. Real good."

More employees dribbled out of the Forest Service offices. If he didn't get out of this parking lot, somebody would be asking him why he was here and he would have to make up a lie. He plopped the Resistol on his head and fired the engine. The old diesel clattered to life, sounding like a thrashing machine in the silence of Dahlia's absence.

A sense of loss gripped him. He had felt it before—
the day he had hung back after the funeral service and
watched his brother's coffin lowered into the ground and
the morning Janet had left the Double Deuce for good
and taken his girls with her.

On a sigh, he shifted into gear and eased out onto
the main street. He crept through town, barely missed a
pedestrian. Somebody he knew, of course. Hell, there
was *nobody* in Callister he didn't know or who didn't
know him. He and the near-victim exchanged hellos and
laughed about his absentmindedness.

Ten miles out, entering the climb up the canyon, the
ache in his chest had only deepened. He cranked down
the window and let the late afternoon cool into the
truck cab.

This part of the winding trip to the ranch always made
him think of Matt. As boys, on their way home from
town, many times they had stopped to look down into
the canyon that plunged a thousand feet. They would
scootch the toes of their boots right to the edge and stare
down at the Snake River that lay like molten silver along
the canyon floor. They would yell into the maw, listening
to the multiple echoes. Life had been simple then, full of
girls and horses and freedom. And plans for rosy futures.

Back then, they hadn't thought about a crazy, wild
mustang or an alcoholic wife. And they had never heard
of FAS.

Lost in his thoughts, he took a curve too fast and had
to skid into the barrow ditch to keep from careening
over the canyon rim. Cussing himself, he shifted into
low gear and plowed back onto the road. Lord, he was
a mess.

On up a ways he reached the fancy scenic overlook
the government had built for tourists. He pulled into its
gravel parking area to gather himself. They had put up
a concrete barrier and a fence with a steel rail on top
and a rock monument with a bronze plaque saying some
stuff about history and geology.

"Waste," he muttered as he slid out of the truck. Ten
tourists hadn't traveled from Callister to Sterling Valley

in the past year and people nowadays couldn't even spell geology.

Leaning on the rail, he looked out to the canyon's opposite side. A chevron of unidentifiable birds silently moved south across the distant, gray-green backdrop of mountains. The solitude began to calm him and he could think.

Dahlia. How had it all gotten so out of hand? How had this one woman sneaked under his guard? Why hadn't the dancing and the movies and the fishing, the weekends of rolling around in bed remained just a good time?

The answer was Dahlia herself, he decided. He had never known a woman of so many intriguing parts— vulnerable, but strong; naïve, yet sophisticated; beautiful, but unaware of it.

Since his divorce, his involvement with the fairer sex had amounted to nothing more than physical indulgence. Most of the time, he didn't trust a woman as far as he could throw her, but he would trust Dahlia with anything he had. She was too loyal and honest to betray a friend. Her good-natured wit and warmth charmed everyone who met her. Even his sisters had succumbed. Hadn't Kathleen told him so just a few nights ago? And Jimmy. Who could ignore how the little guy responded to her gentleness?

Conscience pushed into his thoughts. He had spent the summer learning her in the sweetest of lessons, had pursued and seduced her with little regard for the outcome, his only goal to satisfy his own appetite. Well, he guessed he had gotten more than he bargained for—he had stumbled into a hole damned hard to climb out of.

He glanced down and to the left, looking for comfort in an old friend. And there it stood, halfway down the decline. In the middle of thousands of acres of dark green evergreens, as vivid as a neon sign, grew a single golden tamarack tree. He couldn't remember how many autumns had come and gone since he had first seen it, but he checked often to be sure it was still there.

A phenomenon of such immensity was nothing short

of a miracle. The scientist in him knew the perfectly timed, precisely executed chain of events that produced it. So complicated, yet so simple—one bird, one seed, a fistful of dirt in a crevice. Pondering the process never failed to remind him of man's feeble place in the scheme of things.

And suddenly, in his humbled heart, he identified the reason for his torment. Part of him was missing. Dahlia had taken it when she left him in the Forest Service parking lot.

Back in his rig, he pulled a one-eighty, spewing gravel. He tore back to town, back up the main street, back to Baker's rental. No Blazer in the driveway, no sign of life. He drove like a runaway to the laundry, found only a building empty of people. He thought of checking the bar where he had seen Piggy go, but Dahlia wouldn't be there. She didn't like the bar.

In front of the laundry, he halted, reining in his emotions, remembering Dahlia's words.

Actually, it's just as well. It's time I got back to Texas anyway. . . . There's really no reason for Piggy and me to hang around now that the work's done.

Don't be a damn fool, he told himself. Dahlia was sharp and well educated. She didn't need him. A woman like her would go home and start the company she talked about or hook up with some dude in a suit and get married and live in Dallas, like she had done before. She wouldn't follow some hard-ass cowboy with three half-grown kids and a willful mother out to a mountainside forty miles from the nearest town.

It had been a schoolboy's notion, chasing back to town after her, a waste of valuable time he couldn't afford to squander. He had to get home and try to get a good night's sleep. Before daylight tomorrow, he and his girls would be on their way to a nine o'clock appointment in his lawyer's office in Boise.

Heading north again, he knew one thing for certain— he was through dancing to Janet's tune. This time, she had gone too far. In dealing with her in the past, he had wondered what his limit was. Now he knew. This time, he wouldn't be satisfied with winning a battle. This time, he wouldn't leave the field until he had won the war.

But maybe, when he got back from Boise tomorrow evening, if it wasn't too late, he would drop by Dahlia's house before he went on out to the ranch. Just to talk a little . . .

Chapter 18

Dahlia stood before the bathroom mirror, shocked by
her appearance under the dull light over the medicine
cabinet. Her face was puffy, her eyes red and swollen.
Her sinuses were so plugged she had to breathe through
her mouth.

She knew the pain of spousal betrayal. She knew the
finality of death, the paralysis of bereavement. Twice she
had stared into the graves of people close to her. Rejection by a lover was worse.

Last night, after making flight reservations and arranging for Chuck to pick her up at DFW airport, she had
thrown her laundry into a washer, then driven the back-
roads until late, stopping often and surrendering to bursts
of tears. When the gas gauge showed near empty, she
had been forced back to town.

Somehow, true to her standard of doing what needed
doing even if the earth crumbled beneath her feet, she
sat through drying her clothes, thankful the late hour
gave her the laundromat to herself. Then she went back
to the cottage, packed some things to take on the plane
and organized what was left for Piggy to take home in
the Blazer.

She was exhausted when she sank to her cot, yet sleep
eluded her. Watching the moon travel across her open
bedroom window, she had relived every day and night
she had spent with Luke McRae.

The alarm, heedless of the late hour sleep came,
buzzed at five and she had staggered to the bathroom
and tried to cover the havoc that showed on her face.
Now she could see that thick makeup couldn't hide the

hours of angst. But her appearance no longer mattered, did it?

Nothing mattered—at least not in Idaho.

She twisted her long black hair into a roll and secured it on top of her head with a gold claw clip.

I'll get my hair cut. Who cares now if it's long or short? Soon as I know Dad's okay, I'll go to Fort Worth and get a new do. A makeover.

She finished her makeup with a dash of burgundy lipstick and surveyed for one last time the cramped white bathroom where fixtures barely fit. She would miss the efficiency of being able to stand in one spot and reach anything in the room.

Where the hell is Piggy? You'd think just this once . . .

Two hours to the Boise airport. If they left this minute, she would have less than an hour to check in and pick up her ticket. It would be hot in Dallas. She went back to her suitcase and changed her polo shirt to a tank top and switched from socks and boots to sandals.

She paced, then sat down on a box, drumming her feet on the hardwood floor. She was a snappish bundle of nerves by the time the idle of an engine out front caught her ear. She shoved on her sunglasses to hide her swollen eyes.

Piggy blustered in, grabbed one of Dahlia's bags and charged toward the front door. Dahlia stamped behind her and they were on their way, bulleting along the snakelike highway to Boise, as if it had no blind curves or steep drop-offs alongside it.

Questions about the parking-lot meeting with Luke were inevitable, so Piggy's nosy quizzing came as no surprise. Dahlia told her nothing happened. It hurt too much to say aloud that Luke had brushed her off like lint on his shoulder. Piggy didn't press. Dahlia tilted her seat backward and closed her eyes. "Try not to turn us over while I nap."

The next thing she knew, she was being dumped at Boise's small airport with only minutes to spare. As she headed for the gate, Dahlia remembered she had been so self-absorbed, she hadn't even ask Piggy where she spent the night.

She boarded the 727 feeling detached from everything

familiar. It was hard calling up a picture of Texas after four months in the mountainous Northwest. From Boise to Denver, a blue-haired gnome occupied the adjoining seat, chattering about church work, illnesses and immoral relatives. Dahlia had two drinks of Black Velvet and water instead of lunch and nodded off.

During a layover in Denver, she bought the new issue of *Cosmo* and found every article to be about men. Getting the most out of your relationship. Pleasing your lover. Great sex. If this were a conspiracy to torment her, it was working—she felt like someone was holding her head underwater. She threw *Cosmo* in the trash can and plodded the concourse like a refugee, her purse hanging from one shoulder, her carry-on satchel from the other. Normally the bustle of an airport gave her an effervescent feeling. Today she thought it cold and lonely, the busy travelers pushy and rude.

Passing in front of a dim cocktail lounge, she glanced inside. A place to wait. But when some movie star look-alike—she couldn't think who—gave her a smile and a hitch of his chin and pointed to an empty stool beside him, she ducked her head and quickstepped to the ladies' room.

As she washed her hands, her reflection in the wide mirror startled her. All summer, except for the weekends she had spent in hotels or motels with Luke, she had seen herself only in the notebook-sized medicine cabinet mirror in the cottage's bathroom. The woman staring back looked older somehow than the girl who had gone to Idaho for the summer. It was a silly idea, because she was still the same age as she'd been when she left Loretta last spring.

The difference had to come from within. Because of the potent sexuality of her relationship with Luke, she was aware of herself as a woman in a new way. For the rest of her life, her attitude and behavior around men would be different. This new-sprung knowledge was wondrous in a bizarre way, and exciting, like carrying a concealed weapon through the airport. Okay, so she was a late bloomer. Most women probably *got it* before they were staring at thirty.

Luke. She felt a rush of heat low in her belly. How could just thinking of him cause that? She had to get over it, but could she? Would she ever meet another man she wouldn't compare to him?

Dissolving into a seat in the waiting area, she leaned on her hand and tried to doze, but her thoughts gave her no peace. What if Dad were crippled? Or worse yet, paralyzed and helpless? What if he didn't survive? Would Luke revive his relationship with Lee Ann Flagg or return to seeing women outside of Callister? The questions brought a new threat of tears, so she rose and paced the crowded aisle. By the time she heard her Dallas flight called, she could hardly wait to get on the plane.

Then they were landing and the gold of dusk stained the horizon. She had slept from Denver to Dallas. Deboarding, she felt suffocated by the portable corridor between the plane's doorway and the terminal. The temperature had to be over a hundred. She began to sweat. Her feet hadn't touched Texas soil and already she wished she were back in the mountain valley she had left behind.

Chuck Moore, the butcher and longtime quasi manager of the Handy Pantry, met her with a hug. Because he was Dad's trusted employee and good friend, he was her friend, too.

"I'm sorry, Dally," he said.

Dally—pet name Dad had called her from childhood. A reminder she had come home.

Dahlia's silver Z3 that had been parked all summer in the garage beside Dad's old beige Plymouth started right up and she arrived at Loretta's small hospital at nearly ten p.m. The RN on duty—Loretta Community Hospital had only one per shift—was Piggy's cousin JoAnn. With quick, squeaky steps, she led Dahlia to the ICU's window across the hall from the nurses' station. There, in the dimly lit room's only bed, lay a body, still as death, making an indistinct outline beneath the covers. Her hand raised and flattened on the glass, as if it could snatch from jeopardy the only person who had loved her unconditionally.

"He's just sleeping," JoAnn said before Dahlia asked.

"He—he looks so small."

"All this equipment is intimidating. When you come back tomorrow, we'll let you in to visit for a few minutes."

"Tomorrow?" Dahlia glanced at the two chairs beside the ICU room door. "No, I'll stay here tonight."

"Don't you be looking at those chairs. It doesn't serve any purpose for you to try to sleep here." JoAnn's arm slid around her waist and Dahlia found herself turned away from the ICU window. "We'll take care of him. He's in pretty good shape, considering."

"But I want him to know I'm here."

"We'll tell him. Go home. Get some rest. You look worn out."

"You'll call me if he asks for me? Or if he"—she took a deep breath—"if he gets worse?" She had almost said, God forbid, *if he dies.*

"We'll call. Tomorrow's Saturday. Dr. Webb will probably go fishing, so he'll do rounds early. Get here before nine o'clock if you can." JoAnn hooked her arm through Dahlia's. "Come on. I'll walk you out." They ambled down the quiet, semidark hall toward the front exit. "What's my cousin up to and how was Idaho? I'll bet y'all had fun. My husband's always wanted to go hunting up there."

"Piggy's coming back in a week or so. Idaho was beautiful. In any direction, it looks like a painting. And it's cool. . . . JoAnn, is Dad going to make it?"

"He's in good hands. Talk to Dr. Webb tomorrow."

Nine hours later, Dahlia tiptoed into the ICU. She had spent a fitful night, lost in nightmares of brick walls crashing down on top of her alternating with bouts of half sleep where disjointed memories sawed through her brain like a dull knife.

Now she stared at the body whose impression in the

bed was less than that of a pillow. This *old* man with hollows for eyes, thinning gray hair and pale, crinkled skin couldn't be her father. Dad would be clean-shaven, his hair combed. And he would be wearing Dockers with a clean shirt.

"Hi, Dad," she whispered, schooling her voice not to crack.

He attempted to speak, but seemed to be chewing on his tongue.

Fear pushed into her heart. She felt an odd shifting of the ground beneath her, like seasickness, and a need to catch her breath. Summoning her courage, she picked up his hand, found it ice-cold. A piece of tape had loosened from an IV needle in the back of his hand. She gently pressed it down. "I'm back, Dad," she said, and felt stupid. Obviously she was back.

A tear seeped from one of his eyes and trailed past his temple. Fending off a sob of her own, she turned her gaze to the maze of technology surrounding them. She wanted to cry out, tear loose the tubes and wires and shake her dad back to being the man who held an office in the American Legion, who was known as an honest merchant who gave thousands of dollars' worth of food to needy families. Her only living family. The barrage of emotions so stymied her, all she seemed to be able to do was stand there in silence, holding his hand, weeping inside and feeling helpless.

In what seemed like only seconds, the nurse stuck her head through the doorway and reminded her of the time.

As Dahlia left the room, animal sounds rose from her dad's throat and she began to shake inside. The nurse told her Dr. Webb was in the hospital, then sailed away to find him. Dahlia paced, running through mental exercises to calm herself.

Soon, the balding doctor came up the hall at a brisk gait. Sure enough, he was wearing his fishing clothes. He explained that her father had suffered a temporal lobe stroke, couldn't speak, but could hear and understand what was being said. There was some paralysis on the right side. The doctor expected improvement in both his speech and his mobility. "We'll do the best we can here," he said in conclusion, "and as soon as he's up to it, we'll get him to Abilene to a neurologist."

After the doctor rushed away, Dahlia stood outside the ICU's window, staring at the patient inside who seemed like a stranger. Something touched her arm and she jumped and turned to face a nurse's aide who told her she was needed at the grocery store.

Ten minutes later, Dahlia came to a stop in the parking lot behind the Handy Pantry and entered through the back doorway. A few feet inside the storage room, she saw the Coke driver in with a gathering of employees. They applauded. Her eyes smarted. No one had ever applauded when she entered a room.

The worry on their faces brought home the impact of Elton Montgomery's sudden illness and uncertain future on people other than herself. After the school, the cotton co-op and the hospital, the Handy Pantry was Loretta's largest employer. A few employees had worked at the grocery store for years and had familylike affection for her dad, even for her. They would be concerned for his recovery. Others would be merely worried about their paychecks. For the first time it dawned on her that all these people, her dad's employees, now depended on *her*.

Panic gave her a yank. Not once in her most far-reaching imaginings had she expected or planned to be in charge of the Handy Pantry. From the day she enrolled in college, her future had been mapped out in Corporate America. She hadn't even expected to inherit the grocery store, having always assumed Dad would someday sell it and retire.

Now, two-dozen people peered at her with rapt attention, waiting for . . . what? Then she remembered—tomorrow was payday. That answered the what-should-I-do-next question. She pulled her thoughts together and informed the employees of her dad's condition. She thanked them for their loyalty, told them their jobs were safe, though she had no idea if it were true.

After a short conversation with the Coke driver, she headed for the ladderlike steps that led to Dad's office and the grocery store's checkbook. Fortunately, her name was on the bank account.

She found the office murky and uncomfortable. Someone had turned off both the lights and the air conditioner. Without the window unit blowing, the long, narrow room felt like a sauna and smelled like a stale refrigerator. She switched on the overhead light and the cooler. A deafening roar filled the room and instantly she missed the mountains again, where air was fresh and didn't need artificial cooling.

In the middle of Dad's desk blotter stood a stack of time cards nearly buried by papers and unopened envelopes. The piles of unattended mail seemed larger than her dad would have normally allowed, but she didn't question that. One thing at a time, she told herself. She would write paychecks before thinking of anything else.

Dad's old chair welcomed her with a familiar *screak*. Prowling through the desk drawers, she found the employees' pay records, then the IRS payroll tax table. She grimaced at the sight of it. Her acquaintance with that government agency had been more than a passing one. She had hoped never to see their name again, but there it was.

Chuck had already tallied the hours worked, so all she had to do was follow the procedure already in place. She pulled the vintage IBM Selectric on its metal stand from the corner and went to work.

Toward the end of the check writing, she began to feel queasy. Food was her first thought, though she hadn't been hungry for four days. Noon had come and gone. She went downstairs, took an apple and then a TV dinner from the frozen-food case, aware that employee eyes were on her every move.

Sitting at Dad's desk, eating lunch among the litter, she felt even more alone than usual. And inadequate. Dad had been everything—butcher, buyer, bookkeeper, stock boy and cashier—and still made it home for supper every night by eight. He had never called on her to manage the store, even temporarily. Though she had lived in

his house and worked as his employee every day since
fleeing Dallas, she had been too preoccupied with her
own problems to insert herself into the nuts and bolts of
the grocery store's operation.

She owned a piece of paper declaring her an expert in
business and marketing, but no college course had taught
her how to run a grocery store in a small agricultural
town. All she could rely on now was her common sense
and what she had learned about the grocery business
through osmosis. After all, she had done every odd job
the store required, from cleaning the bathrooms to
butchering to managing the produce; facts that, over the
years, had given Piggy fodder for a thousand crude jokes.

She sat back and scanned the room, reorienting herself. The walls were still the same drab green with only
patches bare of thumbtacked papers and pictures of employees' children. There were pictures of Dahlia
herself—in her tennis whites holding a trophy, in her cap
and gown giving her high-school valedictorian address,
in a different cap and gown, accepting her summa degree
from SMU. Dahlia, the overachiever, the Asian stereo-
type. Of course she had inborn drive and discipline, but
a huge component in her accomplishments had been a
desire to make Dad proud of his only child who was only
half white.

Her eyes came to rest on a framed monochrome picture atop a filing cabinet. Her mother. Though the picture had been there for years, Dahlia had always found
it easier to look through it rather than at it. She had
often wished her dad would put it away.

Memories of her life when her mother had been alive
were distant and scattered, but one remained vivid: the
day seventeen years earlier when she had been taken
from class by the school principal and escorted to the
office where her dad waited. She had gone to school that
morning not knowing her mother was sick enough to die.
Dad. Her shield, her anchor, her best friend.

On the wall behind her mother's picture a yellowed
calendar hung askew. Beneath a faded print of a moun-

tain landscape, 1987 stood out. Dad had dreamed of
spending time in the mountains. Except for his military
years, he had rarely left the flat plains of West Texas.

Guilt assailed her. He had stayed home and minded
the store while *she* had lived his dream. She made a
silent vow: *When he's well enough, I'll take him to see
the mountains.*

Over the weekend, she didn't see Dr. Webb on any of
the hospital visits she sandwiched between unpacking
and resettling. She missed him again Monday morning.

Anxious and determined to waylay the elusive doctor,
she arrived at the hospital before the patients had finished breakfast on Tuesday. He had mixed news. There
was still a danger of restroke. Dad's right side was disa-
bled, but he would likely respond well to therapy and
recover most of his mobility. He wouldn't return to the
fourteen-hour days demanded by the Handy Pantry. And
that meant someone had to take on his job. The grocery
store was their livelihood.

At home that evening, she couldn't remember when
she had been so blue. Sitting alone in the house's quiet,
she tried to think of an old school friend she could call
up and chatter with about nothing, a human voice. Un-
fortunately, she had lost touch long ago with everyone
but Piggy.

Luke eased into her thoughts. Should she call him?
Tell him why she had left Callister so suddenly? She no
longer had his phone number, having torn it to pieces
and flushed it down the toilet back at the cottage.

Swallowing her pride, she dialed Information, had to
ask for Lucas A. McRae, Gerald McRae, then the Double Deuce ranch before she obtained the listing. She
scrawled the ten digits on a notepad and sat there staring
at them, her sweating palm on the receiver. Such innocu-
ous things, numbers written in black ink on white paper,
but they had the power to devastate her all over again.

Don't do this, Dahlia. Don't be weak.

Chapter 19

"You can do this, Dahlia." Dr. Webb spoke as he wrote prescriptions and signed a form dismissing Elton Montgomery from the hospital into Dahlia's care on Friday. "I've known you since you were a little girl and I have confidence in you."

Dahlia had been home nine days, a frighteningly short time in which to reorient herself to her new role.

By the time her father had been home twenty-four hours, she realized the extent of the stroke's devastation beyond his paralysis. He seemed childlike, showing petulance over the smallest of things and an anger contradictory to his gentle nature. He struggled for words, and when he couldn't form them, he wept. Eating left-handed required so much effort, she had to dig deep to find the strength to allow him to feed himself. Dr. Webb and the nurses had told her to force him to be independent. He needed her help in the bathroom, which made him cry.

Home health aides showed her how to brush his teeth and shave him, then how to bathe him. Dahlia looked on in terror as he fought with the aides throughout the process.

They survived the weekend with no major mishaps. Monday began with him messing himself when she failed to get him onto the toilet seat. As she began cleaning him up, nausea overwhelmed her and she broke into trembling and sweating. She dashed to the bathroom off her bedroom and threw up. Returning to his bathroom, she found him where she had left him, half on, half off the toilet, and sobbing like a child. She fought tears of her own.

He was a tall man, weighing close to two hundred pounds, but fitting her shoulder into his armpit as the nurses' aides had taught her, she levered him off the toilet and wrestled him into the tub. He helped as much as he could, weeping the whole time.

You can do this. You can do this. You can do this. Webb's words became a mantra.

As she bent over the tub removing his soiled pajamas, the stench overpowered her. Bile boiled up in her throat. What was wrong with her? She couldn't be sick at a time like this. She dashed to her bathroom. Returning with scented bubble bath, she found him lying where she had left him in the tub, the good side of his face twisted into a grotesque grimace.

She dumped bubble bath under running water and breathed in the clean fragrance, then dug out a fresh washcloth and bathed him. She had to glance away from his nakedness often. They both were embarrassed.

With clumsy help from his functional side, she lifted him out of the tub and dried him, then dressed him in clean pajamas and maneuvered him into the wheelchair. He apologized and thanked her over and over in garbled, broken words.

Once she settled him back into bed, she called the home health aide and told her he had been bathed. After such a bungling experience, he had to be exhausted. She sure was. She sank into a chair beside his bed and began to read to him from the Fort Worth newspaper. In minutes, he dropped off to sleep.

Still weak, she went out to the back porch for the first time since coming home and wilted onto a plastic patio chair. Drenched with sweat, she glanced at the rusted wall thermometer. A hundred degrees and it wasn't yet noon.

Looking over the backyard, she saw it was a shambles. Dad's spent garden took up one corner. Zinnias under the utility-room window lay in withered clumps on the ground. The unwatered Bermuda grass had been burned to white by the sun. Indeed Dad *had* been ill all summer. Otherwise, he wouldn't have neglected the yard and failed to plant flowers. Her mother had loved flowers, had named her only child after one. As a memorial, every summer Dad filled the yard with vibrant blooms.

The method Dahlia had crafted for dealing with life's cruelties was to simply not face them, pretend the bad things were happening to someone else and return to them later. Seeing the backyard, the cold, hard truth refused to be set aside until later and a charge of guilt struck her. Her dad was seventy-seven. What kind of selfishness had made her traipse off for the summer when she should have stayed in Loretta to help him?

As she heaped rebuke on herself, another truth confronted her. Dad was no longer the wise, unselfish man who had guided her through her life. Their roles had reversed. For all the trauma she had faced in her short years, none of it had prepared her for what lay ahead. She wished she smoked. This seemed like a good time for a cigarette.

Heaving a sigh, she left the porch and tackled cleaning the bathroom. At the end of it, she knew she had crossed a threshold. Something inside her had changed.

Leaving the grocery store in Chuck's hands for the day, she stayed home, plowed into rearranging furniture, made the living room wheelchair friendly, moved the TV from her bedroom into Dad's. By nightfall, hot and exhausted, she felt as if she were moving through a crazy house, with distorting mirrors and floors structured to mimic vertigo. Her head and body ached. She was on the verge of tears again. She poured a glass of iced tea, went out to the back porch and sat at the plastic patio table in the humid heat and contemplated the future.

There would be no returning to Dallas. She hadn't seriously considered it anyway. The fire in her belly had been quenched by all that had happened there. Besides that, now she could see she had never had the barracuda personality necessary to survive in the corporate world. She wondered if she even had what it took to make it in this mom-and-pop grocery store.

Spoiled, she admitted, not like a rich kid who had been given everything money could buy, but her father had always taken care of her in one way or another. After her mother's unexpected death, he had set aside his own grief to be two parents. Without a grumble, he had paid for her to attend an expensive college she had thought would launch a stellar business career. And when she buried Kenneth, her dad had been there alongside her, enduring the condescension of Kenneth's snobbish family. Not once had he failed her. She owed him.

"I'll take care of you, Dad," she murmured. "I promise, no matter what I have to do, you'll spend your last days in your own house in Loretta. . . . And somehow, I'll save the grocery store. I'll make you proud of me."

She didn't know if it was fatigue or maybe a virus plaguing her, but in the dark, she thought she saw her mother's smile.

And from out of the blue, she thought of jewelry— her expensive jewelry—lying in her top dresser drawer.

Cash. At the thought of it, Dahlia met the morning inspired. She knew people in Dallas to contact about the sale of her ring. It would take a few days or a week, but she was confident of the outcome. She called and left messages.

To avoid a repeat of yesterday's chaos, she had to be better organized. Readying Dad for the day would take extra time. She switched off her alarm before it had a chance to buzz, dragged herself out of bed and made her way to the kitchen. She still felt as if she were riding ocean waves in a dinghy, but a slice of toast made her feel better. She hadn't eaten an adequate meal since her return, she reminded herself.

A look at the calendar told her she had no time to be sick. Approaching was Labor Day weekend, a holiday important to punching up the Handy Pantry's sales and it was already Tuesday. She hadn't so much as thought about it, much less planned for it.

The big stores in Abilene would already be set for a blowout food weekend. Stock in, advertising out. She was behind. That meant spending more hours in the grocery store and hiring someone to take care of Dad. With what that cost, sales in the store needed to be good.

And they could be, she knew from experience. The lake lovers would pour out of Abilene and the Fort Worth/Dallas Metroplex for the long weekend, pulling boats and hauling jet skis. The campgrounds, the lake-front homes and cabins would fill. The occupants would eat and drink. For the first time, she was grateful for the heat. The hotter the temperature, the more ice, beer and sodas customers bought, as well as steaks and hamburger to cook on outdoor grills.

The store's cash reserve amounted to just enough to bring in extra drinks and snack foods and more beef. The Coca-Cola distributor agreed to share the expense of a last-minute promotion. The Budweiser distributor came through, too, with giveaways. She ran an ad in Loretta's weekly newspaper—a special on prime beef cuts and hamburger, Coke and Bud.

She had hundreds of flyers printed. An employee's son and his friends put them under windshield wipers and in mailboxes. Her efforts didn't carry the cutting-edge excitement of a chain media blitz like those she had once orchestrated in Dallas, but fueled by desperation, her adrenaline pumped just as fast.

She and Chuck had worked long hours all week clean-ing and sanitizing the meat department for the govern-ment inspection, which they had aced. Now they worked equally long hours butchering. The upside, if one could be found, was spending time in the meat cooler. After the pleasant summer temperatures in the mountains, the Texas heat sapped her strength.

To varying degrees, the dizziness and nausea hung on.

Thursday brought Dad's visit to the neurologist. Ex-cept for the challenge of bathing and dressing him and seating him in the Plymouth, the appointment went well. The specialist diagnosed cerebral thrombosis brought on by arteriosclerosis. He sketched a maplike picture on a prescription pad showing her the location of a clot. He scheduled an MRI and told her physical therapy would begin at once. A daily trip from Loretta to Abilene for therapy—how could she do it?

That evening, after Dad had been put to bed, she sat down with her day planner at the kitchen table. The yellow Formica and chrome relic had been parked in one end of the kitchen since before her mother's death. The whole kitchen was a relic, really. The only amenity Dad had added was a fan mounted over the table, flush against the ten-foot ceiling. In its center, three hooded lightbulbs clustered. All but one were spent. Replacing them called for dragging the stepladder from the garage. Dahlia planned to wait for the third one's demise before making the effort.

She mostly avoided the kitchen at night anyway, finding its murk depressing. Tonight she ignored it and turned the planner pages to the current calendar. The next few months would be hard, but now she could organize. She knew more about the future.

Or did she?

Dear God. Her period was five days late.

All the breath whooshed from her lungs and she began to tremble. Like a thunderstorm, the raw, reckless sex with Luke at the mountain hot springs and in his cabin crashed into her thoughts. Those hours now seemed like a fantasy. It had been nearly three weeks. It seemed like three months.

Oh, during sleepless nights she had thought about their carelessness, but there didn't seem to be an empty corner left in her mind to worry over the consequences. They towered in front of her now, like a monolith blocking her path. Hiccuping sobs burst forth. She laid her head on her hands on the tabletop and wept for all of it—her beloved father whose existence had been forever altered, the horror of facing a second bankruptcy in her twenty-nine years and the lost love of her life.

And the real possibility the latter had made her pregnant.

Piggy rolled into town late Saturday afternoon. Like a lantern on a dark night, Dahlia welcomed her return. The ebullient redhead teased Dad as she always did, as if everything were normal, and as always, he laughed—the first time since Dahlia had come home.

After she put him to bed, she and Piggy went to the kitchen. Piggy glanced up at the light fixture. "You out of lightbulbs? This place looks like a cave."

"I have to get the ladder. Now that you're here, you can help me." Dahlia headed for the garage.

Piggy followed. "So what are they saying about Elton?"

"Drugs and therapy. He's going to West Texas Rehab daily. I think he's okay. Not like new, but okay."

"A trip to Abilene every day, huh?"

"Yep. Dad's car never had such a workout. Chuck and I are taking turns driving him."

"I'll help," Piggy said. "The co-op's expecting me back to work next week, but they'll let me take off to drive Elton. They think a lot of him."

Together, they moved the kitchen table, making room for the ladder, and Dahlia climbed up with new lightbulbs. "What happened between you and Pete?"

"We checked out all the better motels between Callister and Cody, Wyoming, and concluded it had been a great summer."

"But I thought you had gotten serious about him."

"What can I say? He's an Idaho boy and I'm a Texas girl. That's never gonna change. Bottom line, I said no."

Dahlia stopped and looked down at her friend. "He wanted you to stay in Callister? With him?"

Piggy answered with a lift of one shoulder. "When it got down to cases, I couldn't. Girl, I'd freeze to death in all that ice and snow. My family's too important to me. I like being close enough to stick my nose in my brothers' business. I want to teach their kids to be monsters. It's the least they deserve."

Piggy's large, close-knit family had always been a source of envy. For all their lives, watching the good-natured pranking of her friend's four brothers, Dahlia longed for siblings, a family group of which she could be a part. And now she had something else to envy: The man *Piggy* had met in Callister had asked her to stay.

Silly, Dahlia called herself, tightening the last bulb. Especially under the circumstances.

In tandem, they carried the stepladder back to the garage, then returned to the kitchen. Out of the refrigerator came a chilled bottle of zinfandel. Piggy made herself at home and reached for wineglasses in the cupboard. "So who's running the grocery store?" she asked as they took seats at the table.

"Who do you think? I've been going through the books. Unless Dad's hidden money in secret accounts, the store's broke, Piggy. Sales have dropped off something awful. Abilene is just too close. A Wal-Mart Superstore and the new Albertson's are too much competition. Dad's been hanging on by his fingernails and I didn't even know it. I sold my wedding ring—"

"No shit?" Piggy's eyes widened.

"I had to. Dad had borrowed money on the store building. The payments were behind. I couldn't think of any other way to get cash. You know what my credit is like."

"Elton mortgaged the store?"

Dahlia nodded. "At least four years ago, before I moved home from Dallas. The balance was small, but the payments were huge." She sighed and went on. "I paid off the mortgage and caught up some past-due bills, but it still takes all I can do to keep the inventory up and find the money for the payroll every week. I've laid off six people, so everybody in town is mad at me."

Piggy's brow crinkled with concern. "Damn."

"I can't believe I didn't know the state of the store's business. I was so focused on my own woes I didn't see it. Now I know why Dad couldn't afford to hire help, why he took on so many of the store's jobs himself. And I added to his stress by leaving for the summer."

"Damn," Piggy said again.

"Besides all that, the store's a huge mess. Dad hasn't been keeping things up like he always did. I'm trying to get on top of it, but I've been so rattled over the finances—"

"Dal, you're babbling."

"I don't think I could survive going through bankruptcy again, Piggy. And I couldn't live with myself if I lost the store. Dad's whole life is invested in it, and what would he do for income?" Tears spilled. Dahlia couldn't restrain her anguish around her best friend.

Piggy reached across the table and took her hand. "Hey, quit worrying. Who's smarter than we are? I'll put on my accountant's hat and we'll dig into the books. We'll figure it out."

Dahlia covered Piggy's hand with hers and dredged up a smile. "I'm so glad you're home."

Piggy poured herself another glass of wine. "Now that we've addressed *that* problem, go ahead and ask me about superstud. I know you're dying to."

"I am not. It doesn't matter." Dahlia toyed with the stem of her wineglass, hating for Piggy to be right. "Okay. Tell me."

"Here it is. I was in the bar Tuesday night with the Forest Service crowd. They were talking about the prince himself. Mind you, this is gossip, but it happened just like you feared it would. Tennis-Bum Dave told Beauty-Shop Tami's husband who then told Luke's ex-wife about the cabin thing, so her lawyer made threats. Beauty-Shop Tami told everybody in town Jimmy was in the cabin while you and Luke were, you know, doing it."

"I hope nobody believed that."

"Oh, it didn't stop there. Janet McRae accused Luke of incest with their oldest daughter."

Dahlia's jaw dropped. "Why, that's just crazy!"

Piggy laughed. "You know Callister. Those people gossip to live and vice versa. McRaes are their favorite topic. Luke went ahead and took those two daughters back down to Boise, but it turned out to be temporary 'cause then"—Piggy hummed a few tension-building notes—"he brought out the big guns."

"What big guns? What are you talking about?"

"Lawyers. Private detectives. Luke had piles of evidence on his ex-wife. Booze is just the tip of the iceberg. She's in a substance-abuse clinic in Boise. Everybody's saying she's lucky she's not in jail. It's not settled yet, but Luke got his kids back in time to start school in Callister. He's filed a suit for permanent custody."

Dahlia snapped her mouth shut. Though custody of his kids had been a never-ending concern, Luke had not once revealed his ex-wife's problems or that someone monitored her activities.

Piggy drained her wineglass and reached for the bottle. "Hey, girlfriend, drink up. You're not helping me celebrate."

Dahlia took only a sip. "I guess I'm not thirsty."

"The range manager told Pete he's never seen Luke so pissed off. In fact, Luke was so mad he told Dave Adams if he didn't learn the meaning of family loyalty and start holding up his end, he was no longer welcome at the Double Deuce. So the atmosphere up at Fort McRae is pret-ty strained."

Dahlia's stomach began to roll. Her hand went to it. She closed her eyes and drew a deep breath. "Being the coward that I am, I'm glad I had to leave."

Piggy frowned. "Are you sick?"

"I've had this . . . virus." Dahlia looked down into the pink liquid that filled her glass, summoning the courage to say, *I may be pregnant.* The words refused to transfer from her brain to her tongue. "Luke fools you," she said instead. "That down-home demeanor is a facade. He does what he thinks needs doing regardless of the consequences." An acid taste grew in her mouth as the ugly memory of the afternoon in the Forest Service parking lot came back. "What did you do with his furniture?"

"The landlord said he'd see to it. Said since he owed Luke for a tank of oil he might even drive that junk up to the Double Deuce himself."

Dahlia gave her an arched look.

Piggy opened her palms. "Looks like your hunch was right. Luke did pay for the oil."

Dahlia's stiff upper lip collapsed. Tears spilled down her cheeks, unwiped. She rose and went to the kitchen sink, tore off a sheet of paper towel, dampened it and bathed her face. "I'm so damn hot. And I'm so miserable."

"Haven't heard from him, huh?"

Dahlia shook her head, all at once aware she had stopped waiting.

"Well, if you're so unhappy, why don't *you* call him?"

Dahlia stared out the kitchen window at the dying grass in the side yard. "Piggy. I'm a week late."

She let out a great breath. There. She had said it aloud, calmly, as if she were speaking about someone else. She had spent the past twenty-four hours yearning for the heaviness low in her belly that signaled the onset of her menses, willing it to appear. In the wee hours of this morning, her last conscious thought before sleep had been, How would her dad take it if she were pregnant? Would he have another stroke?

After a pointed silence, Piggy spoke. "Oh, that's no big deal. I've been that late before."

"Well, I haven't. *Ever.*"

"What did I tell you about being so careless? Didn't I tell you? Hunh?"

Dahlia blew her nose with a loud snort. "I don't need a lecture from you."

Piggy left her chair, came across the room. Her arm slid around Dahlia's waist. "I know. I know. Look, we both know women who try to get knocked up and it never happens. I don't think it's that easy. Everything has to come together just right. Look at all that's gone on. It's probably stress."

Dahlia fell into her best friend's arms. "Oh, Piggy, what would I do without you?"

"Listen, we're not living in the Dark Ages here. You've got pregnancy tests at wholesale, right?"

Dahlia pulled away. "Oh God, I've already thought of that, but I don't know if I have the nerve—"

"Nerve? Either you is or you isn't, girl. There ain't no in between. Wouldn't it be better just to know?"

Chapter 20

While the home health nurses checked and bathed her dad early Sunday morning, Dahlia went to the Handy Pantry. She didn't open it until eleven on Sundays.

She had always thought the store spooky when closed, lit only by the cold-drink coolers and the one small spotlight over the cash registers. This morning, the coolers hummed in harmony with the meat case's compressor, but the sound did nothing to penetrate the palpable stillness Dahlia felt within.

Standing before a four-foot display of home pregnancy tests in the dense gloom was almost an out-of-body experience. This couldn't really be happening to Dahlia Felise Montgomery Jarrett Montgomery, the sexual neophyte who had been a virgin until her senior year in college, who had slept with only two men in her entire life while many of her peers needed both hands and a foot to count their sex partners.

With shaking hands and hammering heart, she selected a best-selling brand and jogged upstairs to the office. The sliver of daylight sluicing between the air conditioner and the window casing only lit the room to gray. Without the air conditioner to freshen the air, the hot room smelled of mildew, nearly bringing up the toast she'd had for breakfast. She went straight to the windowless bathroom off the left side of the office, hugging the apocalyptic cellophane-wrapped box to her bosom.

In a matter of minutes, she knew.

She closed the toilet lid, sank to it and dropped her forehead into her hands. "Oh, Dahlia. What have you done?"

Well, it's a mistake. That's all. It's a mistake.

Sweating buckets, she clicked on the air conditioner, then marched downstairs and snatched a different brand of test off the shelf. Doubt was erased.

Strangely, after weeping almost daily for weeks, now she couldn't cry. Her emotional reservoir was suddenly an empty well. Drained dry. Tapped out. Used up.

She moved out of the bathroom, dropped to the gold velvet sofa and covered her eyes with a trembling hand. She would give herself this private time to punish herself. She deserved it.

How could she have been so thoughtless, so irresponsible, so, so . . . so sex crazed? People had always admired how grounded she was, how reliable. She had betrayed the trust of all who knew her, shamed her dead mother. She was lower than low. And now, at home was a seventy-seven-year-old parent depending solely on her. She had put his welfare in even worse jeopardy.

A baby. What would she do with a baby? Long ago, she had seen herself baking cookies, reading stories, surrounded by the happy children she would have, but the picture had included a loving husband.

Luke. An impulse to call him nudged her—she still had his number—but pride stayed her hand.

She went home and plodded through the rest of the day in a fog. Didn't call Piggy and tell her the news though she knew her friend was waiting on tenterhooks. She functioned with surprising calm, taking one minute at a time. Did some laundry, scrubbed both bathrooms, read to Dad. Thinking of the future would have to wait until tomorrow.

Dahlia sat in the Beemer in front of Dr. Webb's office attempting to collect herself. The doctor had confirmed what she knew and recommended she inform her baby's father as soon as possible.

Memories flooded her mind. *I like my kids, sweetheart, but I don't want any more. . . . Three kids is enough for anybody. . . . No more kids . . .*

Inform the father? She huffed a sarcastic laugh as her

gaze settled on the clock. Nine-thirty. *Damn.* She didn't have time to sit and weep. On the days Chuck relieved her by taking Dad to therapy, she had to squeeze the most into every precious hour.

At lunchtime, Piggy showed up at the grocery store with Dairy Queen hamburgers, and for once, the smell of food didn't make Dahlia sick.

"It's cooled down to ninety-seven today. Let's eat in the park," Piggy said.

They strolled in white-skied heat to Loretta's only park two blocks away. A concrete table and benches, warm to the touch, hunkered under a single oak tree's shade. Piggy brought out the burgers and moved a paper cup of milk toward Dahlia. "I don't think you're supposed to have caffeine. Maybe not greasy hamburgers either, but—"

"Don't start, Piggy. You don't have to monitor my diet."

"Well." Piggy looked around. "This ain't as scenic as lunch on a mountainside, is it?"

Bermuda grass struggled to grow here and there, but mostly, cracked, bare earth showed. Heat waves shimmered above the adjacent main street's asphalt. Dahlia snickered in spite of herself. "Not quite."

"So? You gonna keep me in suspense? What'd Dr. Webb say?"

"He said, 'Young lady, it looks like you're pregnant.' "

"They must learn those stupid statements in med school. Probably part of the penmanship class."

Dahlia snickered again. "I don't know why I'm laughing. It must mean I've finally gone mad."

"So now you've got fact to tell Luke instead of just worry."

"He's never going to know."

"You have to tell him. It's only right."

"*No.* Even if he wanted more kids and even if he wanted me, do you think I could pack up and move to Callister, live at that ranch with his mother hovering and judging? That vicious old bat probably ruined his marriage to Janet."

"He ought to know. If for no other reason, so his conscience will hurt."

"No. I have to think of Dad. I'm all he's got."

"I weaseled a clinic's name out of Dan. He had that girlfriend in Fort Worth who—"

"You told your brother? Good grief, Piggy. Why did you do that? Don't you think this is going to get all over town without your help?"

"Relax. I didn't tell him who I wanted it for."

"He'll know it's me."

"No, he won't. He thinks you're still a virgin."

"I was married, for crying out loud."

"So? Dan knows you." Piggy pulled a small piece of paper from her jeans pocket and held it out. "Here. This place is in southwest Fort Worth. Convenient."

Dahlia ignored the note, her hand involuntarily landing on her stomach. "Don't do this to me, Piggy. This is Luke's baby . . . *our* baby. I couldn't kill it." Tears welled again. *Damn.* She dug napkins from the Dairy Queen sack and dabbed her eyes. "It's all I'll ever have of him. I'm not going to, to . . . get rid of it, like, like . . . it's garbage."

"Dahlia, listen to yourself. I had to look at Elton just once to know taking care of him is a twenty-four-seven job. And *you're* gonna have to keep running that store seven days a week." Piggy began to sniffle. "Going it alone's a noble thought, but you have to face facts. You're not Wonder Woman."

Dahlia had all she could take dealing with her own emotions. She didn't need a friend's, too. "We have to stop crying, Piggy. Dad's getting better every day. I won't have to nursemaid him forever. And running the store won't kill me."

"Okay, fine. But there's another part of this to consider." Piggy dried her eyes and began to stuff the remains of their lunch into the Dairy Queen sack. "Luke's well-off. You're not. He should help you out with a dollar or two. He's a decent, generous guy. He'd want to. I know he would."

"No, no and no. This is not about money."

Piggy's face jutted forward. "No, what it's about is hurt pride. You're pouting. Martyring yourself."

"Piggy, can't you see? This is *my* fault. I knew he didn't want any more kids. I could have insisted we use something."

"Bullpuckey. Getting pregnant is not a solo event."

"I will not, Pegine—repeat, will not—use a baby to club Luke into doing something he has never wanted to do."

"If he doesn't know about it, how can you tell what he might want?"

Dahlia drew herself up and glared at her friend. "I'm not going to keep arguing with you about this. If he finds out, I'll *know* told him. . . . And I'll kill you. Absolutely kill you. Dead, dead, dead."

"Okay. Go ahead. Pout to beat hell. Just remember this—once you've had a baby, you can't put it back. It's forever. Someday you'll wish you'd told him."

"Piggy, stop it. Don't I have enough on my mind already?"

Piggy's eyes scanned Dahlia's body. "By Christmas, you'll be showing."

"I don't know." Dahlia looked down at her stomach. "I'm pretty thin—"

"I'll have a round-bellied maid of honor at my wedding."

Dahlia rose and took their lunch sack to a trash can. "What wedding?"

"I'm getting married. Christmas Eve."

The announcement brought Dahlia to a stop, and she gasped. "To Pete? You're not."

"Not Pete."

"Don't pull my leg. I'm in no mood for it."

"No joke. I'm getting married. William Bailey Porter. The best damn welder in Texas."

Stunned, Dahlia sank to the concrete bench. "Bill Porter? From high school? You just spent the summer in bed with Pete Hand."

"What can I say? He's up there and I'm down here. Bill missed me. He asked me last night and I said, 'Let's go for it.' "

"Why, I don't know what to say."

"Don't act so shocked. You know he and I have had a thing since we were kids. No matter how far I go, I always seem to find my way back to good ol' Bill. He came over with a six-pack. Got down on his knee and everything. Kinda romantic, huh? Said he's been waiting for me to find myself, wanted to catch me before I go off on another wild tear."

"Surely he hasn't really been waiting all these years."

"Patient guy, huh? That's the way he is—solid and dependable. Works hard. Doesn't owe any money except on his equipment. And he's good-looking. We'll have pretty kids. What more could a girl want?"

"You're rationalizing. You may like sex with Bill Porter, but you don't love him."

"Well, he is hell in bed. Makes me shriek like a banshee. That ain't all bad. Who's to say I don't love him? Maybe I always have. Not with thunder and lightning like you and Luke—more like a comfortable old robe, but . . . Anyway, he told me it's high time I got my act together, and he's right. Unlike you, girlfriend, I've never been married and I'm already thirty. I want a kid or two and a steady partner. It's either this or go to Fort Worth and get one of those real jobs."

"That's a terrible thing to say. I feel sorry for Bill."

"You know I'm kidding. I can't wait. I'm tired of the hunt, you know? I'm gonna make him a good wife. I can cook and I'm clean. All four of my brothers like him."

"I suppose there are worse reasons to get married. He *is* sort of like a cousin or something."

"Christmas Eve at my folks' house, we do the deed."

"Good grief. I'd better start planning a shower." Still awed, Dahlia shook her head. "I can't believe it. All of a sudden, *your* life's turning conventional. And here *I* am having a baby with no husband."

"Yeah. Irony's a bitch, ain't it?" Piggy scooted off the bench. "Listen, I gotta get back to the co-op. Without me there, there'll be chaos."

They strolled toward the Handy Pantry. "Okay," Piggy said, "so you're gonna have this kid. We have to find you a good OB doc in Abilene."

"No. Dr. Webb's delivered over half the babies in Loretta, including me. I'm going to stick with him."

"I talked to Bill about it. We'll be here for you, no matter what."

"You told Bill, too? Can't you keep anything quiet?"

"We were in bed, for chrissake."

"And my problems are pillow talk?"

"We were talking above love. I was telling him how much Luke meant to you and how worried I was. And you know what he said? He said, 'You don't need to worry. A love child is always perfect.' "

Love child. Dahlia tried to imagine herself with belly bulging, lifting boxes, sorting fruits and vegetables. A flurry of emotions darted around inside her, including plain old fear. "God, Piggy. Me with a love child. Who'd have thought it?"

"Not me. I remember in school, when we used to say if you ever got pregnant there'd be a new star in the East. . . . So what's the plan? Loretta ain't exactly a mecca of liberal thinking. Around here, single mothers are a Hollywood anomaly."

"I don't have a plan. Crisis management. That's always been my forte."

"It ain't gonna be easy. These old farmers already think you've left the fold because you drive a yuppie car."

"They'll have to get over it."

"And Elton?"

"When he's up to it, I'll tell him. He's looking forward to grandchildren, according to Dr. Webb. This could be the only one he ever has."

Chapter 21

Under Dahlia's management, the Handy Pantry began to recover, if only by inches. Her dad bounced back with nothing more than a limp and a handicapped hand to show for his ordeal.

Dahlia plunged with a vengeance into preparing the grocery store to reap full advantage of the fall holidays, not allowing herself to grieve over her situation. She checked out library books on pregnancy and childbirth and learned what to expect from the coming months.

The calendar pages turned to October. The debilitating fatigue that had plagued her at first went away and she began to feel energized and upbeat. She had always wanted a child and enthusiasm evolved for the prospect of bringing one into the world, even if the circumstances weren't the most ideal.

She decorated the store for Halloween and brought in candy, novelties and costumes, designated a day employees could come to work in costume. Two days later two church women came and met with her about Elton Montgomery's daughter lending support to a celebration of evil for the sake of profit. Her spirits were so high, she was able to smile and serve them coffee and pumpkin cookies in her office.

The week after Thanksgiving, as she stood at the filing cabinet in the office, a faint flutter in her stomach stopped her. In a few seconds she felt it again. Her hand went to her belly and she moved to the desk chair and sat down, fearing the worst. Before she could plunge into a full-scale fit of anxiety, it dawned on her the baby had moved.

Tears sprang to her eyes as profound emotions filled her heart. She stared at the phone, fighting a desperate urge to hear Luke's voice. She couldn't think of anything she had ever wanted as much as to share this moment with the man who had spawned the life growing inside her.

He didn't want you, she reminded herself, and to him, being a father for the fourth time would be viewed, at best, as an unfortunate accident. This precious experience belonged to her and her alone.

She tamped down those maudlin sentiments, dried her eyes and blew her nose, reminded herself she had already resolved she didn't need Luke McRae. But, dammit, she had to tell *somebody.* She yanked up the receiver and keyed in Piggy's number.

Piggy squealed with delight at the news and together they laughed and cried and made a flurry of plans for the baby's room. When they hung up, Dahlia's mood had improved. She placed both hands on her thickening middle and faced that it was time to tell her dad she was pregnant.

Her father was overjoyed at the news. If words of censure passed through his mind, they didn't manifest themselves on his lips. He made plans for turning the bedroom next to hers into a nursery. The room had once been her own nursery. Because he didn't question her, she told him little about her Idaho lover.

As the Christmas frenzy of shopping and cooking swooped down and the grocery store's tasks became increasingly demanding, the next thing she knew, against Dr. Webb's advice, her dad returned to work in the Handy Pantry. Nothing she or the doctor said persuaded him to stay home.

Christmas Eve and Piggy's wedding date arrived. Pegine Murphy and Bill Porter were married beside a beautiful Christmas tree at Piggy's parents' house. Dahlia couldn't make it through the sentimental ceremony dry-eyed. Only the loud family party that followed kept her from sinking into a mire of depression.

In January, as the impracticality of managing a baby

in the Z3 became evident, she sold it and bought a Chevy Lumina. By February, she was into maternity clothes. She had worn oversized street clothes for as long as she could get by with it. Her belly had grown huge overnight it seemed, and Piggy joked about her giving birth to a fifteen-pound kid.

She left the store in her dad's hands after lunch on Groundhog Day and drove to Abilene, shopping for baby furniture and supplies. She returned after dark and found her home lit inside and out and Piggy's car parked haphazardly in the driveway. Piggy met her outside, breathless.

"Elton had one of his spells. He went to the hospital in the ambulance, but he's not . . . He's okay."

A sweep of panic set Dahlia to shaking. "Did he collapse? What happened?"

"He must have felt it coming on. He called 911. My cousin was at the hospital. When she couldn't reach you, she called me."

Dahlia turned back to her car. "I have to go over there."

Piggy came behind her. "I'll go, too. Let me drive."

Dr. Webb had left when they reached the hospital. Her dad appeared to be asleep in the ICU. Piggy's cousin explained as much as protocol allowed. CVA, "guarded" condition. Dahlia could do nothing but get in the way.

"Just five minutes." The nurse opened the door to the ICU.

After spending a sleepless night, Dahlia had arrived at the hospital early. She slipped through the doorway, moved to Dad's bedside and kissed his brow. His face was drawn. He needed a shave. His crinkled skin was as white as the pillow on which he lay. Avoiding IV tubes, she lifted his hand into hers, aware that it was ice-cold. His appearance seemed to be much the same as after the previous stroke. "How do you feel today, Pops?"

He didn't respond. The possibility of his failing to recover flew at her like a giant, evil bird.

She left his room, stopped at the nurses' station and questioned the RN on duty. The nurse gave reassuring answers that told her little more than nothing. She left a message for Dr. Webb to call her and hurried to the Handy Pantry.

Except for the worry over her dad's illness, her day went well. The Budweiser truck's unmarried driver flirted with her as usual, as if he didn't notice her expanded belly. Customers were steadily buying the Valentine's Day candy and gifts she had stocked, and it appeared the store wouldn't be left with heavy overstock after the holiday.

"Dr. Webb's on the phone, Dahlia."

Dahlia looked up from straightening the tomato display and glanced at the clock mounted above the storeroom door. Five-thirty. "I'll take it upstairs." She jogged up to the office and to her desk and lifted her feet to a neighboring chair seat before she picked up the phone. After standing all day, her feet were so swollen even her Nikes felt tight.

"I don't think Dad knew who I was this morning," she told the doctor. "It was worse this time, wasn't it?"

"I'll be frank, Dahlia. It's hard to say about the future, but try not to worry. We're keeping a close eye on him. When he's better, we'll get him in to Dr. Colson again."

She bit her lip. After Dad's first stroke, Dr. Webb's tone had held an expectation for improvement.

"Okay," she said, accepting the pessimistic prognosis.

They discussed her own health and hung up. At the hospital that evening, she found Dr. Webb there. Her dad's condition had been downgraded. He no longer showed any sign of awareness. She followed the doctor out to the hallway, glancing back one more time at the array of equipment around her father's bed. "He looks so bad."

The doctor didn't meet her gaze. He gave her shoulder a pat. "He isn't suffering. Go on home now. I don't want you worrying. You need to rest. I don't expect anything to happen suddenly."

She was left standing alone in the hospital corridor's cool, dim quiet. Dishes clattered in a room down the hall, phones chirped, nurses scurried. Patients were being readied for the night. She melted into the chair outside the ICU room door.

I don't expect anything to happen suddenly. Dad. Her last connection to the planet. Was this the end?

An avalanche of grief rolled over her. She closed her eyes and dropped her forehead into her hand, tuning out the activity in front of her. Though surrounded by people, all of whom she knew, she felt totally, utterly alone. White noise began to roar in her head. She began to shake inside. She leaped from the chair and ran outside to her car.

The ensuing days brought little change except in the increased activity of the life growing inside her. Besides knowing she would give birth to a son, she now knew he must surely have powerful little limbs. His movement became something she enjoyed feeling even when it kept her awake at night. She caught herself often wondering if Luke would find it in his heart to be happy if he knew she carried his son and that the fetus appeared to be hale and healthy, but she tried not to dwell on the question. The answer was too depressing.

Dad breathed on his own, but he was comatose and was being fed through a stomach tube. A knot the size of Dallas had lodged in her throat and she was able to force herself to eat only for the baby's sake.

Dr. Webb ordered Dad moved out of the ICU, into a private room. This is better, she assured herself. She could help the nurses care for him and spend as much time as she wanted when she visited.

On a blustery, chilly day in the middle of March, Dr. Webb placed his hand on her shoulder and said, "Let's go down to the lunchroom and get a cup of coffee."

Dahlia closed her eyes and drew a deep breath. Such a statement always held grave portent. She had seen too many movies, she told herself. She and the doctor didn't talk as they walked side by side to the hospital's tiny cafeteria. The doctor poured coffee for himself and asked the kitchen help for a glass of apple juice for her. She found a seat in the corner, grateful they were the only two people in the room. Dr. Webb's expression was stony as he sat down across from her.

She gathered her courage. "So, what's up?"

"I'd like to remove Elton's feeding tube, Dahlia."

She stared at him, not wanting to believe what she had heard. "But—but . . . He . . ."

Dr. Webb reached across the table and put his hand on her arm. "He can't move. There's little brain activity. We can keep him alive a long time, but . . . it's my opinion he won't improve."

"But he—he makes . . . sounds sometimes." She struggled to remember the last time she had heard anything from him other than raspy breathing. "Doesn't he?" she said in a small voice.

Dr. Webb shook his head.

An out-of-breath feeling overtook her. "If—if you take out the tube, won't he starve?"

The doctor held her gaze.

"That's terrible. No! The answer's no!"

"He won't know—"

"You don't know that."

"Elton and I have been friends since he came home from the war, Dahlia. He's like my brother. He wouldn't want to go on like he is."

She fought for a deep breath. Only a whisper came out of her mouth. "This is what they call pulling the plug, isn't it?"

The doctor frowned and shook his head. "Dahlia . . ."

She stared into space, stifling a scream and groping to put together a coherent sentence. Finally, she swallowed her tears. "Tell me what happens. . . ."

She flew home, barely controlling her grief until she arrived. Sobs racked her. What had she done? How could she live with herself? She went to the phone. It wasn't

too late to call the nurses' station and tell them to keep
her dad alive for as long as possible.

But as she reached for the receiver, something stayed
her hand, redirected it to the nearby cupboard. She took
a glass from the cupboard and filled it with water, carried
it into the living room and sat down on the twenty-year-
old sofa that had so rarely been sat on it looked brand-
new. She held the cool glass against her forehead. Dad
was leaving her. It was really happening. Dr. Webb had
said a matter of days, perhaps a week.

What would she do? What would mornings be like
without him shuffling around the kitchen? Whose opinion would she seek when she had doubts? Who would
look at her with sincere love and call her "Dally"?

No answers came. Her mind was blank.

She heard a car outside and a tearful Piggy burst into
the house. "JoAnn called and told me."

They met in a hug and Dahlia couldn't hold back sobs.
"My dad has things to offer. . . . He's a good person. . . .
He's a good citizen. He's—"

"He's seventy-eight and he's been really sick." Piggy
sniffled. "You know Dr. Webb's right, Dal. Elton
wouldn't want to lie there and be a vegetable."

Dahlia pulled away and blew her nose. "He'll never
see my baby. . . . And he wanted to . . ."

"I know, Dal. I know. . . . But you know what, he *will*
see him. I believe that."

Dahlia shook her head. "Oh, Piggy, he's all I have. . . .
How will I get through this?"

"Just like you've gotten through everything else, Dal.
You're the strongest and best person I know."

Eight days later, Dahlia's anchor left her. The VFW
helped her plan a war hero's funeral. The First Methodist
Church overflowed with mourners and flowers, and her
father was laid to rest beside the woman he had never
stopped loving and the mother Dahlia could remember
only in fleeting vignettes.

She mourned the loss of a beloved parent, but the
person she buried was a virtual stranger she had watched

die a little every day for months. Though she had never wished him gone, in her heart, she had said good-bye sometime back when he still had been the man she had known all her life.

In May, alone but for Piggy and Piggy's mom, she gave birth to a healthy, black-haired, nine-pound, three-ounce son and named him Joseph, her father's middle name.

Chapter 22

The Double Deuce
Three months later

Luke relaxed his favorite saddle horse's reins and let him munch grass. "Lord, it's dry, Roanie." August temperatures had nudged into the nineties several times and lightning storms had danced all over the tinder-dry mountains and valleys. It was a wonder the whole countryside didn't catch fire.

From his vantage point on the miles-long ridge rimming one side of Sterling Valley, he gazed down at the Double Deuce's home pasture that ran the length of the valley floor. Huddled at the far end, partially hidden in a grove of ancient pines, sat Donald Angus McRae's original one-room cabin. Like his predecessors, Luke had done what he could to prevent its rotting to the ground.

A short distance from it, overlooking the Snake River, the McRae family cemetery lay enclosed by a heavy iron fence. It hadn't been disturbed in fourteen years, since his brother, Matt, was put in the ground. It would hold a new resident soon. Luke's paternal grandmother was over ninety years old.

The ridge faded into the horizon beyond the old cemetery and he could see the new pine log house DAM Ranches had built for Brenna and Morgan. It had been vacant, suffering neglect, since they moved to Boise a year ago.

He thought for the ten-thousandth time how he loved this valley and these mountains, how their beauty and his family's history among them held him with unyielding tentacles. Though he had come to be their shepherd by default, he tended them with care and protected them fiercely. He would never part from them even upon his death. He would simply move from life in the Big House to a resting place right down there in that cemetery. Like all McRaes before him, his remains would become a part of Double Deuce soil.

Swallowing the rush of emotion such thinking always brought, he scanned the western sky. Not a cloud in sight. Years of experience told him rain had to be just around the corner and snow by mid-September. He lifted his old straw hat and wiped sweat from his face with his shirtsleeve. Then, clucking to Roanie a couple of times, he nudged him over the berm at the trail's edge and down the hillside toward home and supper.

At the barn, he saw the hired man Shorty herding mares into the adjoining lodgepole corral. He swung out of the saddle and led Roanie toward the new horse stalls.

Shorty fell in step beside him. "You ought to let me ride the fences, Luke, or take one of the ATVs."

Luke untied his saddle scabbard, slipped out his rifle and propped it against a stall. "You got plenty of other stuff to do, Shorty. I like it. Keeps me in touch with what's going on. Nothing like riding a good horse in the high country. Reminds a man he's just a pissant."

Shorty grinned. "See any game?"

Luke fished a piece of carrot out of his shirt pocket and fed it to Roanie. "Few deer. Cows already coming off the mountain."

"Uh-oh. Early winter."

"Suits me. Grass is dryer'n popcorn." Luke dragged the saddle off Roanie's back and toted it toward the tack room.

Shorty came behind him with the scabbard. "Gonna ship 'em all down to the Owhyee then?"

"We'll send the yearlings first. I'm still looking for hay." Every year, Luke resolved to end the summer with enough hay put up for a long winter, but every August he had to scramble.

"How'd the fences look?"

Luke hung up his chaps, left the tack room and scooped a helping of oats for Roanie. "It's too close to winter to get into a fence-building project, but first thing after the thaw, we'll rebuild that whole north line again. Keep the Forest Service happy."

Shorty began to curry Roanie. "I let the girls use the Jeep today. They went over to the Flaggs' place."

Luke's old canvas-topped Jeep sat nose-in outside the barn. His daughters had been taught to drive as soon as they could see over the steering wheel and reach the brake, as he and his siblings had been. "What's going on over there?"

Shorty snorted. "Boys. Flagg's nephews. From back East. I figured they couldn't get into too much trouble in the Jeep."

Luke arched an eyebrow. "I can tell it's been a long time since you were a teenager." He picked up his rifle and headed for the Jeep. "I'm going to the mailbox. See ya' at supper."

Luke switched on the Jeep's ignition and country rock rattled the dash. All the horses and the two mules lifted their heads, ears pointed forward like nosy old women. Luke snapped off the radio. It wasn't that he disliked music, but at the end of a long day's ride, he preferred something soothing.

Wrung out, he left the Jeep in low gear, let it creep down the gravel driveway to the county road and pulled up to the oversized mailbox. He dug out the mail, and as he shuffled through it, a plain envelope addressed to him personally caught his eye. In feminine script, the upper-left corner said P. Porter, Loretta, Texas. A little jolt darted through his gut.

He thumbed his hat back, tore open the envelope and pulled out a two-page note. A small photograph slid out and landed on his lap. He picked it up and saw a black-haired, wide-eyed infant and uneasiness crept through him. Lifting the letter's first page, he looked for the signature. When he saw *Best regards, Piggy,* his fingers began to tremble.

Flipping back to page one, he started to read. . . .

"Jee-sus Christ."

He stared at the picture again and turned to page two. Shaking fingers blurred the second reading. Quick arithmetic—gestation for cows and humans roughly the same . . . The kid was at least three months old. "Jeesus Christ."

Stupefied, he sat there, studying the picture, looking for family resemblance, pinching his lower lip with his thumb and finger. That last weekend with Dahlia flashed in his mind. *Shit.* And Piggy. She was a loudmouth, he recalled, but an honest person and a friend. She wouldn't just up and write him a lie.

His mind lurched to his two daughters, and he looked up at the ranch house. They would be watching TV, arguing over the programs. After the final custody hearing last fall, when the court had decided his girls wouldn't be spending any more time at their mother's house, he had bought a big-screen set and a satellite dish to replace some of what they would miss about Boise. The electronic monster had ruled the household ever since. Even his dad had gotten hooked on *Judge Judy* and *Oprah*.

He stuffed the note back into its envelope and slid it into his shirt pocket. Bypassing the Big House, he drove to the cabin to think. Frosty and Bingo rose from their naps by the front door and looked up at him with guilty eyes. They jumped up on his thighs, wagging their tails for forgiveness, but he wasn't in a forgiving state of mind. He scruffed their hair and scolded them, then shooed them off the deck.

Thoughts stumbling over memories, he went to the bedroom, dropped onto a chair and tugged off his boots, his tired muscles begging for a hot shower's spray. Instead of relaxing him, the shower stall dredged up yet another strong memory that sent a rush of blood to his groin. *Ah, Dahlia.*

He pulled on clean jeans and his boots and settled into his worn recliner to read the letter and study the picture again. The boy looked like Dahlia, dark and exotic. Naturally he would, for that was the way of genetics. His name was Joe. . . . Great kid . . . Dahlia a wonderful mother. Luke wouldn't expect anything less. He had never known a gentler, more caring person.

A vision of the golden-skinned woman with upturned eyes and hair black and shiny as obsidian took shape in his mind. For the past year, she had never been very far from his thoughts. Almost anything could remind him of her, from the upper meadow's deep spring green that was the color of her eyes to Sterling Creek's ripple that tinkled like her laughter.

Good Lord. Had she really gone through pregnancy and given birth all alone? Why hadn't she told him? An overwhelming urge to see the child, *his* child, made his heart crowd into his throat.

His mind sped back to the Forest Service parking lot, the day he had been such a damn fool. After that afternoon, he had gone by Baker's rental house several times, but never found anyone at home, called, but never got an answer. Finally, some computer informed him the number was no longer in service. She had been gone two weeks before Kathleen told him she went home in a hurry because somebody in her family had come down sick. That could only be a lie, he thought. She left, really, because she was pissed off at him.

And now he knew just how mad she had been. Only an enraged woman wouldn't tell a father she carried his child.

He gave himself a mental kick. No, dammit, he hadn't made any serious effort to get in touch with her. Texas was a long way off. He knew she lived with her dad, but he didn't know her dad's name. The name of the little town she came from never really registered in his thoughts until a few minutes ago. Odd, because after she left, he had gone so far as to dig out the road atlas and try to jog his memory about her hometown's name, but with no success. He didn't believe in omens, but he took it as one when he couldn't easily locate her.

Besides, didn't the phone lines run two ways? He hadn't heard from her either, so he figured she didn't care so much about him after all. She never did say so.

He had broken off with women before—one lady friend had told him it was a pattern to avoid making a commitment—so he knew getting one out of his system was a matter of self-discipline and the passage of time. With Dahlia, that method hadn't worked so well. He went months with no sleep. Hell, after she left, it seemed like he had a bad case of indigestion clear up 'til Christmas. He got past it, finally, likening it to when he kicked chewing snoose.

Thump, thump, thump. The sound of a cane on the deck elbowed its way into his thoughts and he blew out a long breath. Never a minute to call his own. "Come on in," he called. Laying Piggy's letter on the lamp table beside the recliner, he stood and greeted his mother.

"Your dad found some hay. Down at Howard's in Caldwell. He told them we'd pick it up this week."

"Good. Shorty can take the truck down tomorrow. I'll get a couple of husky boys from town to help unload it. That oughtta make Mary Claire happy."

"She didn't come back from Flagg's place with Annabeth. The Stripling boy brought her a little later. He's still here. Guess he's staying for supper."

"Jason? Where'd she run into him? Shorty said it was Flagg's nephews they went to see."

"Jason. That's his name. He's putting up hay for the Flaggs."

Luke felt his brows tug together. His overdeveloped fifteen-year-old daughter gave him anxious moments. "That boy's over eighteen. What's he doing fooling around with Mary Claire?"

His mother gave him a piercing look over the top edge of her half glasses. "You don't really want me to answer *that*."

The terse reply and remembering himself at that age only agitated Luke more. Back then, where his next piece was coming from dominated all his thoughts and a considerable number of his actions. The daughter under discussion had been conceived in the bed of his pickup when he was the same age as Jason Stripling. The thought of his Mary heaving under a young stud wasn't a pretty picture. "She's straining against the bit real hard, isn't she?"

"No worse than you and your sisters, I guess." His mother limped across the living room and used her cane to ease down onto one of the two chairs bracketing the large window that looked out at the long pasture. The late-afternoon sun haloed her unruly short hair. "On those TV shows your dad watches, they call it raging hormones. Striplings are good people. She could do worse."

Right now, Luke didn't want to fall into a discussion of how his mother categorized people. With a harrumph, he went to the bedroom and shrugged into a clean shirt. "Supper ready?" he called, tucking his shirttail into his jeans, but he heard no answer. Returning to the living room, he saw why. His mother stood there, holding Piggy's letter. *Jee-sus Christ!*

"Small notes can bring large revelations." Her voice trembled. "Were you going to tell us about this?"

An instant of dread crawled through him. He hated upsetting her. After thousands of dollars' worth of tests, the docs in Salt Lake had diagnosed MS. Her days had become a muddle of drugs and frustration. "I was gonna get around to it."

She thrust the infant's photograph toward him. "I guess you could lay *this* onto raging hormones, too. I assume this child belongs to the woman who—"

"Dahlia. Her name's Dahlia." He took the picture from her, folded it into Piggy's letter and jammed the whole package back into its envelope. *Just no damn privacy.* "It's *my* business, Mom."

"Oh? You know what you do affects everybody here. What does this Dahlia want? A payoff? Child support?"

"She's not that kind of person. My guess is she doesn't know Pig—her friend wrote me."

"You honestly believe the boy's yours?"

"He could be." To Luke's astonishment, he didn't mind admitting to his mother he could have fathered a child with Dahlia. He tried to picture Dahlia pregnant and heard himself mumble, "If only I'd known—"

"How do you know?" Both hands braced on her cane, her chin jutted forward. "You're a wealthy man. This could be an extortion scheme hatched up between her and that friend who was here with her. The wise thing would be to deny it, then alert Brad—"

"No. No lawyers. I've had a bellyful of judges and courts telling me what to do with what's mine. I've got no reason to think this boy's not my son. If it hadn't been for all the hell-raising and all that was going on with Janet and the girls, I might've . . . well, things might've gone a different way."

His mother limped back to the window and stared out at the corral behind the barn. Luke could only guess what might be gnawing at her when she looked down at the corral. He couldn't look at it himself without envisioning his brother's fatal accident.

"It still haunts me how Janet came to be a member of this family," she muttered in a stage whisper.

Christ. His chest felt as if his shirt had shrunk. It haunted him, too, if he let himself dwell on it—coming home his sophomore year at UI, telling his parents he had married a woman from Spokane and she was due to deliver any day. It had been the most gut-wrenching confession of his life up to that moment. Then later, the painful meeting between Janet and his parents, their learning his bride was eight years older than he, a fact that distressed his mother as much as the pregnancy.

She turned back and faced him, eyes moist. "I've talked until I'm blue in the face about the folly of getting outsiders involved with this ranch. What more proof do you need than Janet?"

"I wish we wouldn't do this, Mom—"

"Son, listen to me." She came to stand in front of him. Her fingers closed on his forearm, but it was the glint of steel in her eye that held him like a vice. "It was more than tradition that made your dad give you the controlling interest in this ranch. Neither your sisters nor their husbands are capable of managing it. Nor do they want to."

Luke couldn't hold back a sardonic laugh. "I didn't want to either, Mom."

She went on as if she hadn't heard him, just as she did in all of their conversations about him and the ranch. "The survival of all this"—she made an arc with a flattened hand—"rests in your hands. My future's uncertain.

I don't know how much longer I'll be able to help you. You need a partner you have something in common with. You can't bring an outsider here and expect—"

"Mom, cut it out. I didn't say I'm bringing anybody here. I don't know what's going to happen. But I'm going down there." *Good Lord. Where did that come from?* Until this instant, he hadn't considered a trip to Texas.

"—expect her to be content. This ranch is hard on a woman. Do you think a pretty little thing from clear across the country would handle it any better than Janet did? Why, she'd be hotfooting it back to Texas after the first winter and maybe taking a piece of DAM Ranches with her."

His mood had plummeted into a black hole. "She's not a pretty little thing. And life's no harder here than it is anywhere else. It's just a little farther out of town."

His mother's chest rose on a deep breath, as if she were rallying for a new assault. "We have a right to know if you're planning to claim this child."

"I don't know what I'm planning, but I want to see him. You can't fault me for that."

"And her?"

"Her, too." His mind was busy now, planning.

Silent seconds passed as his mother returned to stare out the window, her head shaking.

"Dahlia's not like Janet, Mom. She's a good, decent person. She doesn't deserve anybody's animosity. I've been sorry ever since I broke off with her."

"I'll tell you this much. If you're of a mind to bring her and her little boy into this family, don't think it's gonna be easy. You've got two sisters and three kids to consider. Your two girls are old enough to have minds of their own, and one of them might have an interest in running this ranch someday."

"I doubt that. Mary Claire's already planning to go to art school in Seattle. And Annabeth wants to be a vet. If that's what she wants, damned if I'll force her into the cattle business."

His mother's jaw tightened. They both knew he spoke of the day she had demanded he leave college and return to the Double Deuce to meet his responsibilities as a

McRae son. Her chin raised another notch. "I guess I had *that* coming."

"I didn't mean—"

A tear dared to sneak from the corner of one of her eyes. "I know," she said, her hand fumbling for her jeans pocket. She pulled out a handkerchief and wiped her eyes. He felt like crying himself. It would have been easier if she had kept up the confrontation. The soft side that had returned since the diagnosis of her illness was disconcerting.

"I didn't say that about Annabeth to make you feel guilty. I admit it pissed me off, being forced to leave school and come back. For a long time, I carried it around like a chip on my shoulder. It's come to me in the last year or so that I couldn't have been happy living away from here."

"It's funny how things happen," she said softly. "I've always puzzled on it. I don't know if the ranch would have survived if the responsibility for it had passed to Matt. If it means anything to you, I think you've made a better manager than he would have. He was a plodder, like your dad. But you're a doer. And you've got vision and spunk."

Resentment of the implied criticism of his dad sprang up in Luke. "Dad's a wiser man than anybody gives him credit for." He deliberately didn't direct the remark at her, not wanting to cause her more distress.

Luke went to her and put his hand on her arm, urged her down to the chair. "Sit down, Mom, and listen to me for once." He took the opposite chair and hunkered forward, letting his hands dangle between his knees. "This boy, if he is my son, may guarantee the ranch's survival. He should be with me, with his family. He won't lean toward being a stockman if he doesn't grow up knowing who he is."

His mother's eyes glistened with unshed tears. She looked down at her lap, shaking her head. "If only Jimmy . . ." She raised her chin with a deep sniff and looked past his shoulder. "Well, no point going into that. If wishes were horses, as Granny McRae says. When are you going?"

Luke could see his words had struck a note. "In a few days. Monday maybe."

"Can't it wait? We could get snow any day. It's a bad time for you to be gone from here."

"Just a few days. That's all I need."

"Your girls will know you're going. Do you intend to tell them about the boy?"

"Not yet. When I get back."

Another sigh, another headshake. His mom struggled to her feet. Before leaving, she stopped in the doorway and looked back at him. "You be careful, Luke. There's been no mischief over inheritance in this family for two generations. Don't do something that will sour the well at this ranch."

An igloo would have held up as a dining-table center-piece in the atmosphere at supper, Luke thought. His mother was as cold and silent as winter fog. At the meal's end, she went to her bedroom.

He and his girls helped Ethel clear the table and would have helped her clean up, but she pushed them out of the kitchen. Luke bolstered his courage and followed his daughters into the living room. He punched off the TV and announced he was going to Texas to see a lady friend who used to be important in his life.

After the shock waves settled, Annabeth warmed to the idea of his having a girlfriend. Mary Claire puffed up, called him a hypocrite and stomped up the stairs. Her reaction didn't surprise him. She believed he had caused her mother's woes.

"I'll bet she can't wait to see you," Annabeth said, her eyes alive with excitement.

"She doesn't know. I'm gonna surprise her."

"Let's go to Boise and buy her a present."

"A present? I hadn't thought about that."

Blue eyes rounded with concern. "Daddy! You can't go see your girlfriend without taking a present."

A smile spread inside him. His younger daughter often instructed him on courtship. She thought it was lacking in his life, and in truth, it was. "I guess you're right, Annie."

"I'll help you. We could go on Saturday and we could visit Jimmy."

Luke laughed at himself for being so dumb. He guessed he *should* take a present, and he hadn't seen his son since the boy's eighth birthday party two weeks ago. "Okay, kiddo. We'll do it."

Annabeth threw herself against him and hugged his ribs. "I love you, Daddy. Everything's gonna be fine. Don't worry about M.C. I'll go talk to her." Hurrying toward the stairway that led to the bedrooms, she stopped and called over her shoulder. "Oh, and Daddy, Chico needs a new blanket so he won't be cold this winter. While we're down there we could get him one."

Luke looked after his younger daughter with warmth in his heart. If he were a crying man, he could burst into tears. The difference in his children would puzzle him forever. Mary Claire, though fleshy and short of stature, was a golden-haired beauty in the classic sense, reminding him of how Janet had looked when they married. Large breasted and round hipped, she looked older than her years. More than a few times, he'd had to force himself to calm down when he saw teenage boys ogling her. For all her beauty, she had inherited more than her mother's good looks—she also had Janet's selfishness and sour disposition.

But fourteen-year-old Annabeth was a breath of fresh air, a bubbling, eternal optimist. She was tall, with curling sandy hair like his, flat chested as a boy and too skinny for her height.

His dad came from the kitchen. "That kid loves that horse."

"I'm glad. I could sell him tomorrow for a pretty penny. Bud Dixon wants him for a barrel horse so bad he can taste it." He gazed up at the stairway. "Mom tell you about the boy?"

His dad nodded. Luke knew he could count on his father not to pass judgment.

"She sure was cold at supper."

"We talked and she agreed to let it lay. I told her it's time we mind our own business. You deserve to be happy, Son. The right woman's a comfort to a man. If this is the one you want, then go get her. You'll get no guff from me."

"It's hard not to think about all that happened between Janet and Mom. Janet had her faults, but Mom was awful hard on her."

"Callister's a small place. And I've given your mother more than enough reason to be bitter."

In all his thirty-five years, Luke hadn't heard his father make such a personal remark. His hands went to rest on his belt, his mind a blank as he stared at his aging parent.

The patriarch tamped his pipe and avoided the stare. "I don't think I ever talked to you about how it was when I met your mother. She had just come from Lewiston to teach school. So much energy packed into one person. Everything was important to her. She could get excited about dew on the grass. Keeping up with her was like grabbing on to a shooting star. More than a dull man who lived in a dull place could ever hope for.

"All of us changed after your brother's death. Claire handled it best. She turned into herself, but she kept moving forward. I was the weaker one. I had to have help. I found it in town."

Dad's youthful mistress. The family's dirty little secret and once the talk of the county. The woman was someone with whom Luke had gone to high school. She lived in a modest house in town owned by DAM Ranches, Inc. The house was hers to keep as long as she chose or until her death, whichever came first. Dad had had it written in legalese.

He walked to the front entry and gazed up at the portrait of Donald McRae. "But for the sake of the ranch and the family, I made sure I didn't leave any catch-colt kids behind."

His dad turned back into the living room and moved toward the bedroom hallway, laying his pipe in a granite ashtray on a massive chairside table. "Guess I'll turn in now. I know you'll make the right decisions. You always do."

Luke was so staggered by his dad's confession he

barely stammered a good-night, but he felt the passing of a torch more than he ever had since assuming the role of leader at the Double Deuce. He stared into the entry at the paintings of his distant grandparents.

Summer sounds wafted through open windows—sawing crickets, the snuffling of well-fed horses, the barks and wails of hungry coyotes. Loneliness settled on him as he studied the one-dimensional face of the ranch's founder, the multidimensional man whose shoes he tried every day to fill.

Old Donald looked down on each succeeding generation with haunting blue eyes that had passed to his progeny for a hundred sixty years. He had bequeathed them more than red hair, blue eyes and strong genes. He had left them a charge to keep. In old-world fashion and rare accidents of birth, a McRae son had always stood as the guardian of the Double Deuce's acres of wild-grass meadows, its miles of rivers and streams and its sections of timber. To keep all of it intact and privately owned, McRaes had fought the elements and epidemics, the Indians and the government and sometimes each other. Some had sanctified its soil with their blood, and every last one of them who had passed on since the beginning was buried in the McRae family cemetery.

This was the legacy he would bestow on his son.

He had begun to worry in recent years who would pick up the DAM Ranches' standard. Like Dad, he had wondered if, breaking with tradition for the first time, Annabeth would be the one. Or if it would be the child of his sister Kathleen, now four months' pregnant, a child who would bear a different last name.

Now he had the answer. It would be his own son, also breaking tradition, for with the exception of Donald Angus himself, no keeper of the Double Deuce had ever been born outside God's country, Idaho.

He would go to Texas and claim his son and heir and the beauty who was the boy's mother.

That is, if she didn't kick his ass clear back to Idaho.

Chapter 23

Beat to life by a hot shower, Dahlia stood in front of the vanity mirror trying to remember how eight hours' sleep felt. She'd had to nurse her three-month-old son twice in the night. The last time was three hours ago, at two a.m. Preparing to begin her morning routine, she wondered why she bothered making up every day, doubted if anyone in Loretta would notice if she didn't.

Well, at least her hair was less trouble than it used to be. The long curly style that once had taken so much time and pampering had grown out and been trimmed to shoulder length. Blow-drying the oversized rollers that curved the blunt ends of her now-straight tresses, she ran through her plan for the day.

Produce would be delivered late morning. A high-school student apprenticing as a butcher would be in after lunch. Once she had assumed management of the Handy Pantry, it hadn't taken long to spot how much of her time and Chuck's was being consumed by doing all the butchering themselves. The struggling store couldn't afford a professional butcher, so she had gone to the high-school principal and volunteered an apprenticeship. Now, to her surprise, several teenagers waited in line for the opportunity to learn the craft of cutting meat.

"It's Monday here at WBAP. It was August a year ago when . . ." The voice of a Fort Worth/Dallas broadcaster came from a radio she kept on the bathroom counter.

August, a year ago. Her son's conception. A date more securely locked in her memory than his birth date or her own.

If her life had a pivotal period, that month had been it. Neither losing her mother and her husband before she reached thirty nor resolving the havoc after Kenneth's death had changed her so profoundly as the events of last August. Prior to then, she had fumbled through time merely reacting to life's trials and wondering what could happen next.

Then, *bam*! A meteor landed smack in the middle of her existence. For the first time, life-altering decisions were left to her alone. She had gritted her teeth and made them, discovering strength she didn't know she possessed.

Gallons of tears had been shed between then and now. Countless sleepless nights had been spent plotting survival, hours pondering her destiny. Now she had a firm grip. Whatever the future held, she could handle it. *Everything happens for a reason.* Indeed. The proverb came to her often, hanging in her mind like a gigantic sign on the side of a tall building.

Temperature over a hundred today, the radio forecasted. *Ugh.* She passed up wearing foundation, which would only make her feel hotter, opting instead for a few swipes of rose blush and a few flicks of black mascara. She finished with Paint the Town Red lipstick and spritzed herself with True Love. She had always enjoyed good perfume, didn't intend to let near poverty deprive her of every pleasant remnant of her former life.

Inside her narrow walk-in closet, she scrutinized the two clothes racks that held her pitiful wardrobe—mostly odds and ends left from her yuppie days in Dallas. Once, her clothing had cost big bucks, but now, being fashionable had been reduced to much less importance than her son's first smile or the quality of the meat sold in the Handy Pantry.

Her gaze landed on a plastic garment bag in the very back of the closet. It held the expensive red silk dress she had worn one time. She hadn't so much as looked at it since her return from Idaho. As she fingered the bag's zipper, a flood of memories washed over her. Like echoes in an empty hall, Luke McRae's soft baritone voice reverberated through her mind. *I was starting to wonder if I was gonna get to dance with the belle of the ball.*

She stopped herself. *Good grief.* Where had that flashback come from? She thought she had dispatched him to a far corner of her memory, alongside her deceased mother. It wasn't fun being reminded how desperate for his affection she had once been.

Redirecting herself to choosing clothing, she picked a cherry-red poplin skirt that hit her midknee, then searched for a coordinating top. Her tops these days consisted of mostly T-shirts. More convenient for nursing.

Snuffling cries came from down the hall, and she smiled. Her baby boy was waking up again, ready for breakfast. She went to his room, and as she approached his crib, he let out one blatant "Wah" and looked up at her with sky-blue eyes that assured her she would never be able to forget his father.

"Hiya, Joey." She cooed at him as she removed his diaper. He fretted and shook his tiny fists while she washed him and dressed him in dry clothing. Then she carried him to the rocking chair that had belonged to her paternal grandmother, the only extended family she had ever known.

The infant nuzzled at her breast, and as soon as she lifted her T-shirt and loosened her nursing bra, he latched on and settled down to eat. She relaxed and relished the connection to this tiny human who was surely the most wonderful child ever born.

"You look good, Dal. Just like always."

Dahlia froze. Her head jerked in the direction of a deep, familiar voice and her world spun off its axis. "Luke!"

Her heart hammered so hard her vision blurred. Gulping air, she braced herself against the edge of a sturdy round produce display. "Wha-what are you doing here?"

"I came to see the boy."

His family's lunatic ideas about heirs rushed at her. *Joe.* He had come for Joe, just as she had feared he might someday.

Fighting for calm, she forced herself back to her task— building a shoulder-high pyramid of apples on the round display island. An apple slipped from her grasp. She grabbed for it and her elbow struck the stack of fruit. "Oh! Ohmygod."

Like a red waterfall, a hundred costly, top-quality apples cascaded to the floor. Effort to stop them left her clawing the air. She dropped to her knees on the splintery wood floor and grabbed up the apples, throwing them back into the perforated box from which they had come.

Luke laid his hat on top of a bin of oranges and crouched to help. "I didn't mean to scare you." He grasped her wrist and stopped her hands. "You should have told me, Dal. We could have worked it out."

She looked into his face and nearly came undone. His eyes were even bluer than she remembered, a reflection pool threatening to drown her. "How did you find me?"

"Piggy. She wrote me."

"She did not. She's my best friend." Dahlia freed her wrist and returned to rescuing her investment. In front of her, as distinctive as his face, were his size-twelve, full-quill ostrich boots. They had probably cost more than today's produce shipment.

"Guess she's my friend, too." He moved crablike on the balls of his feet picking up the fallen fruit. Her stomach clenched. Upstairs in a playpen in the office, she had a live trophy to show for intimate knowledge of those long shanks and lean haunches.

Her shaking hands fumbled the last of the fruit into the box. She gripped the edge of the display island to pull herself up, but before she succeeded, he stood, slid his hand under her forearm and easily lifted her to her feet. An uninvited warmth stole through her.

Not daring to risk a second look into his face, she moved her arm from his hand—she felt safer leaning on the display island. "You shouldn't have come here."

"Shouldn't have come? You thought I wouldn't?" His voice shook with . . . what—anger, emotion?

A flash of guilt flared, but she drilled him with the coldest stare she could muster. "Actually, I hadn't thought of you at all lately, although once you took up a lot of room inside my head. Fortunately, I got over it."

His eyes made a sweep of the produce section. "Piggy says you keep him here. Where is he?" His tone would have frozen a beef carcass.

"Well, he isn't hidden under the lettuce. I'm sure he's asleep. And I don't like waking him."

The heat in his eyes told her he didn't buy that lame excuse. He stood there glowering, hands on his hips, one knee cocked. His damn John Wayne stance. How many times had she seem him do this? Thanks to him, she'd ceased watching her favorite Gary Cooper and John Wayne Westerns. She glanced around to see who might be watching and listening, then gave up. "He's upstairs. I'll take you up there."

Passing through the storeroom on the way to the stairs, Dahlia's throat felt as if she had swallowed an oversized bite of one of her premium apples. Seeing a teenage part-time helper tearing down empty boxes, she forced her voice and ordered him to sort through the spilled apples, wash them, then restack the ones that weren't too badly bruised.

She jogged up the stairs with Luke behind her. As his boots made scuffy clomps on the wooden steps, her mind raced. Piggy had written to him? Unbelievable. Still, Dahlia wouldn't put it past her. Piggy nagged her constantly about telling Luke she had given birth to his son.

By the time she reached the office door, the shock of Luke's arrival and her best friend's betrayal had metamorphosed into fury. She clenched her jaw and opened the door.

They found Joe awake in his playpen. Realizing breastfeeding would require him to be with her every day, she had borrowed the playpen from an employee and set it up with a white lamb-patterned mattress in the office.

She didn't usually leave him alone unless he was asleep, but today he had evidently awakened early. He was making baby noises and clutching at the air. His eyes brightened when he saw her and his chubby arms and legs churned. Much of her anger melted away.

Before she could say a word, Luke had laid his hat on the old gold sofa and was on his knees, his gaze roving over her baby, his arms reaching over the playpen's side and his fingers touching the tiny hands. To her dismay, an anxious part of her waited for his approval.

"He's perfect," Luke murmured, and she drew a needed breath. He looked at her across his shoulder as if waiting for her to tell him it was okay to pick the infant up. She bit her lip and said nothing.

Luke lifted him out of the playpen anyway, tucked him into the crook of his elbow and began a stream of baby talk. If she weren't so irate, she might have been amused, for it was the last thing she expected. The baby's mouth and tongue made sucking motions and he nuzzled at Luke's shirtfront.

"He—he's hungry," she managed. "And probably wet."

Luke laid him back on the playpen mattress and began to unsnap the short blue romper she had put on over the puffy diaper. It came back to her how Luke always took charge of any situation, a characteristic that had added to her sense that his presence was larger than the space around him. In Callister, she had allowed him take control of their relationship, and look where that had led her.

In a renewed gust of panic, she grabbed a clean diaper from the Pampers box on top of the filing cabinet and went to the playpen. "I'll do it."

Luke grinned up at her and took the diaper from her hand. "You think I don't know how? It's been a while since my kids were babies, but I still know how to change a diaper."

Of course he did. His son Jimmy had worn diapers until age five. Joe was in a red-faced, full-decibel squall by the time Luke finished. She carried her son to the desk chair, turned her back on his father and positioned the screaming infant at her breast. He calmed down with a great sigh and began to drink. Tears brimmed her eyelids. How could she get through this?

She didn't know what Luke was doing behind her back, but he hadn't left the room. She heard his footsteps and then felt her chair was being swiveled, turning her and Joe to face him.

"Dal," he said softly, looking into her eyes. He was so close she could see the navy blue ring outlining his blue pupils and giving his eyes their arctic look. She could smell Polo, smell his breath made minty by flavored toothpicks, smell *him*. Shaking her head, she swallowed her tears and looked away. Joe was undeterred. He clung to her breast in the football grip and suckled in contentment, unaware his mother was close to screaming.

Luke placed his finger beneath the baby's hand, barely missing her breast. The baby gripped it and hung on, a link between his father's finger and his mother's breast. Luke leaned forward and placed a long kiss on her temple.

Emotion plugged Dahlia's throat and paralyzed her vocal chords. When she could speak, she said, "I would appreciate it if you would sit on the sofa."

He stepped back as if she had punched him, his gaze intense on her and the baby.

"He'll be finished in a few minutes," she blurted, not moving her eyes from Joe's mouth and jaws, fighting to come to grips with how events had spiraled out of her control.

Luke sat down on the sofa, forearms resting on his thighs, his hands dangling between his knees. "It's six o'clock. Maybe we can go to supper somewhere."

She glanced at her desk clock. Good grief, where had the day gone? *Okay, so he's here.* He wouldn't, *couldn't* stay away from that ranch long. All she had to do was keep her wits and get through this visit without incident. "Essie's and the Dairy Queen are all there is in Loretta, and everything's fried. I guess I could fix supper at my house. I'll get something out of the freezer case downstairs."

The corners of Luke's mouth turned up in a wide grin. "Home cooking, hunh?"

Damn. His teeth were still perfect. Perfect to nip her neck, then kiss the bitten spot. Suddenly the room seemed to tilt and she felt as if she needed help to stand. "Something frozen is mostly what I cook. I'm too busy to be Betty Crocker."

"Working like you do and all, you almost don't have time to be a mother to the boy here, do you?"

His expression revealed nothing, but she took that remark to be threatening. Maybe he had a bevy of Boise lawyers waiting in the wings. "Joe is a perfectly contented baby who has all the attention he needs. Everyone dotes on him, especially me."

Joe had finished. Dahlia hooked her bra cup back in place and covered herself, then put the baby against her shoulder to burp. She nodded toward the end of the sofa where she had stashed the infant carrier. "If you want to put that on the sofa—"

Before she could finish, Luke squatted and lifted the carrier onto the sofa, then took the baby from her and positioned him in it. He brushed Joe's hair into place with his fingers. "He's got your pretty black hair. And McRae eyes."

"I suppose you can feel relieved he doesn't look Chinese."

Luke picked up the infant carrier and tucked it under his arm. "You know what, darlin'? I'm not gonna let you pick a fight with me. We hashed that race thing out a long time ago. He's a fine-looking boy. Just fine."

"I'm not your darling," she snapped, going to the door. She nodded for him to leave the office ahead of her. She locked the door and they moved down the dim stairs.

She plucked two Hungry Man meatloaf dinners from the freezer case as they passed it, then detoured by the bread rack. "White or wheat?"

"I'm not fussy. You know me."

Indeed. And the knowing had her strung tight as a banjo string. She picked up a loaf of whole-wheat bread and led the way out the plate-glass front door. The grocery store's night-lights and Loretta's three pink street-lights bathed the pocked sidewalk in front of the store in eerie amber.

"You can follow us home. Our house isn't far from Piggy's. I assume that's where you're staying."

"Nope. Gonna get a room."

"Humph. Not in Loretta. All we have is the Prairie Bed & Breakfast. They have only two rooms and they're usually full."

"Then where am I sleeping?"

"There's motels on the highway between here and Abilene. About sixty miles."

His face scrunched into a pained expression. "Did you expect *me* to put you up?"

"I don't know what I expected. This isn't the easiest place to get to. I left home at four o'clock this morning. I drove three hours to Boise, rode on two airplanes, then drove two hundred more miles in this roller skate. I'd just like to get a bite to eat and stretch out a little."

Dahlia thought frustration might strangle her. She swerved a look to the pay phone mounted on the wall outside the Handy Pantry. "I'll call the Prairie B & B. Maybe you'll get lucky."

A call to the bed-and-breakfast yielded zilch. She looked at his rental car, a Taurus. Sleeping in it would serve him right. She returned to where he waited on the sidewalk. "They're full."

He shrugged and she could see the weariness on his face. A déjà vu feeling nearly smothered her. She remembered the look from last summer, after he had worked a long day, then made the hour-and-a-half drive into town from the Double Deuce just to visit her.

"Abilene it is, I guess." He turned and opened the car door.

Damn. She had never been a mean person and she couldn't be mean to him, though a cranky old hen that had popped into her head thought he deserved it. She closed her eyes and pinched the bridge of her nose. "We've got an extra room, but you'll have to make do with a regular-sized bed."

Chapter 24

Dahlia clicked on a Winnie the Pooh lamp, and soft light filled Joe's room. Luke laid the infant in his crib, then stood there watching him, his solemn silence as unnerving as any words.

Dahlia watched, too, chewing on the inside of her lower lip. When Luke stepped back at last, his hat collided with a Pooh and Friends mobile hanging from the ceiling.

She went to the crib, removed the baby's lightweight blanket and straightened his clothing, but didn't undress him. She kissed his cheek, then looked up at Luke. "It's too hot for covers." As soon as she said it, she berated herself for having felt the need to explain her action. Joe heaved a baby sigh and continued to sleep.

After the brush with the mobile, Luke had removed his hat. It hung on his fingers in front of him. "It's sure 'nuff hot, all right."

She nodded at his arm. "One thing I do *not* recommend is a starched, long-sleeved shirt in a Texas August."

His gaze shifted from one sleeve to the other. "This is all I've got with me. I'll get along."

She had forgotten how unaffected he was by circumstances he saw as not worth worrying about. If a long-sleeved shirt was all he had to wear and the temperature melted a thermometer, he would endure without complaint.

"Whatever," she said. *Just go ahead and suffer.* "Come on. I'll heat the food."

The scrape of his leather-soled boots behind her in the hallway emphasized the age of the turn-of-the-century house's linoleum floor, which had been laid during her childhood. She remembered the shining oak floors in the Double Deuce ranch house and wished she had spent the money to have the outdated linoleum replaced with new vinyl. What if Luke thought she couldn't afford to provide a decent home for Joe?

They passed through the living room on the way to the kitchen, and she directed him to lay his hat on the sofa arm. At the kitchen counter, she pulled the two frozen dinners from the plastic sack. "Do you want one or both of these?"

Luke looked at the boxes with a puzzled expression. "One's okay, I guess. What do *you* think?"

She shrugged. "I can always heat the other later if you want it."

As she tore one open and slid it into the microwave, she suspected he may never before have eaten a TV dinner. She was reminded, as she had been often in Callister, how little she knew of the way her son's father lived his daily life.

She moved to the refrigerator and stood with its door open, perusing the sparse contents—a jar of apple juice, a shelf of fresh fruits and vegetables, a plate of sliced boiled chicken.

Luke joined her and peered over her shoulder. "For somebody in the grocery business, you sure don't have much to eat in there."

His hand came to rest on her hip as if it had a right to be there. She lifted it, dropped it and stepped sideways, then pulled out the plate of chicken slices covered with plastic wrap. "Do you want some chicken? I boiled this last night."

She thought he repressed a grimace. The pallid slices on the white plate didn't look particularly appetizing, but these days, sustenance was all she sought from food. How it looked made little difference.

"Boiled, huh? Guess you don't have any beef."

"Chicken's better for you."

He gave her a lopsided grin. "Whatever you say. I'm so hungry right now, I could eat the feathers."

While Luke's TV dinner turned in the microwave, she made a green salad, then for herself, built a thick chicken sandwich with tomato slices, lettuce and avocado. She placed small bunches of white grapes on each plate. "Fruits and vegetables are what I eat. With nursing, I'm cautious about my diet."

She filled two huge glasses with ice cubes and lifted the jar of apple juice off the refrigerator shelf.

"Apple juice?" Luke asked.

"I don't have anything else but water. I don't drink anything with caffeine."

"Apple juice is just fine. Water down here tastes like shit."

She rolled her eyes at the coarse comment, but at the same time, appreciated that to someone whose drinking water came from a mountain spring, the heavily mineralized water of West Texas probably wasn't pleasant. They ate in silence except for her grandmother's mantel clock ticking in a monotonous cadence from the top of the TV set in the living room.

Luke wolfed down the TV dinner and several slices of chicken covered with salsa. She hadn't eaten a bite since a light lunch, but her stomach felt as if a rock nested in it. She nibbled at her sandwich, finally picked it apart with her fingers and ate only the vegetables. "Would you like my chicken?"

"Well, I *am* still a little hungry. They don't feed you that good on airplanes anymore, even in first-class."

A dart of anger flew through her as she thought of the cost of first-class plane tickets. "First-class? You flew down here first-class?"

His eyes widened in a defensive expression. "I always fly first-class. Those seats in the back are too cramped up."

"Well, how nice." Had she lost her mind? Why should it annoy her for him or anyone to fly first-class? She rebuilt her sandwich sans the vegetables, slid her plate to him and sat back in her chair, hugging her elbows and hoping his first-class ticket had a short time limit.

"Piggy said your dad passed on." Luke appeared to be studying his plate as if it required concentration, treading lightly, no doubt after her caustic comment. "Said he meant a lot to you."

"He's . . . He *was* the only person who was always there when I needed someone."

Luke raised his eyes to hers. For several seconds their gazes held. "He's why you left town in such a hurry, isn't he?"

Memories of the devastating day before she departed Callister came hurtling back—learning of Dad's collapse, followed by Luke— She shook her head to clear it. "He had a stroke."

"I thought you left because . . . Well, I figured you were so pissed off when I put a stall on things you just hit the road."

"It's water under the bridge. Things have worked out for the best."

He exhaled a tight breath, obviously searching for a follow-up. "I know all about sick folks. I could have bought a herd of new bulls with what I spent on doctors in the last year."

"Who's been sick?" She scolded herself for asking. She didn't care, so what difference would knowing make?

"They finally said Mom's got MS. She's not old enough for Medicare. We've got insurance, but it doesn't pay the bills all that good."

Claire McRae's effort to rise from the sofa that horrible night in Luke's cabin came back, but Dahlia refused to offer words of sympathy. "MS?"

"She's walking with a cane now. Her and Dad both."

"I assume your kids are okay."

"They're just fine." He reached back for his wallet, removed three pictures and handed them across the table. "I got settled up with Janet. The girls live at the ranch for good now. I told you I'd get things straightened out."

Dahlia didn't look up, unwilling to face another you-didn't-give-me-a-chance glare.

"They're pretty girls," he said. "Look like their mother."

Dahlia stared at the photographs of Luke's daughters. Never having seen even a picture of their mother, she couldn't confirm or deny a resemblance, but his daughters had *his* stark blue eyes.

Just as it appeared Joe would.

Dear God. Her baby's half sisters. The realization was as shocking as a slap.

Her gaze lingered on the third photo that had come out of the wallet. "And how's Jimmy?"

Luke's eyes settled on the picture, too, and she saw a glimmer of sadness. "He's still in that school in Boise. They tested him a few months ago. They say he's about as good as he's ever gonna get. He'll always need supervision, but he's learning to be independent, taking on a little responsibility."

Dal-la. Jimmy, with his limited abilities, had pronounced her name in two broken syllables. She almost blubbered again. "His health's okay, then. I mean, the heart condition . . ."

Luke shrugged. "About the same."

Recalling Jimmy's life expectancy had been placed somewhere around twenty and thinking of Joe, healthy as a horse and normal, aroused a queer feeling of guilt. The air conditioner clicked on, scattering chill bumps down her bare arms. Then again, maybe it wasn't the cool air at all. She handed the photographs back to him and rubbed her palms up and down her arms. "I'm sorry about that, Luke. I truly am."

"Nothing for *you* to be sorry about. It's none of *your* doing." He slipped the pictures back into the wallet sleeves.

"But I remember him. He's such a sweet little boy."

Luke made a circle on the tabletop with the wet bottom of his glass, then looked up and smiled. "Boy, you should see him now. He's getting tall. Seems like he's grown a foot in just a year. I stopped off to see him on my way to the airport this morning. He read me a story."

"That's good, he's learning to read, right?"

"Yeah, it is. We didn't know if he ever would."

"And—and your father? You said he's crippled?"

"Got pinned to the fence during branding. Banged him up pretty good. Broke his leg and some ribs. He's still not over it." Luke leaned back in his chair and sighed, a man resigned to the burdens he carried, had always carried, alone. "He's different. Doesn't care much about anything anymore. He mostly takes care of small details that aren't too complicated. Don't know what I'd do without Mom. She's always been the strong one. 'Course, now that she's sick—"

"How long are you planning to visit?" Dahlia interrupted. Luke and his problems. If she listened, she might care.

"Can't stay long. Bad time of year." Another punishing silence passed while the air conditioner blew and the clock on top of the TV ticked.

"We've made a good cross in that boy, Dahlia. DAM Ranches is his legacy. Just as it became mine when Matt—" He paused, holding her gaze. "Bring the baby and come back with me."

What? She had no name for the emotion that pushed a primal part of her to remember where she had stashed her suitcase. She shunned the traitorous urge. His seductive voice had already coaxed her into thorny territory and the fifteen-pound result was sleeping down the hall. Besides, this was the man who thought he had all the kids he wanted or needed. "You can't be serious."

"I am."

"Perhaps you should have called first. You've made the trip for nothing."

"I'm the father of your son. I'm not denying it for a minute. We're a family."

"You didn't feel that way last summer."

"You don't know how I might have felt."

"You're right. You never told me."

Bewilderment spread over his face, as if he couldn't believe she could be so dense. "I figured you knew. I didn't think I *had* to tell you."

Her jaw went slack. She splayed her hand across her chest as tears burned her eyes again. "My God, how could I have known? You broke up with me. Sent me packing."

"No. I told you we oughtta cool it. I had problems to deal with. But *you* didn't even let me know why you left town in such a hurry. Didn't say a word about your dad."

Her defenses sprang up. She had a vivid memory of the scene in that parking lot, had tortured herself with his fatal words a thousand times. She *wasn't* the bad guy here. Was she? She glowered across the table. "As a matter of fact, Luke, what you *told* me, numerous times I might add, was you didn't want any more kids."

"That weekend at the ranch, when we went to the hot springs, when Mom . . . That's when we got him, wasn't it?"

Dahlia closed her eyes. Her throat had filled with such a huge bubble she couldn't speak.

"*Wasn't* it?"

She fumbled for her napkin to dab the damn tears she couldn't seem to stop.

Luke shook his head. "How could you think I didn't care? If there's anything I know, Dahlia, it's how babies are made. We took chances. You *know* I wouldn't have done that with just any woman."

She stared him, blinking. Then why had he ended their relationship? Why hadn't he gotten in touch with her, given her the tiniest indication he cared about her? If he had, everything now might be so different. "I'll bet," she said coldly.

He pushed his chair back and stood, his fists jammed against his hips. His head lowered and he appeared to be studying the faded blue floral pattern on the worn linoleum floor. "I was afraid this was gonna be hard."

She could take no more. She sprang to her feet and planted her palms on the table. Her chair tipped over backward and banged the floor. "Hard! Don't tell *me* about hard! Hard is taking over a small business that's floundering, single-handedly dragging it up from bankruptcy. Hard is burying your only living relative when you're seven months' pregnant."

She reached across the table for his plate and silverware and stacked them on top of hers with clattering jerks. "Hard is giving birth alone and taking care of an infant whose father didn't want you. Do you have any idea what it was like for me, coming back here pregnant and dumped by the man who made me that way? Facing the sniggers and snide remarks of the customers, people who have known me and my dad all our lives?"

She stamped toward the sink, carrying the stack of soiled dishes. "I couldn't even go to another town to hide my embarrassment. Dad was too sick!"

She dumped the dishes into the sink, grateful it was stainless steel and not likely to break the plates. "Just because the rest of the world accepts unwed mothers as normal doesn't mean Loretta, Texas, does. This is the Bible Belt. They prayed for me at the Baptist church, for chrissake."

Luke bent and picked up the tipped-over chair, but she strode to it, yanked it from his hands and reset it with a clunk. "Our neighbor even asked me point-blank if I knew who my baby's father was. I'm my dad's only child. And I"—she shot him a pointed glare—"*we* humiliated him."

Good God, I'm raving.

She went back to the sink and turned on the faucet full stream, squirted in dish-washing soap. Her eyes stung, but she would not cry again. She had already shed a bucket of tears for Luke McRae.

"You chose your own path, Dahlia. All you had to do was pick up the phone. I would've been here like *that*."

She heard the snap of his fingers, but didn't turn to face him. "I don't believe you."

She braced for a verbal assault. What came instead was a soft voice. "I can see I shouldn't have barged in on you. I'm much obliged for supper."

She heard his footsteps as he went to the sofa, pictured him putting on his hat. The front door slammed as she reached for the dishrag.

Luke had never been lost in his life and he wasn't now, though he didn't know where he was going. He drove back to town and parked in front of the Handy Pantry.

He was shaken. Dahlia's words had torn through him like a dull knife. He could imagine too well what she had faced in a small town that didn't look much different from Callister. He felt bad about his own contribution to the stress on her dying father. But a greater worry gnawed at a place deep within. Had he been such an ass he made her think he would reject his own kid? Or her? Evidently he had, because any fool could see that was what she thought.

He guessed he shouldn't have come down here assuming so much without laying some groundwork or finding out first how she felt, shouldn't have been so abrupt stating what *he* wanted. But he couldn't have stopped himself. After seeing Joe, then her, the year since the Forest Service parking lot melted away like fog in sunshine. He had been filled with an uncontrollable yearning to sweep them up and carry them away.

A wave of fatigue prompted him to dig into his pocket for his watch. Nearly midnight. He sighed. He sorely didn't want to drive another sixty miles to rent a room—not that he wouldn't do it—but a trip back and forth used up time, something he had in a limited amount.

Piggy and Bill had offered him a bed, told him to come back regardless of the hour. He had no trouble finding their house a few blocks from town. Its windows were dark, but a porch light shone, so he rang the doorbell.

Chapter 25

Six o'clock. Dahlia had overslept by an hour. But that was a small problem compared to the one she saw in her vanity mirror. Her pupils looked like olives caught in red cobwebs and they had a right to. Last night after Luke's departure, she had cried through washing supper dishes, then slept little as resentment and memories pushed and pulled inside her.

Leaning closer to the mirror, she examined the darkened pouches under each eye. She hadn't looked this bad since her last encounter with Luke.

While she brushed on blush, she wondered if he had slept at Piggy's. Last night's outburst that sent him running from her kitchen had been extreme, but she didn't regret blowing up or that he left. He had touched all her most private places, emotional as well as physical. Having him sleep in her house was a torment she didn't want to endure.

She nursed and bathed Joe, then left him to play in his crib while she dressed. For comfort in what would be a hundred-degree day, she put on a yellow cotton T-shirt, a denim skirt and tan sandals. Lacking the time or patience for the hairstyling process, she brushed back her hair and clasped it with a leather barrette at her nape. She had just hooked silver and turquoise drops into her ears when she heard a knock at the front door.

Luke, looking cool and well rested.

He was wearing his usual Wranglers, starched and creased. A pale yellow button-down with white pinstripes looked delicious with his ruddy coloring and cinnamon hair. A familiar frisson passed down her spine. The pesky question of where he had spent last night wouldn't leave her alone. In Loretta, beds where a man like him would be welcome were aplenty.

He asked if she intended to invite him in or make him stand out on the porch. She stood aside and allowed him into the house, then followed as he sauntered up the hall toward Joe's room.

Her baby boy was in a jovial mood and googled when Luke spoke to him. Luke picked him up and held him, and Joe squealed and lapped up the attention. Soon he returned the baby to the crib, then straightened and faced her. "I was hoping we could talk, Dal. I don't have much time—"

"Nothing new about *that,* is there? I don't have much time, either, so why inconvenience both of us?"

"You afraid to talk to me?"

She stared at him bug-eyed. She had always been willing to talk. He had been the one with nothing to say.

"Crap," she mumbled, tramping toward the kitchen. She went to the wall phone and keyed in the Handy Pantry's number. When Chuck Moore came on the line, she told him she would be late. Then she snatched a banana from a fruit bowl on the counter.

Luke was standing a few feet away, which was too close. She moved to the opposite side of the square kitchen, braced her hip against the sink's edge and began peeling her banana. "We spent four months eating, drinking and sleeping together and we didn't talk." She bit down hard on the soft fruit, chewed as if it were caramel and swallowed with a gulp. "So now that we're two thousand miles apart, we're going to start up a dialogue? Why bother? You're off the hook."

She finished the fruit, opened the cupboard door underneath the sink and threw the peel in the trash. "I take responsibility for getting pregnant. And I accept that you can't help it your family and your ranch came before me."

"It wasn't like that." His head bowed and he appeared to be studying the toes of his boots. "Well . . . maybe it was. A little." After a pause, he looked up at her. "But I know now last summer was special. And I didn't treat it like it was. I guess I was hoping you might still feel a little something."

She saw a look in his eyes she couldn't remember ever having seen. Like air leaving a punctured tire, the desire to make the pious speech she had rehearsed countless times fizzled into a sigh. "It was a hundred years ago, Luke."

A frown creased his brow. "Look, I'm not gonna make a pest of myself and I'm not gonna beg you. Maybe it's *not* like it used to be, but if you still care just a little bit, well . . . I mean, since we've already got the kid and all—and he can't help it 'cause he's here—wouldn't it be worth it to give him the best shot we can give him?"

"Such as?"

Luke spread his open hands. "Two parents?"

What was he suggesting—some kind of bizarre living arrangement? Last night she had dismissed a similar remark as a reflex to his seeing his son for the first time. But he had slept on it since then. She crossed her arms under her breasts. "He has two parents who happen to live in two different places. And, I might add, who function on two different wavelengths."

Luke crossed his arms, too. "You didn't used to be so closeminded. If we can't work things out between *us,* I guess we oughtta try to work something out about Joe."

"There's nothing to work out. You have no rights where Joe's concerned."

She hoped her bogus confidence in that remark didn't show. In truth, she didn't know his rights. Consulting a lawyer was another of those things she had meant to do but never made time.

"It may disappoint you, darlin', but you're wrong about that."

The kitchen suddenly felt as chilled as a meat locker. If anybody knew his legal parental rights, Luke did. He *would* fight her, just as she had feared all along.

"I'm not blind," he said. "I can see things are hard for you. When I get back to Callister, I intend to get with our lawyer. Draw up support papers. I was hoping—"

"Don't you dare throw money at me."

"Then what *do* you want?"

She stared at him, stumped. Last summer, she thought she knew. Now here it stood right in front of her, all dressed up in cowboy garb, and she was confused and upset and unprepared for the way her heart and mind were dueling. "Well, one thing I *didn't* want was for you to drop out of the sky."

"Okay, I'll tell you what *I* want. And that's for my son to be in my life and my family's."

She might not know what she wanted, but she knew this much—Luke and the McRae clan weren't going to travel between Idaho and Texas to be around Joe. "What did you have in mind? Shuttling him back and forth on an airplane every other weekend, like luggage? Maybe we could ship him UPS." All her maternal instincts to protect amplified. Her head began to shake back and forth. "Nuh-unh. No. No. Nada. My little boy isn't going *anywhere* without me."

"Fine. Then you come with him."

"Not a chance. My life and his are in Loretta, Texas."

Luke pushed away from the counter, his fists on his hips, his eyes hot as lasers. "So what're you gonna do? Turn him into some kind of a damn store clerk?"

We look like gunfighters, she thought, facing each other across the kitchen. "Are you demeaning what I do? My grocery business may not be as glamorous as your cattle ranch, but it makes our living."

Luke's palms raised in surrender. "I shouldn't have said that. I just meant—"

"I agree. You shouldn't have said it. But we both know you meant it. I don't have time to argue. People are waiting for me."

"Where you taking the boy?"

"Stop calling him 'the boy.' He goes with me. He nurses several times a day."

"I'll come, too. Help you take care of him."

Dahlia huffed out an exaggerated breath. *Damn you, Piggy.*

At the grocery store, while she went about her tasks, Luke played with Joe and changed his diapers, read to him from Dr. Seuss, making odd animal noises for each character. When Joe became hungry and fussy, Luke watched intently as Joe nursed, then stunned her by saying he had seen plenty of calves and colts suck, but never a baby. Janet hadn't breast-fed any of their kids. When Joe drifted off to sleep, Luke lifted him from her arms and tucked him into the playpen.

No way did she intend to be confined alone in the small space with a man who made her question every thought she had. "You may as well see the store," she told him.

He trailed behind her as she took him on a tour of the grocery store, including her pride and joy, the butcher shop, and as they went, she couldn't keep from wondering when he had been in a grocery store for thirty minutes, let alone all day. He made dutiful comments like, "That's real good," and "That's real nice," and "You do a real good job."

He couldn't have cared less, she suspected. A small-town, mom-and-pop grocery store was indeed small potatoes compared to a ninety-thousand-acre working ranch. She wanted to smack her forehead in frustration. Or better yet, smack him. "Not that you're really interested, but I do, in fact, do a real good job. And I like it."

The presence of a ruggedly good-looking cowboy who obviously wasn't struggling to make his truck payments was a huge distraction to the female employees. They blushed and giggled if he went near them. And why not? Hadn't she once behaved the same way? She overheard even the male employees prattling about the observable fact that Luke was her son's father.

At lunchtime, Luke walked down the street to Essie's Café to pick up sandwiches. As soon as he left, one of the cashiers approached her and asked if he was a model. "Yeah," Dahlia growled, "he's the Marlboro Man."

Near the day's end, instructing the teenager in her butcher training program, she sliced her finger on a sharp blade. As she taped on a Band-Aid. Luke asked if he could help her. "Yes," she said, "you go back to *your* home and I'll go to mine."

She gathered Joe and his stuff and didn't try to prevent Luke from helping her load them into her Lumina.

Leaving Luke standing in the parking lot as she drove away, she watched him in her rearview mirror, their last parking-lot meeting still as vivid in her memory as if it had happened yesterday and ugly as the grasshopper that had splattered on her windshield. She could see him watching her, too, his hat tipped back and posed in his damn John Wayne stance. She felt something turn over inside her. He was just so, so . . . so friggin' *macho*. . . .

That evening, after Joe's bedtime feeding, she held the baby close for a long time, recapping the day.

Fine. You come with him. How *could* she believe Luke wanted *her*? He pursued his goals with a vengeance. If he had really wanted *her* last summer, wild horses couldn't have stood in his way. Knowing him that well was what had made his breaking up with her so painful, a thorn that pricked her anew every time she thought of him.

No, it was Joe, only Joe, that Luke *wanted*. Maybe last summer he said he didn't want more children, but now that he had another one, possessiveness took over. It wasn't an uncommon phenomenon.

And what would she do if he tried to take Joe or sued for equal custody or did something else bizarre? Where would she find the money to fight him?

It was foolish to treat him coldly and risk angering him, she concluded—like poking a sleeping dragon with a stick. Or to be uncooperative when he wanted to do something good for Joe, and indirectly, for her. Even a patient man had his limits. Hadn't what he had done to his ex-wife proved it?

She would be kinder, she decided, and friendlier.

And again, she wondered where he might be sleeping.

"You have a manager, so you don't have to be at that store every day. I hope you, Joe and I can spend the day together."

For the second day in a row, Luke was on her front porch at a ridiculous hour of the morning.

"It's hot and it's really difficult taking a baby—"

"I know all about that. I'll help you. We can drive over to that bigger town, have a nice dinner, maybe go to a movie. C'mon. You owe me that much. I won't take no for an answer."

Dahlia knew the latter statement to be true. She gave in and changed into loose khaki shorts, a red T-shirt and Nikes, bunched her hair and clipped it at her crown. When she appeared in the living room, Luke told her she still looked as pretty in red as she had the first time.

He said he wanted to buy a cap, so they stopped by the Handy Pantry. A bill cap embroidered with DALLAS COWBOYS was all the store had to offer. Near one cash register sat a rack of short-sleeved T-shirts also imprinted with the football team logo. She pulled a size XXX off a hanger. A quick frown crossed Luke's brow when she handed the hat and shirt to him. Knowing he had almost no interest in football, she gave him a bland look and shrugged. "You may as well be comfortable."

"They'll do." He flashed her a heart-stopping smile, reached back for his wallet and offered the cashier two twenties.

Dahlia pushed away his hand. "It's a gift. I don't think I've ever given you anything."

He looked at her intently. "You're wrong about that."

She felt her cheeks grow warm and swung a quick glance at the cashier. Dahlia could almost see antennae shoot up from the young woman's head. By nightfall, a dozen tales about her and this tall stranger would be circulating around Loretta.

In the parking lot behind the store, while Luke changed from his long-sleeved shirt to the T-shirt, she glued her gaze to the dash. If there was anything she didn't need in her fragile emotional state, it was seeing his sculpted torso without a shirt.

As soon as they were underway, Joe dropped off to sleep and she did, too. When she awoke, Luke reached across the console and patted her thigh. She shifted her knees to the right, away from his possessive pats.

How odd, she thought, as she watched the landscape fly by. Last summer in Callister, she wouldn't have dreamed of evading his touch or of dropping off to sleep while he drove. Back then, his displays of affection and savoring every waking moment with him had been the epitome of bliss.

She suggested they eat before the movie and directed him to a steak house near the mall. A hostess led them to seats in a booth with room to park an infant carrier. They ordered and the waitress bustled away, leaving silence. Even Joe, who appeared to be fascinated by the overhead lights, added nothing to fill the void.

This is going to last all day, she thought, *so we might as well be comrades.* She was determined to stick to last night's resolution to be friendlier. "So what happened to Lee Ann?"

She squeezed a lime slice into her glass of ice water, feigning nonchalance about the Callister woman who had been her nemesis. "I assume you went back to seeing her after I left. I'm a little surprised you didn't go ahead and marry her, given your mother's feelings."

"She married somebody else. Moved to Oregon."

Dahlia's heart went *ka-thunk.* "How sad for your mother."

The waitress came with their meal and Dahlia occupied herself cutting her steak into smaller-than-necessary pieces.

"Dal, I never—I haven't been with anybody since you left." An urgency in his tone made her stop and look up. He was looking at her with that concentrated gaze she knew indicated his sincerity.

"Well"—she cleared the lump that had swelled in her throat—"I'm sure you'll find someone. Old girlfriends are easy enough to replace."

He put down the roll and leaned back with a sigh. "I don't want to replace you. I couldn't replace what we had. I think about it a lot. You remember how it was . . ."

That did it. Tears bunched in the corners of her eyes. Damn. She had become a waterfall since he showed up. She snatched up her napkin and attempted to salvage her eye makeup.

"I don't mean to make you cry, but I don't have much time to get the things said that I want to."

"I'm not crying," she snapped. "Please. We're in a restaurant. Let's just get this, this . . . *trip* over with."

"Okay. But I gotta ask one more question, Dal."

"What is it?"

"How about you?"

"How about me what?"

"You making it with anybody?"

Blood rushed to her face. She looked down at her lap. *Tell him it's none of his damn business. Tell him now.* "Don't be ridiculous," she said to her steak.

When she looked up, his face held a sparkling-eyed, white-toothed grin. Oh, God. If only she could hate him. She had called him every gutter name she knew. She had cursed him in the night, wished evil upon his house and his mother's head, but as she looked into eyes that matched her son's, she couldn't deny that a weak-willed part of her was doomed to always love him.

Joe stretched and sighed in the car seat strapped in the backseat. Luke watched him through the rearview mirror. "Our boy was good," he said.

Dahlia didn't reply. An irrational jealousy flew through her when he made proprietary remarks about Joe. She hadn't thought of her son in terms of "ours"; he was "mine."

Twilight softened the air around them to deep blue as they motored toward Loretta. Joe *had* been good on his first trip to the movies. She'd had doubts they would be allowed into the theatre with an infant, but admission to a weekday matinee had been no problem. She fed him as soon as they were seated and he slept through the whole movie. She made a mental note to write the event in his baby book.

They rode for miles in silence. Luke appeared to be lost in his thoughts. She wouldn't attempt to guess what they might be.

"When's his birthday?"

The question snapped her to attention. "What?"

"His birthday—when is it?"

"May fifteenth."

"Hey, *my* birthday's the tenth. He didn't miss it by too far." He laughed, a deep huh-huh.

She cut him a sidewise glance. "I know."

"What's his whole name? Nobody's ever told me."

"Joseph. After my dad's middle name."

"What's his middle name?"

"Lucas," she said, her voice almost a whisper.

"Lucas?" His head turned toward her. "That's *my* name."

"I would have named him after my mother, but her maiden name was De la Fuente." She crossed her arms and looked out the window.

"If you named him after me, I guess you weren't too mad when he was born. How long were you in labor?"

Joe's birth came back to her—the hours of excruciating pain, Piggy's mom holding her hand and telling her to breathe. Piggy wisecracking and popping in and out of the room like a jack-in-the-box until the pains got serious, at which point she disappeared altogether. And the overwhelming swell of love in her chest at the first look at her little boy. "Long enough."

"Guess things went okay?"

"We survived."

"Guess somebody was with you . . ."

"Piggy. And her mom." Dahlia kept her gaze glued to the landscape. Seconds turned to a minute.

"Sure wish I would've known."

"Be glad you missed it. It hurt like hell. He weighed nine pounds and I wasn't exactly stoic."

"If I'd known, maybe you would've been with *me,* where you should've been."

And maybe Claire McRae would send her a congratulations card. "I doubt it. Just how would you have dealt with your mother? Somehow I can't see you muzzling her and chaining her to a tree."

"It could have been handled—"

"We're going over old news here. I did you a favor."

"Mom's not as mean as you think, Dal. I hope someday you'll be able to forgive her."

"Not likely. She ruined my—" Dahlia almost said *my life,* but her life wasn't ruined. In reality, it was better. The past year had made her lean and mean. She felt like an adult in control—or at least she *had* felt that way until Luke came to town. And she wouldn't trade Joe for anything. "It wasn't just her. *You* didn't stand up for me. I'll never forget that."

"That's not true. Maybe I didn't do it the way you would have liked, but—" He let out a long breath. "Guess I hope you can forgive me, too."

She hesitated and pulled at an earring, softening inside. Had she already forgiven him without admitting it to herself? Put to the question, she couldn't think of another man she would rather see as the father of her child—including the one with whom she had lived as a wife. She had even begun to rehearse what positive things she might someday tell Joe about his father. "I don't hate her, okay? . . . And I can't hate you. You gave me Joe. There have been times when he was all I had to look forward to."

"Guess that's better than a snakebite. I wouldn't like to think about you hating me, Dal."

"Why are we having this conversation? It goes nowhere."

"What's the rest of his name? Is he a Montgomery? Or is he a . . . McRae?"

She couldn't answer.

"Is my name on his birth certificate, Dahlia?"

She stalled until she could speak in a strong voice. "Of course it is. You think I'd put 'father unknown'? . . . But his name is Montgomery."

He placed his hand on her thigh. She moved it and concentrated on the landscape whisking by the window.

Damn. Life was getting complicated again.

Chapter 26

After the heavy lunch Dahlia and Luke had eaten, they settled on a milk shake for dinner and reached Loretta at nine. She put a blanket on the living-room floor and laid Joe on it. She wanted to keep him awake until eleven. She and Luke cuddled and played with him. He even rolled from his back to his stomach once and Luke laughed and bragged on him.

The display of fatherly pride sent a little ping through her heart, and she couldn't block out images of the future, of Joe with Luke as the baby grew into being a little boy.

Dahlia bathed and fed him and Luke watched, letting Joe hang on to his finger, linking the three of them. The profundity of that made her brain hurt, so she tried to make a mental plan for tomorrow.

"How long before you'll have to feed him again?"

"He's sleeping longer now. Sometimes he'll last three hours. For a while he was eating every two hours."

When she put the sleeping baby in his crib, Luke stood so close behind her she could feel his heat, and a shiver traveled through her. She stepped away.

"Let's go outside," he said. "We haven't had a chance to talk, and I can't get used to this blowing air."

The porch's old, wooden floorboards felt spongy underfoot as they stepped out the front door. Veranda style, it spanned the front of the seventy-year-old house that had seen better days. Dad hadn't been able to make home repairs after his first stroke, and money had been so tight, except for emergencies, she dared not spend it hiring work done to the house.

Luke seated himself on the rickety wooden swing hanging by chains on one end of the porch. He dug out his pocketknife and began to manicure his fingernails, something she had seen him do countless times. Cricket sounds reverberated in the hot, still night. She reached back inside the front door and switched off the porch light, defending them against flying bugs.

She eased down to sit on the top step, leaving him to her back, seeking safety from the emotion the day had aroused. In the corner of the yard, moonlight cast the old, gigantic oak tree in a silvery nimbus. "Full moon," she said.

"Yep."

Feeling the weight of his eyes on her back, she toyed with her fingers. "It would be cooler if we got some rain." An old saying she had heard all her life popped up: *People who have nothing else to discuss talk about the weather.*

"Never gets this hot in the mountains," he said at last.

"I remember."

More silence. She wrapped her arms around her shins and smiled, thinking of how trouble free Joe had been all day.

"Your dad was sick a long time, huh?"

"He had the first stroke while I was in Callister, then the fatal one a couple of months before Joe was born. But I'm sure he was sick long before I knew it."

"We never talked much about your family."

"We never *talked* about anything. We were too busy— well, you know what we were doing."

He chuckled. His teeth showed white in the moonlight.

She jerked her gaze back toward the night. "You can stop laughing."

"Not laughing. I wouldn't make light of what we had, especially after seeing what we got."

"I always knew what we had, but you—" She stopped herself. She had already made the point. Why belabor it?

"Sometimes a man's choices are all hard ones, Dahlia. And sometimes what seems right one minute looks different a few minutes later. . . . After that speech I made in the Forest Service parking lot that day, I turned around and went back to town, but you weren't home. You weren't at the laundry, either."

Something inside Dahlia went still. In all the times she had relived the brutal parking-lot breakup, not once had she considered he might have come back. "Hunh. Fate must not have been on our side. I was upset. I took a drive."

He dropped to sit on the porch floor a step above her. His denim-covered thigh touched her bare arm. His boots came to rest on the ragged concrete step beside her. "I knew I hurt your feelings, but at the time, I couldn't see what else to do."

She twisted from the waist and stared up at him. His face was shiny with perspiration, his expression grave. "Let me get this straight. You made a conscious choice to hurt my feelings instead of doing something else?"

"When you put it that way, I guess I did. It's hard to explain, but Janet was an outsider. Me marrying her and bringing her to the Double Deuce, then all that happened afterward, caused a lot of pain in my family. I decided it was better to hurt you and me than to hurt them any more. I'm not saying it was right."

Dahlia huffed and looked out into the night again. Outsider. She hadn't heard that word since coming back from Callister.

"I was spread pretty thin last summer. Mom being sick and nobody knowing what was wrong with her had everybody wondering what would happen next. Then Janet—well, my kids' futures were on the line, Dal. The problems were like a sore that wouldn't heal. I had to fix things once and for all."

"So the solution was to give up *us*"—she snapped her fingers—"just like that?"

"It wasn't that simple or that easy to do. I didn't *want* to give us up. After that night when Mom walked in, Janet went after my ass. Things got real mean before they ended."

"Sorry, Luke. I'm not convinced." But Dahlia understood more than she would ever admit to him. She knew his rigid sense of responsibility, knew that with soldierly ardor, he was capable of ignoring his heart to do what he saw as his duty. It was chilling.

"It's not just people that depend on me, you know. You live here in the middle of cow country. You know what a rancher's life is like. I *had* to get ready for winter. When the snow's six feet deep and it's thirty below, those poor old cows and horses don't give a damn if Luke McRae wanted to go a'courting instead of putting up hay."

"Our relationship was more than courting. If you had wanted, if I had been important, you could have gotten in touch with me. I didn't hear a word from you. Not one word."

"I tried. Not as hard as I should've, maybe. I didn't hear from you, either. Do you think it's right that you— well, no point going there."

She heard him sigh again, sensed he had leaned back on the porch. Having this conversation without looking him in the face felt awkward, but it was easier by far.

"At first," he said, "I figured I'd try to patch things up after the judge made the custody decision, but it kept dragging from one hearing to another. Then we had to get calves to the sale, and getting the girls settled down was rougher than I expected. The holidays were real hard on them and—"

Dahlia interrupted with a humorless chuckle. Was Luke the Stoic groveling? "There's no end to it, is there? The saga of Luke McRae and his kids and cows."

"Those kids needed all I had to give. Mary Claire felt responsible to take care of her mother. She ran off and went back to Boise twice. The last time, when I went to get her, I found her nursing Janet out of one of her binges. A guitar player with earrings stuck all over was all my Mary had for help. She's a good little trooper, but she's having a time of it, even now."

"So you rescued your daughters from the jaws of alcoholic hell and have sole custody now. Does their mother see them?"

"Only if I let her. And only if she's sober."

So he had backed his ex-wife into a corner. Dahlia had never thought of him as being mean-spirited, but he was as tough as bullhide and ruthless when he thought it necessary. Didn't she know from firsthand experience? She felt a need to jockey for position. "I can't imagine anything that would make me give up Joe."

"No reason why you should. You're not a drunk."

Her fists clenched. "And I'm not rich, either. But don't think for a minute I wouldn't find a way—"

"Whoa. Just hold it. I'm not somebody you've got to fight."

"I'm not fighting. Just understand, I won't be steamrollered by you."

He mumbled an expletive. "Okay. I guess I've said my piece. I was hoping you might see it as reasons instead of excuses. Guess not, huh?"

Her anger at him was dangerously close to subsiding. His thigh touching her arm had become too comfortable, and perspiration had her clothing sticking to her body. "Well," she said, pushing herself to her feet, "I think we've beat this subject to death." Wanting to appear unaffected, she looked across the yard at the oak tree. "I fell behind today, so I'll have to run twice as fast tomorrow."

"Dahlia." He stood up, too. "He's all a man could hope for. You're gonna share him with me, aren't you?"

She hesitated, crafting a reply with care. "Callister is a long way from here. Someday, when he's older, maybe he can spend time with you. I suppose that's one of those bridges we can cross when we get to it."

Tension so thick it was almost tangible thrummed between them, a too-familiar feeling. Her heart began to hammer. His hand reached out and closed around her arm, turning her to face him. His eyes peered into hers, his mouth inches away. "Eyes like a spring meadow," he said softly. "You're still the prettiest woman I know. And you've never stopped being my girl."

His head descended and he placed his lips on hers. And just as surely as she had known he was going to kiss her, she knew she was going to let him. Closing her eyes as his mouth shaped hers, she gave in to the volcanic fever rising inside her.

Stop this right now, Dahlia!

She parted her lips and let in his tongue. His mouth tasted clean, just as she remembered. She slid her arms around his neck and pressed against him. *This is dangerous, Dahlia.*

One of his hands closed over her nape; the other slid down her back and kneaded her bottom. Instinctively, her hips thrust forward. He was hard, and the heat of him radiated through his jeans. He maneuvered her, fitted his erection to the notch of her thighs. A dreamy memory of how he felt inside her swept into her mind. All she had to do was unhook his belt, open his zipper and . . . She pressed her palm against him, rubbed him up and down, remembered the smooth feel of his velvety penis in her hand.

She heard his deep groan. His lips left hers and cruised down her throat, the woodsy scent of his shampoo filled her nostrils. "Dahlia, Jesus . . ."

She let her head tilt back as his warm mouth and tongue played on the slope of her breasts and chipped chunks out of her willpower. Then she felt his warm fingertips under the leg of her shorts, touching her bare thigh, and the pain and hardship of the past year screamed in her ears. She broke away with a sideways jerk of her head. "No," she said, gasping for breath.

"Why not?" he growled beneath her ear, tightening his arm around her waist.

She pushed away from him, her breath coming shaky and fast, her heart pounding. "It's not the same as it was."

His eyes locked with hers. "It *is* the same. You want it as much as I do. You wouldn't have kissed me like that, rubbed my cock with that pretty little hand if you didn't want it."

"No! I don't. I'm a year wiser now."

His fists jammed against his hips, taking her attention to the front of his pants. His fly had a prominent bulge and he was breathing hard. "You're talking in circles again."

She forced her gaze back to his face. His brow glistened with sweat. "If some crisis crops up at the Double Deuce or with some member of your family, or a cow gets sick, or a horse goes lame, you'll leave me lying in the dust just like you did before. That's never going to happen again."

He took a step toward her. "That's BS."

She stepped back, keeping distance between them. "Luke, please . . . I said I'll share Joe with you. When he's old enough." Her voice sounded almost falsetto.

Luke shifted his weight to one leg and looked away, wiping sweat from his forehead with the back of his hand. "Okay, Dahlia." He jerked his handkerchief from his back pocket and wiped his hand. "I shouldn't have pushed it. But I thought—"

"I'm—I'm a different person now. I own the store, and I'm proud of the direction I'm taking it. I have ideas to grow it into something better. . . . My feelings aren't the same as they were last summer."

Luke's features fell. She saw pain in his eyes, but she rambled on. "I don't know why I let you kiss me. Or why I kissed you. It was wrong of me to—to . . ." *Just shut up!* "I'm sorry."

He stepped back and went into the house, returned carrying his hat and running a hand through his hair. "I'll go on back over to Piggy and Bill's." His voice sounded stiff, distant. He set his hat on and adjusted it. "They told me I was welcome."

She drew a calming breath as her heartbeat slowed from a gallop to a trot. "That isn't necessary. It's late. They'll be asleep. You may as well stay here. Surely you and I can behave like adults."

He puffed his cheeks and blew out a long breath.

"I've got an extra toothbrush," she added lamely.

"I don't need it. My bag's in the car. I intended to get a room at that bed-and-breakfast place."

She watched as he went to the Taurus and dragged a duffel and a suit bag from the backseat. "I must be out of my mind," she muttered.

Chapter 27

Dahlia led him to the guest bedroom, the one with walls higher than its width and furnishings older than she was, the one where no one had slept in years. A spread crocheted by her mother covered a bed that filled more than half the room.

His gaze swerved from the bed to her. She diverted her eyes and directed him to put his bag on top of a carved mahogany chest her mother had brought from the Philippines. Her extended hand shook and she quickly put it behind her.

He laid his duffel on the chest and she opened the narrow closet that contained nothing but a few cardboard boxes of who-knew-what. After he hung up his suit bag, she showed him the household bathroom up the hall, rummaged in the linen cabinet for a towel that wasn't threadbare and handed it to him. "If you're up before I am, feel free to make coffee or whatever. I presume you still like eating breakfast early. There's cereal and fruit."

She said good-night, then watched him return to the bedroom and close the door. Soon, the bed squeaked. He had sat down on the edge of the mattress to pull off his boots. Left boot, left sock, then right. Always the same. How many times had she lain in bed and waited while he completed that routine? She drew in a deep breath and placed her hand on her stomach as if by doing so she could hold herself together, then walked the eight steps to her own room.

In her bathroom, Dahlia dribbled scented oil and skin softener into a warm bath, then slowly settled into it. She hadn't allowed herself this luxury for months, but after the past two days, she had earned a little stress relief. Tranquility *was* her goal tonight, but a bubble bath wasn't where it lay.

Luke. She closed her eyes, allowing the soothing water a chance to calm the tremors rocking her world. She wished she had touched him—just unzipped his fly, slipped her hand inside and folded it around his erection. He loved for her to touch him.

She missed sex, or at least sex as it had been with Luke. There had been times during her pregnancy when need had made her wish she could forget consequences and take up with one of the local men who would have happily relieved her of her self-imposed celibacy. Mick Ivey, for one. Or Rob Ellis, Loretta's new deputy who had asked her out several times, even while she was pregnant.

But they were the wrong men. Luke had ruined her. She couldn't imagine sharing herself with another man.

She climbed out of the tub and dried. Her bath had done nothing to calm the turbulent desire to feel his hands and mouth on her body, nor had it cooled the fire he had ignited between her thighs. She studied her naked self in the vanity mirror. Two faint stretch marks showed on her stomach, which was still slightly rounded and flabby even with the number of times she jogged up and down the stairs to the Handy Pantry office. Her nipples were enlarged, her breasts weighty with milk, but they didn't sag she was happy to note. She did enough lifting in the grocery store to keep her pec muscles toned. She sighed. Even if her body didn't look as svelte as it once had, the aftermath of childbearing wouldn't be unfamiliar to a man who had fathered three children.

Closing her eyes, she cupped her breasts and caressed them, remembering how well they fit in Luke's hands, remembering the heat of his mouth closing around her nipples. She smoothed her hands over her belly, thinking of the times Luke had kissed her there. And lower.

One thing she knew with certainty about Luke McRae—he was a sexual being. Her rebuffing his kiss on the front porch wouldn't keep him from coming to her bed.

She creamed and perfumed her body. Then she searched her dresser drawers for the one fancy nightgown she still owned. He loved sexy lingerie.

She slipped the black gown over her head, straightened it and adjusted her breasts into the peekaboo lace cups held by thin spaghetti straps. Then she slid between the sheets and waited, her heart beating a tattoo.

Minutes passed. She reached for a magazine from the bedside table and thumbed through it. Finding no article to distract her or quell anticipation, she switched off the light, plumped the pillows and plopped back against them. Soon. Soon he would appear in her bedroom doorway, her name soft on his lips. . . .

He didn't come.

What did come was three o'clock. She went to Joe's room and picked him up before his fretting could awaken Luke. After changing his diaper and nursing him, finally, she fell into a sound sleep, only to be jarred awake by the alarm at five.

She started her makeup, listening for Joe again, glad she had bathed last night. One thing less to do this morning.

At the same time, she gave herself a mental tongue-lashing. How could she have stooped to waiting for Luke to come to her bed? How pathetic was *that*? Her jaw tightened at the thought of how she had abandoned her pride.

So he didn't want her. Fine. She had already proved his rejection wouldn't kill her, and he was an itch she couldn't let herself scratch anyway. Today she had things to do and places to go and none of her plans included an unwelcome cowboy. Luke McRae could take a hike back to the mountains and jump off a high one for all she cared.

But just in case he didn't, she applied her makeup with care—rose blush to emphasize how her high cheekbones framed her eyes, lavender shadow and black-black mas-

cara to make them look catlike. She twisted her hair into
a loose knot and secured it on top of her head with a
silver claw clip from which tendrils escaped immediately.

Moving on, she dressed in a white T-shirt and a soft
rayon gored skirt, coral with a large white peony print.
Cinching her waist with a leather and silver belt in front
of the vanity mirror, she saw the outline of her nipples
showing through her T-shirt's thin knit fabric and decided something more conservative was called for.

Then a mischievous thought danced past. She had
heard Piggy say some men were "ass and leg" men and
others were "breast" men. Luke was definitely a breast
man. She changed her mind about finding another shirt.
Eat your heart out, Luke McRae.

Adding a slash of Sun-Kissed Melon lipstick and
dangly earrings gave her the exotic appearance she knew
fascinated Luke. Last, she added several spritzes of Red
Door perfume and pushed her bare feet with their bright
coral toenails into tan woven-leather mules. Ta-daaa!
Ready to face the cowboy.

She found Joe's room empty. Luke's voice came from
the kitchen and she double-timed toward it. At the Formica table, she saw him cradling Joe in the crook of his
left arm, feeding him from a bottle and making gooing
sounds. Had she slept so soundly, he hadn't even awakened her this morning?

She hadn't heard Luke making noise in the hall bathroom, either, but she wasn't surprised to see him looking
starched and pressed in Wranglers and a button-down,
the light blue color coordinating with his eyes as if he
had planned it.

The *Fort Worth Star Telegram* lay folded on the table
in front of him. He would have already read it from front
to back. The comingling scents of Polo and freshly
brewed coffee filled the room. Coffee aroma hadn't been
present in the kitchen since her dad's demise.

After the night she had spent, none of it was what she
needed to see, hear or smell first thing this morning.
Aggravation pecked at her. The cantankerous old hen
was back.

Luke smiled up at her, his expression giving no indication he had any emotion about what had happened on the front porch. She felt an unwanted pang of disappointment.

"I found some milk bottles in the fridge," he said. "I checked the dates."

The bottles came from expressing milk to relieve breast engorgement as well as to have milk available when she couldn't conveniently nurse Joe. She seldom used them, more often than not, poured the milk down the drain. "I try not to feed him from bottles," she said righteously. "It affects my milk production."

She lifted Joe from Luke's arms and put the infant against her shoulder to burp, felt his dry diaper and looked at Luke. "Did you change him?"

"Well, he was wet." Luke's gaze moved to her chest and back. "I bathed him in the sink, so you could catch some extra z's."

Damn. He thought her inadequate as a mother. "I don't recall mentioning I was suffering."

"Don't be nervous, Dal. I'm not a threat. I'm just trying to help you out."

Double damn. He was too good at reading her mind. Being reminded of *that* didn't improve her attitude, either. "I'm not nervous," she said sharply, and sat down to let Joe finish his breakfast at her breast.

Luke went to the cupboard and took out a tall glass, then moved to the refrigerator and poured the glass full of apple juice. He returned to the table, took a seat and scooted the glass within her reach. "I didn't forget. No caffeine."

Her anger subsided as she sipped. Staying mad at him was impossible. And silly, considering that by not coming to her bed, he had done only what she demanded. Now she wished she were wearing something besides the spiteful thin T-shirt.

He rested his forearms on the tabletop and clasped his palms together, giving her a measured look. "I always liked your hair put up like that. It shows off your neck. It's real pretty."

She ducked her chin and smoothed her hand up the back of her head, attempting to catch loose tendrils and avoid his eyes. "That's just one more thing I've never understood about men. They like long hair, but they like to see it put up."

"Guess it's 'cause we think it's fun to take it down." He kept grinning and shifting his gaze between her and Joe.

"It's cooler like this." She would never let him know she hadn't had time to do her hair because she had over-slept after waiting half the night for him.

"There sure is a lot of killing around here. The news-paper's full of it."

"Only in Fort Worth and Dallas. Even there, they say the murder rate is down."

"There's never been a murder in Callister and damn few in Boise."

"There's never been a murder in Loretta, either," she parried, "and we aren't affected by crime in the Metro-plex."

He shrugged. "Good. That's real good."

She felt smart at winning that exchange.

Luke's gaze lowered to their son's pumping jaws. "You're a good mother, Dahlia."

"Well, I won't be writing any books on parenting. The fact that he's survived shows what a hardy kid he is. I didn't know much about babies when he was born. It's taken me, Piggy's mom and half the Handy Pantry em-ployees to get us to this point."

"You like being a mother, don't you?"

She smiled, thinking of her childhood goals. "Yes. I wanted a lot of kids once. I still do. I know how lonely being an only child is."

Luke stood, stepped to her side and unexpectedly placed a quick kiss on her neck beneath her ear. "That was always one of my favorite spots," he said softly.

Her throat closed. She stared into his eyes as her free hand sprang up to touch the spot.

Luke's heart flipped backward. Her eyes had that soft, shimmery look, the one that made his backbone wilt and his dick swell, but he willed away those urges. He had been cussing himself all night for grabbing her like some horny teenager out on the front porch.

He guessed he shouldn't have kissed her, but he couldn't have stopped himself. He had found her mouth as hot and sweet as he had known it would be, and she still kissed him back in that hungry way that made every other woman he had ever known vanish from his memory. She didn't even know how sexy she was.

My feelings aren't the same as they were last summer. The declaration had pounded with the thud of a splitting maul inside his skull all night. He had lost her, and he could cuss nobody but himself. She had loved him last summer. She never said so, but he had suspected it. Hell, why kid himself? He had *known* it. But like a dumb-ass, he had been thoughtless of her feelings. Who could blame her for getting on with her life without even trying to reach him?

And when that thought hadn't been keeping him awake, there had been the knowing she was in bed in the room down the hall and imagining her coming to him, smelling all female and flowery, on golden legs that went on forever. . . .

He had sweated like a pig in spite of that roaring monster blowing air across the bed from an overhead vent which only made a healthy erection throb that much more. It seemed as if he had been in a smoldering state ever since he hit Texas, and that kiss on the front porch had only added a log to the fire.

Now there was more to it than sex. Besides being the woman who haunted his nights, she was the mother of his child and he longed for the binding ties, a ring on her finger for the world to see she and Joe were his. But to his heart-crushing distress, she wasn't interested in making a life with him and it didn't appear she was ever going to be.

He didn't believe in prolonging agony, so he said, "I've been thinking about things, Dal. I shouldn't have come down here without warning. I've decided to go on back home."

Her chin lifted, her cheeks were flushed. "Oh?"

He thought he saw a flicker of disappointment in her eyes, but hell, it was probably poor light. He was giving up trying to read her thoughts. Besides everything else that had been going on in his mind and body all night, he had wrestled with his decision to go, had made it only after exhausting every option he could think of. She had neither said nor done anything to make him think he should do otherwise. "I'm mostly in the way here and I'm needed up there. The ranch has a lawyer. I assume you have one, too. They can work out something about Joe."

She gave him a tight-lipped stare, which puzzled him. He had figured she would be glad to get rid of him. Was he wrong?

"I don't have a lawyer," she said. "But if it's necessary, I'll hire one."

Shit. It hadn't crossed his mind she wouldn't have a lawyer lined up. "It won't be necessary. You've got nothing to fear from me. There's a trust fund set up to educate my other kids. I'm gonna add Joe, so maybe knowing that will take a worry off your mind. Support and visiting can be resolved between you and the lawyer. I'll have him get in touch with you. Just tell him what you want. As for me, all I'm asking you for is fair treatment."

And the opportunity to get to know my son.

He turned toward the phone. "I'll be going tomorrow. Guess I need to do something with my ticket."

She didn't reply and he couldn't read her expression. She placed her little finger into Joe's mouth and unlatched him. Luke's gaze dropped to her nipple, dark and puckered, then to the infant, his milky little mouth still working and his tiny fingers folded into fists and for a crazy minute Luke's chest felt so full he didn't know what to do with himself. A fierce longing seized him. The idea of his son, the product of his seed, growing up without him was suddenly as heavy as a cross. With Joe in Texas and himself in Idaho, how was he going to forge a place in the little guy's life?

Dahlia broke into his thoughts by standing up and passing Joe to him. Automatically, he placed the infant against his shoulder and began to rub his back, as he had done hundreds of times with his other children.

Dahlia went to the cabinet and lifted a phone book from a cabinet drawer. Plunking the heavy tome onto the counter, she pawed through the tissuelike pages. He moved to stand beside her and looked over her shoulder, still unable to make out her mood.

"Here's 'Airlines.' " She took Joe from him, stamped back to the chair and sat. She began cooing at the baby, who smiled and waved his arms.

My feelings aren't the same . . . Luke couldn't erase that pronouncement from his mind as he hid his eyes in the phone book.

Flight confirmed, he turned to her. "Flight's at noon tomorrow. I'll leave here early, maybe before you get up." He guessed now was as good a time as any to tell her the other half of the decision he had made. "For today, I'm gonna get out of your hair. Drive on over to Abilene, look up a guy we sold some bulls to a couple years ago. When I get back, if you've got time, I'll take you somewhere to supper."

Chapter 28

While Joe slept upstairs in the office, Dahlia worked in the butcher shop, trimming a long strip of tenderloin for slicing into filet mignon. A lake resident had ordered a dozen of the premium steaks. Thank God she was skilled enough to do it automatically, because her concentration had been gone since Luke drove away this morning.

A confusing mix of emotions stewed inside her—relief, regret. And anger.

His leaving proved what she had always known. In Luke McRae's world, it was his way or the highway. She hadn't kissed up to him, so he was leaving. Just as well, she told herself. A complication out of her life. Once he was gone, she could get back to a routine.

At the same time, she was frustrated. They hadn't discussed important details, and she had to take the blame for that. Every time he had tried to talk, she had dug in her heels and thwarted the conversation. Now he would be gone in a matter of hours. A bleak mirage crept into her head—Luke, mounting his horse and buttoning his parka, gathering his reins and tugging his hat brim, riding away without looking back. A traitorous part of her wanted to throw her arms around him and beg him to stay.

A familiar freckled face peeked around the corner of the butcher shop. Piggy. Dahlia continued her task. "What are you doing here, Judas?"

"Just in the neighborhood. Thought I'd stop by." Piggy looked around. "Luke here?"

"You mean he didn't leave his itinerary with you?"

Piggy's brown eyes held a shimmer. "Is Joe with him?"

"I'm not discussing Joe with you. The next thing I know, you'll be helping Luke take him away from me."

Piggy came closer. "Aren't you just a teeny-weeny bit glad to see him?"

"Are you insane? You've screwed up my life royally, Piggy. I'll never forgive you."

A tear sneaked down Piggy's cheek. "I know. Damn me. I should be killed." She sniffled and jerked a piece of parchment paper from its box on top of the meat display case. "I thought I was doing a good thing for everybody. I can't stand you being mad at me."

Dahlia felt a lump in her own throat and put down her butcher knife. She and Piggy had always looked out for each other. They had shared every major milestone in each other's lives.

"Damn you is right, Piggy. I can't think of anything bad enough to say to you."

"Call me names. Beat me up. Just don't be mad at me."

They fell into each other's arms, weeping and wiping eyes, and Dahlia realized for the first time how much her anger at her only friend had weighed on her. "After what you've done, you're going to owe me, big time," she told the crazy redhead.

"I'll do your laundry, clean your house," Piggy said.

"Damn, I got beef blood on your shirt."

"I don't care. I've got lots of shirts, but I've got only one best friend."

A few chores and an hour later, Dahlia climbed the stairs to the office. She fed Joe and clicked on a musical for him to hear. Making up with Piggy had improved her attitude. She felt as if a burden had been lifted. Determined to keep herself too busy to think about Luke, she sat down at the computer to catch up the sales data that had been neglected for two full days.

Her efforts to bring the Handy Pantry into the nineties had included replacing the two antiquated cash registers with computerized point-of-sale equipment that scanned UPC codes and software that kept track of sales item by item. Having it would have been of no benefit to her dad whose mind had worked like a computer, but to her the electronic aide was priceless.

She looked at August's numbers, chewing on her jaw. The meat department was producing good sales again, thanks to targeting a market that had money to burn— out-of-towners and second-home owners. Thick, top-quality steaks on barbecue grills at the lake helped them endure the hot summers.

Several times a week, she thanked her Dad for teaching her butchering the old-fashioned way. Since leaving Dallas, her university education hadn't been as beneficial as knowing how to carve excellent cuts of meat.

She was building a following. More and more often, on their way to the lake, instead of bringing meat with them, people from Abilene, Fort Worth and Dallas stopped in to shop at the Handy Pantry. Often they ordered cuts to take back to their tables in the Metroplex. Shipping steaks in dry ice had become routine.

That modicum of success prevented the Handy Pantry's being just another convenience store. Still, it had a long way to go. She was getting by on what Dad had paid himself five years ago.

Deciding to add a new function to her spreadsheet, she dug into her bottom drawer, lifted out a new box of computer disks and reached the software-program manual on the bottom of the drawer. As she fanned its pages, a white envelope fell out on the desk blotter, and she paused, knowing what it contained.

She opened it and slid out two snapshots. One she had snapped of Luke smiling. The other was of her and Luke wrapped in each other's arms beside his river boat in the Callister cottage's driveway. They were her only pictures of him. She hadn't looked at them for months, though once she had wept over them every day.

She reached for the framed newborn shot of Joe on the corner of her desk, looking for her baby's resemblance to his father. *This little boy's got my blood in his veins.* . . . Luke's words confronted her, and for the first time, she saw the magnificence of Joe's birth from his father's eyes. Like their ancient Scottish ascendants, in light of the incapacity of Luke's firstborn son, Joe was the successor, a prince. The blood of heroes coursed through his veins, the stuff of legends lived in his soul.

She hadn't given this a moment's thought before. To her, devotion to family tradition had scant meaning. If she had relatives on her mother's side, she didn't know them. She couldn't remember her father's father at all. Her grandmother Montgomery was nothing more than a dim white-haired chimera from childhood who sang songs in a high-pitched voice and moved to and fro in the antique rocking chair used of late to soothe Joe.

What logical excuse was there, really, why her son shouldn't know and love his father?

She reached for the scissors in her middle desk drawer and trimmed to an inch square the snapshot of Luke's face and tucked it into the corner of the frame that held Joe's photograph. Then she replaced the frame on the corner of her desk and sat back to admire the man she had once believed was her soul mate and the child of their union.

It was too late for the three of them as a unit. The breakup in Callister had trampled the arcane connection that had been the glue of her attachment to Luke. Her bitterness was deeply seated. Last night she had shunned him, but how she had loved him last summer. Whatever the future held for her, she would never love again in the same way.

The snapshot of the two of them by his boat lay in the center of the desk blotter. She leaned and lookd closer at the tiny images. The picture had been snapped prior to leaving for a day of fishing at Hells Canyon Reservoir. Having not seen each other for a week, they were lost in mutual adoration when Piggy darted out of the house with a throwaway camera.

Another memory from that day pushed into her mind, blocking out all else. . . . Luke's high-sided river boat tied to a rock on a deserted beach. The electric blue of the Idaho sky . . . Luke motioning her to the back of the boat with a hitch of his chin, pulling her down to lie on the flat deck. With a wink and a grin, stripping off one of her boots and one leg of her jeans and panties, unhooking his belt . . .

She had laughed and pushed at his hands, told him somebody might see them, but did she stop him? Hardly . . .

Then, maddening, wet friction. And heat. His hard, thick penis thrusting deep and fast, her bare buttocks grinding against the deck's abrasive surface, his belt buckle and pocket change jangling in steady beats; the boat bouncing, rocking, water slapping its aluminum sides; the sun a red weight on her eyelids. She buried her face inside his shirt collar, the pungent scent of him flooded her nostrils. She grew dizzy, disoriented, acutely sentient. "Come," he had whispered, but she couldn't. Too inhibited, too exposed.

He stopped and withdrew, stretched and reached for something, lifted her hips. A cushion slid under her—a life preserver, its vinyl cover sun warmed and buttery smooth, relieving the deck's chafing. His hand slid up the backs of her thighs, hooked her knees over his shoulders. She was pinned, couldn't move. Then his whisker stubble on the insides of her thighs, his breath riffling her pubic hair, his mouth . . . his tongue . . .

Speeee! The scream of a hawk pierced the solitude. She soared to meet it, her own outcry echoing through the steep walls of Hells Canyon.

The *burr* and *peep* of the computer brought her back with a jump. She felt warm all over, her pulse drummed in her ears. She was throbbing down there, racing toward a cataclysm she had to force herself to stop.

"My God," she whispered. This couldn't be normal.

She rose and moved on shaky legs to the privacy of the bathroom. Her panties were damp, and she felt hot and swollen between her legs. She removed the underwear and bathed herself with cool water, then dabbed at her arms and neck with a wet paper towel. The sweet scent of her moisture seemed strong in the airless bathroom, but she had no fresh panties to put on. Using hand soap, she rinsed them under the faucet and hung them on the towel hook to dry.

A supply of perfume and cosmetics stayed on a shelf over the toilet tank. She gave herself several sprays and glanced at her reflection in the medicine cabinet's cracked mirror. She looked unkempt and Luke would be returning soon.

Why do you care? You're over him.

She washed her face and applied fresh makeup.

Why are you doing this? It means nothing.

She took down her hair. After being pinned up all day, it fell to her shoulders in a soft wave. She brushed it vigorously, making it shine. Then she went downstairs to wait.

"The accountant's on the phone, Dahlia."

Dahlia looked up from straightening the green vegetable display and glanced at the Pepsicola clock mounted above the storeroom door. Five-thirty. "I'll take it upstairs." She jogged up to the office, keenly aware, as she had been all afternoon, that she wasn't wearing panties.

As she hung up, thumps sounded on the wooden stairs. Luke.

She left her chair, switched on the bulb that lit the stairway and stepped out onto the square landing. When he reached the landing, he handed her a box, leaned down and kissed her cheek. "Umm," he said. "You smell awful good."

Her heart made a leap as she thought of being without panties, and she quickly stepped back, bumping her shoulder on the door facing and stumbling. Both his hands jerked up to catch her, but she swung around him, out of his reach, leaving his hands suspended in air.

"You okay?"

"Fine. I'm fine." She carried the box into the office, sat down on the sofa and pulled loose the ribbon. "You look hot. There's cold beer if you like." She nodded toward the small square refrigerator on the opposite end of the room, then regretted offering him a beer. If he drank beer, he might have to go into the bathroom.

"That sounds fine." He headed for the portable unit, stopping to look down at Joe. "Baby good today?"

"Yes. He's good most of the time."

He reached inside the refrigerator for a beer and cracked it open, then thumbed back his hat, propped his elbow on the filing cabinet and drank down half the can in one long swallow. Dahlia couldn't take her eyes off the muscles working in his throat.

"I've been thinking about dinner," she said, freeing the box of its paper. "It's hard, going out of town. I cut some great filet mignon today. I'll take a couple home and we can cook them on the grill on the back porch."

"Okay," he said, "if that's more convenient."

She could see the difference in his demeanor. He seemed stiff and reserved, not like himself, like he was putting one foot in front of the other until he could get out the door and on his way to the airport tomorrow morning.

She returned her attention to the box and saw the tiniest pair of cowboy boots she had ever seen. She looked at Joe, then up at Luke.

He smiled. "So he'll start out knowing his roots."

Luke bent over Joe's crib, closed his eyes and placed a long kiss on Joe's forehead. "Sleep tight, pardner."

A lump congealed in Dahlia's throat as she stood in the doorway waiting. "I'll, uh, make a salad."

She had gathered two of the prime filets, some salad vegetables and baking potatoes, even a box of Texas Toast, which she loved but seldom ate. When she had fed Joe a few minutes earlier, instead of watching and hanging on to to the baby's finger, Luke had busied himself in the bedroom repacking, and Dahlia had felt his absence.

She had seasoned the steaks and put them on a plate, and now he took them outside and stayed. As she put the finishing touches on the salad, he returned carrying the cooked steaks, which looked to be done to perfection. He came to her side and idly picked up each of the three bottles of salad dressing she had brought home and read the labels.

When she could stand the heaviness in the air no longer, she spoke. "Do your daughters know about Joe?"

She could tell by the crimson fan that spread over his face they probably didn't.

"I'm gonna tell 'em when I get home."

Dahlia snorted. "Do you think they'll be happy to have a bastard half brother?"

Luke's long fingers gripped her wrist and he froze her with a cold glare. "Don't call him that. I won't allow anyone to call him that."

She glared back and freed her wrist. "I wasn't calling him that. I was making a point. And the point is, some things are out of your control."

He backed off. "I'll do right by him, Dahlia."

"Whatever," she said. Left jittery by the vehemence of his reaction, she sacked up the extra vegetables into storage bags and took them to the refrigerator. "Here's two beers Piggy and Bill left. They've been in here for months. Do you want one?"

"Okay." Luke took the can of Bud she handed him and popped the tab.

Luke ate, but she had no appetite, even for filet mignon. She couldn't stop the anger that had been growing ever since his announcement that he would go home sooner than planned. Nibbling, but not tasting, she stared at her plate, sneaking peeks at him across the yellow tabletop.

"When do you think you can bring Joe to the Double Deuce? Spend some time, let him get to know his sisters and brother, his grandparents?"

"Me? At your ranch, with *your* family? Do I look like I'm into self-torture?" She shook her head. "Oh, no. I remember the last meeting I had with your parents. Do you think I would subject myself to being humiliated like that again?"

"You'd be a guest. Most folks think we're pretty good hosts. I'm asking you for Joe's sake."

"You're asking me for *Luke's* sake." As if she weighed three hundred pounds, she flattened her palms on the tabletop, pushed herself up from her chair and took their dishes to the sink.

Rinsing the plates, she stared out through the small window over the sink. *His family?* What had he told them? He had already said his children knew nothing about Joe. And why ask herself these questions? None of it made any difference. She had no intention of ever returning to Callister, Idaho. For any reason.

Luke wrapped his hand around his third can of Budweiser. Three beers hadn't made him drunk, but he wished they had. He couldn't be in a darker mood. And it was Dahlia's fault. For three days she had kept him at arm's length and brushed off his efforts to make some ground rules about Joe.

He hooked his elbow on the back of his chair and stared at her working at the sink. He narrowed his eyes, homing in on her straight, slender nose and high cheekbones. The light over the sink emphasized her hair's clean shininess. The profile of her full breasts was defined in that thin shirt. He knew damn well she had worn that to tease him, and it had, all day.

He finished off his beer and thought about what he knew of the other sex—how they knew tricks that ignited a man's senses and dulled his mind, turned him into a fool; how marriage to one small woman had threatened his very survival as a man and how close he had come to losing the fight. But he hadn't lost it. He had hung on and prevailed. Since then, his senses had been lit up plenty of times, but he had never lost control of the situation mentally.

Until now.

Like she did that summer, Dahlia had put a stamp on him again, and now, here she was, acting like she didn't need him. Well, by God, since when did he back off pursuing something he wanted just because the road got rocky? Nobody had ever called Luke McRae fainthearted.

She and Joe were alone in the world. She did need

him. And his kid needed him, whether *she* wanted to admit it or not, and time was wasting.

Dahlia felt Luke's eyes. They burned through her clothing. She heard the scrape of chair legs on the linoleum floor, then the soft thud of boot heels.

"Pretty soon, you're gonna wash all the pictures off those plates," Luke said, coming up behind her.

She turned off the faucet, reached for a dish towel and pivoted to face him. The soft fabric of her skirt brushed her pubic hair as she turned, and she thought of her panties hanging on the towel hook in the Handy Pantry's office bathroom. The erotic episode in her office earlier had left her with a need that overlapped her brain and simmered behind every thought and deed. It had begun last night, really, when she bathed and perfumed herself and waited.

"Well, they *are* my plates."

Luke stood a few feet away, his mouth grim, his eyes hooded and focused on her mouth. His palm flattened on the counter, and a fist went to his hip. His John Wayne stance. She half expected him to call her *Pilgrim*. "I believe you when you say you're not doing it with anybody."

She blinked, stunned at his audacity. She tossed the towel aside and swept a sheaf of hair off her forehead. "What I do or whom I do it with is absolutely none of your business."

"That boy sleeping down the hall says different. Piggy told me there's a couple of guys in town after you."

Her jaw dropped. A basket of fruit sat on the counter at fingertip's reach. She thought of crowning him with an apple, but couldn't summon such out-of-character aggression.

"I'll tell you this. With either one of 'em, it'll never be like it was with me."

She gasped. The basketful of apples was alarmingly tempting.

He stepped closer. His scent surrounded her. His gaze traveled down to her breasts and back up. "You're a woman who likes fucking, Dahlia. And you like it with me. You can deny it with words, but you can't hide how you kissed me out there on that front porch last night. Or how your nipples are sticking out in that shirt."

Her arms flew to cross over her breasts. "You're the most arrogant jerk I've ever known."

He backed her against the counter. His probing gaze held hers for several beats. "That may be, but I'm right."

Breath left her. Her chest felt like a trapped bird flapped inside it. Her bravado collapsed. "Luke, listen—"

"No. No more games." He tipped her face up, his head descended and he covered her mouth with his.

She *would not* kiss him back!

His tongue nudged for entrance, her lips parted.

Well okay, maybe she would let *him* kiss her . . . but she would *not* kiss him back.

His kiss was deliberate, his mouth gently suckling, his tongue rubbing hers in a slow, carnal rhythm. No man had ever kissed her as he did. She hung there on the counter edge, weak-kneed and helpless.

He raised his head, frowning. She couldn't tell whose breath was more ragged. "You didn't kiss me back," he said.

"Kissing you is more expensive than I can afford."

"That day in the Forest Service parking lot—what if I told you I know I screwed up? That I've kicked myself ever since?"

She knew his pride and ego. For him to admit he had been wrong was akin to his skinning a buffalo with his pocketknife. A tide of emotion surged from her deepest place. She gripped the counter's edge tighter. "It's too late."

"Only if you want it to be," he said softly, and flicked the corner of her mouth with his tongue. "Only if you want it to be."

Did he think she was last summer's same silly fool? Even then it had been too late. She simply had been too blind to see it. A tear escaped, leaked down her cheek. She fought it, but a sob burst forth. Her shoulders quaked from the force of it. "Damn you, Luke. You—

you broke my heart. . . . All I wanted was . . . to be with you . . . but you didn't . . ."

"I know." His hand cupped her head and pulled it against his chest. "Shh. Shh. I'm a hardheaded ass. I know it."

"That's an understatement." Her arms went around his ribs, and she clung to him, weeping and spilling a year of pain and struggle. "You're worse than that. . . . You're contrary and single-minded and . . ."

"I know." He ducked his head; his lips brushed her wet cheek.

"And—and manipulative. You used me—"

"No. I didn't, Dal. *That* I didn't do. Some of that other stuff may be true, but . . ." He tipped up her chin and wiped her tears with his thumb. "I didn't mean to hurt you so much. I'd take away every tear if I could. I wish I hadn't been absent when you needed me. I'll never be again, if you give me another chance."

He was so close. His breath touched her face in little, heated puffs. Pleasing heat was spilling through her, pooling in the tips of her breasts, in her belly and thighs. Her head burrowed up and she found his lips with hers.

A powerful arm banded her waist and he hauled her against him. They went at each other like starved creatures, tongues connecting at a violent, primitive level. The hard ridge below his belt buckle pressed against her belly. She wriggled against it, seeking more.

The cranky old hen screamed from a distant niche in her brain. *He's going home. You don't know when or if you'll ever see him again.*

She heeded it not, because somehow her belt had been unbuckled and had fallen to the floor. She unsnapped his shirt and ran her hands over his furry chest. He released her and whipped off the shirt, then pulled her T-shirt over her head. At the same time she unhooked the clasp of her bra. Her breasts spilled free and her arms went up around his neck.

A keening sound came from his throat as his tongue plumbed her mouth again. The room spun. She whimpered, making no attempt to hide how much she wanted him.

"The neighbors can see us." Her voice sounded faint, yet she had never felt stronger. Reaching behind herself for the switch near the sink, she clicked off the overhead light. The gloaming colored the old kitchen in pale gold and limned his bare, wide shoulders in amber. A day's beard shadowed his lean cheeks. He looked as solemn and menacing as she had ever seen him as his gaze settled on her breasts.

She kicked off her mules, hooked her thumbs into the elastic waist of her skirt and slid it to a pool around her feet.

Still as a statue he stood. His darkened stare raked over her body. She knew what that look foretold, and something in her stomach rose and fell. Ponderous seconds passed, but she didn't waver. As much as food, water and shelter, she needed this. Now. With him.

The air conditioner cycled off, leaving the room in blaring silence except for the ticking of the antique clock. It resounded like cymbals from the living room.

He swallowed audibly, slid his arms behind her waist and knees and lifted her off her feet. She wrapped her arms around his neck and pulled his earlobe between her teeth. As he carried her through the living room's shadows, she ran her tongue along the curve of his ear.

At the entrance to the hallway, he stopped. "Look at me."

She looked into his eyes. "I'm sure. . . . My room's at the end of the hall."

Chapter 29

"I'll get him." Luke threw off the sheet that covered him. They could hear Joe fussing himself awake. Dahlia had fed him late, then the little guy had done his parents a favor and slept through the rest of the night.

"Hey, pardner." He entered Joe's room. The infant blatted and chewed on his fist. "Let's get you cleaned up and ready for Mama." Luke changed his son's diaper with deftness born of experience, then took him to the bedroom. Dahlia turned on her side, her arm crooked behind her head, and Joe nuzzled and found her nipple.

"Isn't he sweet?" She smoothed her hand over his black hair, bent her head and kissed his temple.

"He's a smart kid," Luke said. "He knows how to find what he wants." He stretched across the baby, tipped up Dahlia's chin and placed a tender kiss on her lips. "That's for giving me Joe," he whispered. "I know you could have made a different choice."

"No, I couldn't have. I wanted him."

Luke propped himself on his elbow studying the image, imprinting it into his memory—Dahlia's thick hair all tousled from hours of lovemaking, his healthy son drawing nourishment from her breast. She had never been more beautiful.

He could hear the baby suckling and swallowing. "Now he's getting the good stuff," Dahlia said with a laugh.

Luke traced the baby's jaw with his finger. "How long are you gonna nurse him?"

"The doctors say a year, but a lot of women tell me they stop when teeth grow in."

"I forgot how long that takes."

"Six or seven months."

Luke let his finger move from the baby's jaw to the mother's breast. "You look like a mother should look. I always wondered what my other kids missed, not having this."

Dahlia rolled her head and smiled at him. "What, breast-feeding? It really is more convenient and much cheaper than formula. And I enjoy it."

He stroked her hair, his heart hurting as he thought of the hours she worked and how difficult her life must be. "What are we gonna do about this, Dal?"

A frown creased her brow and she looked down at the baby. She didn't answer. Shit. He guessed he couldn't assume that one night in the sack had changed her mind about his family or the ranch, or for that matter, *him*.

They lay there in awkward silence watching Joe. Finally she said something. "When he's finished, you can bathe him and dress him if you like, and I'll fix breakfast for us."

"You don't have to cook for me. I'll get something between here and the airport."

"I want to. I didn't eat in the mornings before Joe, but now I have to."

He shrugged. "Okay."

Now what? Dahlia stared at the kitchen floor bestrewn with clothing—everything she had been wearing yesterday along with Luke's shirt—and thought about what she had done. It was lust, plain and simple, nothing but lust that had driven her to strip and practically beg him to carry her off to bed.

They had made love no less ardently or urgently than they ever had. Luke had been tender and patient, and the initial discomfort melted into the heat of their reunion. The depth of their passion, even after the bitterness she had harbored toward him and his family, stunned her. More shocking were the heady emotions that had raised their heads, emotions like feeling protected and safe lying in his arms again, sensing the connection that had fostered the making of a child.

Thankfully, every time her thoughts drifted in *that* irrational direction, she heard the squawk of the cranky old hen that had carped in her head since his arrival, reminding her she couldn't risk giving him her heart again. His priorities were still his Idaho family and the Edge-of-Civilization Ranch. No way could she let herself assume last night had been anything other than an intense romp in bed.

Now he would go back from where he came, and with two thousand miles between them, maybe she would never see him again. She wanted to be glad about that, but the unexplainable anger that had sprung up yesterday began to seep back.

She bent to pick up the scattered clothing and her head throbbed. Three nights with little sleep had left her with a headache. A stitch of pain caught in her back. Come to that, she ached everywhere. A night in bed with Luke McRae wasn't for the physically unfit. He was a strong, athletic man. In a night of unbridled sex, she had used muscles she had forgotten.

As she laid his shirt across the end of the kitchen counter, she thought about the handling of the clothing he had worn and the strangeness of such intimacy with someone who had never told her his hopes and dreams. But then, she hadn't opened up with hers either. Last summer, they had been nebulous and drifting—

Dear God. Last summer had been another life in another world. There was nothing else to say for it.

In the bedroom, Luke put on his jeans and boots, then gathered up Joe and took him to the bathroom sink for a bath. The little guy's mouth formed into an O when Luke submerged his spindly legs and narrow butt, and he smiled and squealed while Luke washed him. Just as he was awed by every newborn calf or colt he saw, Luke was no less fascinated by baby humans. He loved all of his children, but in only a few days, this one had found a special place in his heart. He couldn't escape the intuition that little Joseph Lucas was the fruit of an ordained union.

Luke wrapped him in a thick towel and took him to the crib to dress him. A smile tugged at his mouth as he dried the miniature toes and feet, the wee fingers. He had forgotten how delicate a baby was.

Dahlia had left one of those one-piece knit things with snaps for him to wear. He squealed with delight and his fragile arms resisted being fed into the soft clothing, and Luke laughed and told him he was a pistol.

Sorrow washed over Luke as sparkling blue eyes looked up at him. This was *his son,* without so much as a shred of doubt. He pulled the baby to his chest, cuddled him close. How could he go back to Callister and leave him? And how could he leave the mother who had supported him with her body and borne the pain of bringing him into the world?

But he had to go home. People, animals and chores awaited him. A feeling of helplessness nearly overwhelmed him.

Cradling Joe in the crook of his arm, he sighed, regret running rampant.

He thought about sharing his life with a woman again. He missed it, *wanted* it. And he wanted it with Dahlia. He wanted every morning to be like this one, where he had eased into semiconsciousness with his hand cupping her breast. They had lazily loved their way through layers of sleep and that tension had built again—until the baby awoke. . . .

He knew what had to be done, and it couldn't wait any longer.

He kissed Joe's forehead and laid him back in his crib. "I'm gonna leave you this morning, Son, but before too long, we'll be together. I've got a fine horse just waiting for a good little cowboy to ride him." He clicked on the mobile hanging above the crib. Cute little animals began to move in a slow circle. "You just lay there and watch this for a while. I'm gonna go have a talk with your mama."

Dahlia heard Luke cross the living room and turned toward the sound. He swung his suit bag over the back of the sofa—as if she needed to be reminded of his leaving—and came into the kitchen. Bright-eyed and shiny faced, he didn't look as if he had missed *any* sleep. His hair, still damp from the shower, curled in little "c's" at his collar. His khaki shirt with its embroidered Cinch logo was striking with his eyes and coloring, and he smelled like he had bathed in Polo.

Rat! He would encounter dozens of women between Loretta and Callister today. The cranky old hen popped up and told her to forget it, she didn't need him. Still, she wished she had put on something more attractive than a denim smock dress. "Joe okay?"

"Gave me a razz before I left him. How about you? You okay?"

"I'm a little tired. We didn't get much sleep."

He smoothed a hand over her bottom and nipped below her ear. "Care if I make coffee?"

"No," she said curtly. "Oh. I put your shirt on the end of the counter."

She went to the refrigerator and inventoried its contents, attempting to be casual. "Cereal or toast and eggs? I'm afraid eggs are the only cholesterol-laden food we have in the house." You need your head examined, the old hen said.

"Whatever's easiest. I'll help."

She handed him a partial loaf of bread. "Make toast."

He took the loaf without comment, and they worked in strained silence. She could see the tic in his jaw muscle. She scrambled eggs, her bad mood mollified by their sharing a task. Deciding to have an egg herself, she sat opposite him, each of them eating without speaking. As ugly and brown as smog in the Metroplex, gloom hung around them.

Luke cleaned his plate and pushed it aside. "Good breakfast, sugar. Guess you'll do as a cook."

"It doesn't take a chef to make scrambled eggs."

He took a sip of coffee, then rested his forearms on the table. He had that fish-or-cut-bait look in his eye, and she could see something serious was going on inside his head.

"You can't ignore last night," he said. "And I don't intend to ignore my son. It's time we quit this BS and got married."

The bite of egg Dahlia had just swallowed lodged in her throat. She didn't know if she wanted to laugh or cry.

Seconds turned to a minute. His mouth tipped into a faint smile. "Cat got your tongue? . . . I told you the day I got here why I came."

"Well . . . I just—"

"Come on, Dal," he said softly. You know it's the right thing to do. . . . Now, while he's a baby."

The right thing. Is this what she owed Joe, to marry a man whose affection she would always doubt? Could she pretend Luke held a deep, undying love for her? That she loved *him* in the same blind-idiot way she had loved him last summer? That they would stroll hand in hand into the happy ever after?

Of course she couldn't. On a long list of foolish presumptions she had made about their relationship, letting herself believe in a fairy-tale ending would be the most unreasonable one yet. "It isn't that simple. Here, you can't just go get married."

"Okay. Then I'm willing to make a commitment to the future. I'd like the same from you."

The future. Hers spanned a twenty-four hour period at a time. A long-range forecast was as blurry as an Idaho snowstorm. Marrying Luke could solve that problem except for a few obstacles—like the grocery store. Employees depended on her. Loretta needed the Handy Pantry. And what of the hours of time and energy, not to mention money, she had spent rescuing it? Didn't she owe herself the opportunity to see it successful?

That was the Texas dilemma if she said yes, the simple-to-solve issue. On the Idaho end were the critical challenges—Luke's nearly grown daughters, and Jimmy, who would be a child forever, and the rest of the McRae family.

And its matriarch.

The thought of Claire McRae's hawklike eyes scruti-
nizing her life and her son's flooded Dahlia with hope-
lessness. She put down her fork slowly, stalling, giving
the flutter in her stomach a chance to cease. "I, uh, don't
think I can."

"You saying you wouldn't even give it a try?"

"How do you give *marriage* a try? It's not like something you can take back if it doesn't fit, is it?"

Luke rose and brought his chair around the table and
set it down beside her. He took her arm and turned her
to face him. His thumb stroked her forearm. "I won't
say moving to the Double Deuce wouldn't take some
adjustment, but I'd do my damnedest to make it easy.
You know I wouldn't be mean to you. Your foot
wouldn't be nailed to the floor, either. If you got cabin
fever, well, there's things to do, places to go, and I'd
take you—as long as it's not shopping," he hastily added.
"I'm not much for shopping."

She gave him a quirky smile, teased him with her eyes.
"You're making a statement like that to somebody who
makes a living in retail? Shopping's my life."

Evidently he didn't appreciate her attempt at light-
heartedness. He frowned. "I want to be around my
son, Dahlia."

Oh, you'd marry me all right. To get Joe. Her teeth
clamped together.

"I can afford to give him things you can't."

She looked away, explored a cobweb on the ceiling to
her right, rationalizing the insult. Why be angry? He had
only stated the facts, lined up priorities, put their son
first. *Things* would include a college education, financial
security for the rest of Joe's life and an enviable position
in an old, respected family.

She, too, should be thinking of Joe before herself. But
she wasn't happy to be included like a two-for-the-price-
of-one special, where you take an extra one you don't
want so you can have the one you *do* want.

"You, too," he added, as if he had read her thoughts.

She had never made a snap decision in her life except
for what *he* had talked her into. Now he was trying to

persuade her to tackle the impossible. She wanted to tear her hair and wail, she wanted an aspirin for her aching head. She let her gaze travel back to him and found her voice. "I guess I'd have to say the last reason I would ever marry someone, Luke, is because he can afford *things*. My former husband could afford things. I was miserable."

"I guess I said that wrong." His shoulders sagged and he looked away. "I feel chicken about all this, Dahlia."

And just when I thought he couldn't make things worse. "Chicken. You mean guilty. I think the second-to-last reason I'd marry someone, Luke, is because he feels guilty." She hooked a sheaf of hair behind her ear. "Look, you don't have to marry me just because we slept together. And we don't have to be married for you to have a relationship with Joe. I've thought about it. I won't keep you from seeing him, and if I ever marry again, you can be sure Joe will always know who his father is."

Color drained from Luke's face. Pure savagery boiled up in his eyes. "What the *hell* are you talking about? What kind of games are you playing with me, Dahlia?"

"None. I mean, I don't think we have that much in common anymore. I don't know if we ever did, really. It was mostly sex between us, right?"

Luke knelt on one knee. He pulled her close. His fingers touched her chin, lifted her face. "Dal . . ." He kissed the corner of her mouth, gently drew her lower lip between his teeth, ended by cupping the back of her head with his hand and kissing her deeply and so very, very sweetly and . . . Oh, hell, she kissed him back until they were both out of breath and her blood began to heat again.

He drew back, his breath unsteady against her mouth. "You can kiss me like that, do what we did last night and try to tell me we don't have anything in common?"

"There's more to it than sex," she said on a pathetic choke. "We don't want the same things."

"No? Maybe you better tell me what is it you want that you think I don't."

A man who loves me. "For starters? More children. Brothers and sisters for Joe."

He stiffened and tucked back his chin. Oh, she had nailed him with that one as surely as if she had punched him.

He stood abruptly and stared down at her. "It's too late for me to start having babies again, Dahlia. My girls are practically old enough to have kids themselves."

"I know. The next kids in your life will be grandchildren, but that doesn't have to be true of me."

His expression had gone from hurt to puzzled. "You said you aren't seeing anybody. You're past thirty. What're you gonna do—go for insemination? Raise a bunch of kids with no daddy? Because if you are, no son of mine is gonna be a part of that."

"Don't threaten me. I may not know what I'm going to do, but I know what I'm *not* doing—I'm *not* packing up and taking off two thousand miles with, with—" She stopped. She had almost said *with a man who doesn't love me.* She couldn't extort a specious declaration of love from him now any more than she could have tried to make him marry her against his will last summer.

"It's not a decision I'm ready to deal with," she said.

"Dammit, what's there to deal with? It's a simple thing. Why are you making this harder than it has to be? There's something else on your mind. You might as well let me have it."

"Okay, I will. This is my home. The grocery store's my business now. It was close to bankruptcy when Dad got sick. It's coming back. I saved it." She splayed her hand over her chest. "I'm rebuilding it into something that's working. Me. My personal accomplishment. If I went with you, I'd have to sacrifice it, and I don't know if I'm ready to do that. If I asked you to give up your ranch at the drop of a hat, could you?"

"I was hoping you'd see the Double Deuce as replacing what you've got here with something just as good. I believe men and women have places in life, Dahlia, and a woman's place, especially if there's a kid, is with the man who's willing and able to take care of her."

"A woman's place? That's the most obsolete idea I've ever heard." She started to clear away their breakfast dishes. "Even if I bought into that, which I don't, I've never lived so far away from things. If I didn't go crazy in the isolation, your mother would probably poison my food."

She added an exclamation point by clacking a mug onto a plate and carrying the stack of dishes to the counter by the sink. She ran water over a dishcloth, went back to the table and began to wipe away their breakfast crumbs. "This sounds more like a negotiation than a marriage proposal. I feel like I should ask what I get in return for my agreement."

"Anything you want that I can afford. I'm not stingy."

She took the dishrag to the sink, leaned her backside against the counter and crossed her arms under her breasts. "I told you what I wanted, but you've already nixed the C word. What about the L word?"

There. She had thrown it out there to sink or swim.

"What's that? C word, L word?"

Dahlia rolled her eyes. "Children. Love, for crying out loud. We just bypass love and base our future on sex?"

He gave her another one of those how-can-you-be-so-dense looks. "You think we were bypassing last night? You think I came to this hot, damn place 'cause I needed a vacation in Hades?"

Dahlia let a few beats pass, knocked off-balance again by the convoluted way he expressed himself. As declarations of affection went, it could be labeled a joke, but she didn't doubt his sincerity. "And children? I'm serious about that, Luke."

He shook his head and dropped his hands to his side. "Damn, Dal. That, I can't make a promise to. But I'll put it this way. I'll think on it. That's as honest as I can be."

Emotions volleyed. Her stomach did somersaults in rhythm with the pulse in her temples. She thought of deep green trees and cool mountain mornings. She pictured head-high snowbanks and tried to imagine how thirty below felt. And she pictured Joe, alone among Luke's three older children. She gave a puny laugh. "When you came here, you surely didn't expect . . . just because we slept together—"

He cupped her chin with his hand and kissed her hard and quick. "Stop calling what we did sleeping together. We made love. There's a difference."

Well, that's something. He knows the difference.

"And just for the record, I wanted, but I didn't expect a damn thing. There's a difference in that, too."

He stepped back, jerked his watch from his pocket and snapped it open. "I gotta go. I'll miss my plane. I'm gonna say 'bye to Joe."

The hardened cowboy was back. She knew too well how capable he was of setting aside his feelings. Her chest felt like her ribs had caved in on her heart. She didn't follow him to Joe's room, didn't want to witness his good-bye.

He returned to the living room wiping his nose with his handkerchief as she battled a wave of guilt. He picked up his hat and bag. He had said nothing about ever returning to Loretta.

"Now that we're friends again, guess we'll hear from you someday?"

"It'll be night before I get to Boise. Real late when I get home. I'll call when I get the chance."

She nodded, fighting the old hen that wanted to say, *Just leave a hundred dollars on the dresser.* And fearing that saying anything at all might bring tears.

On the front porch, they stopped and looked out at the bright morning, the cloudless, sun-bleached sky. It was already hot. She scolded herself for it, but couldn't keep from saying, "You could stay. Another day. Like you originally planned."

He shook his head. "Nope. Wouldn't make any difference. It's better that I go. I've still got winter to deal with. You need the freedom to do what you have to. And to think about things."

"I'll see," she said, but the truth was, while she loved

being Joe's mother, she couldn't picture herself as Luke's wife. And she couldn't imagine leaving the Handy Pantry or Loretta. Now she had roots.

He dropped an arm around her shoulder. "Just a simple yes or no is all I'm asking. No pussyfooting around."

"Is this an ultimatum?"

"No, but you know I'm not a frivolous-minded man. Your decision has consequences for all of us. Nobody knows it better than I do."

"I hate consequences."

"They're always there, sweetheart. They're always there." He smiled and pulled her closer. "Looks like it's gonna be another hot day for you. You ever have those badass storms?"

"You mean tornadoes? Don't worry. We won't blow away."

"We don't have those in the mountains."

"You have blizzards." She couldn't let a point go unrefuted.

She stood on the sidewalk as he opened the trunk and shoved in his bag. "I'll be damned. I forgot . . ." He reached into the spare tire well for a shiny pink sack emblazoned with BON MARCHÉ. Dahlia recognized the logo of the Boise department store.

He handed her the crumpled sack, holding the handle between his thumb and two fingers. "I brought you a present. I forgot about it."

Sheesh. There was no hope. He didn't have a romantic bone in his body. Cocking her head, she squinted up at him as she pulled a small gift-wrapped box from the bag. She tore the package open and found a gold neck chain lying on a blue cut-velvet lining. It held a delicate, free-flowing heart encrusted with a near-blinding galaxy of diamonds. She blinked twice and looked up at him. "But—but this cost a lot of money."

He hooked his thumbs in his front pockets. "I'm ashamed to admit it, but it was Annabeth's idea. When she heard I was coming down here, she made me go shopping."

"Annabeth?"

He shrugged. "She thinks I need a girlfriend."

Tears brimmed in Dahlia's eyes. She wiped them with the back of her hand.

He looped an arm around her shoulders and pulled her against him. "Hey, don't cry, sugar. It was her idea, but I'm the one who picked it out. Honest. I thought it looked soft and ladylike, like you. When I saw it, I thought about those stars I used see in your eyes when I did something that made you happy."

Well, maybe he did have one or two romantic bones. "I just—well, it's just . . . It's so expensive."

"Let's see how pretty it looks." He took the necklace and stepped behind her. She lifted her hair for him to fasten it.

As she touched it with two fingertips, his hands slid around her waist and she turned in his arms. "You are such a jerk. Every time I think I'm in control of myself around you, you do something I don't know how to react to." She slid her arms around his neck, rose to her tiptoes and kissed him.

They parted and he pressed his forehead against hers. "Dal, you know I'm not any good with words. I wasn't bypassing last night, honest." He kissed her again. "Promise me you'll think serious about things and promise you won't forget me."

"That works both ways. Don't you forget me, either."

"After last night, I don't think I will. I'll be going around from now on with my hat on my lap."

Her cheeks warmed and she gave him a coquettish squint. "That was your fault. It's true, you know. You do bring out the worst in me."

He chuckled in the old sexy, intimate way. "If that was your worst, darlin', you just keep on being bad." He kissed her again. "I gotta go."

"I know." She stood back.

"I'll call you soon as I can." He folded himself into the Taurus, closed the door and reached for her wrist. "I told you, but you didn't tell me."

Well, he hadn't really told her, but she supposed in his own mind, he thought he had. "I—I do. . . . I think."

"You think? No, sweetheart. You *know*. And I know it, too. Say the words."

She rolled her eyes. "Okay, I love you. . . . Maybe."

His face beamed. "Don't forget it."

He started the engine, and she sniffled in spite of herself.

"Don't cry now. This is gonna work out. Just takes a little patience. Kiss my boy and tell him every day that I care about him." Luke pulled his handkerchief from his rear pocket and wiped his nose.

And he was gone.

"Be careful," she mouthed as his car left her sight.

Chapter 30

Luke stewed all the way from Texas to Idaho, then from Boise to Callister. And he still stewed on the winding trip home. If he didn't succeed in persuading Dahlia to marry him and bring Joe to live at the Double Deuce, the only future he could envision for himself looked bleak and lonely. Dahlia filled a place inside him that had been empty far too long. If he had a destiny with a woman, she was it. No part of him doubted it.

He had thought he was making progress 'til she bowled him over by saying she wanted more kids. He couldn't relate to her feelings. His brother, sisters and he were close in age and had been in each other's way forever, it seemed. Still, because it was of serious importance to her, he had to give it earnest consideration.

He didn't dislike kids, but Lord, could he raise a second family? And under the circumstances, *should* he? Then he reminded himself, with Joe, he had already started one.

Dal was right about the resentment combining two families could generate. Could he do it and maintain peace and harmony at the ranch? Bringing a new wife and *one* kid into the Double Deuce's communal lifestyle might be like throwing a cat into a pack of dogs. What would happen if Dahlia gave birth to a second child? Or a third?

The matter occupied his thoughts until he reached the Double Deuce's front gate well after midnight. A silvery moon gave enough light to see, so he switched off his headlights as he headed for the Big House.

At the driveway's Y, he changed his mind about rousing the family and took the left leg to the cabin. As usual, Frosty and Bingo had taken advantage of his absence and were sleeping on the deck. They began to bark as his truck neared. He tried to shush them when he slid out, but to no avail. So much for sneaking in.

The master bedroom's king-sized bed welcomed him. Opening every window, he breathed in the fresh mountain air. Air-conditioning—he hated it. His sojourn in Texas had been the longest five days he had ever spent anywhere. He stripped, sprawled in a bed that fit him and fell into a dreamless sleep.

He awoke before daylight, showered and pulled on the jeans he had worn yesterday. He no longer kept clean clothing in the cabin. His mother had insisted he take over the office in the Big House, so now the cabin was used as a guesthouse.

As he shaved, he heard tapping on the front door and the whine of the hinge. "Come on in," he called, knowing the invitation was gratuitous only. Such an early visitor would be his dad, who would come in whether invited or not. He suppressed the irritation the lack of regard for his privacy caused him. That would have to change when he brought Dahlia and Joe here to live.

He guessed he would move his flock back into the cabin. The new house DAM Ranches had built for Brenna and Morgan, though vacant, was too small for his family of six and located too far away from the barns and corrals. He would give Dal free rein. If she wanted to remodel the cabin and paint it pink, that was okay, as long as she and Joe were in it.

Luke wiped remaining patches of lather from his face and craned his neck around the doorjamb. His dad limped in, his unlit pipe clenched between his teeth. "How did you find Texas?"

Back in his familiar surroundings, Texas *did* seem to be as far away as the moon, just as Dahlia had said. And he was glad, because that part of the world felt a whole lot like hell must feel. "Hot and far."

"I saw. I watched the weather down there on TV."

"Over a hundred every day. Remember John Woods—bought bulls from us a few years ago? I looked him up. Took a look at his operation." Luke reached for the shirt he had hung on the chairback the night before. "Ethel got breakfast ready? I haven't had but one decent meal since I left here."

Piggy's letter still lay where he had left it on the table beside his recliner. His dad picked it up and glanced over it again. "What does she want?"

"Nothing."

"The boy's not yours, then?"

"He is. When you see him, you won't doubt it."

His dad removed his pipe, lowered his head and shook it. "They're waiting breakfast for you. Brenna and Morgan came yesterday. Let's go on up there."

In the Big House's entry, Luke's children met him and hugged him. Brenna's and Morgan's presence reminded him it was Saturday. They often came up from Boise for weekends. Luke thought it a puzzling thing. When they lived at the ranch, his sister and brother-in-law spent nearly every weekend in Boise; now that they lived there, they came back to the ranch.

He felt his family's curious glances. None of them had been to Texas for any reason, and each knew some part of why *he* went. Breakfast conversation went as usual—the weather, the upcoming cattle sale, hunting season, political gossip from Boise. He ate with little comment, fortifying himself for the unavoidable conversation with his mother.

At the end of breakfast, Brenna announced she was two months' pregnant. Morgan squeezed her hand and blushed. Luke glanced at his mother, whose eyes became shiny. The soft side of her always showed when it came to her grandchildren, and he wondered how she would react when she saw his second son.

Brenna wanted to look at his new stallion. Except for his mother and him, all left the table and trooped to the barn. No one wanted to be present for the upcoming discussion.

Mom spoke the minute the family cleared the door. "Well?"

"Well, what?"

"Are you going to tell me about the new addition you've brought to the family or am I going to have to hear it secondhand from your dad and your sisters?"

"He's stout and healthy. His name's Joseph Lucas and I'm proud he's mine."

She leaned to the right and began stacking the breakfast plates. "I see. You're sure of that fact, that he's yours?"

"I am."

"What does it mean to us here?"

"He's your grandson." Luke helped her by handing her soiled plates. "As much kin as my other kids. I'd hope you'd want to know him."

"With him in Texas, that's not likely."

"I might as well say what's on my mind, Mom. I'm not gonna fight you about this. I intend for my family to treat Joe like my son and his mother like the good woman she is."

His mother leaned against the chairback and folded her arms across her chest. "Your arrogance is ill placed, considering you've exposed all of us to the risks of a paternity suit."

"What do you expect of me?" Luke snapped, out of patience. For the second time in forty-eight hours, somebody had accused him of arrogance. "Lee Ann's married, so that possibility is out. It's always been out. Have you picked somebody else now?"

"Don't be disrespectful. When it comes to women, we've seen evidence of *your* judgment, Son. Your motivation dangles between your legs. What am I supposed to tell family and friends about this catch-colt child?"

Anger flew through him, white-hot. No one could set off his temper like his mother could. "Tell them anything that's easy for you. I'm gonna say this just once and I'm not gonna argue about it. If Dahlia ever says she'll marry me—and just so you'll know, I did ask her—I intend to bring her here to live, and it's not gonna be like it was when Janet was here."

He kicked up his nerve and said something that had

gnawed at him for years. "Janet was a far cry from a perfect wife and mother, but she didn't get much encouragement around here, either. If you had ever given her a chance, she might have been different."

"You don't believe that any more than I do."

He scooted his chair back with a jerk, stood up and threw down his napkin. "It's a new day, Mom. I'm thirty-five years old and I'm lonesome. If the woman I choose to be my wife can't be treated decent by my family, then I'll build a house clear up on Sterling Mountain. And you'll never know my son Joe. If that's what you want, then I'm willing."

He strode toward the front door, swearing under his breath.

"You know I don't want that."

Hearing a catch in her voice, he stopped and looked back.

"I just hate to see you make another foolish mistake," she said. "Bring in here some cute little thing with dollar signs in her eyes and no idea what she's getting into."

"Dahlia's not a cute little thing. She's a beautiful, accomplished woman. I'm lucky she gives me the time of day. She runs a business and takes care of our son. And she does it all without my help. And that fact galls me more than you'll ever know." He yanked on the front door latch. "Back off, Mom. I've made up my mind."

The ranch's chores awaited him. He walked down to the barn and his horses. In what seemed like the blink of an eye, Brenna ducked her head inside the barn and announced the cocktail hour.

He had been too busy to think often of his Texas trip. As it and Dahlia resurfaced in his thoughts, so did the daunting task ahead of him—telling his daughters they had a half brother, a confession he dreaded.

Kathleen and Dave showed up for supper, which, with Brenna and Morgan home for the weekend, was inevitable. Luke barbecued a grill full of steaks and they ate outside on the back deck and visited and had a good time teasing his sisters about both of them being pregnant at the same time.

Kathleen told them she could feel her child's movement. Dave beamed like a flashlight and rubbed her belly. Luke listened and watched heavyhearted, hating he hadn't been around to share that moment with Dahlia.

Before that thought could drive his mood to the bottom of a black hole, Morgan pulled him aside. "Brenna told me you've been down to Texas. If you need some legal help, I could do it on the QT, without involving Brad or the family. I don't know Texas paternity law, but—"

"It's not a problem, Morg. And nothing's gonna be done under the table. It may cause Mom a heart attack, but one of these days, Dahlia Montgomery's gonna marry me."

"That's great, Luke. Brenna and I thought she was the one when we met her last summer."

After supper, Luke left the family playing games and watching TV and drove the Jeep down to the cabin to think. The lamp beside his old tan recliner lit the living room in a soft amber. The cabin held a chill, so he sat on the cold hearth and laid a fire in the stone fireplace.

Behind cupboard doors in the fireplace's stonework, a small bar hid. Once its shelves had been filled with assorted liquors and glasses. Opening the doors, he recalled how, after a bitter fight with Janet, he had cleared out every bottle and glass, including some expensive, fancy crystal, and hauled all of it to the landfill in town. Now, a single bottle of Jack Daniel's sat on one shelf.

He took a tumbler from the kitchen, poured a splash of whiskey and slid a Willie Nelson disk into the CD player—the cabin was the only place where he found the opportunity to enjoy music—and kicked back in his recliner.

He had no sooner sat down than he heard light steps on the deck, then a soft tap on the front door. He opened it to see Annabeth standing there shivering, freckled nose and rosy cheeks even redder than usual, blue eyes watering from the nighttime cold. A halo of undisciplined, russet curls shone in the light that spilled from the front doorway. "Hi, Daddy. Can I come in?"

He stepped back for her to enter. "Did you walk down here without a coat?"

"I didn't know it was so cold." She seemed tentative, anxious. "They're playing Monopoly up there. I didn't want to watch TV. I wanted to, I don't know, just come see you."

Luke dropped an arm around her bony shoulders and guided her to the sofa. "What's bothering you, honey?"

She shrugged away with a nervous laugh. "You smell like Mom."

He felt a little ping in his chest. With what his kids experienced with their mother, he rarely let them see *him* drink hard liquor. He set the glass of whiskey aside.

"We didn't have school yesterday. Aunt Kat took Mary C and me shopping in Boise. We bought you a George Strait CD." She handed him a flat sack.

"Hey. Thank you, honey. Let's play it." He dug out his pocketknife and sliced through the cellophane wrap. "Now, tell me what's on your mind."

"We went by Mom's house. I know we weren't supposed to, but Mary C talked Aunt Kat into it."

Luke felt his eyes narrow. Involuntarily, his pocketknife stopped. "Yeah?"

"She was real sick."

Hung over. "What was wrong with her?"

"She had the stomach flu. A guy was there, taking care of her. She told Aunt Kat she needed some money so she could go to the doctor. She said since the lawyers took away our child support she doesn't have enough to live on."

Luke felt his teeth clench. Why in hell did Janet unload crap like that on the kids? And why did she expose them to the barflies with whom she associated?

"Why is Mom like she is, Daddy?"

All of his defenses went on alert. His chest felt like a truck tire had rolled across it. Jesus. He had avoided a serious conversation with his daughters about their mother's problems.

He concentrated on removing Willie Nelson and inserting George Strait. "She's got some weaknesses, as we all do. Hers have affected other people a little more than some."

"She and Aunt Kat got into this big argument. Aunt Kat told her she had taken all the money away from you she was going to and if she wasn't careful you'd stick her back in a hospital. Mom called Aunt Kat a smart-aleck bitch and Aunt Kat called her a trashy tramp and said it was her fault Jimmy's like he is."

Luke glanced up, a throb of anger pounding in his temple. A tear seeped from the corner of his daughter's eye, and she quickly swiped it away with her hand. He turned off the CD player, his desire for music suddenly quashed. He couldn't imagine how his children must feel in dealing with a mother who used them as pawns. During his boyhood, his own mother had been a caring parent. Suppressing his emotions, he drew Annabeth into his arms and hugged her.

"I wasn't gonna tell anybody about it," she went on, "but I've been so worried. Mom said Jimmy's *your* fault, Daddy. And grandma's. Mary C believes her, but I don't."

"What do you believe?"

"Aunt Kat said when women drink too much it makes their babies deformed. Is that true, Daddy? Did Mom do that? Aunt Kat said the lawyers said—"

"Come here, Annie." Taking his daughter's hand, he made a silent vow to muzzle his sister. He led Annabeth to the sofa, drew her down beside him. Hunching forward, he interlocked his fingers between his thighs. She sat there waiting and looking back at him with troubled eyes. "Maybe we should have talked about this already, honey, but it's a hard thing to discuss. We can't know for sure, but some suspect that's the truth about Jimmy. They call it fetal alcohol syndrome. It *can* happen when mothers drink while they're pr—er, expecting."

Annabeth assumed a posture to match his, crossing her scuffed boot toes and staring at them. "She told us you and Grandma made her so upset all the time she *had* to drink."

Good, ol' Janet. Blame her faults on somebody else.

Yet it wasn't in him to denigrate her to the daughter they shared.

"Your mom's got serious problems. I know you've heard the word alcoholic describing her. One thing alcoholics do is look for excuses to drink and keep drinking. Some folks think it's a sickness, but some think it's a weakness in character. Your grandmother happens to be one of the latter. Grandma's never been sharp with you, but you've seen how tough she can be on other people. That's how she was with Janet."

Annabeth nodded, which gave him the courage to go on.

"But Grandma's not the reason your mother drinks or the reason she drank while she was carrying Jimmy."

His daughter looked up at him, took a deep breath and asked exactly what he feared she would. "Then what was it?"

A hundred excuses careened through his head. Should he try to explain that Janet came from alcoholic parents, that she had probably been well on her way to doomsday when he met her and that Annabeth herself and Mary Claire carried the same propensity in their genes? God knew, he had worried enough about *that* fact.

How could he explain the depth of Janet's resentment back in those first days of their marriage when she learned he didn't have control of the DAM Ranches checkbook?

"I guess Jimmy *was* partly my fault. After you came, your mom didn't want any more kids. When she turned up pr—er, expecting—with Jimmy, she was real upset."

"Aunt Kathleen said Mom wanted Jimmy to be an abortion. Is that true, Daddy?"

Jesus! He couldn't remember if, at fourteen, he knew or cared what an abortion was. Oh, sure, he had known what happened when a cow slipped a calf, and for that matter, Annie knew, too. Ranch kids just did. But *that* was different. Jesus. He felt as if he were trying to swim across the Snake with his boots full of water.

How could he tell his daughter the rotten state to which Janet's and his marriage had deteriorated by the time she got pregnant with Jimmy? Should he reveal it was possible he wasn't even Jimmy's father? How could he explain to a teenager his own failure in character and common sense that drove him to share a bed with Janet after he had sworn never to touch her again. And that after he had *done* that, he couldn't deny Jimmy even if he had wanted to?

"Your granddad and I—well, mostly me—talked her out of it. She agreed to, uh, have Jimmy, but I didn't make her promise anything about the drinking. It was a real bad thing. Besides what happened to Jimmy, she nearly killed herself."

Annabeth's expression remained as it was—inscrutable. A few beats passed. "She did it to get even, didn't she, with you and Grandma?"

Luke sighed and shook his head. Without a doubt, revenge had been a factor in Janet's screwed-up thinking. "I know it's hard for you to understand. I have a hard time reasoning through it myself."

His daughter's eyes teared again, sending an ache all through him, and he pulled her into his arms. Never had he wanted his actions to cause his children tears.

"I hate her," Annabeth said with frightening intensity.

"Don't do that, Daughter. In her own blurry way, she loves you. She gave you life and that's just about the best thing somebody can do for somebody else."

Annabeth pushed back and looked up at him, her wet blue stare piercing his. "But you hate her, too, don't you?"

"No, I don't." For the first time in longer than he could measure, Luke realized he had put the years of bitterness behind him. Knowing a woman as good as Dahlia had healed his wounds and given him the impetus. "I guess I'd have to say I don't feel anything at all, Annie, but I promise you, I'm not being mean to your mother and I never will be."

"I didn't think so." She sniffed and wiped her nose on her sleeve. "I wish . . . I wish we were a real family. I mean, I love Grandma and Grandpa, but I wish we could live in the cabin and be a real family. . . . And I wish—

I wish you had somebody to love, Daddy, and somebody to help you."

No doubt, she had heard the "help" part from her grandmother. He had heard it a thousand times himself. For a moment, he was tempted to tell her he *had* found someone, but he couldn't tell her about Dahlia without also discussing Joe.

Telling his kids about Joe was something he wanted to ease into, when there was time to try to make them understand that besides being *their* father, he was also the father of—what had Mom and Dad called Joe?—a "catch-colt son" he wanted them to accept and love as their brother.

But right now, it was past eleven o'clock. "You don't be worrying about me. I've got you and Mary Claire and Jimmy to love. And Grandma and Grandpa. And Aunt Kathleen and Aunt Brenna. I'm not suffering."

She gave him a wet, rueful smile. "Did your girlfriend in Texas like the necklace we bought her?"

"She did." A mixture of emotions threaded through him—relief that Annabeth had gone to a different subject and how happy he had been over Dahlia's jubilant reaction to the diamond pendant. "And I told her it was my youngest sweetheart who helped me buy it."

"I didn't even tell Mary C we got it. I was afraid she'd tell. Grandma would have a fit if she knew what we paid for it."

He hid a laugh at the teenager's assumption they were engaged in a conspiracy. "You worry too much, Annie." He stood up and tugged her to her feet. "It's past your bedtime, gal. You'll doze and fall off that horse tomorrow. We'd better get you back up to the Big House so you can get some sleep."

Luke found her a heavier jacket in the coat closet and they returned to the Big House. He went to bed, determined to wring Kathleen's neck. Lord, she must have caught foot-in-mouth disease from Dave.

And he was more determined than ever to unite his family. His daughters had never seen the soft side of being a wife and mother. His mom had done her best, but she was tougher than a boiled owl, hadn't worn a dress in more years than he could remember. The feminine gentleness that had been there once was buried in two deep holes—his older brother's grave and the survival of the Double Deuce. His girls needed a positive female role model in their lives, an unselfish woman who had good instincts and a heart big enough to embrace him and his whole flawed family. A woman like Dahlia.

Chapter 31

Brenna and Morgan left at noon the next day. As soon as they were out of sight, he told his parents that in the coming evening, he would be revealing to his daughters his intention to marry Dahlia.

He was still working on how to tell them about Joe.

His mom was quiet all day. After supper, she limped to her bedroom—to show her disapproval, he presumed. His dad put on a jacket and went outside to smoke his pipe. Luke led the two girls to the leather sofa in front of the rock fireplace, took a seat on the ottoman opposite them and made his announcement, wondering what he would do if Dahlia didn't say yes.

Mary Claire gasped. "You *lied*! You said you went to visit an old friend. . . . Well I hope you don't expect *me* to like her."

Luke felt a twitch in his jaw. He hated getting caught in his own trap. "If you don't want to like her, I can't make you, but I expect you to treat her with respect."

Mary Claire crossed her arms over her chest and cinched her mouth into a bright red pout. Tears shimmered in her eyes.

Annabeth's eyes rounded with concern. "Gosh, Daddy. What if *she* doesn't like *us*?"

"She'll like us just fine."

Annabeth moved beside him on the ottoman and hugged him. "I'm so proud of you, Daddy. I knew you could find somebody. If *you* like her, I know I will. I'll bet she's pretty. What does she look like? Show us her picture."

"Well I don't have a picture, but she *is* pretty. She's

got long black hair. Big green eyes. And she's tall—tall as you, Annie."

Annabeth looked at him with worried eyes. "Do you think she'll like Jimmy?"

"She's met Jimmy. She'll be just fine with Jimmy. If I didn't think so, I wouldn't marry her."

Mary Claire remained wedged against the arm of the sofa, her mouth set in defiance. Though disappointed, Luke wasn't surprised. Lately she seemed to blow up about everything.

She rose abruptly and stalked toward the kitchen. Annabeth's eyes grew even rounder. He squeezed her hand, then followed his older daughter.

When he entered the kitchen he found her taking a Coke from the refrigerator. She spun and left through the doorway on the large room's opposite side.

Annabeth came up behind him. "Do you want me to talk to her?"

Luke figured he may as well go the whole route. "Come over here and sit down, Annie." He guided her toward the round oak table in the corner of the kitchen and pulled out a chair for her. "I want to tell you something."

She dropped to the edge of the chair seat, her hands clasped between her knees, worried eyes waiting.

"What would you think if I told you Dahlia and I have a son together?"

A range of expressions volleyed across her face. After a silence, she responded in a tenuous voice. "Is—is he very old?"

"He's three and a half months old."

A dummy Annabeth wasn't. She blinked and a corner of her mouth twitched. "Dahlia's that woman who—"

"No, honey. No." Luke reached out and put a hand on her shoulder. "She's not 'that woman.' She's somebody I care a lot about. I cared about her last summer, but things were hard then."

"Mom will just die—"

"Annie, your mother and I haven't been married for

over six years. Lord, she's had another husband since me."

"I know, but she didn't really love him. Mary C says she loves you. That's why she's so mad at you all the time."

"No, Annie. It isn't love. It's a need for somebody to hold her together and be responsible. We talked about her problems just last night, remember? She'll always be looked after. You and Mary don't have to worry about that."

"Does Dahlia know about Mom? Won't she be mad if you're taking care of *our* mom?"

Gratitude almost burst from Luke's mouth. Annabeth had accepted the idea of his taking another wife, though she hadn't yet said much about having a half brother. But that couldn't be said of the fifteen-year-old who now stood in the kitchen doorway skewering him with a fiery glare.

Luke reached out. "Mary Claire, come and sit down with us."

"*No.* Mom told us all you really cared about was somebody who put out." Her upper lip curled into a sneer. "What happened, Daddy? Did you get caught?"

He wanted to grab her and shake her for her insolence. She was so like her mother she sometimes scared him. Before he could speak, she ran from the kitchen. He closed his eyes, blew out a tense sigh and fell back in his chair.

When he opened his eyes, Annabeth was staring at him. "I don't think I can talk to her this time, Daddy."

Luke heard the front door open and knew his dad had come back inside. "It's not your place to talk to her. You go watch TV with Grandpa. I'll see what I can do."

He didn't find Mary Claire in her bedroom, but when he descended the stairs, he met Annabeth waiting at the bottom.

"She's in Grandma's room, Daddy."

Shit! The hard part just got harder.

He stared down the hall toward his parents' bedroom,

debating if he should risk a confrontation with his mother in front of his children. "We'll just let it ride 'til we all sleep on it, Annie. Things will look different in the daylight."

Brushing his teeth the next morning and mulling over his approach to his older daughter, he heard his mother's cane thumping up the hall. He glanced up and saw her framed by the doorway, leaning on her cane. He couldn't guess her reason for coming to his bathroom at daylight, but he knew she had one. Wary, he lathered up to shave.

"Your daddy says you just have to have this Texas woman."

"Morning, Mom." Luke made a razor swipe down his jaw.

"I guess if you just have to have her, there's nothing for it. Annie's more excited than when you brought Chico home."

Luke made another swipe, watching his mother's reflection in the mirror with one eye.

"Kathleen says she's Chinese. I presume she's a citizen."

Luke ran his tongue over his teeth and concentrated on rinsing his razor. "She's not Chinese. She's half Filipino. And yeah, she's a citizen. Born and raised in Texas."

"Humph. Might as well be from a foreign country."

Luke arched an eyebrow, but she had looked away.

"I was thinking." Her gaze appeared to be focused on something outside the bathroom. "I don't know when your daddy went upstairs last. I haven't been up there myself for months. Seems a waste, that nice new house we built for Brenna and Morgan just sitting there empty. . . . It's all on one floor."

"Yeah." Luke kept his tone bland and made a swipe down the opposite jaw.

"Kathleen says this Texas woman's smart. Says she's educated in business. Maybe she could understand all this red tape the government puts us through these days. I don't know what's going on with it half the time."

Luke wiped stray lather from his face and turned to

face her. She dug a Kleenex from her apron pocket and wiped her eyes. He stepped to where she stood and put his arms around her. He hadn't hugged her in years; she hadn't allowed it. "What's this about, Ma?"

"For godsake, don't call me Ma. I don't need to be reminded how damned old I am." She wrapped her arms around him and hugged him hard, and he felt her tears against his bare chest. He fought back a tear himself.

"You're a good son. You always have been. You've always done your duty to this ranch and this family. And you're a good rancher, a fine stockman."

"I learned it all from Dad and you, Mother. I couldn't have done it without your help."

She pulled back and wiped her nose. "Yes, you could have. You would have found a way. You were the determined one, the responsible one. Matt was like your dad. Always had his head in the clouds. With all we've had to battle, Matt wouldn't have survived here. He might have lost the whole damn place. I always knew it."

"Mom—"

"If you just have to have this Texas woman, then her and her boy will be welcome. Mary Claire will come around as soon as she gets over her snit."

Luke cupped her shoulders and looked into her face. "*Our* boy, Mom. He's *our* boy."

She nodded and stuffed the Kleenex back into her apron pocket. "You bring your Texas woman and raise your son in this house like McRae men have always done. Gerald's already quit the ranch and it's time I did."

"Dahlia, Mom. Her name's Dahlia." He smiled as he thought of the night he met Dahlia. "Like the flower."

"Don't understand people naming their kids after flowers." She thumped away and Luke didn't try to stop her. Or add to what had been said or implied. Instead, he looked up, waiting for a rumble from heaven. A mountain had moved. He couldn't help but wonder if anyone else on the planet had felt it.

Dahlia had stayed busy with the rush for the coming Labor Day. She had heard nothing from Luke. The excuses she made for the lack of a phone call varied from hour to hour: Maybe he had been injured, he was too busy. . . .

Maybe he had lied. . . .

Labor Day came and went. The daytime temperature hung in triple digits for the tenth day in a row, dropped no lower than the high eighties at night.

On Tuesday, as she sat at her computer, someone tapped on her door. A female employee entered. "There's a guy downstairs from Abilene. He's got a bunch of flowers. You want 'em up here?"

"Flowers?" Had she ordered mums to sell? She couldn't remember. "No, I'll come down."

By the time she reached the grocery store floor, several bouquets of roses in an assortment of colors had been lined up in front of one cash register. When the delivery-man had put down the last one, she counted ten. He handed her a card with a message: *For every day I've been gone and haven't called. I'll call you at home tonight.* It was signed, *Me.*

Under the scrutiny of every employee in the store, she felt her face flush.

She sailed through the rest of the afternoon, then stopped off at the hospital on her way home and left bouquets of roses at the nurses' station. She fed Joe, played with him and put him to bed. At nine-thirty, the phone hadn't rung.

Disappointed, weary and hot, she put herself to bed. The phone woke her at eleven. Luke. They talked for an hour, covered Joe's new feats and she thanked him for the flowers.

"I just wanted you to know I didn't forget," he said.

Her chest and head would scarcely hold her joy, but she said, "You don't think ten-dozen roses was a little overboard?"

"You said I'm not romantic. Just trying to make up for lost time. . . . Lord, I miss you. I think about you all the time. If I'm eating breakfast, I picture you in the chair beside me, your pretty black hair shining in the sunlight. If I'm working in the barn, I pretend you're there, sitting on a hay bale, watching me, telling me what to do in that soft Texas drawl. And at night . . . hell, I don't get any sleep, Dal."

She scrunched down into the covers. "No one has ever said anything so sweet to me. Maybe I'll change my mind about your not being romantic."

"I told the girls, Dal. That's why I'm just now calling. I wanted the dust settled. It took a week to smooth Mary Claire's feathers, but she's coming around. Mom's helping me work on her."

"Your mother?"

"Yep. Told me to tell you you're welcome at the Double Deuce."

Dahlia fell silent, letting her thoughts catch up with her heartbeat. Another obstacle removed from her giving him an answer. She couldn't make the leap.

"If Mom's on your side, it's sort of like hooking up with a bulldozer," he added.

Dahlia could see that picture. "How much did you tell them?"

"I told them about Joe, that I want us to get married."

"Luke! You didn't." The statement came out louder than necessary. Her heartbeat escalated again. "I haven't said . . ."

"Now, don't get upset. I'm not saying rush into anything. I told them I wanted you to come up—"

"I can't do that."

"Bring Joe and come just for a visit. When you're ready. I'll see that you get plane tickets."

"I can't leave. The fall seasons are too important to sales in the Handy Pantry."

Silence. Then, "Dal? . . . You know what we talked about—about more kids and stuff?"

Her heartbeat suspended altogether. "Yes, I remember."

"It's been on my mind because I told you I'd think about it. And well, I've always felt like I was a good dad, and it's not like I can't afford to take care of more kids. I guess I should ask just exactly how many it is you're wanting."

Her heartbeat picked up where it had left off, and a tear spilled down her cheek. "Considering my advanced age, I would settle for two more."

"We're talking three total, counting Joe?"

She wiped away a tear. "Before I'm forty."

"I guess two or three babies aren't much more trouble than one. I've already done it once. I guess I haven't forgot how."

She relaxed and made a low chuckle into the mouthpiece. "If you were here right now, Luke McRae, we wouldn't waste another minute getting started."

He laughed. "Look out your window, sweetheart."